ENEMY WITHIN

THE ATERNIEN WARS BOOK #2

G J OGDEN

Illustration © Tom Edwards
TomEdwardsDesign.com

Editing by S L Ogden
Published by Ogden Media Ltd
www.ogdenmedia.net

ONE

OLD HABITS

MASTER COMMANDER CARTER ROSE walked toward the briefing room on Station Alpha, with his XO in lockstep at his side. The news of the Aternien invasion of Terra Six was still rattling around his brain like a pinball, but with his warship the Longsword Galatine still little more than a wreck, he was powerless to do anything about it. All he could do was gather what remained of his biologically- and technologically-augmented crew – those who had survived the last hundred years ostracized from Union society – and prepare for war.

"Do we even need to attend this briefing?" Major Carina Larsen complained. She was struggling to keep pace with him, to the point where she was almost jogging. "The specifics of the invasion don't matter to us. We need to find the rest of your old crew."

"I want to know how bad the situation is," Carter grunted, maintaining his furious pace. "The Aterniens are merely dipping their toes in the water to test our capabilities.

If we fail to stop them at Terra Six, they will only grow bolder, and future invasions will come harder and faster."

"All the more reason why we need to get the Galatine ready," his XO countered.

Carter stopped dead at the entrance to the briefing room. It was so sudden that Carina almost ran into him, and her boots screeched across the polished metal deck plates as she halted. He was about to open the door, but paused and looked his human first officer in the eyes.

"To fight the Aterniens, we need to know how they've changed and adapted in the century since I last faced them. Sometimes, war requires patience, even when every cell in your body is screaming at you to act."

Carina blew out a sigh and nodded, though she was hopping on the spot and rubbing the backs of her hands, as if she were about to enter an important interview. He gently took hold of her shoulders and used his own genetically-enhanced muscles to absorb her nervous energy, like a mass damper keeping a skyscraper steady during an earthquake.

"There will more than enough time to fight, Carina," Carter said. "Soon enough, you'll wish for calmer moments like these. Trust me, I know."

The door to the briefing room opened and Admiral Clara Krantz appeared behind it. She looked at them with curious eyes, and Carter quickly removed his hands from his XO's shoulders, as if caught in an embarrassing moment.

"Is everything okay?" Krantz asked.

There was an unusual degree of concern in the admiral's normally hard-edged voice, and Carter couldn't help but notice that she had directed the question to his XO, rather than himself.

"We're all good, Admiral," Carina replied, straightening

to attention. "We're just keen to learn more about the invasion and get on with our mission."

"Good," Krantz said, with more of her usual pep. "Then come inside; the rest of the team is already assembled."

Carter invited his XO to enter first and she huffed a laugh and bowed like a medieval courtier before accepting his offer. Carina may have mocked his chivalric gesture, but Carter didn't have a problem with his old-fashioned habits. After all, but he was considerably more than a century older than anyone else in the room.

Carter entered last and the door thumped shut behind him, as if announcing his arrival. It didn't take long for all eyes in the room to fall upon him. It didn't matter whether the eyes belonged to a lieutenant, colonel, commander, or commodore, they all looked at him with deep suspicion and unease. While his XO and Admiral Krantz had treated him no differently, it was clear that the deeply-ingrained fears and intolerances toward post-humans were still very much alive in the Union military.

"Good morning people," Krantz began, and the room fell silent. Carter welcomed the fact that attention had now switched from him to the admiral. "Time is of the essence, so I'll get straight to it. At 0540 Union Central Time, a significant Aternien force invaded Terra Six. This is what we know."

Krantz stepped back and a series of physical and holographic displays lit up the back wall of the room, each presenting information on a different aspect of the invasion.

"Terra Six has a total population of eighty-two million citizens, spread across seven major cities and their suburban districts, all in the north-western continent." Krantz highlighted one display in particular and it expanded. "The key conurbations are Enterprise City in the far north and Blue City in the east which, as you know, is the Union's primary source of cobalt for electronics production. Both cities are already under Aternien control."

The room erupted into a chaotic jumble of disjointed murmurs between the officers of the different branches of the Union military that were present. To anyone else, it would have been impossible to pick out one conversation from another, but Carter's augmented hearing was more acute. There was shock at how easily their forces had been subdued, and anger at how they had been caught unprepared. Some of that anger was directed toward the admiral herself.

"Admiral, how was it possible that our forces were so easily overcome?"

The question had been asked by a Navy Commodore, and the critical and almost accusatory tone of the man's voice had not gone unnoticed by the delegation from the land warfare branch of the Union military.

"Commodore, as you know, our resources are extremely limited," a general spoke up in reply. "Terra Six has barely more than seventy thousand troops, of which nine thousand are combat-capable."

"Terra Six is a frontier world, so why so few?" the commodore answered.

Carter thought it staggering that the man didn't already know the answer to this, and his ignorance, combined with the continued tone of condemnation, only served to get the general's hackles up.

"Peacetime has made us lazy, Commodore," the general replied, with a touch of embarrassment but much more bitterness. "We have been underfunded and under-resourced for decades. I have made this point repeatedly, yet my calls for more troops fell on deaf ears. This is the result."

The commodore looked ready to continue his attack, but Admiral Krantz intervened.

"Enough! Bickering amongst ourselves serves no useful purpose," Krantz cut in, and both officers at loggerheads stood down. "The General is correct. The difficult truth is that we have been caught napping, but this is the situation, and we must deal with it."

Krantz turned back to the screens and highlighted another display.

"The Aternien forces in orbit number four hundred ships, many of which are the new Khopesh-class Destroyers that we first encountered at the diplomatic outpost."

Anxious glances were cast in the direction of Carter and Carina but were quickly returned to the admiral as she continued her briefing.

"Within hours of their arrival in the system, Aternien troop transports had landed over forty-thousand Immortals on the surface, plus support vehicles and craft. This is how we were so easily overcome."

"Those synth-bodied post-human soldiers are worth at least three of our own," the commodore said, shaking his head. "It is no wonder the cities fell so easily."

"My troops fought valiantly, Commodore," the general cut in, angry at the commodore's continued disrespect. "Where was the fleet when this invasion occurred, might I ask? How many of your warships stood against the Aterniens?"

The commodore was now the one to bristle, but Krantz raised a hand, and the man bit his tongue.

"All branches of our military were unprepared," the

admiral admitted. "We have enjoyed a century of peace, but it has made us soft, and now we are paying the price for that complacency."

The admiral's brutally honest statement silenced the officers in the room for a time, until a Navy Captain tentatively raised a hand to get Krantz's attention.

"Admiral, what of the reports that the Aternien invasion was aided by Union citizens on the ground?" the officer asked.

Krantz drew in a deep breath and let it out slowly. Carter knew that the captain's question referred to the so-called 'Acolytes of Aternus'; the human cultists he and Major Larsen had encountered on Terra Three, while searching for Master Engineer Kendra Castle. He could see that she was weighing up how best to present the information to the assembled officers, all of whom were already spooked and on-edge. The knowledge that some of their own citizens had aided the invasion was another bitter pill to swallow.

"We believe that close to fifteen thousand of these Aternien sympathizers were actively engaged with the Aternien efforts to seize control of the major cities."

There was a sharp intake of breath from almost everyone in the room, including himself. Carter knew the acolytes existed, but the number had shocked him as much as it had the others.

"The acolytes have since been armed by the Aterniens, and are working with them on the ground," Krantz added.

"Fifteen *thousand*?" the army general repeated, struggling to take in the news. "How did we not know about this?"

"We've known about these acolytes for some time, but in truth, we have never considered the movement a credible threat," Krantz admitted. "Since the end of the last war, their movement has never been thought of as anything more than a collection of small, isolated cults. Mere rabble-rousers and armchair warriors. Clearly, we were wrong."

The reveal about the scale of the insurgency had hit the assembled officers even harder than the news of the invasion itself. Krantz needed to focus on solutions, but Carter was painfully aware that they had none. The admiral then glanced at him, and he felt suddenly exposed, like a raw nerve. She pressed her hands to the small of her back and stood tall.

"A plan is already in place to bolster our defenses and retake Terra Six," Krantz continued, trying to present a more defiant air. "The President is likely to authorize conscription in the coming days, but in the meantime, we must fight with what we have."

The mention of a plan caused the officers in the room to look nervously toward Carter, but this time the admiral addressed the literal elephant in the room.

"This is Master Commander Carter Rose," Krantz said, gesturing toward him with the flat of her hand. He felt like he'd just been identified as the target of a firing squad. "He is a remnant of the post-human soldier program that was conceived to combat the Aternien threat a century ago. With his help, we have recovered the Longsword Galatine, and are in the process of preparing it for war."

The room burst into another chaotic jumble of murmurs, and Carter wasn't surprised at the content of the whispered conversations. At the time the Longsword program was conceived, the intolerances toward post-humans had already been festering for several decades. Now, however, it had been close to two hundred years since the first post-human experiments by Markus Aternus had gripped the Union with a mixture of interest and dread fear. In that time, he and those like him had remained hidden from the eyes of the worlds, but people hadn't forgotten, not even for a second. His comeback was no more welcome than the recurrence of a cancer that had long been in remission.

"Is it wise to place our trust in this post-human and its ancient war machine?" the general asked, addressing Krantz as if Carter wasn't even in the room. "Such a decision would undo a century of progress."

Carter was unable to stifle a laugh. The notion that it had been progress to cast aside all of the lessons and advancements of the last war had always seemed farcical to him.

"Is something amusing to you, Master Commander?" the general snapped. Now, the man was focussed only on him.

"No general, there's nothing about this that I find funny at all," Carter answered, grimly.

He felt suddenly weary in a way that his post-human biology shouldn't have allowed. He could feel the room's collective anger and fear as if it were a thousand hot needles poking into his skin, and in that moment, he would have rather been anywhere else in the galaxy. For a time, it looked like Krantz was going to address the general's hostility toward him, but instead she chose to continue the briefing. Another screen on the wall of displays was highlighted and a map of the Union worlds appeared.

"Since the invasion of Terra Six, a significant number of these acolytes have crept out of the shadows in other Union systems." The screens switched to images of burning government buildings and people lying dead in city streets. "We already have reports of terrorist acts being committed on four other worlds. The targets are indiscriminate and intended to create fear and panic."

Krantz switched the display again, and this time the faces of various mid-level government officials were shown. Carter scanned the names and saw that the list included local leaders, such as mayors, police chiefs and similar.

"The acolytes are trying to recruit more people to their cause, and are focusing on those in positions of authority," Krantz continued. "They are being lured with the prospect of ascension for them and their families. This is the Aternien process of mind transference from human to neuromorphic brain. A promise of eternal life. We believe this is how Terra Six was so easily infiltrated."

"You're saying that some of our own people conspired against us?" the commodore asked. "Even inside the military?"

Krantz remained stern as she nodded. "In truth, we've yet to scratch the surface of who is involved, but we need to remain vigilant. This all happened right under our noses, without even a hint of corruption. The Aterniens have clearly been planning it for some time. We are talking years, perhaps even decades."

The room was suitably cowed by yet another shocking revelation, which allowed Admiral Krantz to progress her briefing. She highlighted another display and the face of a man appeared. Carter felt his throat tighten; it was a face he knew well, but one that he'd not seen for a very long time.

"The leader of the Acolytes is this man, Damien Morrow."

Carter cursed under his breath as the admiral spoke the name. Carina glanced in his direction, eyes scrunched, but she stayed silent.

"Morrow was the Master Commander of the Longsword Rhongomiant during the first Aternien War. He was believed dead, but now it is clear that Morrow has been working with the Aterniens to infiltrate the Union."

The general looked ready to explode, but his jaw remained clamped shut, at least for the moment.

"We also believe that Morrow's former Master-at-arms, Marco Ryan, has joined forces with the Aterniens," Krantz added, as a picture of the post-human soldier appeared on one of the other screens.

"Admiral, this is intolerable!" the general roared. "By your own admission, the leader of this rebel group is a former comrade of the man standing right there." A shaking fist was pressed toward Carter as the officer said this. "Commander Rose should be placed under arrest, and interrogated, not given command of a powerful warship, so that he can deploy it against his own people. For all we know, he is their true leader, and we have merely invited a fox into our den!"

Carter felt like ripping the general's stars off his collar and feeding them to him through the man's nose, but his intervention was not required, because Admiral Krantz quickly leapt to his defense.

"Master Commander Rose has my *complete* confidence," Krantz snapped, shooting the general a look that could melt lead. "He agreed to return to Union service despite his better judgement, and despite knowing the persecution he would receive. He has already risked his life and scored a major victory for the Union by recovering a weapon that is vital to our survival. I will not have any officer in this room, or outside of it, call his loyalty into question. Those who have a problem with that can tender their resignation to me right now."

The general was cowed into silence. The admiral's eyes swept across the sea of stony faces gathered before her, and not a single other officer dared voice their protest.

"Now that is dealt with, Commodore Chapman will continue the briefing and deliver your specific assignments," Krantz continued. She was practically shaking with rage.

Then without another word, the admiral marched toward the door and swept past Carter like a tornado, before stopping in the threshold and turning back.

"Master Commander Rose; Major Larsen, you are with me..." she barked, before vanishing into the corridor outside.

Carter raised an eyebrow, glancing at Carina who, to his surprise, was smiling as if she had enjoyed the admiral's dressing-down of the senior staff.

"After you, Commander," Carina said, gesturing toward the door, as Carter had done before they entered the explosive briefing several minutes earlier.

Carter grunted a laugh, impressed that his XO had weathered the briefing with more resilience than he had done, and wasted no time in fleeing the suffocating atmosphere of the room. Stepping into the corridor felt like having a plastic bag pulled off his head. However, while he'd escaped the prejudices of his fellow officers for now, he had a sinking feeling that it wouldn't be the last time his loyalty was called into question.

TWO
RESCUE OPERATIONS

ADMIRAL KRANTZ WAS ALREADY HALF-WAY along the corridor by the time Carter and Carina had exited the briefing room, forcing them to jog to catch up. Despite their arrival at her side, however, the admiral remained surly and silent, continuing on her way to whatever location she had in mind. Eventually, their destination became clear, and Carter was glad of her choice of venue. He grabbed the railings overlooking the Galatine's repair dock and discovered that the sight of his old ship had a calming effect. The briefing had been hostile, at least toward him, and had reopened old wounds that he'd tried hard to forget. Even after a century, the misgivings about his post-human nature remained, and were arguably stronger than ever.

"How long before she's ready?" Major Larsen asked.

She had also grabbed the railings and was admiring the Galatine with almost the same amount of a pride and reverence as Carter felt.

"With teams working around the clocks, perhaps two weeks," Admiral Krantz replied, in a brooding tone that suggested the briefing had soured her mood too. "However, depending on how quickly the situation with the Aterniens escalates, we may not have time to repair her fully."

"Kendra will get her where she needs to be," Carter said, buoyed by the knowledge that his Master Engineer was in charge of the repair efforts. "And at a certain point, the Galatine will begin to repair herself."

Krantz nodded but was still distant. Carter chose to allow her the space and time to work through whatever thoughts were circling her mind, and to her credit, Major Larsen did the same. Young officers were often too eager to impress their superiors, and unable to cope with periods of silence. Instead, many chose to fill such voids with what they believed to be insightful comments, cynically chosen with the intention of making them sound more intelligent. Carter knew that this was almost always a bad idea and that, often, nothing was the best thing anyone could say.

"I apologize for what happened in the briefing just now," Krantz said, still staring through the viewing gallery windows into space. "I had hoped that with the recovery of the Galatine, I would be able to introduce you to the senior staff in a more positive light. To reset the bar, as it were. But Damien Morrow put paid to that idea."

Carter was grateful for the apology, and for the admission that Krantz was at least trying to reset the relationship between human and post-human officers. However, much in the way that trying to impress admirals with ill-timed comments was a fool's errand, so was trying to wipe out nearly two hundred years of ingrained intolerance in a single meeting.

"I appreciate the effort, Admiral," Carter replied. "Unfortunately, the fact that Markus Aternus is succeeding in recruiting former Longsword officers will only make it much harder for people to trust me."

He then thought back to the admiral's speech during the briefing, in which Clara Krantz had given him her full confidence. In hindsight, he realized that had been a risky statement for her to have made, in light of the revelations about Damien Morrow and the rumors of possible Aternien conspirators within the Union. She would have known that allying herself closely with Carter – a post-human who had already been approached more than once to turn his coat – would shine an intense spotlight on her. The other officers would now be wary and suspicious of her actions, which would make her job even harder.

"I also wanted to thank you for speaking up in my defense," Carter said, turning to the admiral. "But perhaps it would be wise for you keep me at arm's length. With everything that's going on, you don't want to be known as 'the admiral who supports post-humans'."

"Do not concern yourself with me, Master Commander," Krantz replied, quick to rebut his suggestions. "I can deal with my staff, and I can deal with the President if needs be. I will not tiptoe around for the benefit of ignorant men and women who cannot see beyond their own bigotries."

Carter was taken aback by her forthrightness and found himself smiling. In his one hundred and seventy-two years, it had been vanishingly rare to find anyone who treated him no differently to a regular human. The fact he had found two such people, in Admiral Krantz and Major Larsen, in the space of only a few weeks was doubly surprising. Yet, it was a very welcome surprise.

"For now, however, while the Galatine is out of commission, perhaps lying low is all you can reasonably do," Krantz continued. She was drumming her fingers on the metal railings that ran along the long wall of viewing gallery windows, much in the same way that Carina drummed on her thighs. "I cannot risk giving you another ship and losing you to a lucky Aternien shot."

"I understand, Admiral, but without a full crew, the Galatine isn't going anywhere," Carter said. The fact that Krantz was at a loss as to what to do with him gave him an opportunity to push his own idea. "Three of my original crew are still alive, and I need to find them."

Krantz turned away from the windows and looked him in the eyes. He could tell that he'd piqued her interest.

"You propose an expedition of sorts, to recover the rest of your team?"

Carter nodded. "That's exactly what I propose, and since it would only entail traveling to Union worlds, rather than the front line, it doesn't put us as risk."

Admiral Krantz raised one of her sharp eyebrows. "Your endeavor in finding Master Engineer Castle would seem to contradict that statement."

Carter held up his hands. "Okay, we may run into some acolytes, but we've proven that we can handle them. And along the way, we might even learn more about them and who else they've recruited."

Krantz took a moment to consider what he'd said, measuring the risks against the benefits, in the same way that Carter had done already. Carter was well aware that the situation on all Union planets had evolved rapidly. The Acolytes of Aternus were everywhere, which meant that no Union world or city was truly safe any longer.

"Who are these three officers?" Krantz enquired. She

hadn't committed to the plan, but nor had she dismissed it. "And do you even know where they are?"

Major Larsen sprang into action, plucking her comp-slate out of her pocket and unfolding it to letter-paper size.

"I've taken the liberty of putting together a brief report," Carina began, while cycling through the entries on her comp-slate until she reached the first record. "This is the Galatine's former Master-at-arms, Brodie Kaur. I've had Union Intelligence searching for him for some time, and I believe he's in Goldrush City on Terra Seven, or possibly Venture Terminal."

Admiral Krantz did not appear enthused. "Terra Seven is a precarious place at the best of times, but with all the new acolyte activity it's even more dangerous. Is this man worth the risk?"

Carter understood the admiral's hesitation about sending them to Terra Seven. The world was almost as distant as the backwater planet and moon he'd chosen for his own self-exile, but whereas Terra Nine was agricultural and dull as dishwater, Terra Seven was a magnet for thrill seekers and adventurers. The planet was rich in precious metals, including gold and titanium, but was also the hub of the galactic jewel trade, after the discovery of a 4,200 carat, gem-quality rough-cut diamond in 2354.

"The Master-at-arms is a combat specialist, Admiral," Carter began. "There isn't a weapon in existence that Brodie Kaur doesn't know how to use, modify or adapt, no matter whether it's a firearm, mortar or an Aternien particle rifle."

While he was talking, Carter was looking at the image of Brodie on Carina's comp-slate, which had been taken from the Union archives. He was impressively square-jawed and had a kind face for someone whose principal occupation was violence; beneath the man's congenial exterior was an alpha-level predator as dangerous as any creature that had ever walked the earth.

"On top of that, Brodie is a demolitions expert, saboteur and master assassin," Carter continued. "Hell, the guy took down more Immortals during the first war than the rest of us combined."

"You're not exactly a slouch when it comes to killing Aterniens, Master Commander," Krantz replied, seemingly unimpressed. "From your description, this man sounds like a sociopath who is better left forgotten."

Carter shook his head. "I perhaps painted a harsh picture, but Brodie isn't what you think. The man is an undeniably formidable destructive force, but he's not a blunt instrument, quite the opposite. And his nature is surprisingly gentle."

Not for the first time, the admiral raised one of her sharp eyebrows to illustrate her skepticism, so Carter chose another tack.

"Admiral, we're at war with a superior enemy that hates our guts and will wipe us out without giving it a second thought. We need fighters, and Brodie is a one-man army. Besides, I want to get to him before Damien Morrow does."

The mention of the former Longsword commander turned traitor woke the admiral to the danger of losing another post-human officer to the enemy like a bucket of ice water over her head.

"Very well, Master Commander, I will authorize you to recover Brodie Kaur, if only to ensure the man does not fall into the hands of the Aterniens." Krantz nodded toward Carina's comp-slate. "Who else?"

Carina cycled to the next record, which was the Galatine's former Master Navigator, Amaya Reid.

"Is a pilot really necessary?" Krantz cut in, before either Carina or himself could make a case for a mission to recover Amaya. "From what I understand, the Longswords can practically fly themselves."

"They have a certain level of autonomous ability, aided by our gophers, but I'm a firm believer that nothing can replace the instincts of a human, or in this case, post-human pilot," Carter said, jumping to the defense of his former navigator. "The Longswords are big ships, but in the right hands they are capable of maneuvers that defy logic and physics. Amaya has a unique spatial awareness. Her augmentations allow her to interface with the Galatine and fly her almost as if she were the ship itself. The best defense, Admiral, is to not get hit in the first place, and since we only have one Longsword, we need to make sure it survives."

Krantz wrinkled her nose then shrugged. "That is both a more convincing and more reassuring pitch than the one you gave for Brodie Kaur. Where is Amaya Reid now?"

"Our intel suggests she's on Terra Eight," Carina replied. "We believe she's working as a contract pilot for the scientific expeditions that are constantly ongoing on that world."

Krantz thought for a moment, her brow and nose still wrinkled. "After the occupied planet of Terra Six, Terra Eight is the closest to the Aternien demarcation line. It may become their next target."

Carter wasn't so sure. "Terra Eight is a tropical world with a small population and no real strategic value. Most of the people who live there are scientists who scour the jungles and rainforests for flora and fauna that can be adapted into new drugs. The rest are big pharma execs and drug barons who make use of the jungle's treasures for more nefarious reasons. I can't imagine the Aterniens will focus on it next."

Krantz folded her arms and shot Carter what could only be described as a dirty look.

"Considerably more than half the Union's medicines are produced on Terra Eight, including all the key pain-relief drugs, antibiotics, and antivirals the military requires. You may be immune to sickness, Commander Rose, but the rest of us are not. And in the coming weeks and months, I expect the demand for such medicines to rise exponentially."

Carter felt a little foolish, and also selfish. "Sorry, Admiral, I hadn't considered that."

Krantz huffed and unfolded her arms, apparently satisfied that she'd made her point. "You are authorized to recover Amaya Reid. Given her location, she should be your priority, unless the third errant member of your crew is in greater immediate danger?"

Carter winced and clenched his teeth together, and the thorny expression on his XO's face showed that she was similarly uncomfortable.

"What is it?" Krantz said, picking up that something was wrong. "Out with it, both of you…"

"The final crew member we need is Cai Cooper, the ship's Master Operator," Carter said, taking the lead from Carina, who was tentatively recovering the record on her comp-slate. "He's our ops officer and scientist, and the next best thing we have to a medic, since my actual Master Medic is dead."

"A medic would seem to be a key member of your crew, especially considering your XO does not have the benefit of post-human physiology," Krantz cut in. "Unless your ship can accommodate her needs?"

Not for the first time, the admiral had displayed some deeper level of concern for Carina. Clearly, Krantz was keen to ensure that his XO had some form of medical support while away from Union doctors, and Carter understood this.

"The Major will be fine," Carter replied. He had almost said, "looked after…" before catching himself, and remembering that Carina did not want to be coddled. "The Galatine has the medical facilities to cope with regular humans too."

Krantz appeared to be reassured and returned her gaze to Carina's comp-slate.

"So, where is this Master Operator of yours?" Krantz asked, since neither of them had yet specified the man's location.

"That's where things get a little tricky," Carter replied, facing the situation. "The last known location of Cai Cooper was Enterprise City on Terra Six."

Admiral Krantz sighed, and her expression soured. "As you are well aware, Master Commander, Enterprise City is under Aternien occupation. You cannot seriously think I will authorize such a mission?"

"Admiral, I need as many of my old crew as I can get," Carter hit back, eager to push his case. "Terra Six is currently still in turmoil. With a fast ship, we can sneak past the blockade, find Cai, and be in and out before the Aterniens realize."

Krantz shook her head firmly. "Negative, Commander, that is too much of a risk."

"Admiral, I won't abandon my crew, not again," Carter said. Anger and frustration had bled into his words. "I cut them loose a century ago and I've always regretted it. This time it has to be different."

"Commander, you did not 'cut them loose'. You were ordered to decommission and disband your team. All you did was carry out your orders."

"Admiral, I won't…"

Krantz raised a hand and cut him off mid-sentence. "Master Commander Cater Rose, you are ordered not to attempt a rescue of Cai Cooper from Terra Six. Is that absolutely clear?"

Carter clenched his fists and clamped his jaw shut. He was desperate to fight his corner, and even felt like telling the admiral where she could shove her orders, but experience had taught him when to bite his tongue. He forced his clenched fists to the small of his back and stood to attention.

"Yes, ma'am, perfectly clear."

Krantz eyeballed him for a few moments longer, then appeared to relax. "Good, then I suggest you begin by recovering Amaya Reid. You will need a good pilot in order to navigate the treacherous waters of Venture Terminal."

"Yes, Admiral," Carter replied, briskly.

This time it was Major Larson's turn to raise a skeptical eyebrow, but she remained silent, despite her thumping heartbeat giving away the fact she was brimming with nervous energy.

"I await your report," Krantz said. She then turned to Carina and nodded. "Major…" she added, almost as an afterthought, before marching away.

Carter remained at attention until Admiral Krantz had slipped out of sight and earshot then blew out a heavy sigh and unfurled his clenched fists.

"What are you up to?" Carina asked. She had folded her arms across her chest in the exact same way that Krantz had done.

"I'm not up to anything," Carter lied, flexing his throbbing fingers.

Carina nodded but seemed far from convinced. "So, do you want to start planning our op to recover Amaya Reid?"

"Later," Carter said, rubbing his neck and trying to appear tired, despite the fact he felt nothing of the sort. "I'm beat. I think I'm going head back to my quarters for a few hours. I'll give you a call when I'm ready to go through the details, okay?"

Carina's eyes grew wider, but then she simply shrugged. "Okay, Carter, give me a call when you're ready to meet." She dropped a hand on his shoulder and patted it gently. "I know how you old-timers like to take a nice little nap in the afternoons."

"It's still morning," Carter grunted, not finding the joke funny.

"Well, you are really, *really*, old," Carina replied, with a smirk. She patted his shoulder again, then strutted away. "I'll be waiting for your call."

Carter watched Carina leave, feeling pangs of guilt over the fact he'd lied to her, but he didn't want his choices to affect the career of his XO. What he was about to do was his decision, and the consequences were his alone to bear. There wasn't a chance in hell that he was going to leave Cai Cooper to his fate on Terra Six. He was going to get him back, and orders be damned.

THREE
CLOAK AND DAGGER

CARTER ROSE EXITED his quarters on Station Alpha and stole along the corridor, moving as quietly as his augmented body would allow. However, even with his inhuman speed and nimbleness, the fact he weighed the same as an adult silverback gorilla, and was even stronger, made it impossible to move silently over the noisy metal deck plates. Every tap of his boot heels carried through the air with the resonance of a hammer striking a stone, but it was toward the end of the middle watch on the station, and all was quiet. Finally, he reached the next junction and pressed his body to wall. JACAB hummed to his side and let out a frustrated warble.

"I *am* being quiet," Carter whispered, annoyed that his bot had the audacity to chastise him while bleeping and warbling like a broken computer. "You should try it too…"

JACAB blew a raspberry then hummed out ahead of him. Carter cursed and followed, initially with the intention of grabbing the bot and bundling the spherical machine beneath his long frock coat. However, it seemed that JACAB's scanners had already checked that the coast was clear.

"A little warning next time, buddy?" Carter said, arriving at the next junction. "It may be the dead of night, but there are still security patrols and on-duty crew."

JACAB screeched, causing Carter to clench his teeth, and nervously look around him, but there was no-one close by.

"Will you cut it out?" Carter said, as the bot chuckled to himself. "I'm on-edge enough as it is, and don't need you horsing around and making things worse."

JACAB grumbled then nodded, before humming closer and appearing penitent. He immediately felt guilty and patted the bot affectionally.

"Thanks, buddy. I couldn't do this without you."

His plan was to steal a warp-capable shuttle and conduct a unilateral mission to rescue his former Master Operator, Cai Cooper. To achieve this would require more than just stealth and guile; it would require his bot's unique ability to hack computers and confuse security systems.

"We need to reach dock four, which is where they keep the lighter warp-capable craft on this station," Carter said, checking that his frock coat was still covering his plasma cutlass, before pulling the straps on his backpack tighter. "Can you find a route that avoids people completely?"

JACAB's lights flashed then he shook from side to side and released a rapidly descending tone, like an electronic trombone. Carter cursed and checked his comp-slate. JACAB had highlighted two crewmembers who appeared to be conducting routine maintenance on an access panel directly between them and where he needed to be.

"Are you sure there's no way to go around?" Carter asked.

The bot answered with an 'uh-uh' sound, like the buzzer gameshow hosts use when a contestant gives the wrong answer to a question. Carter cursed under his breath again and resigned himself to the fact he'd need to engage in a little casual deception.

"Okay, come on, and stay behind me," Carter said, taking the right fork along the corridor toward dock four. "I look suspicious enough as it is, without a gravity-defying high-tech robot flying by my side."

JACAB chuckled but did as he was asked, and tucked in so tightly behind Carter's back that it was almost as if the bot was physically connected to him. Before long, the two maintenance crewmembers became visible up ahead. They were both wearing work overalls and had tools, replacement parts and several wall panels strewn across the deck. A half-assed barrier had been erected around them, which appeared to be a token nod toward health and safety regulations. Considering the amount of gear they'd left on the floor, it was hardly adequate, but Carter bit down his urge to reprimand the crew and continued.

"Oh, sorry, I didn't think anyone would be up and about at this hour," one of the crewmen said, as Carter approached, trying to look natural. "Mind your step; if you slip and fall then we get to spend another week in workplace-safety seminars."

The two men broke into laughter and Carter joined in. JACAB also chortled, though thankfully the bot's electronic guffaws were drowned out by the voices of the three men.

"Don't worry, I'll be careful," Carter said, dancing over

wrenches and screwdrivers, like he was avoiding landmines. "Hopefully, it won't take you too long to finish up," he added, breezily, before hurrying past and picking up the pace again.

"We'll be here all damned night at this rate," the first man grumbled, while scratching his backside with a pair of wire strippers. "This is the third time this week we've had to pull this system apart." The man used the wire strippers to point to a circuit board held in his partner's grime-blackened hands. "All we have left to do is fit this module, but whoever designed this station must have been the size of a damned rodent, because neither of us can reach the slot to push it in."

Carter laughed politely and was about to turn away, when he noticed that JACAB was no longer glued to his rear. He stopped and searched around, even looking inside his frock coat, before realizing that the bot was humming back toward the workmen.

"JACAB, what are you doing?" Carter hissed through gritted teeth, while hurrying after the machine.

The comp-slate integrated into his forearm vibrated and he saw that JACAB had sent him a message. He hurriedly read it and discovered that his bot had formulated his own wild idea about how to reach dock four undetected.

"What on earth is that?" said one of the crewmen as JACAB hummed merrily up to the barrier surrounding the two engineers.

"Oh, sorry about that," Carter said, rushing to his gopher's side. "It's a prototype engineering assistant. I was taking it to the lab for a tune-up. As you can see, it has a few screws loose."

Carter and the crewmen laughed, but JACAB merely

scowled at him with his single red eye and flashed his lights angrily.

"It's actually a nice bit of new tech; and you know how rare it is for the Union to develop anything new."

The lead crewman nodded, knowingly,

"Tell me about it," the man said, while his partner ducked back inside the crawlspace, so that only the lower half of his body was visible. "The software in this security scanner hasn't been overhauled in a decade, and the hardware components are even older. Fixing it is like trying to sculpt marble with a wooden chisel."

"I hear you," Carter replied, with a knowing nod of his own.

Carter's acting performance appeared to be causing JACAB some amusement, but he was quick to rap his knuckles against the bot's spherical hull to drown out its chuckles.

"Hey, why don't you let my bot have a go at plugging in that module?" Carter said, finally instigating the plan that JACAB had suggested to him, via his comp-slate. "Despite its foibles, this machine is very dexterous, and can get to those hard-to-reach places."

The lead workman rubbed his chin and appeared wary. "I don't know; we could get into trouble for allowing unauthorized tech in here." At the same time, the crewman's partner cursed and banged his head in the roof of the crawlspace. "Then again, I guess it couldn't hurt to try."

The second man, who was shorter and rounder than the first, backed out of the crawlspace, rubbing his head and muttering curses under his breath.

"Here, see what you can do with the blasted thing," the

man said, practically throwing the circuit board at Carter. "I don't care if we do get double-time for working nights, I've had it up to here with this job!"

JACAB swooped in and seized the circuit board using a claw that had sprung from an internal compartment. To the evident astonishment of the crewmen, the bot then swooped inside the crawlspace and disappeared.

"It's not going to cock things up worse than they are already are, is it?" the shorter of the two men asked, while still rubbing his head.

"No, these sorts of tasks are easy for it," Carter said, dismissively. "You'll all have a machine like this in a year or two."

The man snorted like an angry bull. "It'll be taking our jobs, you mean. Bloody technology! Next thing you know that little robot will sprout guns and start trying to kill us like those Aternien bastards."

An indignant electronic rasp echoed out from the crawlspace and Carter couldn't help but smile. Moments later, JACAB reappeared, minus the circuit board.

"It is done, already?" the taller workman asked.

"See, nothing to it!" Carter replied. JACAB hummed past the workman and blew a muted raspberry at him. "Glad we could help."

"We?" the taller crewman said, snorting a laugh. "You talk like that ball of nuts and bolts has a brain of its own!"

The two men burst into laughter and Carter tentatively joined in, aware that JACAB was glowering at him.

"Anyway, you can clock off now, and we'd best be going too," Carter said, trying to usher his bot away, before he decided to do anything rash.

"Yeah, no worries," the taller man said. The pair were

already hastily packing up their gear. "And thanks for your help. Just don't work too hard on fixing up that machine; I still want to have a job in the morning!"

The men chuckled again, but this time Carter left them to it and walked away. JACAB stayed close, though the bot's warbles, squawks and bleeps sounded like the angry cusses of someone who'd just accidentally whacked their own thumb with a mallet.

"Did you manage to hack the security scanner?" Carter asked, turning the next corner, and entering the home straight toward dock four.

JACAB didn't answer and continued its string of electronic curses.

Carter shook his head and stopped in front of the door to the dock. "Well then I guess I'll just have to find out for myself," he added, huffily. Carter stared into the security scanner and pressed his hand to the pad. The system analyzed his biometric readings then his face appeared on the screen, surrounded by a green border, and the door opened. He was about to head through, when he spotted ID data that the scanner had detected and shook his head again.

"Major Jack Pott? Are you serious? You couldn't have just come up with a normal name for me?"

JACAB giggled electronically then hummed through the door with the imperiousness of a Roman general. Carter sighed, then followed his gopher, this time making less of an effort to remain inconspicuous, since his bot had effectively cleared him to be in the dock. For a moment, he lost sight of JACAB then saw the bot on the observation deck, overlooking the small docking garage. He climbed the steep flight of steps to join him and found that the bot had discovered the perfect vantage from which to scout the available ships.

"Okay, show me what we've got," Carter said, casting his eyes over the twenty-seven available options. "It needs to be warp-capable, of course, and maneuverable enough to get out of a sticky situation if needed, but also small to enough to slip past the Aternien blockade, without attracting attention."

JACAB produced the robot equivalent of a snort and muttered to himself as he continued his assessment.

"I know it's a tough gig, buddy, but I trust you to pick the right ship for the job," Carter added, while patting the machine like a pet cat.

A holo emitter on JACAB's lower hemisphere brightened, and the data for eight of the available ships was projected in front of him. Carter stroked his silver beard then pulled the image of the closest ship toward him.

"This is a Ferryman-class short-range shuttle," Carter said, discarding the vessel by swiping the image away. "It may have warp, but it would barely get us to Proxima Centauri, before needing to refuel."

JACAB squawked then moved three more ships into his line of sight. Carter studied them, still stroking his beard. They were all Volans-class transports, in various configurations.

"I don't think they'll work, either, buddy," Carter said, shaking his head. "It would take maybe three jumps to reach Terra Six, by which time our ploy would have probably been rumbled, and Krantz will have sent a ship to intercept us."

JACAB's lights and indicators blinked rapidly as the machine thought for a moment, then three of the four remaining options were wiped away. The bot projected the eighth and final choice in front of Carter and bleeped a 'ta-da' sound.

"A Lacerta-class scout, eh?" Carter said, while casting his eyes over the ship's specifications. "It's almost perfect, and it's even armed, but at twenty-four meters long, do you think we could sneak down the planet's surface, without being spotted by the Aterniens?"

JACAB's lights flashed again, then the bot rotated from side-to-side, as if he were shaking his head. Carter cursed and rested forward on the railings.

"Are you sure there's nothing else in here that might work?"

The bot's eye widened then he looked away.

"JACAB, what are you hiding?"

His gopher didn't answer.

"Come on, buddy, don't hold out on me," Carter said. "You're a computer, so there's either an option that will work, or none at all. A binary one or zero, right?"

JACAB warbled gloomily then turned back and projected the image of another vessel. Carter checked the spec and laughed. It was an ambassador-class executive shuttle, and perfect for the job. However, he understood why his gopher had been reticent to suggest it.

"I'm sure Admiral Krantz won't mind if we borrow her personal ship," Carter said, already setting off down the stairs to the garage level.

JACAB blew a raspberry then meekly followed, hiding behind Carter's frock coat, as he strode across the landing area toward the admiral's private shuttle. At the same time, he became aware of the many security cameras that were probing the garage for the precise reason of spotting intruders, such as himself.

"See if you can blind the security systems, while I detach the mooring clamps and fuel line," Carter said. "And see if you can input a departure schedule for us too."

JACAB hummed away, while Carter kept his head down and continued toward the shuttle. Even so, by now it was a good bet that he'd been spotted. All he could do was hope that the middle shift security officers were as keen to skive off as the crewman in the corridor had been.

Carter worked fast to detach the mooring locks and fuel pipe from the shuttle, while carefully avoiding the eyes of the skeleton workforce that was in the garage with him. Soon, the ship was prepared, and JACAB was humming back toward him. The bot bleeped and he checked his comp-slate, noting that his dependable gopher had succeeded in all the tasks he'd assigned him.

"Good work, buddy. What would I do without you?" Carter said, winking at the bot, who merely rolled his red eye in reply. "Now, can you get this tin can open?" he added, rapping his knuckles on the side hatch of Admiral Krantz's shuttle.

JACAB worked on the lock mechanism using the digital equivalent of a skeleton key. At the same time, Carter had become aware that a couple of crewmen in the dock were paying closer attention to him, and he redoubled his efforts to appear casual, like he was supposed to be there. Suddenly, there was a hiss of escaping gas and the hatch swung open. Carter was about to jump into the shuttle, when he realized there was already someone inside.

"I was wondering when you two would finally show up," Major Larsen said. She was in the pilot's seat and had her feet up on the dashboard. "I've been here for an hour already."

Carter was not easily startled, but the shock of seeing his XO made him jump out of his skin and crack his head on the hatch door. "What the hell are you doing here?"

Carina frowned and appeared disappointed.

"I know how you can go for days without sleep, so you didn't really think I was going to buy the whole 'I'm beat...' horseshit, did you?" she said, imitating Carter's gruff voice. She then folded her arms, appearing genuinely wounded. "I'm actually pretty pissed that you still don't trust me."

"I do trust you, Carina, but I also don't want to get you court-marshaled," Carter answered, ducking inside the shuttle to get out of sight. "They can bitch and moan about me disobeying orders all they like, but the truth is, I'm the only Master Commander they have. They won't kick me out, but they could easily demote or transfer you, or worse."

"Admiral Krantz wouldn't do that," Carina said, sliding her boots off the dash and getting to her feet. "Trust me, I know her."

Now it was Carter who frowned. "Why do you say that? What is it between you two, anyway? Not long ago, I saw her dressing down a group of senior officers like they were first-year cadets, but for some reason she actually seems to like you."

Carina smiled and threw her arms out to the side. "What's not to like? Everyone likes me."

Carter snorted, but JACAB bleeped in agreement then hummed beside Carina and hovered by her shoulder, like a mascot.

Carter narrowed his eyes at the bot. "Damned traitor..."

"Look, we're a team, so either we both go to Terra Six to find Cai Cooper, or neither of us does."

Carina had made her point firmly, and Carter knew she wouldn't take no for an answer. Even so, it still irked him.

"Last time I checked, I was the commander, and you were the XO," Carter said, adopting a standoffish pose of his own. "I give the orders, not you."

Carina was not intimidated in the slightest. "When it comes to stealing a Union Admiral's shuttle, I don't really think you have the authority to order me around, one way or another…" She smiled. "Either I'm coming, or I hit this little comm switch on the console here, and call station operations."

Carter narrowed his eyes. "You wouldn't dare."

Carina reached out and hovered her index finger next to the comm system. His senses spiked, and he realized she wasn't bluffing.

"Damn it, okay," Carter snapped. He removed his backpack and angrily slung it into the hold. "You're a real pain in the ass, do you know that?"

Carina shrugged off his comment and slid back into the pilot's seat, seemingly without a care in the world. Carter then noticed that the two crewmen who had been watching him earlier were snooping around, comp-slates in hand.

"JACAB, we need that launch clearance, buddy. How's it coming along?"

His gopher warbled then interfaced with the shuttle's systems, and his indicator lights began flashing so rapidly it was like they were stuck on. The crewmen scowled and started to approach, and Carter could sense that they were suspicious. Then JACAB stopped flashing and dropped into the co-pilot seat, like an old man lowering himself into his favorite armchair. At the same time the crewmen's comp-slate chimed an update. The men stopped, scratched their heads, then walked away.

"Good work, JACAB!" Carina said, holding up the flat of her hand. The bot hopped out of the chair and bounced off her palm, as if giving the Major a high-five.

"Yes, good work, buddy," Carter added, holding up his hand too, but JACAB merely blew a raspberry at him, then sat on Carina's lap, chuckling.

"You're supposed to be *my* gopher, remember?" Carter said, annoyed that his bot's little games were actually getting to him.

"Now all that excitement is out of the way, how about we get going?" Carina said, scooting JACAB out of her lap so that she could fasten her harness.

Carter closed the hatch then slid into the co-pilot's seat and fastened his own harness. JACAB hovered over once he was done and rested in his lap, perhaps feeling guilty for his earlier trick. Carter smiled at the bot, relieved that he still had his affections, then the shuttle's engines fired up, and Carina lifted the craft off the deck, and aligned it with the launch tube that JACAB had unlocked for their departure.

"Are you all set?" Carina asked, hand poised on the thruster controls.

Now that crunch time had arrived, Carter was suddenly wracked with doubt. *Maybe the admiral was right, and this is too much of a risk just for one man...* he thought, as Carina regarded him with curious eyes. *Maybe it's my own guilt that's making me do this...*

"Hey, Carter, are you still with us?" Carina said. "We're all set, so let's go and get your friend."

Carter rubbed his beard then cast a sideways glance at his

XO. Despite their mission being unauthorized, and despite the fact they were breaking a hundred regulations by stealing Krantz's ship, Carina appeared to have no reservations whatsoever. Her confidence that they were doing the right thing blew away the fog of doubt clouding his own mind. It was just what he needed. *She* was just what he needed.

"Take us out, Major," Carter said, smiling.

FOUR

BLOCKADE RUNNERS

THE WARP DRIVE ENGAGED, and the shuttle was instantly transported hundreds of lights years from Station Alpha in the literal blink of an eye. From staring out at the bright blue orb of Terra Prime, Carter now found himself confronted by the steel-grey world of Terra Six. He'd selected an exit point far enough from the Union fleet, so as not to attract unwanted attention, but it still wasn't long before their arrival had been detected.

"We're receiving a message," Carina said, turning to a blinking indicator on her console. "It's a warning from the Union, broadcast in the clear."

"Let me guess; it says, 'abandon hope all ye who enter here', or words to that effect?"

Carina laughed. "Yep, it's pretty much along those lines."

Carter turned to his console and waited for the navigation screen to populate with all the ships that were in the Terra Six system. To remain as stealthy as possible, he'd set their scanners to low-power mode, so the process was taking longer than usual.

"It looks like the main Aternien fleet is comprised of six-hundred and eighty-six warships, but there are also dozens of seven-ship squadrons patrolling in orbit, keeping an eye out for smaller formations that might try to sneak through." Carter scowled and rocked back in his chair. "Seven's a strange number for a squadron, don't you think?"

Carina shrugged. "Maybe for a Union squadron, but not for the Aterniens. Seven was an important number in ancient Egyptian mythology; it symbolized ideas such as perfection, effectiveness, and completeness."

Carter continued to frown. "So why do the Immortals come in squads of ten?"

Carina thought for a moment. "The ancient Egyptians used a base-ten numerical system, and they had ten-day weeks, so I guess ten was important too."

Carter snorted with derision. "It sounds to me that Aternus is so obsessed with modeling himself on a Pharaoh that he's just mashed together different element of ancient Egyptian culture to create his own society. It wouldn't surprise me if the bastard lives in a pyramid."

The consoles updated again, and Carina accessed the new data.

"The Union seventh and ninth fleets are holding position, just out of weapons range of the Aterniens," his XO continued. "That's close to eight hundred and fifty ships, but even with that number, the Union Fleet is no match for the goldies."

"No, but Krantz knows she can't overcommit," Carter answered, while stroking his beard. "From this position, the Aterniens could try a coordinated warp to Terra Eight or Terra Five, or even the inner worlds. She has to keep ships in positions to defend the other systems to make sure we're not caught with our pants down."

Another update populated the screen and Carter muttered a curse. His sharp eyes could read the new information, even from his reclined position.

"The Mesek-tet is here too," Carter said, looking out toward the planet. "Markus Aternus wants his people to see him as a divine conqueror."

"It looks like the god-king isn't alone," Carina worked her panels and an image of the Mesek-tet and its escorts appeared on the main screen. "There are seven Khopesh-class Destroyers escorting it."

Carter noticed something different about the escorts that marked them out as special. "Each of the destroyers are decorated with Royal Court hieroglyphs," he pointed out. "That means they'll be commanded by High Overseers, the highest-ranking members of the inner circle, besides the Grand Vizier."

Carina sucked in a deep breath and blew it out. "That squadron alone could probably take out thirty or forty ships."

His XO's comment sounded like an exaggeration, but Carter had faced these elite officers before, when they each commanded solar barques. All considered, forty might have been a gross underestimate, he reasoned.

"So, what's our play?" Carina finally asked, after a rare few seconds of silence had passed. "We could make our way around to the far side of the planet and enter there, away from the fleets?"

Carter sucked in his bottom lip and considered Carina's suggestion, along with a dozen other ideas that his augmented mind had already been working on.

"No matter where we choose to enter, we'll have a squadron of Aternien ships on our ass long before we hit atmosphere," Carter said, cradling his chin in his hand, in a thoughtful repose. "And we don't want to reach the surface too far from Enterprise City, or we'll likely be intercepted before we can land."

Carina narrowed her eyes at him. "This was your crazy idea in the first place, so you must have had a plan, right?"

"A plan that you highjacked and went along with, unquestionably," Carter countered, making his gaze even sharper.

"Well, I'm asking the question now, because at the moment, we're stuck up here, with nowhere to go," Carina said, giving as good as she got.

The truth that Carter wasn't willing to admit was that he hadn't planned the mission in any detail and was largely making it up as he went along. *Sometimes, the lack of a plan was a plan in itself*, he thought.

"In circumstances such as these, we observe and react," Carter said, trying to make out that he had everything under control. "Right now, those two fleets are just squaring-off, like pieces on a chessboard. When they move, we countermove."

Carina raised an eyebrow. "If you ask me, that's just some jazzy bullshit for, 'I don't know what I'm doing'…"

An electronic chortle floated toward them from the direction of the hold, and Carter saw JACAB's lights quivering in the darkness, as the machine chuckled to himself.

"No-one asked you…" Carter called out, as his bot slid out of sight again. "Just be patient. An opportunity will present itself, and we need to be ready when it does." No sooner had he finished speaking than the navigation console began chirruping a series of alerts.

Carina leaned forward and assessed the updates. "The Union fleets are repositioning…" she reported, frowning at the data. "A large contingent of ships are moving to attack the Aternien's right flank. They're drawing the enemy ships out of formation."

Carter sat up and studied the ship deployments on the scanner. However, it wasn't the bulk of the Union fleet he was focused on, but a small taskforce that appeared to be breaking away on the other side. He concentrated a scan on that sector and displayed the ships on the main screen.

"The Union attack is a decoy," Carter decided, feeling his senses begin to sharpen. "The Aternien redeployment has opened up a gap in their blockade. There's a landing force of Union troop carriers that's going to try to punch through."

He grabbed the controls and engaged the main engines at full thrust. The acceleration kicked him and Carina back into their seats like they'd been fired from a catapult.

"Woah, what the hell?!" Carina called out, struggling to fight the g-forces that were suddenly pressing against her body. "At this speed, they'll see us a light year away!"

"This is what we've been waiting for," Carter replied. Thanks to his augmented strength and stamina, he could endure long periods of high-g acceleration without discomfort. "Remember the briefing by Krantz? The Union doesn't have enough combat troops on Terra Six to fight the Aterniens, so they're trying to land boots on the ground."

Carina adjusted her seat so that it was both closer to her console and tilted toward it. She was looking at the navigation system and appeared consternated, though he admitted that her expression could have simply been due to the g-forces.

"We're flying toward the landing force?" Carina queried, through gritted teeth.

"The destinations of those landing craft will be Cob City and Enterprise City, where the bulk of the Aternien forces are deployed," Carter replied. They were now pulling a steady nine-g burn. "If we can slip in amongst those ships, we can ride on their coattails right down to the surface."

Carina didn't answer and he glanced across to see that she'd passed out. Cursing under his breath, he craned his neck and tried to spot JACAB in the hold.

"Buddy, can you get up here and give the Major a shot?" Carter called out. The blinking lights of the bot suddenly appeared. "And adjust her battle uniform to increase the pressure around her legs."

JACAB warbled and hummed into the cockpit, while Carter returned his attention to intercepting the Union taskforce. The bot interfaced with Carina's battle uniform first, before injecting her in the neck. Moments later, her eyes sprang open, and she sucked in a panicked gulp of air that sounded like a scream in reverse.

"What happened?"

"You blacked out from the acceleration," Carter said. "I had JACAB adjust your uniform so that it acts like an old-fashioned G-suit and give you a cocktail of drugs to help maintain your cardiac output and keep you awake."

"I feel like ass…"

Carter laughed, which in hindsight he realized was a little cruel. However, the forces acting on his XO meant she couldn't shoot him her usual, surly scowl.

"Don't worry, I've already begun the deceleration burn, so just try to hang on for a couple more minutes."

Carter began to ease down, and as their acceleration decreased, the pained expression on his XO's face also began to lessen.

"How do you plan on slipping in amongst those ships?" Carina said, rubbing the spot on her neck where JACAB had injected her. "We're not a part of this taskforce; they might consider us an Aternien trojan horse and blow us out of the ether."

Carter rubbed his beard; that thought had, admittedly, not crossed his mind. He had an idea and turned back to JACAB, who was still humming close by.

"JACAB, do you think you can modify our AIS so that we look like another escort frigate?"

JACAB's lights flashed and the bot's eye sharpened as it considered the suggestion.

"Whatever we do, it needs to be quick," Carina cut in. She was able to lean forward and check her console again. "The Aterniens have cottoned on to the Union's plan and have sent a force of Khopesh destroyers to intercept the landing force."

JACAB warbled and shrugged its maneuvering fins, before interfacing directly with the shuttle's computer system. Suddenly, flashes of Aternien particle energy lit up the void, and straight away the Union ships escorting the landing craft came under heavy fire. Two frigates exploded instantly, while another half a dozen ships were crippled and set adrift, with flames dancing across their stricken hulls.

Carter maneuvered the shuttle through the debris and maintained his course. However, it wasn't only the Aternien guns he had to watch out for. Without a proper identification transponder signal, Carina was right that the Union would consider them a threat too. JACAB warbled, then backed away from the console and tucked his spherical body in beside Major Larsen, like a cat curling up into a ball.

"Nice work, buddy!" Carter said, reading the update that his gopher had transmitted to his uniform's comp-slate. "Now, unless anyone physically looks out of a window, we'll appear as a Union frigate to the fleet's scanners."

A particle blast from a Khopesh destroyer flashed over the top of the cockpit, so close it momentarily blinded him.

"That means the Aterniens will see us as a more tempting target too," Carina replied. She was hugging JACAB, though whether she was trying to comfort the bot, or comfort herself, he couldn't tell. "I hope some of your hundred and seventy-two years of life were spent in advanced pilot training programs?"

Carter hurled the controls left and right, pushing the nimble shuttle through space like it was a speedboat. Smaller chunks of debris pelted their hull, sounding like hailstones on a tin roof, but his focus was on avoiding the larger hulks, as well as the Aternien guns.

"This is Amaya's domain, not mine," Carter said, as another frigate was hit dead center and turned into a raging fireball. "But I'll do my best..."

The lethal game of laser tag continued for several minutes, but it quickly became clear that the Aterniens were the far superior team. Union escorts fought bravely to fend off the Khopesh destroyers, but soon the forerunners had been all but destroyed, leaving the troop transports exposed and vulnerable.

"We've got another couple of minutes before we reach atmosphere," Carina said, as a twisted piece of metal whacked the side of the cockpit glass, scoring a groove into it, like a lathe cutting an LP record. "But I don't know how many of these ships will be left by then."

Carter was suddenly forced to evade as a trio of Khopesh destroyers unleashed an intense barrage of particle energy into the center of the landing force. Two transports were damaged and forced to turn back, but a third was hit cleanly and split open like a coconut. Alarms rang out inside the cabin as wreckage exploded outward like a starburst, but this time there was no chance of going around it.

"Hold on!" Carter called out.

He ignored the sensors and relied on his own acute eyesight and reactions to avoid the debris, but there was simply too much. Twisted components and fractured hull plating gorged holes into their armor, while hundreds of smaller pieces of burning wreckage pockmarked the cockpit glass like buckshot.

Suddenly, a body hit the nose of the shuttle and was drawn over the cockpit glass, leaving a smear of blood in its wake. Carina froze in shock, and if it weren't for his own augmented responses, Carter would have surely locked up too. Then dozens more bodies began flying toward them like organic meteorites.

Carter tried to evade, but it was impossible to miss them all, and they were forced to witness the last moments of hundreds of Union soldiers. Bodies hammered against their hull and already half-dead faces were smashed against the cockpit glass, leaving images of tortured men and women imprinted on his retinas, like gruesome tattoos. It was all over within a matter of seconds, yet he knew the horrors he'd just witnessed would remain with him for the rest of life.

"Twelve troop carriers are down, already," Carina said, her voice little more than a ghostly whisper. "That's over five thousand dead…"

"Try to put it out of you mind, Major," Carter said, pulling in behind one of the few remaining destroyers and using it as cover. He glanced at his XO and knew that his words had simply washed over her. "Those that followed protocol would have been wearing combat helmets. There's a chance that the SAR teams might get to them before…"

He chose not to speak the final words of his sentence, "before they die." It didn't need to be said, and Carina didn't need reminding.

Suddenly flashes lit up the cabin and the destroyer ahead of them was ripped to shreds by Aternien weapons fire. The ship's forward section exploded, but the engines continued to burn brightly, causing the vessel to spin away and begin tearing itself apart. Carter reacted instantly, pushing below the bulk of the debris, before pulling up and flying through the fireball left behind from the burning fuels tanks. More alarms sounded and their already beleaguered hull was subjected to more impacts. Then a more strident alert followed, and Carter knew that they were in trouble.

"Hull breach!" Carina called out. At the same time, her head covering automatically engaged, cocooning her inside her battle uniform. "It looks like it's on the port side, near the base of the cargo doors!"

"I'll handle it!" Carter yelled, as the air in the cabin rushed toward the rear of the shuttle. "Take the controls."

He unclipped his harness and jumped out of his seat, using his incredible strength to ensure he wasn't blown aft. He could see the breach, and though it was almost microscopically small, he knew it wouldn't be long before there was a hole in the hull large enough for JACAB to fit through.

"We're through the blockade!" Carina called out, though her voice was almost lost in the rush of air. "But we've only got about sixty seconds before we hit the upper atmosphere."

"Stay on course, no matter what," Carter called back. He was already halfway through the hold, using the cargo netting and structural supports to brace himself. "We can't afford to slow up, or the Aterniens will tag us before we're clear."

"Understood," Carina replied, though her voice was shaky and uncertain.

Carter continued to pull himself toward the rupture, grabbing a breach-sealing kit from the wall as he did so. Energy blasts crisscrossed space all around them, and Carter could see flames beginning to creep around the ship as friction with the atmosphere heated their hull.

"Hurry up, or it's going to get pretty warm in here!" Carina added, not yet too afraid to make a joke.

Carter snorted a laugh and dropped down beside the breach. The suggestion that he was doing anything other than hurrying amused him, despite their dire circumstances. Cracking open the sealing kit, he cleared the debris from around the breach and placed the device over the hole, which had already grown to the size of a walnut. The plunger adapted its shape and molded to the contours of the ship, but still the hiss of air remained.

"Damn it, the sealing kit hasn't worked."

"Structural integrity is still falling," Carina called back. "I don't think we'll survive entry!"

Carter cursed under his breath and leaned in closer. The

sealing device, which was essentially a malleable metal plunger, had failed to properly mold itself around the breach.

"Carter, what's happening back there?" His XO now sounded frantic but turning back meant certain death. The only way to survive was to make it down to the planet's surface, which meant he had to seal the hull breach, no matter what.

"Stay on course!" Carter shouted back, while grabbing the metal plunger with both hands.

Gritting his teeth, he pushed on the device with all his strength, not only bending the metal to his will, but warping the hull plating around it too. Suddenly, the device latched on, the rush of escaping air ceased, and the alarms stopped wailing. He blew out a sigh and flopped onto his back, but all he could see was the outline of Carina's head, silhouetted against a backdrop of fire.

They were on course to Terra Six, but despite their close call, the irony was that reaching the planet's surface was only the first part of their hazardous assignment.

FIVE

SCARABS OF THE SKY

CARTER CLIMBED BACK into his seat and fastened his harness, relieved to finally see the gleaming blue sky of Terra Six, instead of the inferno of atmospheric entry. Yet, while the immediate risk of being blown to pieces by Aternien destroyers, or burning up in the atmosphere, had been averted, they were still in significant danger.

"Get low as fast as you can," Carter said, as the shuttle dipped below the clouds, giving them their first glimpse of Enterprise City. "The Aterniens will have set up surface-to-air batteries around the city and will be patrolling the skies with drones and single-seater combat craft, called Khepri fighters."

"Descending now," Carina said, pitching the nose of the shuttle more sharply toward the ground. "We'll need a place to set down that's out of sight."

Carter could hear the thump of her heartbeat and see the sweat coating her face and neck but considering how close they'd come to dying only moments earlier, his XO had held it together well.

"The closer we can get to the inner city the better," Carter replied. "I'll scout a location, just as soon as the shuttle's scanners come back online."

He slapped the side of the navigation computer with the side of his hand, causing the screen to judder and distort, before turning black again. Cursing, he pulled a panel off the console, tearing it free rather than bothering to unlock it, and tossed it over his shoulder. JACAB warbled his annoyance, and Carter realized he'd almost struck the bot with the slab of metal.

"Sorry, buddy," he said, genuinely apologetic. "Do you think you can get in here, and fix these damned scanners? Right now, the major is flying using mark one eyeballs, only."

JACAB bleeped in agreement then hummed underneath the dash and set to work interfacing with the systems. At the same time, a long streak of fire caught his attention off the starboard side, and he looked out to see two troop transports crashing through the clouds. They were accompanied by six other troop carriers, which he was heartened to see were in much better condition. However, he still felt a twist of anger in his gut, knowing that another eight or nine hundred Union soldiers were about to die, and there was nothing that he, or anyone else, could do to stop it.

Carter maintained a solemn silence as the stricken transports smashed into the hills beyond the city limits, turning a lush green woodland into a lake of fire and death. He could see that Carina had witnessed the crash too, but she was following his earlier advice to put any feelings of remorse or sadness aside and focus on the mission. It was an easy lesson to teach, but a hard one to follow, even for a veteran like himself.

JACAB warbled cheerfully, and the scanners rebooted. Dozens of new contacts appeared, but it was a mess of readings that made it impossible to discern friendly from foe. Even so, it was enough to survey the city and assess a suitable landing site.

"Enterprise Stadium has a private shuttle garage, which is under cover and secured, so I think that's our best bet," Carter said, highlighting the garage on the scanner for Carina to see.

"It's on the opposite side of the city to where we're coming in," his XO replied. She was flying low over the suburbs, where panic-stricken residents were desperately loading vehicles and flyers, in an effort to flee. "Do we try to skirt around, or go straight through?"

Suddenly, a tremendous roar filled the sky and Carter saw a Union troop transport and a frigate both spiraling toward the ground. They hit hard and exploded like bombs, then a formation of three Aternien Khepri fighters burst through the flames, heading directly for them. Carter was about to call out to Carina to evade, but she'd seen the danger and reacted with a swiftness that almost matched his own. Particle cannon fire flashed past and slammed into a block of condos, causing half of the building to collapse.

"Head into the city and stay low," Carter said, twisting his body to keep sight of the Khepri fighters. "If we stay out in the open, we're an easy target. At least in the city, we get to test the Aternien's piloting skills."

"And my own…" Carina added, increasing speed, and nudging the nose down by another half a degree.

The Khepri fighters, which resembled scarab beetles, but with sleeker and thinner bodies, continued on course for a few seconds, then turned sharply and began heading back toward the city.

"Damn it, I'd expect those bastards to go after bigger fish than us," Carter said, fearing the worst. "JACAB, try to jam their targeting scanners. This bucket doesn't have any weapons, not that we're in any condition to fight."

JACAB warbled then plugged itself into the tactical system, its many indicator lights flashing chaotically as it did so. A target lock blared out, but Carina was already on it, cutting a hard right and putting a business center between them and the Aterniens. Particle cannon blasts ripped through several floors of the building, causing shattered glass and debris to rain down on the empty streets below, but their shuttle wasn't hit.

"We can't outrun them forever," Carina said, practically skimming the surface at road level, while weaving through the Enterprise City's war-torn streets. "And if they follow us to the stadium, we'll have an entire regiment of Aternien Immortals on our asses before you can say, 'Mesek-tet'."

Carter cursed under his breath then removed his harness. "Keep evading, but when I tell you to fly straight, fly straight..."

Carina looked at him like he'd lost his marbles, but he jumped out of his seat and headed aft, drawing his 57-EX from its holster as he did so.

"Carter, come on; even you can't shoot down enemy fighters with a handgun!"

"We'll see about that," he grunted in reply. He was then thrown hard against the wall, as Carina jinked left to avoid another volley from the Aternien particle cannons. The impact only served to make him more determined to shake the flying scarabs off their tail. "Just keep flying; I'll do the rest."

He was about to pull the emergency release lever to open the rear doors, when he spotted a set of tactical webbing hanging on the wall and stopped to look at it.

"What gear did you bring with you?" Carter called back.

"Nothing much; just whatever I could sneak out of the armory," Carina answered, weaving from avenue to avenue like a downhill skier running a slalom course. "Some gauss pistols, mags, a few grenades…"

Carter smiled then grabbed a grenade from one of the webbing pouches and continued aft, using his super-human grip-strength to anchor himself in place. "Standby…" he called out, before yanking the handle and causing the rear ramp to fly open.

"Standby for what?!" His XO's cry was consumed by the rush of air that flooded inside the shuttle. The craft shimmied and vibrated as its aerodynamics was suddenly disrupted, but Carina wrestled the craft back on course, and Carter held on too.

"Take the freeway and level off!" Carter yelled, grateful that his augmented biology also gave him the ability to shout at volumes that could deafen normal human ears.

If his XO had a spoken a reply, he didn't hear it, but soon the shuttle changed course, and the long expressway that linked the north of the metropolis to the south began unfurling behind him. Small arms fire crackled, and Carter saw squads of Aternien Immortals battling against Union ground troops, who were fighting block-to-block to retake the city. However, right at that moment, it was Khepri fighters that concerned him the most, and before long, the scarab-shaped craft were swooping in for the kill.

"Hold her steady!" Carter yelled.

Dagger-like splinters of particle energy flashed past, but Carter didn't flinch. He drew back the grenade, armed it, then flung it at the lead Khepri fighter with the force of a cannonball. The explosive thudded into the craft and detonated, blinding its pilot to the route ahead. The fighter lost control and collided with its wingman on the port side, sending both vessels crashing into the freeway like falling stars.

The third and final Khepri fighter banked hard to avoid the collision but was back on their tail in a near instant. Particle cannons flashed from beneath the craft's stubby nose and the shuttle was hit, but not badly. Steadying himself again, he aimed his 57-EX and squeezed off all five rounds in the blink of an eye. Combined with the forward velocity of the fighter, the impact of the bullets was like being hit by a series of miniature supernovae. Sparks and flames erupted all across the vessel's hull, then it exploded in mid-air like a firework on steroids.

"We're clear!" Carter called out, holstering his revolver then flipping the handle back to the closed position to seal the door. "Take us into the stadium's garage, before anyone else comes after us."

Returning to the cabin, he jumped over the back of the seat and dropped down into the padded cushion with a satisfied groan of pleasure. It was then that he noticed his XO giving him the side-eye.

"What?"

"What do you mean, what?" Carina said, astonished. "You just took out three Aternien fighters with a frag grenade and a revolver!"

Carter shrugged. "I know…" he said, trying to sound

nonchalant, though in truth, he was feeling pretty smug about the achievement. "Now stop gawping and set this shuttle down, before it finally decides to give up the ghost and drop out of the sky."

"Well, since you asked so nicely…" Carina replied, before guiding the craft toward the stadium on the south-west edge of the city. Gunfire continued to crackle all around them, while both Union and Aternien fighter craft wrestled for supremacy of the skies. Smoke was rising from all corners of the metropolis, but it looked like the operation to land troops on the planet had ended. He had no idea how many of the original forty landing craft had succeeded in reaching Terra Six, but he had a sinking feeling that no matter the number, it wouldn't be enough.

"JACAB, can you hack the garage door, please?" Carina said, maneuvering in front of the entrance. "Understandably, there's no-one on duty to take our call."

JACAB bleeped an obliging tone then a few seconds later the heavy slabs of metal began to separate and slide into their housings. Carina inched the shuttle inside, and it soon became clear that no-one else was home.

"It looks like all the rich folk who can afford a permanent parking spot here have already bugged out," Carter said. He'd spotted maybe half a dozen craft inside the four-hundred capacity garage.

"They're the smart ones, and the lucky ones," Carina replied. "Most people in the city don't have the luxury of escaping off world."

Considering the garage was practically deserted, Carina availed herself of one of the VIP parking slots, close to the exit elevators and stairwells. The shuttle hit the asphalt with a hard thump, then creaked and groaned like an old pirate galleon as the battered hull took up the strain of the ship's mass.

"We'd best not hang around in here for long," Carter said, leaping out of his seat again. It felt like he'd spent more time out of it than in it. "I wouldn't be surprised if Aternien scouts saw us come in here, so we should expect company. And not of the pleasant kind…"

SIX

STADIUM PERFORMANCE

MAJOR CARINA LARSEN opened the rear ramp of their stolen Union shuttle and headed outside. Carter followed, immediately picking up the high-pitched metallic chime of the ship's engines and reactor as they cooled. The timbre was off, which didn't instill him with confidence, nor did the sight of the pockmarked and scorched armor plating, and cracked glass panels.

"It's a miracle we made it to the surface at all," Carter said, placing a hand to one of the broken armor panels, which felt hot to the touch. "I'll say one thing for Krantz's shuttle; it's a tough little sucker."

"These VIP landing bays have auto-repair and auto-valeting stations." Carina was inspecting a bank of industrial-looking machines next to the bay. "I doubt there's much they can do to patch up the shuttle, but anything is better than nothing."

Carter nodded then looked for JACAB, but the machine was already beside Major Larsen, inspecting the contraptions. "What do you think, buddy? Is it worth activating?"

JACAB continued to examine the machine then looked at him and shrugged his maneuvering fins.

"Do it anyway. Even if it can just patch up the holes and fix the glass, it will increase our chances of this thing reaching space again."

JACAB nodded and interfaced with the machine. It sparked into life moments later and a troop of automated drones trundled out from a compartment beneath the main console. Compared to the hovering, intelligent orb that was JACAB, they looked almost laughably crude. Then there was a sound and Carter's senses jumped up a notch. His hand went to the grip of his 57-EX revolver, and he began to carefully survey their surroundings, but besides the other parked craft, the garage remained empty.

"Let's get out gear and move out," Carter said warily, backing toward the open cargo door of the shuttle, hand still wrapped around his revolver.

Carina jogged inside and equipped her energy pistol before pulling on a long military frock-coat, similar to the one Carter was wearing.

"Great minds think alike," he said, smiling at his XO. "But if you're going to be Longsword crew, you'll need a sword too."

Carina snorted-laughed. "Honestly, I would advise against that. Not unless you want to lose an ear or a hand, or an entire arm for that matter."

Another faint sound wiped the smile from Carter's face, but even with his acute hearing, he couldn't place the origin of the noise. Carina stepped to his side, wearing a backpack over the top of her coat, and shut the cargo bay door. She had her personal comp-slate in her hand, and the device was unfolded to letter-paper size.

"I pulled the latest intel on Cai Cooper from the Union Intelligence mainframe before we set out," Carina said, holding the slate so that Carter could see it. "From what we can gather, it looks like he's in a relationship with a doctor called Lola Carney, who's registered at Mount Leeman hospital in the city."

The news almost bowled him over. "In a relationship? With a real woman?"

Carina raised an eyebrow. "Yes, a *real* woman. What were you expecting; a sex doll?"

"I wasn't expecting him to be seeing anyone at all," Carter hit back. Carina's sarcasm had gotten his hackles up. "Cai was always such a cold fish. Always so logical and direct, almost to the point of being uncaring. I guess I just never saw him in a relationship."

"People change, Carter, especially after a hundred years." Carina folded the comp-slate and slid it into her pocket before side-eyeing him again. "You're telling me you never hooked up with anyone? Not ever?"

Carter folded his arms and looked down his nose at his XO. "That's none of your damned business."

There was now a twinkle in her eye. "I bet you did, a hunky silver fox like you... I'll bet you had your own little harem on that forest moon, tucked away in that cabin, out of sight."

"I'd focus your thinking on trying to find this doctor, if I were you," Carter said. Even during the best of times, he was disinclined to talk about his personal life, but especially now, and especially since his personal life was non-existent.

"Fine, be like that," Carina said, with a dollop of sass.

"Besides, I already know where to find her, because the hospital records list her home address. She lives in the city, close to the hospital. 1725 North 45th street."

"Well, why didn't you say so?" Carter said, feeling particularly grouchy. He then had a disquieting thought. "How did Union Intelligence find out about this relationship? Cai might have changed in a hundred years, but if it means he's become careless, that could be a problem."

Carina quickly slipped the comp-slate out of her pocket and reviewed the records.

"It says he was caught on a hospital security camera, with Lola Carney," his XO revealed. "Still, we've only been able to tag him a handful of times in the last few decades, so I'd say that's pretty good going."

Carter grunted and stroked his beard. Then the noise came again, and this time his ears pinpointed the location. Someone was stalking up the stairs on the opposite side of the garage.

"Fall back, away from the shuttle," Carter whispered. He moved quickly and quietly toward an exit that placed structural supports and a parked vehicle between him and the approaching footsteps.

Carina stayed close and JACAB hummed silently behind them. Then doors across the far side of the garage were gently eased open, and a group of armed men and women stole inside.

"Could it be Union resistance fighters?" asked Carina, noting that the arrivals were not in uniform.

Carter watched the group for a few more seconds, but his instincts told him otherwise. "I don't think so. They don't move like soldiers. My guess is they're acolytes." He turned to JACAB and spoke quietly into the bot's audio receptor. "Create a scanner inference bubble. Try to extend it around this whole level if you can."

JACAB nodded and set to work; his various antennae spinning and reconfiguring on the fly. At the same time, the final member of the six-person group entered the docking level. He thought that was it, until a seventh man walked inside, making far less of an effort to disguise his arrival. At first, the man had his back to Carter; then the figure turned around and he got a clean look at his face.

"That's Marco Ryan," Carter whispered. "He was Master-at-arms of the Longsword Rhongomiant, but he's now Damien Morrow's turncoat lapdog."

Marco Ryan relayed orders to the acolyte squad then walked into the center of the garage. The man had lifted his chin and scrunched his brow, as if trying to place an unusual scent that had just wafted past his nostrils. However, Carter understood the look well; Ryan's senses had just been piqued; the man knew that danger was close by.

"Should we take them out?" Carina asked. "After three Aternien fighters, these goons should be no sweat."

Carter shook his head. "They don't know for certain we're here. It's best we remain undetected, for as long as we can." He checked their surroundings and saw there was still a clear route to the exit that would keep them hidden from Marco Ryan's probing gaze. "Let's go. Nice and slow…"

Carter took the lead and Carina followed, both of them creeping like cats in the night, and soon they had reached the exit. He nodded to JACAB, who understood his intent and quickly bypassed the lock, allowing Carter to slowly force open the door by just enough to squeeze through. Carina went through first, followed by JACAB. Carter was about to exit as well, when the voice of Marco Ryan filled the docking garage with the intensity of the PA system.

"I know you're here, Carter Rose!" the man bellowed. Ryan's coat fell open, and Carter spotted a sheathed sword tied around the man's waist. "Acolyte Commander Morrow would like to speak with you, Longsword-to-Longsword."

Part of him wanted to march out and cut down the traitor then and there, and he had to force himself to take his own advice and stay hidden.

"We just want to talk," Ryan called out, as Carter pushed himself through the narrow opening into the stairwell beyond. "You know the Union can't win this war. Don't give your life fighting for people who despise what you are. There's still time to join us, Carter. There's still time to make the right choice."

Carter gritted his teeth and slid the doors shut, partly to disguise their exit point, but also in the hope it would shut out the man's sermonizing. Staying low, he crept down the first flight of stairs to where Carina and JACAB were waiting, then together they hurried to the ground level.

"You took your time," Carina said, with a mildly accusatory tone that didn't sit well with him. "For a moment, I thought you'd signed up with psycho-at-arms, up there."

"I don't mind jokes, Major, but not about that," Carter said. His blood was pumping, and he was feeling combative. "My oath is all I have. I didn't break with it a century ago, and I'm sure as hell not going to now."

Carina seemed to recognize her error, and quickly backed down. "I'm sorry, Commander. I was out of line."

"Yes, you were," Carter hit back. "While we're at it, my personal life is off limits too. I don't ask about your sex life, even though I'm sure you'd love to regale me with stories of your many conquests."

"That's kinda presumptuous, but point taken," Carina replied, reaching the bottom of their stairwell first. "Besides, I don't think your old ticker could handle my dating anecdotes. They're a bit saucy for someone of your advancing years."

Carter snorted a laugh and shook his head. Even when she was being borderline obnoxious, Carina still had a charming manner about her. Pushing through the door, he stepped out into the street, then his senses spiked, and he stopped dead.

"What is it?"

"Someone's coming," Carter said, feeling that danger was near. "Keep moving but act casual."

Carina nodded then pulled her coat more tightly around her body to hide as much of her uniform as possible. Carter did the same, and JACAB hummed behind him, hugging the recess at the small of his back to remain out of sight. Then a group of four people climbed out of an underpass and began walking toward them. They were dressed the same as the acolytes in the garage, and Carter could see they were concealing weapons inside their jacket pockets. In that moment, he knew he had to act.

Reaching inside his coat, he gripped the handle of his plasma cutlass and rested his thumb on the switch to ignite the blade. The four drew closer, hands inside their pockets and eyes locked onto him, like scallywags looking for a fight. The front two pulled weapons, but Carter had preempted their actions, and had already drawn and ignited his blade.

His first cut severed the lead man's arm off at the elbow, while a downward strike sliced open the neck of the second acolyte as if her flesh was nothing more than air. Then he sprang at the remaining pair, spinning the blade at them like a helicopter rotor. Two heads thudded into the ground a second later, like coconuts falling from a palm tree.

The fight was over in seconds, and with barely more than a whimper escaping from the lips of his victims. He disengaged the blade and sheathed his cutlass, before turning back to a pale-faced Major Larsen, who was watching the severed heads roll off the sidewalk and into the bushes. Then he caught movement in his peripheral vision and saw Marco Ryan peering down at him from the upper-level balcony. The man clenched his hand into a fist and shook it at him.

"Get them!"

SEVEN
OLD WARRIORS DUEL

CARTER EXITED the underpass and was met with the rattle of gunfire and flashes of Aternien particle weapons. Pitched battles were being fought all around them, with Union soldiers desperately trying to push back a superior enemy that was already entrenched in the beleaguered city. Recon drones and scarab-shaped Khepri fighters roared overhead, pursued by Union Talon H1 heavy fighters, one of which took the full brunt of a surface-to-air-missile and exploded violently directly above his head.

"Which way do we go?" Carina called out, ducking as more particle blasts flashed along the street.

"We stick to the plan and head to the doctor's house," Carter replied. His augmented biology, along with his combat experience, allowed him to remain calm and assess their situation without panic or fear.

"But that must be ten kliks from here," Carina pointed out. "At this rate, we'll barely make it five hundred meters on foot, before being cut down."

Suddenly, the remains of an Aternien squad of Immortals marched around a corner directly ahead. Carter pulled Carina out of the line of fire, moments before shards of energy cut through the air where she'd been standing. He returned fire with his revolver, killing three of the five warriors with headshots, before the final two were put down by his XO. Despite her human nerves jangling like a bag of spanners, he was pleased to see that her aim remained steady.

"Nice shooting," Carter said, while reloading his 57-EX. "You're right, we can't hope to make it on foot, especially with Marco Ryan looking for us." He turned to JACAB, who was tucked into cover, beside Carina. "Buddy, I need you to find us a transit or flyer that isn't surrounded by goldies."

JACAB nodded then his antenna swirled so quickly Carter thought it might fly off. His comp-slate vibrated, and he pulled back the sleeve of his coat to see that the bot had uploaded a map of their immediate vicinity. JACAB had highlighted a block directly across from a public park that was currently clear of enemy action.

"Nice work, we can likely find a private ground transit there that will get us to the doctor's house," Carter said, rapping his knuckles against the shell of the bot. He was about to move out when gauss slugs hammered into the wall next to him, chipping splinters of bricks and mortar into his face. He spun around and fired, driving Marco Ryan's Acolytes of Aternus into cover. However, from what he'd already seen of the fanatics, he knew they wouldn't stop coming for them.

"Let's hustle. We don't want Ryan to see where we're headed."

JACAB lit up the underpass with blasts from his own plasma cannons, then they all made a dash for the park on the other side of the street. A group of Immortals spotted their run, and particle blasts chased them, but the Aterniens were shooting indiscriminately, not caring whether they were attacking military or civilian targets. JACAB continued to harass the acolytes with his needle-like shots of energy, until they'd all gathered at the boundary of the grassy common.

"I had no idea it would be like this…" Carina said, stealing through the trees and into the open, greener space beyond.

"You had no idea what would be like this?" Carter replied, jogging backwards to cover their rear.

"War…" Carina spoke the word as if understanding its true meaning for the first time. Like all Union officers, she'd studied war, and even played war games, but nothing compared to the brutal, bloody reality of armed conflict. She, like all of the other members of the Union, were finding that out to their cost.

"I'd like to say you get used to it, but you don't, not really," Carter said. Even though he hadn't seen action for a century, the memory of it never faded. "But you will become more accustomed to fighting, so long as you stay calm and don't drop you guard even for a…"

Carter's senses spiked and he didn't have time to finish the sentence before an acolyte ran through the trees, weapon held outstretched. He reacted like the snap of a scorpion's tail and shot the man clean through the heart, but soon more of the Aternien sympathizers had gathered, and were trying to surround them.

"Take cover over there!" Carter called out, leading Carina toward a brick-built café in the center of the common.

They ran hard gauss slugs tearing up the turf around their feet. Since his body was more resilient, Carter kept himself between Carina and their attackers, soaking up shots like a sponge. Reloading on the move, he returned fire, and three more acolytes were hit and killed, but the others were zeroing in on them, and gauss slugs continued to bite into his flesh.

Carina then took a hit to the calf and was sent crashing to the grass. Carter put down two more acolytes then grabbed his XO and hauled her into cover behind the café. However, while the brick wall functioned as an effective barrier, Carter knew their respite would be short-lived.

"JACAB, how many more are out there?" Carter asked, as the bot zipped around the corner with the nimbleness of a racing drone.

The machine warbled and squawked, and the positions of the acolytes appeared on Carter's comp-slate. Four were directly east and slowly approaching the café, while another four were moving in from the northwest corner, trying to get behind them.

"Did you pack any more of those frag grenades into your gear?" Carter asked his XO, while showing her the information on his comp-slate.

"Yes, in the left side-pocket of my pack," Carina replied.

She was crouched in a firing position, watching for the acolytes that were stealthily approaching from the northwest. Blood was trickling down her leg where she'd taken the hit, but the battle uniform had spared her from serious injury, and she was ignoring the pain and staying focused on their enemies.

"Cover the east; I'll deal with the four trying to sneak up behind us," Carter ordered.

Carina nodded and allowed Carter to remove two frag grenades from her pack, before they swapped positions. He attached one grenade to his battle uniform, which gripped the explosive with a localized magnetic force, then set the fuse on the other for three seconds.

"Let's see if we can't smoke out our traitorous friends," Carter said, gripping the grenade tightly in his fist.

He updated the location of the acolytes on his comp-slate, then darted out from cover and hurled the grenade at their position like a pitcher throwing a fastball. The charge exploded and cries of pain filled the air. Two targets blinked off his comp-slate, while the other two acolytes staggered away, clawing burning-hot metal from their faces and necks.

Fear and panic are a soldier's worst enemies, Carter thought, as he picked off the two injured men with carefully-aimed shots from his 57-EX. *Fear and panic are what get you killed…*

"Come out, Commander Rose!"

Carter recognized the voice of Marco Ryan and tried to spot the former Master-at-arms amongst the trees to the east, but the augmented soldier was hidden well. Even so, he could still see the man on his scanner readout.

"This is pointless!" Ryan continued, his anger and frustration laid bare. "You can't kill us all. Why throw your life away, fighting for these people? You're better than this. You're better than the humans!"

"I'd pay serious money for that guy to shut up," Carina hissed through gritted teeth.

Carter holstered his revolver and drew his cutlass. "I find that the best way to shut people up is to take off their heads."

"That's… dark," his XO replied, suddenly looking like she'd rather face a troop of Immortals than be next to him.

"War is dark, Major," Carter replied, plainly. "Better get used to it."

Carter checked JACAB's scanner reading and saw that three of the acolytes were standing further back from Ryan's position. He grabbed the second grenade from his uniform, turned the dial to four seconds, then hurled it over the top of the café. To Carina, it might have seemed like a casual lob, when in fact he'd weighed and measured the throw precisely. With the grenade still in flight, he then marched around the side of the building and headed directly for the acolytes.

"Carter, what are you doing?!" Carina called out, her voice strained and panicky.

There was no time to explain before the grenade exploded in the midst of the three acolytes to Ryan's flank. One was torn apart, as if the explosive had detonated inside his body, while the other two were blown five meters clear. Both thumped into the grass, crying out in pain, and trying to claw themselves under the cover of the trees.

In contrast, Marco Ryan hadn't flinched. Smoke wisped from the man's jacket, where smoldering fragments of metal had lodged into his clothing, while more shrapnel had peppered the right side of his face. The former Longsword officer simply advanced toward Carter, like two boxers moving out from their respective corners to meet in the middle of the ring.

"It doesn't have to be this way," Ryan said, pulling back his jacket to reveal the sword sheathed at his hip. Carter recognized it as a revolutionary war saber. "You could be a leader in the new dynasty; a civilization where people like you and me are treated as gods."

"Spare me any more of your horseshit, Ryan," Carter countered. He ignited the plasma-edge of his blade and activated his buckler. "You're a traitor and that's all there is to it."

Ryan shook his head. "Have it your way, Commander..." The former Master-at-arms drew his sword and the saber fizzed with golden Aternien energy.

"I see that your overlords have given you a new sword," Carter said, admiring the weapon in his opponent's hand. "It's a shame you chose to waste your talents fighting for the enemy."

"You are my enemy now, Commander," Ryan answered, taking a guard. "But out of respect, I'll make your death a quick one."

Marco Ryan attacked, thrusting the energized saber towards Carter's gut. He parried and countered, but Ryan deflected the strike and came at him again, forcing Carter to retreat out of range.

"I heard you were good," Ryan said, flourishing the sword, which hummed like an electricity substation. "I've always wanted to find out how good."

Carter flourished his saber and inched forward. "Let me show you."

The two blades clashed, spitting sparks of energy into the air like flint striking metal. To normal human eyes, the exchanges would have appeared feverish and chaotic, but each move and countermove was precisely orchestrated. Recorded and replayed at half speed, it would have been beautiful to watch, like two dancing masters, exposing the best of their deadly art. Then Ryan scored a glancing blow to Carter's shoulder, and he backed out of range, drawing an arrogant smile from his opponent.

"Perhaps you have lost a step, old man," Ryan said, mocking him with a sinister smile. "Maybe you're not worthy of the blessings of Aternus, after all?"

Growing in confidence, Ryan thrust for his neck, and Carter barely managed to parry. The blow affected his balance and Ryan seized his chance, slicing through his coat and battle uniform, and cutting into his flesh. The pain was numbed, and the energized edge of the sword cauterized the wound, but Carter knew he'd been lucky not to receive a crippling blow.

"You have no idea how many of us there are," Ryan said, continuing to harangue Carter with words as well as his blade. "Our acolyte movement was formed in the shadows over decades, right under the Union's nose."

Carter snorted with derision. "Such a proud traitor… You're a disgrace to everything we fought for."

"And what did we fight for?" Ryan snarled. The man danced forward and forced Carter to defend against a flurry of whirling cuts and strikes. "We bled for the Union, and they discarded us like trash!" Their blades clashed again, and sparks burned Carter's face. "But by joining with Aternus, I will live forever."

Carter parried another attack, then pushed his opponent back, and battled Ryan to a standstill, but the man's traitorous words were still ringing in his ears and making him nauseous with rage.

"You can't live forever, Ryan," he growled, tightening the grip on his cutlass. "Especially if you're dead."

Carter advanced and cut upward, but his opponent

evaded the strike, and responded with a lunge to his throat, forcing him to protect his neck both with sword and buckler, before counterattacking to the body. Ryan parried and for several seconds their swords clashed in a furious ballet of parry-riposte, until Carter exposed an opening, and hammered the guard of his cutlass into Ryan's face. The former Master-at-arms reeled back, and Carter pursued, forcing his opponent to scurry out of range. Dabbing blood from his nose, Ryan looked down at his shirt and pulled open the sliced fabric to reveal golden, scale armor beneath.

Carter laughed and shook his head. "Another gift from your Aternien masters, I take it?"

"And what have your masters ever given you, besides disrespect and hatred?" Ryan replied. The smirk had been well-and-truly wiped from the man's face. "You're the real traitor, Commander. A traitor to your own kind."

"Save it, Ryan, we knew what we were signing up for," Carter answered.

"I didn't sign up to be hated!" Ryan spat. "We should have been hailed as heroes. Instead, the Union treated us like lepers."

"I'd rather that than be a traitor." Carter raised his guard. "Now shut up and fight."

The two squared-off, then Carter's senses spiked, and he felt another, even greater danger closing in. His eyes were drawn to a full squad of Aternien Immortals marching toward the park and closing fast.

"Looks like your time is finally up," Ryan said. The smirk had returned. "Get on your knees, and I'll make it quick."

Suddenly, the turncoat Master-at-arms was hit in the chest by a series of plasma blasts that knocked the man off his feet. Then Major Larsen came running at him, smoking energy pistol in hand.

"You can finish your swashbuckling another time," Carina called out. She was rightly more concerned with the squad of Immortals than Marco Ryan. "Right now, we have to run!"

EIGHT
ROAD RAGE

THE SQUAD of Aterniens opened fire in concentrated bursts, pulverizing the brick-built café and reducing it to rubble, but Carter, Carina and JACAB were already long gone. Using his plasma cutlass to hack through the trees and dense bushes lining the park, Carter pushed through onto the street beyond. It was deserted, with destroyed vehicles and dead Union soldiers and civilians littering the road and sidewalk, giving the impression of a post-apocalyptic wasteland, instead of what should have been a bustling, thriving city.

"JACAB, find us a vehicle. Something hardy," Carter said, taking cover behind an upturned bus.

Carina was hot on his heels, but instead of keeping a look out for Aternien Immortals, she was checking the bodies of the dead soldiers. "We're going to need more firepower than a couple of handguns can deliver, even when one of those handguns is your 57-EX."

She removed a gauss rifle from a fallen soldier and slung it over her shoulder, before recovering as many magazines as she could find. Carter found that he was impressed with his XO's ability to detach her emotions and focus on the mission. It was a macabre and unsettling thing to be proud of, but the harsh reality was that mourning the dead would have to come later. In the heat of battle, it was fatal to get hung up on the loss of life.

The bus was suddenly hit by Aternien particle fire, and Carter was showered with sparks and flying shards of glass. He chanced a look around the side of the mangled vehicle and saw the squad of Immortals that had been pursuing them through the park working their way toward them. It was formed of nine regular Aternien warriors and a Warden; a capable warrior who was subordinate to an Overseer.

"JACAB, we could really use that vehicle right now," Carter called out, while harassing the approaching Immortals with shots from his high-powered revolver. There was no reply, and he couldn't see his bot anywhere. "Where the hell has that machine got to?"

"He'll be back," Carina said, her back thumping into the upturned belly of the bus. "We just have to hold them off for a few more seconds."

Carina hustled to the other end of the vehicle then opened fire with the gauss rifle. The weapon fizzed and Carter saw the solid slugs rattle and clang off the armored bodies of the Aternien Immortals.

"Shit, it's like I'm shooting blanks!" Carina cursed, releasing the spent magazine, and slapping a new one into place.

"Aim for the head, it's the only way you'll stop them with conventional weapons," Carter answered. By way of a demonstration he then picked off an Immortal with a precise shot straight between the eyes, which blew the Aternien's head off like popping a champagne cork.

"What I need is one of those damned revolvers," Carina called back, ducking deeper into cover as particle energy ripped into the bus close to where she was hiding.

Suddenly, the sound of a horn honking made Carter pull back and spin around. A pick-up truck was racing toward them, horn still blaring as if the driver was in the throes of road rage. Aternien particle energy was redirected at the vehicle, which quickly sped behind the upturned bus to avoid being hit.

"Here's our ride!" said Carina running for the passenger side. "I call shotgun…"

"Shotgun?" Carter cried, diving over the tailgate into the bed of the pickup. "If you're in the passenger seat, who the hell is driving?"

There was a series of cheerful bleeps and warbles and Carter looked through the rear windows to see JACAB attached to the steering wheel. He waved his maneuvering fins at him then the truck suddenly accelerated hard, leaving a trail of melted rubber on the road behind them.

"Buddy, I didn't know you could drive!" Carter called out, clinging on with one hand to stop himself from being thrown out of the back.

JACAB warbled and shrugged his maneuvering fins, which Carter took to mean that his gopher hadn't known he could drive either, at least not until a couple of minutes ago. However, the surprise and relief at finding his trusty bot at the wheel was short-lived, as shards of particle energy began chasing the vehicle. One shot smashed though the floodlight above the cabin, missing Carter's head by inches. Ducking lower, he peered behind and saw that the squad of

Immortals were in pursuit and gaining fast. Incredibly, they were still on foot.

"What the hell is up with these people?" Carina said. She had the passenger side window wound down and was hanging out of it, weapon in hand. "Don't they know when to quit?"

"They never quit," Carter replied, with an air of weary resignation. He opened the cylinder of his revolver and shook out the empty cartridges. "They don't tire. They don't get frustrated. They just keep coming, and the only way to stop them is to take them out."

Sliding five more rounds into his 57-EX, he closed the cylinder then maneuvered himself to the rear of the truck's bed. JACAB must have been pushing fifty miles per hour through the narrow streets of Enterprise City, yet the Aterniens were keeping pace.

"Let's see you run without legs, you synthetic bastards," Carter muttered under his breath. He took aim and squeezed off the first round, hitting the lead warrior in the kneecap and blowing the Aternien's lower leg clean off. The warrior went down hard and skidded across the road for another twenty meters before finally colliding with the burned-out carcass of another vehicle.

"That's one…"

He aimed and fired again, sinking the powerful, armor-piercing .50 caliber round into the left hip of a pursuing Immortal. This time, the limb remained attached, but the joint was destroyed, and the warrior fell, tripping up another to its rear and taking both out of commission.

"That's three…"

He was about to fire again when the squad suddenly split up. Two darted left and two went right, moving along an adjacent street and using the buildings for cover. That still left three directly to their rear, including the Warden.

"Keep an eye on upcoming junctions," Carter called out to his XO. "They'll be coming at us from the sides."

Carina nodded and got into position; gauss rifle aimed at the road ahead. Moments later, the truck raced into an intersection and Carter's senses spiked. The warriors that had cut right had put on an incredible boost of speed and gotten ahead of them. Flinging themselves into the air like missiles, the Aterniens hammered into the side of the truck, momentarily tipping it onto two wheels. Carter almost fell out, but managed to hang on, as JACAB wrestled with the wheel to keep the vehicle in motion, like a stunt driver on a movie set.

Carter hurled himself to the other side of the bed, using his mass to rebalance the truck and force it down onto four wheels again. At the same time, the Immortals that had climbed onto the cabin and were preparing to blast JACAB through the roof. Carter expended the last three rounds in his revolver to neutralize the threat before the pair of warriors had chance to fire, but now his weapon was empty, and there were still five more Aternien soldiers to deal with.

"On our left!" Carina's cry was followed swiftly by the rattle of her gauss rifle. Two more warriors were racing toward them, trying to succeed where their comrades had failed, by either tipping the truck over, or neutralizing its pilot. He glanced behind and saw that the remaining three hostiles had also closed to the gap and were almost on top of them.

"JACAB, brake hard, now, now, NOW!"

The truck's brakes locked up and Carter was thrown against the rear window, denting the frame and smashing the glass. The Aterniens that were trying to side-swipe them surged past and crashed through the wall of the building opposite, like ram raiders.

"Go!"

JACAB accelerated hard and the acrid smell of burning rubber filled his nostrils for a second time. Then he heard the reverberant clang of metal striking metal. The three remaining Immortals were clambering inside the bed of the truck, dragging themselves toward him like undead warriors clawing their unnatural bodies from the pit of a grave.

Carter got to his feet, drew his sword, and ignited the blade. The closest Immortal blasted him at point-blank range, but he'd just managed to activate his buckler and parry the shot. Even so, the force of the blast destroyed the shield and cooked the flesh on his forearm. Protected from the pain, he swung his cutlass and severed the warrior in half, before whirling his blade and destroying the particle rifle of the Aternien to its rear.

The disarmed Immortal charged and tried to wrestle the cutlass from Carter's grasp, but despite the warrior's synthetic muscles, he was by far the stronger of the two. The effect of in-built chemical and electrical stimulants, combined with his already super-human muscle density, meant that Carter could have grappled three Immortals at once and still emerged the victor. Grabbing the warrior by the neck to immobilize the Aternien, Carter repeatedly hammered the guard of his cutlass into the Immortal's head, until the synthetic man's neuromorphic brain was flattened like a crumpled tin can.

Carter tossed the defeated Immortal over the side of the truck and adjusted his stance to face his final opponent. The

Aternien Warden met his challenge and ignited the bayonet attached to his rifle, causing it to crackle with golden energy.

"Aternus is immortal," the Warden said, speaking the opening line of the Aternien motto with reverence. "Aternus is forever."

The Warden attacked, thrusting the energized bayonet at his neck, but Carter parried and whirled a cut at the Aternien's body. The skilled soldier evaded the strike and scored a glancing hit to his lower leg. Blood trickled down his shin, and a twinge of pain seeped through his barrier of sensation blockers, but it only served to sharpen his senses, and heighten his human compulsion to survive.

Emboldened, the Warden came at him again, this time trying to drive the bayonet into Carter's gut, but he parried then grabbed the barrel of the Aternien weapon and crushed it in his grasp. The bayonet fizzled and sparked then sputtered out completely. He released the rifle and hammered a backhand strike into the Warden's face, which almost sent the Aternien flying off the back of truck, but the warrior managed to regain his balance and stay in the fight.

The brief pause allowed the Warden to examine his broken weapon, but there was no fear in the Aternien's glowing blue eyes. The man tore the bayonet from the barrel, before tossing the rifle over the side of the truck. Then, holding the dagger in a reverse grip, the Warden flung himself at Carter, and tried to stab the blade into his throat, but he caught the Aternien's arm and smashed the warrior's face flat with the pommel of his cutlass. The Warden staggered back again; his once magazine-cover perfect features now mangled like a dented fender. One of the warrior's blue eyes had also been destroyed, and the Warden could barely stand, but surrender was not in the Aternien vocabulary. Unarmed and crippled, Carter's opponent loped forward, teeth gritted and bared, hands outstretched toward him, but it was a desperate and futile effort with no hope of success.

Carter almost took pity on the Warden, before realizing that its death would only be temporary. His Soul Block would be retrieved from the battlefield, and the Aternien would simply rejoin the ranks of the Aternien army, wiser and more experienced than before, and still without remorse. Anger flushed through his veins, and Carter cleaved the Aternien in half from shoulder to hip, like the warrior had been struck by the axe of Hephaestus. Both halves of the Warden toppled over the rear tailgate, and Carter disengaged his blade and sheathed the cutlass. The burn to his arm and cut to his leg were now asserting themselves, but the pain only served as a reminder that he was still breathing.

"Hey, are you good?" Carina called out.

Carter backed up and dropped to a crouch near the cab, where Carina was peering at him through the smashed rear window. Not for the first time, his XO seemed in awe of what she'd just witnessed.

"My wounds aren't severe," Carter grunted in reply. "They'll heal on their own, in time."

JACAB turned to look at him and waved with a maneuvering fin.

"I'm fine, buddy, but keep your eye on the road!" Carter added, sternly.

Despite his concern, JACAB appeared to be driving just fine, despite not looking where he was going. It was then that Carter noticed they didn't appear to be going in the right direction.

"Isn't the doctor's address over that way?" he asked, pointing toward where he thought the hospital near North 45th Street was.

"We can't head there yet," Carina said. Carter scowled and his XO pointed upward. "We have a tail."

Carter peered skyward and saw the scarab-like outline of an Aternien Khepri fighter shadowing them.

"Why hasn't it strafed us?"

"My guess is that it's trying to figure out where we're going, and have a welcoming party there when we arrive," Carina answered. "By now, it wouldn't surprise me if they've figured out what we're doing on Terra Six. And while you haven't taken up Morrow's offer, there's nothing to say the other members of your old crew won't turn their coats."

Carter snorted in disgust at the suggestion. "No way; Cai wouldn't betray his oath."

"Marco Ryan and Damien Morrow did..." his XO hit back.

"I don't give a damn about Ryan and Morrow." Carter emptied the spent rounds from his revolver and reloaded. "They weren't my crew, and they didn't follow my example. Cai won't join the Aterniens, nor will Amaya or Brodie. That I can promise you."

Carina shrugged. "I'll take your word for it. But what do we do about our shadow?"

Carter pondered on this for a moment, allowing his augmented mind to race through dozens of possible solutions. Then he got to his feet, aimed his 57-EX at the Khepri fighter and squeezed off all five rounds in less than a second. Each shot hit the Aternien fighter craft in the exact same location, burrowing through its belly armor and destroying its engine block. The vessel burst into flames, lost control, and crashed into the side of a tower block like a wayward cruise missile.

"Now we don't have a shadow," Carter said, holstering his weapon and tapping JACAB on the top of his shell. "Driver, take us to 1725 North 45th street."

JACAB warbled a laugh, saluted him with a maneuvering fin, then turned off at the next exit.

NINE
AN ORDINARY LIFE

"THERE, JUST UP AHEAD." Carina pointed to an attractive ranch-style house on the right of the leafy street they were driving down. "1725 North 45th. This is the place."

"It looks deserted, like half of the houses on this street," Carter replied, watching a family hurriedly pack up their car with what seemed like everything bar the kitchen sink. "Most folk have left already, and it looks like the rest are finally bugging out too."

JACAB pulled the battered truck off the road and into the car port to the side of Cai Cooper's house. The motor whirred and clicked and finally shut down with a dangerous-sounding fizz and hiss.

"Nice driving, JACAB," Carina said, rubbing the top of the bot, like ruffling a toddler's hair. "You're a natural."

The bot bleeped and squawked, sounding incredibly pleased with himself, and pleased with the compliment too. Carter jumped out of the truck and Carina pushed open the passenger side door, which creaked like a rusted gate. The sound of weapons fire was more distant, but Carter could still see the scarab-like Khepri fighters circling around the inner city, scouting for Union soldiers. The perihelion of their orbits was little more than a kilometer from the house. However, it wasn't the proximity of the enemy that had given him pause, but the sight of a swing and other play equipment in the back yard of the house.

"Is there something wrong?" Carina asked, a curious expression furrowing her brow.

"I don't know yet," Carter grunted. "But it won't be long before the Aterniens push out into the suburbs, so we shouldn't linger here too long."

He cautiously made his way up the porch steps, hand twitching close by the handle of his cutlass. However, while he stayed alert and ready to spring into action in a moment, his senses hadn't become elevated, and there were no signs of immediate danger.

"This is a really nice area," his XO said, admiring the wide, tree-lined street and rows of compact, but attractive houses on either side.

"Soak it up while you can, because it won't look like this for much longer," Carter replied.

His answer drew a disappointed glower from his XO, but while he may have come across as unnecessarily morose, Carter had seen too many pretty suburban districts reduced to apocalyptic wastelands to feel any hope that North 45th street would meet a different fate.

"JACAB, scan the interior of the house. Let's see if anyone is home."

The bot bleeped then moved in front of the door, his indicator lights and antenna flashing and twirling as he did so. A few seconds later the bot spun around and shrugged its maneuvering fins at him.

"There's no-one home, or you can't tell if there's anyone home?" Carter asked, unsure of what his gopher's unhelpful response meant. His comp-slate vibrated, and he checked the screen, scowling. "A disruption field? That's Longsword tech."

"We could try knocking?" Carina suggested, with a shrug of her own.

"I have a better idea…" Carter slammed his shoulder into the door, which yielded like it was made from cracker bread. Drawing his sword, he hustled inside, and quickly checked the rooms that led directly off from the hallway, but there were no signs of life.

"It looks like Cai and Lola already left," Carina commented.

Carter still wasn't convinced but he beckoned the others inside. His XO even paused to wipe her feet on the mat, which Carter found amusing, considering the floor was littered with splinters of wood from the broken door. Together, they continued to check the ground floor, and Carter's attention was quickly drawn to a framed photo on a console table at the end of the long hall. He picked it up and sighed; the image confirmed his suspicions, and his fears.

"Look at this…" Carter said.

He held out the photo of Cai Cooper, Lola Carney and two young girls, who he guessed were around nine or ten years old. It was a picture-perfect image of family bliss. The girls, dressed in the baggy, brightly colored denim style that was popular on Terra Six, looked carefree and happy. Lola smiled brightly, her arm wrapped around Cai's waist, while his old Master Operator was barely recognizable. Gone was the serious, consternated expression of a man obsessed with logic and order, replaced by one of contentment and joy.

"Cai has a family?" His XO took the frame and studied it more closely. "I thought you said that Longsword crew were sterilized so that they couldn't have kids?"

"I adopted them…"

Carter spun around to find Cai Cooper in the hallway. His old Master Operator was pointing a gauss pistol at his head.

"After finding the security photo of you at the hospital, I was worried you'd lost your edge, but sneaking up on me is no mean feat," Carter said.

There was pride in his voice, but also apprehension. Cai had never so much as spoken a cross word to him before, never mind aimed a weapon at his head.

"I've had to be on my toes of late," Cai replied. The man appeared fraught, and on edge, and Carter knew to tread carefully. "Are you with them?"

Carter scowled. "With who?"

"He means the acolytes," Carina cut in. She had her hands up, though it was a fairly half-hearted gesture.

"The major is correct," Cai said, studying Carina with the inquisitiveness of a scholar. "I do not recognize you from the original roster of Longword officers. Are you part of a rebooted program?"

Carina smiled and shook her head. "No, I'm a home-grown human, I'm afraid. Just regular flesh and blood."

Cai appeared to be confused by his XO's response. "Then why are you with the Master Commander? Standard humans and Longsword officers were never mixed."

"A lot has changed, Cai," Carter said. "We need to talk."

"A former Master-at-arms named Marco Ryan said the very same thing to me, only two days ago. I did not like what he had to say."

"Neither did we." Carter took a step toward his old crewmate, but Cai slid his finger on to the trigger, and Carter's senses suddenly spiked. "Woah, Cai, it's me. What the hell are you doing?" He knew instinctively that if he took another step, his old friend would shoot him.

"I have a family now, sir," Cai said; his use of the honorific, 'sir' spoke volumes. "My obligations are to them. I have already moved them to a safe location, and only returned to collect a few personal effects."

"At least hear me out, Cai," Carter continued. He had also raised his hands and taken a step back so as to appear less threatening. "The Aterniens won't stop at Terra Six. Your family will never be safe unless we defeat them."

Cai Cooper's clever, sharp eyes narrowed. "Speak your piece, sir, and I will listen."

"It comes to this," Carter went on, lowering his hands to his side. "I'm putting the crew back together to fight Markus Aternus and beat him for the last time. We've already recovered the Galatine. It's at Terra Prime right now, getting fixed up by Kendra."

Cai's finger was removed from the trigger and slid back along the frame of the gauss pistol. The man also slightly relaxed his aim, though the barrel of the weapon remained pointed in Carter's direction.

"Kendra is still alive?"

"Very much so," Carter replied, with a knowing smile. "She gave me a hard time, and in truth I deserved it, but once she learned that our old enemy is back, she was all-in. I was hoping the same would be true of you."

Cai made his pistol safe then slid it into the waistband of his pants. "I am gratified to hear that Kendra is safe and well. And my senses detect no ill intent from you." Carter felt a swell of hope, but his Master Operator quickly dashed it. "But I regret that I cannot rejoin your crew, sir. I have a wife and family. I must protect them. That is my sole duty now."

Carter sighed and rubbed his beard. He wanted to argue, but he knew that once Cai Cooper had made up his mind about something, he could not be swayed.

"You still can't stay here, Cai," Carter said, focusing his thoughts on the safety of Lola and the two carefree and happy girls in the photo. "The Aterniens are planning something big. I don't know exactly what, but Terra Six isn't safe, no matter where you go."

"I know…" Cai replied.

Carter was shocked at how deflated his old friend sounded. Cai's shoulders sagged and he sat down on a bench that doubled as a shoe-storage rack. Pairs of muddy sneakers and boots were shoved inside it, untidily. Carter huffed a laugh, realizing that this single item of furniture and its messy contents revealed everything he needed to know about the new Cai Cooper. While serving together, his Master Operator wouldn't have tolerated so much as a strand of hair out of place on his head. That he could live anywhere that was not in laser precise order meant that Cai had changed far more than Carter first realized.

"The Aterniens have placed a device in the city," the former Master Operator said. "I believe it to be some kind of weapon, though I have been unable to discern precisely what kind."

Cai's revelation was shocking, but timely. If there was anyone who could find such a device and figure out its purpose, it was Carter's old Master Operator.

"Do you know where it is?" Carter asked. "This time, the

Aterniens mean to kill us all, Cai, so whatever this weapon is, we need to find it."

"My resources are limited, but I have monitored significant activity at Enterprise Stadium," Copper replied. "They have been moving equipment through the underground transport network and appear to be guarding something at that location."

Carina cursed. "Enterprise Stadium is where we parked our shuttle. Marco Ryan and his cronies were on us in a flash once we landed. If they're hiding something there, it makes sense that the acolytes were already so close by."

Carter thought for a moment. The news of a potential doomsday device on Terra Six was more than enough incentive to convince Cai Cooper to leave with him. Yet he respected the man's choices and the life that he'd built – a life that he'd never thought possible for people like them. Despite how much he needed his old Master Operator, he wasn't going to take that away from him.

"I need your help to find and take out this weapon, Cai," Carter said, making his choice. "Then, I'll help to get you and your family off-world, and somewhere safe. What you do after that is your own business."

Cai thought for a moment then nodded. "Agreed, thank you, sir."

The man then hurried to another bench on the opposite side of the hall. Flipping open a panel in the ornate wooden item, he revealed a biometric scanner. The device probed his thumb print then scanned his right eye, before a lock thudded open.

Carter, Carina, and JACAB gathered closer, all intrigued to see what was contained inside the mysterious chest. Cai lifted the lid, rummaged inside, then removed a sword.

Carter smiled; he was more than familiar with the weapon, which was a Celtic short sword design.

"Another one?" Carina said, eyeing the weapon with suspicion. "What is it with you guys and your swords, anyway?"

Cai ignited the blade, which fizzed and hummed with more elegance than the more brutish cutlass that Carter chose to wield.

"Swords are efficient, and do not attract attention," Cai said, performing a few practice cuts.

"How did you get that off the Galatine before we decommissioned her?" Carter asked. The fact his Master Operator had managed to squirrel away his sword, and he had not, made him embarrassed.

"This is not the same weapon," Cai replied, disengaging the blade. "I forged this sword myself and fashioned the components to energize the edge. It was a difficult but rewarding project."

Suddenly, a warble and bleep filtered into the hallway, but the noises hadn't emanated from JACAB. Carter listened carefully, trying to place the sound, but his gopher had already pinpointed the location and was humming above the open chest, squawking excitedly.

"What's up, buddy, what do you sense?" Carter asked. His hand moved to his sidearm, but Cai was quick to intervene.

"It is okay; there is no cause for alarm."

A spherical bot levitated from beneath a pile of neatly folded coats and scarves and hovered next to JACAB. The machine, which was the same size as Carter's bot, warbled and waved its maneuvering fins; a greeting which JACAB happily returned.

"Is that TOBY?" Carter asked. To Carina, who looked puzzled, he added. "It means Tactical Operations Bot Y-Series. A starship operations gopher, basically."

"Yes and no," Cai answered, somewhat vaguely.

Carter frowned and studied the bot more closely. It certainly looked and sounded the same as TOBY, but there were subtle differences that made him question his confidence.

"I removed TOBY's core block before we decommissioned the Galatine," Cai continued. "What you see is TOBY in mind, but with a body that I designed in my spare time on Terra Six."

Carter let out a long, low whistle. "Kendra would be impressed. Even she would struggle to construct an entirely new gopher body from scratch."

"No, she would not." Cai's rebuttal was definitive, and Carter realized that his old Master Operator was absolutely right. "She would find it rather trivial, whereas I found the task to be vexing and problematic, though ultimately rewarding."

"I guess you're right," Carter agreed, smiling as the two bots bleeped and warbled to each other in their own unique language. "There's nothing that old grease monkey can't fix or build."

Both bots suddenly stopped chatting and sounded alarms in perfect synchronization with one other. The comp-slate on his arm vibrated, but Carter didn't need to read the message, because his own early-warning system had also kicked in.

"Get behind us," Carter said to his XO, while readying his weapons.

Cai's short sword fizzed into life at the same time, and

Carina backed up, pistol raised, with TOBY and JACAB by her side. Moments later, a gang of acolytes charged up the driveway and through the open door, rifles raised, but the first man had barely made it an inch inside the house before Carter's cutlass had sliced the weapon in half. He then dodged aside as the man careered forward, straight into the waiting blade of his Master Operator.

Two more acolytes charged forward, this time spraying bullets while they were still on the porch outside. Carter activated his buckler and deflected the slugs, while Cai dodged into cover. Carina opened fire with her energy pistol, killing the closest acolyte and forcing the second to withdraw.

Carter gave chase and battered the retreating man in the back of his head with his buckler, but three more were waiting for them outside. Gauss rifles fizzed and he was hit and forced to dive for cover, using his shield to protect his head.

The acolytes pursued, but they hadn't counted on Cai Cooper. Carter's old Master Operator sped through the open door like a runaway freight train and removed the head of one of the men with a swift and elegant swing of his sword. One of the remaining two acolytes fired at Cai, but the Longsword officer danced out of the line of fire and sliced open the man's wrist with another graceful strike of the blade. The acolyte cried out then dropped his rifle and clutched his wrist, which had been cut through to the bone. However, the yelp of pain was soon silenced, as Cai opened the man's throat, severing and cauterizing the jugular in one slash of the blade.

The final acolyte panicked, not knowing who to attack first, but Carter made the decision for him. Marching out of cover, he deflected several panicked shots from the man, then thrust his cutlass through the acolyte's heart. The look of surprise and fear in the man's eyes was one that he was not used to seeing. An Aternien's eyes merely faded to black, like the flame of a candle burning itself out. The dying seconds of a human being felt more real, and more tragic as a result.

Carina stalked onto the porch, weapon still raised, but the fight was already over. JACAB and TOBY hummed through the door and Carter's comp-slate vibrated with another message. He checked it, confirming with his gopher that the danger had passed, even though his own senses had told him the same thing.

"This one's still breathing," Carina said.

She was aiming her pistol at the acolyte Carter had hit with his buckler and sent flying over the banister that enclosed the porch. Carter disengaged the plasma-edge of his cutlass and stormed over to the man, grabbing him by the jacket and hauling him up with barely any effort.

"How did you know we were here?" Carter snarled, pinning the man to the outside of the house with his feet suspended off the ground. The acolyte was barely conscious, and he slammed the man's body repeatedly against the red brick wall, trying to jolt him awake. "Answer me, damn you!" he growled. "Tell me what I want to know, and you'll live."

The man's eyes, which had been rolled into the back of his head, suddenly sharpened and focused on Carter's face. The acolyte smiled, revealing bloody gums where the buckler had smashed his teeth and broken his jaw.

"The eye of Aternus sees everything…" the acolyte mumbled, blood dripping from his chin. "He sees it all." The man then sneered at Cai. "Even where he's hidden his family."

Carter felt a swell of panic fill his gut. It was a sensation he was not accustomed to, and it unsettled him more than he expected. "You're lying..." he hissed, but the acolyte simply shook his head.

"We're coming for them... We're coming and you can't stop us..."

Carter tightened his grip and was about to swing his cutlass, when another sword punched through the man's chest and impaled the acolyte to the wall. The man rasped his last breath, then slumped onto the energized blade, which sliced him in half like a laser.

"We must hurry," Cai said, pulling his sword free. "There is not a moment to lose."

TEN

SIT BACK, SERGEANT

"MY FAMILY IS at my mother-in-law's farm, outside the city to the North," Cai Cooper said, pulling open the door to the truck and jumping into the driver's seat. "TOBY has tried to warn them, but there is too much interference, so I cannot be sure the message got through."

"They'll be alright, Cai," Carter said. "Just get us there as fast as you can."

He had no reason to believe this, but he could sense the unease in his old Master Operator and felt that a reassuring voice might help. Carina jumped into the passenger seat, while Carter again seated himself in the bed of the truck, so that he could function as a gun turret should more acolytes or Immortals try to stop them.

Cai reversed the truck off the drive then floored the accelerator. The screech of the tires was barely audible over the sound of heavy weapons fire, which was growing closer by the second. Even in the short time they'd been inside the house, the few residents that were still packing up when they'd arrived had gone. The streets were clear and eerily calm. It was like a ghost town.

"How far away is this farm?" Carina asked.

"It is seven point two miles from my house," the Master Operator replied, with typical precision. "Without traffic, I should be able to cover the distance in nine minutes and thirty-five seconds." Cai shrugged. "Give or take…"

A squadron of Aternien Khepri fighters raced overhead and Carter could see heavy fighting in the skies west of the city, close to Enterprise Stadium; the suspected location of the Aternien weapon. The Union officer inside him was screaming for then to turn around and tackle the major threat, but the human being in him refused. Cai Cooper was as close to family as he'd ever known, which meant that his family was as his own. A century ago, Carter put duty above family, and he swore to himself that this time would be different. He intended to keep that promise, to himself as well as to his crew.

Suddenly, the squadron of Khepri fighters banked sharply to the right and began heading back in their direction. For a moment Carter thought their truck might be the target of the Aternien ships, but his senses told him otherwise. A concentrated volley of particle energy erupted from the cannons of the flying scarabs and a Union platoon drop ship was hit. The vessel's engines flashed out and the craft began to lose altitude at an alarming rate. Carter could only imagine the terror gripping the drop ship's pilot in that moment, but despite efforts to arrest its fall, gravity always won in the end.

Out of control and on fire, the drop ship shrieked through the air like a dive bomber and smashed into the freeway directly in their path, less than a mile from their current location. His first thought was for the crew on-board the ship, but its downing also presented another problem.

"JACAB, are there any other routes out of the city?" Carter asked.

The bot flashed its lights and warbled as it conferred with TOBY. The update was relayed to his comp-slate, but it wasn't good news.

"What's wrong?" Carina asked.

"That drop ship crashed on the freeway up ahead, and it won't be long before squads of Immortals are crawling all over the wreckage to pick off any survivors."

"Can we go around?" asked Cai.

Unusually for the normally ice-cold officer, the tone of Cai's voice betrayed the stress and worry the man was feeling. Carter switched his comp-slate to a map view of the route ahead, but his bot was right. The other good roads were blocked or too dangerous to traverse, which left the only other choice as a circuitous, long detour.

"The only other safe route would take us an hour out of our way," Carter said, lowering his wrist. "We should press on, and deal with whatever lies ahead."

Cai nodded and sped up, pushing the truck to one hundred and thirty miles per hour. Carter was used to moving at speed, but traveling in the battle-scarred vehicle felt like he was in a horse drawn carriage that was careering out of control down the side of the mountain. Before long, the billowing smoke of the crashed drop ship dominated the view ahead of them, and Cai was forced to slow down. The flash of Aternien particle fire and fizz and rattle of Union gauss rifles signaled that the surviving troopers were already engaged in a fight for their lives.

"Give me a sit-rep, buddy," Carter said to JACAB.

The bot nodded then hummed out of the vehicle and raced into the sky like a rocket. The flashing indicators on TOBY's body told him that the two gophers were still in communication: one surveying the scene and the other assessing it. Cai's bot then turned to his keeper, warbling and bleeping in the unique machine language that his Master Operator had managed to learn.

"Two squads of Immortals have already moved in on the downed drop ship," Cai said, relaying TOBY's analysis. "One squad is entrenched on the roof of Century Market to our east and are keeping the Union platoon pinned down. The other is advancing from the north, across the parking lot from the direction of Clarence and Baymore."

Carter rubbed his beard, first glancing at the market building and spotting the Aternien sniper fire with his keen eyes, before turning his attention to the drop ship. The craft had crashed through the corner of a shopping mall, which had collapsed around it. There was no way out, other than to advance toward the approaching squad of Immortals and expose themselves to a brutal crossfire.

"What are your thoughts, Cai?" Carter asked. He knew what to do, but he was curious to see if his Master Operator's mind was still as keen as he remembered.

"Major Larsen and I will approach the market from the southeast and neutralize the Immortals on the roof," Cai replied, without a moment's hesitation. "This will allow Commander Rose to move up behind the downed troop carrier, make contact with the soldiers and co-ordinate an assault on the remaining squad."

Carina seemed surprised. "I was expecting you to suggest that we just blitz past and not get involved, so we can reach your family faster."

"I estimate a more than seventy percent chance that we would come under heavy fire, should we attempt to race through the engagement zone," Cai replied, coolly. "Clearing this obstruction is the most efficient method of reaching my family." The Master Operator then glanced at Carina out of the corner of his eye. "Also, it is not in my nature to ignore those in need of help."

The earlier unease that Carter had sensed in Cai was gone. The Longsword officer's augments had kicked in, flooding his body with hormones and chemicals to boost his capabilities, and keep his human anxieties and emotions at bay. However, what their augments could not do is change who a person was, and Cai Cooper was a fundamentally good and caring man, which is why he could not cross over and walk on the other side of the street.

"Let's make it fast," Carter said, as Cai pulled the truck into a lay-by. "Every second we delay, is more time for Damien Morrow and Marco Ryan to reach Cai's family first."

Cai and Carina moved out, with TOBY assisting them at a safe height and distance. Carter waited for a few seconds, knowing that his part couldn't begin in earnest until his team had neutralized the snipers on the roof of the market building.

While he was waiting, Carter removed his long frock coat and folded it neatly before placing it in the bed of the truck. The garment had proven useful in the beginning as a way to hide his uniform, but now it was an unnecessary encumbrance since his cover had already been blown. He also hoped that the Union soldiers holed up by the drop ship would recognize the uniform, and not try to blow his head off the moment he popped up.

Next, Carter activated his buckler and drew both of his

weapons. He could shoot just as well with either hand, but he preferred wielding his sword in his right. His left hand was more finessed, but his right was more brutal. *Now is no time for finesse…* he told himself.

His comp-slate vibrated, and he read the message for JACAB. His gopher was holding position above the downed craft, like a spy drone relaying vital intelligence to the troops on the ground.

"I'm moving out now, buddy," Carter said, stealing away off the truck. "Keep me apprised. You know I don't like surprises."

Carter stalked through the streets around the mall, using trees, wrecked vehicles, and barrier walls for cover. His comp-slate continued to update with the live positions of Aternien Immortals, along with the location of Cai Cooper and his XO. They had already made good ground, and were working their way up to the roof, ahead of schedule. Then he felt his senses sharpen and knew instinctively the time for action was near.

Suddenly, Cai and Carina appeared on the roof of the market and assaulted the Aternien position. His XO, aided by TOBY, pounded the entrenched Immortals with energy weapons, while Cai charged ahead, energized plasma sword in hand. Carter smiled as he watched his old Master Operator go to work. As in all aspects of his crew member's life, efficiency was paramount. There were no flourishes of the blade, no wasted movements. Everything Cai did had a singular purpose, and in this instance, that purpose was to kill.

Before long, the glow of Cai's plasma-edged short sword vanished and the Aterniens on the rooftop had all fallen. His comp-slate relayed a message from JACAB, which simply read, "You are clear to proceed."

A boost of strength and stamina-enhancing chemicals and hormones kicked in, and he raced out of cover, accelerating harder and moving faster than any human being could hope to match. The Aterniens were caught by surprise, and he opened fire with his 57-EX, squeezing off all five shots in the blink of an eye. Five shots; five kills.

The Aterniens returned fire, but Carter was already in cover, and the particle blasts pulverized the upturned vehicle at his back. Across from him was the nose of the downed drop ship. Bodies littered the road between him and the craft, and he could see through the smashed cockpit glass that the pilot and co-pilot were already dead. One Union soldier stood strong and was firing at the Aterniens with a light machine gun, despite clearly suffering from serious injuries of his own.

Carter reloaded his 57-EX and moved out, using the powerful weapon to drive the Aterniens into cover. Flashes of energy came flying back at him, and he managed to block most with his buckler, but took a glancing blow to his side before he made it across to the drop ship and found the platoon sergeant.

"You're a sight for sore eyes," the sergeant said. The man's breathing was heavily labored, and his hands were shaking, though Carter could see it was as much from exhaustion as it was due to fear. "I didn't think there were any other units nearby."

"I'm not from what you'd call a regular unit," Carter replied, while again reloading his 57-EX. "How many of your troops are still trapped inside?"

"Half of us were killed in the crash, and we've lost

another squad to these bastards since then, but the LT and maybe half a dozen others are still holed up in the ship."

Carter nodded. "Sit back, Sergeant, I'll take care of this."

Carter stepped away, but the sergeant grabbed his arm, his eyes wide with surprise.

"Woah, you can't go in there on your own!" the soldier called out to him. "These Aterniens are killers. It takes an entire magazine just to put one of the bastards down."

Carter noticed that the sergeant taken a hit to his chest that had not only burned through his armor, but also his flesh down to the bone. The only thing keeping the man on his feet was adrenaline.

"Sit down, Sergeant," Carter said, placing his hand on the man's shoulder and using his strength to force the soldier onto his ass. "This won't take me long."

The sergeant was about to protest again, but Carter had already moved away. He focused on the apex of the drop ship and exploded upward like a jack-in-a-box, leaping a full six meters into the air and landing on top of the troop craft like a comic book superhero. Creeping over the charred and dented hull, he spotted the remainder of the Aterniens stalking through mall, toward the smashed-open side of the drop ship.

Igniting his plasma cutlass, Carter plummeted into the middle of the pack, trampling an Immortal underfoot, like stomping on a bug. Springing up, he spun his sword like a whirligig, cutting down two more of the five with savage swings of his blade. The Immortals reacted without panic, and a bayonet was thrust at his gut, but he deflected the strike then cut the Immortal's arm off at the shoulder. His senses spiked, and he dodged aside as the last moment, evading a particle blast at close range that would have surely killed him.

Carter's cutlass flashed again, and the Immortal was cut down, leaving only the dismembered Aternien and the warrior he'd trampled underfoot after leaping from the drop ship. The first he decapitated in the blink of an eye, while the second scrambled to his feet, desperately searching for a weapon. Wasting no time, Carter buried his sword into the warrior's chest and the Aternien froze, as if he had been doused in liquid nitrogen. The man's eyes grew wide and flickered, and in that moment, Carter knew that the so-called Immortal feared death, no differently to a flesh-and-blood human. Primal instincts outweighed the rational certainty of his rebirth, and Carter was quick to finish the kill before the warrior came to that realization.

Perhaps it'll make no difference, Carter thought, *but I want that bastard to wake up remembering my face, and my sword in his synthetic heart…*

"Who the hell are you?"

Carter shoved the dead Aternien away then turned to see the platoon's officer hobbling out of the wrecked craft toward him. The woman's arm was in a sling and her head was bandaged with a blood-soaked tourniquet that covered her right eye and ear.

"Your uniform is Union, but I don't recognize your rank," the Lieutenant continued, struck with a mix of awe and confusion.

"It doesn't matter who I am," Carter said, unwilling to open that particular can of worms. "But I'm here to help."

The lieutenant looked at the sea of Aternien bodies that Carter had left in his wake and huffed a feeble laugh. "I think you already helped," she said, appearing distant and confused, perhaps as a result of her head injury. "Though how you did it, the Lord only knows."

Carter checked his comp-slate and was stunned to discover that the soldiers were from Second Brigade, Sixteenth Regiment, Terra Prime.

"You guys are Terra Prime infantry?" he asked the officer, unable to hide his shock. "Where are the troops from Terra Six?"

The lieutenant gingerly shook her head. "I haven't seen a damned one of them. It's like they were never here. Either that, or they were wiped out before we even arrived."

Carter looked up, hoping that more troop carriers were en route, but all he could see were formations of scarab-like Khepri fighters patrolling the city. The battle for the sky had been lost, he realized.

"How many of you got through?" Carter asked. Whoever was already on the ground was all the Union had.

The lieutenant rubbed her eyes and sighed. "We lost more than three-quarters of the troop transports before they even reached the surface, then command called off any further attempts to reach us. It's just a goddam waste of life."

Carter noticed that the sergeant he'd spoken to earlier was walking toward them, oblivious to the hole in his chest. He signaled the platoon medic, hoping it wasn't already too late to save the man, despite the grave nature of his injuries.

"I don't know how you did it, but thanks," the sergeant said, dropping heavily onto an ammo crate that had been tossed free of the drop ship, and allowing the medic to tend to him. The man then eyed Carter suspiciously. "You're one of those Longsword guys, aren't you?" He wagged a bloodstained finger at him. "You know, the super soldiers from the first Aternien war?"

The lieutenant laughed feebly. "Those are just urban legends, Sergeant," she said, shooting her NCO a kindly smile. "Though I wish they weren't. We could use a few fighters like them right about now."

Carter smiled and laughed along with the soldiers, but still chose not to reveal who he was. The fact that the lieutenant wished there were Longsword officers fighting for them didn't necessarily mean she was any less prejudiced than other humans when it came to his kind. The truck then pulled up alongside the wrecked drop ship, serving as a timely reprieve. Cai was driving, and Carina was in the passenger seat, as if they'd never left.

"TOBY says the area is clear, for now," Carina called out of the window. "But there are more Aterniens heading this way."

Carter nodded then turned to the lieutenant. "Did you copy that?"

"Loud and clear..." the woman replied, gravely.

The officer turned to what remained of her platoon and ordered them to fall in. The sergeant, who appeared a little stronger thanks to the meds and field dressing, began orchestrating the soldiers, most of whom were wounded. Carter stole away while they were busy and slid into the rear seat of the dual cab truck. JACAB hummed down from his observation point above the wreckage and slipped in through the broken rear window.

"You okay, buddy?" Carter asked his bot.

JACAB nodded then set himself down on his lap. Carter rested a hand on his bot then reached through the window and slapped the side of the door with the flat of his hand.

"We're all here, so let's get moving."

Cai accelerated, and again pushed the battered truck to the limit of its capabilities, but Carter's mind was elsewhere. Then there was a boom like thunder far out to the west, and a Union Frigate fell out of the sky like a meteorite. As he watched, the lieutenant's words suddenly rung out in his mind.

"It's just a goddam waste of life…" he said out loud.

Carina scowled and turned to him. "What was that?"

"Oh, nothing," Carter answered, waving her off. "I was just thinking that it's like the last hundred years didn't happen, and we're right back where we started, at war again."

Carina smiled and rested her hand on his arm, which was still hanging out of the rear window. "Then let's make sure this war is the last war."

ELEVEN
A DAY ON THE FARM

CAI MADE it out of the city without further incident, and before long they were driving on open roads with the sound of fighting fading into the distance. Even so, evidence of the Aternien invasion was all around them, from burned-out vehicles to destroyed buildings and the remains of crashed Union warships, which blackened the hilly suburban towns and villages like a blight.

The respite from action had allowed Carter's injuries to heal and the holes in his battle uniform to self-repair, so that he was feeling stronger and more ready than ever. Carina had also used the time wisely, but in a different way. With JACAB's help, she had reviewed the recordings of their enemy engagements, in order to learn more about their enemy.

In spite of his earlier concerns about the 'normie' human major, she had acquitted herself well, and not been an incumbrance, as he'd feared. In fact, despite him cautioning his XO against the idea, he admitted that with augmentation, she would make a formidable Longsword officer. Carina suddenly turned her head and frowned at him, as if she could sense his thoughts, but he looked out of the window and pretended not to have noticed.

"There appears to be a roadblock ahead," Cai said.

Carter slid between the driver and passenger seats and stared ahead. His Master Operator had already reduced speed in order to buy them some extra time before reaching the checkpoint.

"I see four Union soldiers," Cai added in his precise manner. "Judging from their uniforms, they are from second battalion, first infantry brigade, Terra Six."

Carina recoiled from the man. "You can see all that from here? I can barely tell which of them is male and which is female."

"Two male, two female," Cai answered. "If you like, I could also relay their ranks and approximate ages?"

"There's no need to show off," Carina said, with a wry smile.

"Extraordinary is ordinary, where Cai is concerned," said Carter, stepping in to deescalate the situation, since his Master Operator had clearly taken offense at the accusation of being a braggart. "You'll get used to it."

The checkpoint was now only a hundred meters away, and despite it appearing to be a standard military roadblock, Carter was developing a strong sense that something was wrong.

"Everyone be on your guard," Carter cautioned. "We'll have to blag our way through, since we're not officially supposed to be on Terra Six."

Cai raised an eyebrow at this admission, but there was no opportunity for his Master Operator to question Carter, before one of the guards stepped out and flagged them down. Cai slowed to a stop, the truck rattling and clunking like an old banger, and wound down the window, smiling vacantly at the approaching soldier.

"I'll do the talking," Carina said, suddenly stone-cold serious. "And I'd suggest that JACAB and TOBY hide under my coat. "They'll only raise questions that we don't have time to answer."

Carter nodded to the bots, and the two gophers burrowed themselves beneath Carina's long frock coat, which was lying on the rear seat beside him. Carina beckoned to the soldier, who scowled at her, then changed course to approach the passenger-side window instead. It wasn't long before the corporal noticed the golden oak leaf on her collar.

"My apologies, I saw a civilian truck and assumed you were locals," the corporal said. "We've been told to check all vehicles leaving the city."

Carter narrowed his eyes at the soldier. The corporal hadn't addressed Carina with the correct formality, and instead of saying he'd been "ordered to check" all vehicles leaving the city, the man had said, "told to check."

"Quite alright, Corporal," Carina replied, offering the man a friendly but professional smile. "We commandeered this truck to stay off the Aternien's radar; I'm sure you understand."

"Of course," the corporal replied, smiling, and again showing a lack of proper conduct.

Carina then pointed to the roadblock. "Now, if you'll raise the barricade, we'll be on our way."

The corporal glanced into the rear of the truck, briefly making eye contact with Carter, before taking a longer, harder look at Cai in the driver's seat. "Who are the two people with you?" The corporal asked, his tone bordering on rude.

Carter's senses kicked up another notch. The three other soldiers were standing in the road, gauss rifles at low-ready. He could feel the thumping of their hearts; all of them were far more anxious and on-edge than the situation merited.

"That's none of your concern, Corporal," Carina replied, sternly. "Now raise the barricade. That is an order."

The corporal ignored the command, then moved to the rear passenger side window and rapped his knuckles against the glass.

"I'll need you to step outside," the soldier demanded.

"Corporal, I have given you an order, and you will obey it," Carina barked.

She reached for the door handle, and the barrel of the soldier's rifle was immediately pointed at her head. At the same time, the other three soldiers, raised their weapons and slipped their fingers onto the triggers.

"Stay where you are!" the corporal yelled. Carter could hear his heart beating faster than a hummingbird's. "Put your hands where I can see them!"

Carter glanced at Cai; it was a simple look that to the untrained eye would appear to mean nothing, but between Longsword officers, a look could convey as much detail as a spoken command.

A split second later, Carter made his move, ripping the door off its hinges and smashing it into the corporal's head. The soldier was sent flying over the crash barrier at the side of the road and was knocked out cold. It was then he noticed that the corporal was not wearing standard issue boots, but regular store-bought footwear.

The other checkpoint guards opened fire without

warning, and Carter was forced to use the door as a shield. With gauss slugs hammering into the metal, he charged at the trio of soldiers, flattening two, but the third managed to step aside and was merely knocked off balance. The soldier's rifle was swung in his direction, and Carter raised the car door to protect his head, but the shots never came. Instead, there was a dull, organic crunch, followed by a gargling sound, like someone drowning in a vat of treacle.

Carter lowered the door to see the soldier on her knees. Cai's short sword was impaled through the back of her head, and was protruding out of her mouth, in the same way that a suckling pig might have been skewered in preparation for a hog roast. However, his Master Operator's hand was not connected to the weapon. Instead, Cai had launched the sword like a javelin. A few of inches in either direction and the throw would have missed the soldier and skewered him instead.

"Nice work," Carter said, tossing the bullet-ridden door aside. "You really haven't missed a beat, have you?"

"Our abilities are innate, sir," Cai replied, modestly, while pulling his sword out from the back of the soldier's head with a nauseating squelch that made Carina pucker up like a fish. "It is like riding a bike; you never forget."

"I never actually learned to ride a bike," Carina cut in. Carter and Cai both frowned at her, and she shrugged. "Sorry, I just felt like contributing."

Carter pointed to one of the bodies. "Contribute by figuring out who these people were," he said. "Because they're not Union soldiers, that's for damned certain."

Carina and Cai began to search the bodies, aided by TOBY, while JACAB hummed higher and functioned as lookout. It wasn't long before his officers had uncovered evidence that the checkpoint guards were not who they purported to be.

"Look at this," Carina said, pulling open the corporal's jacket. "This isn't Union-issue gear." Instead of the regular sand-colored t-shirt, the corporal was wearing a rusty brown tank-top that also had a different neckline to the uniform standard.

"The socks are wrong too, and the boots," Carina added, getting back to her feet. "In fact, only the helmet, jacket and pants are Union gear, but if you look at the name tags, they all belong to different soldiers."

Carter grunted, understanding the macabre conclusion that his XO had drawn, which was that the guards had scavenged the gear from the bodies of dead Union troopers. He idly wondered if the trio had killed the soldiers, or just found them already dead in the streets, but that wasn't the important question to ask.

"You're right that these aren't Union troopers, so who the hell are they?"

TOBY hummed beside Carter, bleeping and squawking with excitement. His comp-slate vibrated, and he checked the update with interest, with Carina and Cai both looking keenly over his shoulder.

"The left arms of all three bodies have been surgically amputated at the elbow then reattached," Carter said, scowling at the medical scan of the body that TOBY had provided. "That makes no damned sense."

"Their elbow joints have been replaced," Cai added, pointing to the area in question. "From these readings, I would say that the metal used is an Aternien alloy."

Carter nodded; thanks to another keen observation, the mystery had been resolved, at least in part. "They're acolytes," he said, clearing the data from his screen. "This mutilation may be a sort of initiation ritual, maybe?"

Cai nodded. "Perhaps, but regardless of its purpose, this discovery works to our benefit. It will make identifying other acolytes easier."

"Good work people," Carter said, addressing his current and former crewmembers, as well as TOBY, who chirruped with pride. "Now, let's get back on the road, and hope we don't meet any other obstacles."

Carter marched to the barricade and forced the metal beam out of their path as easily as bending a spoon. The truck pulled up beside him and he jumped in, taking advantage of the fact there was no longer a door to impede his entry. JACAB continued to scan ahead, able to keep pace with the truck due to the winding roads that limited their maximum speed. It wasn't long before they were headed toward the farm in the valley where Cai's family had been hidden. A hundred meters before the turn off, TOBY bleeped and squawked, causing his owner's eyes to sharpen.

"JACAB reports that there are six men in the grounds of the farm," Cai said, driving past the farm lane so as not to draw suspicion. "From this distance, he cannot be certain, but there are indicators of Aternien metals, which suggest they may also be acolytes."

"What about inside the house?" asked Carter.

"There is movement, but the number of individuals is unclear," Cai replied.

Carter grunted then surveyed the farm and the area surrounding it as they drove past. They'd been surprised once already, and he didn't intend to be caught off guard again. "Pull off the road in that lay-by up ahead," he said, pointing out of the open door. "It's out of sight of the farm and will allow us to approach on foot."

Cai complied and soon the truck had trundled to a halt and its fatigued motor was turned off. There was a moment of stillness, punctuated only by the chirping of birds and the percussive ping of the engine as it cooled.

"We have to do this right," Cai said, breaking the silence. "I cannot risk my family, Master Commander. Whoever is inside that house, no matter how vital they are to your mission, must come secondary to the safety of my wife and children."

"Don't worry, Cai," Carter said, resting a hand on the man's shoulder. "I don't give a damn if Markus Aternus himself is in that house; your family comes first."

Cai nodded, then the group exited the truck and began to gather their gear and weapons. At the same time, TOBY and JACAB took off high above the farm, and began forming a detailed map of the area, including the locations of the acolytes that were walking the perimeter.

"The house is almost in the dead center of the plot, surrounded by farm buildings," Carter said, referring to the map as it built in real time on his comp-slate. "The acolytes have split into two groups of three and are patrolling on opposite sides of the farm. Major Larsen will approach from the east, using the grain tanks for cover." He magnified and highlighted his suggested route. "I'll approach from the west and move through the farm buildings. We hit them hard and fast. Silent takedowns."

Carina nodded then turned to Cai Cooper. "What about you?"

"The acolytes have tried to recruit me once before and failed, so the likelihood is that they are planning to use my family as leverage," Cai replied, still as cool as ice. "This means they will not hurt them – not yet, anyway."

"Cai will take the truck and drive directly up to the farmhouse," Carter cut in. He could sense that he and his Master Operator were in sync, even without needing to use words. "He'll surrender to whoever is inside, which will keep them off guard, and give Major Larsen and I the element of surprise."

Carina seemed convinced; moreover, she appeared eager to get into action. She drew her energy pistol then activated the comm system built into her battle uniform. A near-invisible bone-conducting transducer snaked up from the rear of her collar and attached to the side of her head. A similar device sprouted from his own uniform, and he heard a soft chirrup as the connection was established.

"Ready when you are," Carina said.

Carter couldn't help but crack a smile, but then forced his mind and body to focus.

"Silent takedowns," he said to his XO, who was steely-eyed and ready. "We don't want to risk alerting the acolytes inside the house and putting Cai's family at risk."

Carina pressed her finger to her lips, then slipped away through the trees. At the same time, Cai returned to the truck and drove back along the road to the farm turnoff, while Carter snuck into the wheat fields and began to pursue his own targets, like a tiger stalking through long grasses.

Soon, Carter heard the truck driving along the farm lane, crunching dirt and gravel beneath its wide tires, and he checked his comp-slate. As expected, the acolytes guarding the farm had begun to cluster together, with several of them moving toward the vehicle. Suddenly, one of the contacts blinked off the scanner display, and he smiled again.

Carina is moving fast. I'd better up my game…

Picking up speed, he approached the closest of his three targets, who was also in the wheat fields. He scooped up a rock, made sure the man had his back turned, then hurled it with the force of a musket ball. There was a nauseating crunch, not dissimilar to the sound of Cai's sword piercing the skull of the acolyte who'd posed as a soldier, and the man went down like a felled tree.

Carter checked his comp-slate again and saw that two of Carina's targets had been wiped off the grid. Realizing it wouldn't be long before the others became suspicious, he advanced more quickly, yet still without making a sound. The second of his targets stood beside a farm building, covering the truck with his rifle. Cai had already pulled up in front of the house and was walking toward it, ignoring the acolyte guards.

Stealing out of cover, Carter snuck up behind the man and whistled. The acolyte spun around and ate a crushing right hook that could have knocked out a rhino. Carter dragged the man out of sight then spotted Carina's final target on the far side of the driveway, inching closer to the house with each passing second. Trusting his XO to get the job done, Carter focused on his last acolyte, who was inside the farm building. Peering through the wooden slats, he saw the man reclining against the side of a tractor. Wisps of smoke were snaking into the air as the acolyte sucked on a cigarette, oblivious to his advance. Creeping through the open door, he approached the man on tip-toe, his footsteps masked by the covering of matted straw that lined the floor.

He was almost on top of the acolyte when his foot kicked a spanner that had been buried beneath the hay. It spun away and struck a heavy metal upright, causing it to toll like a door chime. Cursing, Carter tried to take out the acolyte before he could react, but the guard had already spat out his cigarette and pulled a pistol. He slapped the weapon away, then took a hard punch from the man, but it was like hitting a stone wall. The acolyte yelped and Carter leapt at him, covering the man's mouth with his hand to stifle any further cries. The guard squirmed like a cat that was refusing to be picked up, and Carter clanged the man's head on the side of the tractor, finally shutting him up.

"What the hell was that?" Carina said, whispering over their comm link. "It sounded like a dinner gong."

"Are you finished with your three, Major?" Carter replied, ignoring his XO's remark.

"Yes, all taken care of…" Carina replied. There was a brief pause before she added, "…and I did my three quietly…"

Carter scowled but chose not to dignify his XO's snarky response with a reply. "Head to the house; I'll meet you there."

Exiting the barn, Carter saw that his XO was already on the porch, approaching the entrance with her energy pistol at low ready. He sped across the front of the house, ducking to keep his head below the window line, and drew up on the other side of the door. Nodding to his XO, he moved inside, closely followed by his partner, and they were at once confronted by Damien Morrow and Marco Ryan. The turncoat Master-at-arms was holding the edge of his energized war saber to Cai Cooper's neck.

TWELVE
THE OFFER

CARTER DREW his cutlass and energized the blade, sending a ribbon of searing-hot plasma along the razor-sharp edge of the sword. Flickering light illuminated one side of his face, while casting the other into deep shadow.

"Step back from my officer or I will take your head," Carter snarled, aiming the cutlass at Marco Ryan, who showed not even a flicker of emotion in reply.

"Relax, Carter, we're only here to talk," Damien Morrow cut in, speaking to Carter as if they were old drinking buddies having a minor disagreement.

Carter kept the sword aimed at Ryan but looked the former Master Commander over. Unlike the silvering of his own hair, Morrow had changed little in last century. The man had the strong jawline and engaging blue eyes of an actor, though because of his chiseled face and sharp features, Carter had always thought he cut the look of a villain, rather than a hero, and he had the confident swagger to match. He was dressed in hardy civilian clothes, but the glint of Aternien armor was visible beneath. There was also an energy pistol of a design unfamiliar to Carter in the man's right hand, but it was not aimed at him or Cai.

"Holding a sword to someone's neck is a strange way to strike up a conversation," Carter replied, still keeping half-an-eye on the turncoat Master-at-arms. "And you can refer to me as Commander Rose. We're not friends. Not anymore."

"That's hurtful, Carter, especially after everything we've been through."

Carter found his fellow Master Commander's blasé tone to be insulting and inappropriate. It was as if the man thought he'd already won.

"That was a long time ago, Morrow," Carter hit back. "Now call off your dog, before I cut him down."

"I'd welcome a rematch," Ryan said, bristling because of Carter's insult. "Though it wouldn't end well for you."

If it wasn't for the fact the former Master-at-arms could have severed the vertebrae in Cai's neck with a flick of his wrist, Carter would have faced down Marco Ryan at once. As it turned out, it was the man's own commander who stood him down.

"That's enough, Marco," Morrow said, with the authoritative tenor of a military leader. "I told Carter that we're here to talk and I meant it."

Ryan nodded respectfully to his commander then disengaged the blade of his saber and stepped back. Even so, the man's eyes remained fixated on Carter, and his hand hovered close to his holstered pistol, like an old West gunslinger, preparing for a shootout.

Cai backed away from the traitors and stood beside Major Larsen. His XO had also kept her energy pistol in hand, though her eyes flicked from Ryan to Morrow, unclear as to which of them was more of a threat. Carter, however, was under no illusion who posed the greater danger. In all of Union history, only twelve human beings had survived both the trauma of augmentation and the ordeal of leadership trials, to attain the rank of Master Commander. And though he had been the first, Carter could say without ego that none of those people were to be trifled with.

"Master Operator Cooper was merely a little over-eager to learn about the welfare of his family," Morrow continued, still with a breezy tone of voice. "But, as I explained to him already, we did not come for them. We merely wanted to meet your Master Operator."

"If you just wanted to talk then you should have said so before we slaughtered all your acolyte friends outside," Carter replied.

He was continuing to disregard Morrow's pretense of friendship, but the turncoat Master Commander merely laughed and shrugged off Carter's comment.

"There are literally tens of thousands more where they came from, and more wishing to join our ranks every day," Morrow explained. "But until the acolytes have proven themselves worthy of ascension, they're just humans, like her."

Morrow turned his attention to Major Larsen as he said this, and his penetrating stare seemed to petrify her like a fossil.

"Why is she even here?" Ryan snapped. "She doesn't deserve to stand in our presence or wear the uniform of a Longsword officer."

This time it was Carina who laughed. "You mean in the presence of traitors?"

Morrow smiled, appreciating the joke, though Ryan remained hostile and indignant.

"One person's traitor is another's patriot, Major Larsen," Morrow replied, diplomatically. "I am simply choosing to fight for my own kind, against a regime that has discriminated against people like me for more than one hundred and seventy-five years."

Carter sighed; he had no intention of being subjected to another self-righteous lecture by officers who had forsaken their oaths.

"Your Master-at-arms already gave me the sob story, so you can you save it," Carter grunted. His tone remained deliberately acerbic and aggressive. "Yes, we were treated like shit, and no, we didn't deserve any of it. But you took an oath to defend the Union, same as I did, and you broke it. That makes you a traitor."

"Call it what you like, Carter, it makes no difference," Morrow answered, dismissing the personal attack like it meant nothing. "What's important is that I'm not here to fight you; I didn't even expect to find you here." The man turned to Cai. "It's him I wanted to meet."

"Invading my home and laying siege to my family's farm is no way to set up a meeting," Cai replied.

Carter had always been impressed with how his Master Operator was able to keep cool, even when provoked. As someone who was prone to anger, it was a skill he'd never been able to master, despite the long years of his life.

"I apologize for our methods, Master Operator Cooper, but you haven't made it easy for me," Morrow answered. "I mean no harm to your family; despite the fact they are humans. I actually came to make you an offer."

"We already know what you're offering, and we're not

interested, so save your breath," Carter cut in.

There was a flicker of anger in Morrow's eyes as Carter cut across him. He and his contemporary had never been bosom pals, but he knew the man well enough. Out of the twelve Longsword commanders, Damien Morrow had the highest opinion of himself, though not without reason. He was an exceptional battle commander, but despite his augmentations, he was still human at his core, and still flawed.

Carter knew, for example, that Morrow was intolerant of other people's views, and quick to anger if he didn't get what he wanted. Even so, the Master Commander always managed to skillfully navigate his relationship with the admiralty, displaying a duplicity that had always led Carter to distrust him. He was both pleased, and disappointed, to learn he'd been right about the man all along.

"I urge you not to be hasty," Morrow continued. It seemed clear to Carter that his patience was wearing thin. "I am extending to Master Operator Cooper the same offer that Markus Aternus himself made to Commander Rose, only to have it thrown back in his face." Morrow cast a sideways glance at him. "Despite this, the hand of Aternus remains outstretched to you too, Carter."

Carter snorted in disbelief. "Aternus still wants me to sign up with the goldies, despite the fact I nearly blew up his precious Solar Barque, and him in the process?"

"It is precisely for that reason that the great Markus Aternus has not withdrawn his offer," Morrow replied, becoming suddenly more agitated and excited. "The god-king was impressed with you. You would be a formidable ally. Only your misplaced sense of honor, as noble as that is in its own way, is stopping you from seeing sense."

Carter was equally animated in his rebuttal. "Honor is the only thing the Union didn't take from me a century ago, and I'm sure as hell not giving it up now. Not for you, and certainly not for some self-proclaimed god-king."

Morrow hissed with exasperation and shook his head, before returning his attention to Cai.

"Nevertheless, you do not speak for your former crewmembers. Think carefully, Mister Cooper, and make your own decision; not the choice that Commander Rose would want you to make."

Morrow was almost pleading with Cai to see his point of view, and although the Master Operator's expression rarely betrayed the emotions swelling beneath his calm exterior, Carter had learned to read his tells. He could see that Cai was tempted.

"Don't answer yet," Morrow added, seemingly buoyed by the fact Cai had not immediately dismissed his offer. "Hear what I have to tell you. Then, if you still wish to remain tethered to the Union, I'll respect your decision, and leave."

Cai turned to Carter. Despite the fact his old officer was no longer under his command, Cai was still seeking his permission before responding. In truth, he didn't want to give it, but Morrow had been correct about one thing; it was not his place to interfere. So he acquiesced and nodded his approval.

"Very well, say your piece," Cai replied, coolly.

Morrow's body language immediately changed. Instead of looking like a coiled viper, he had the confident and assured manner of a professional public speaker addressing a crowd that had paid specifically to hear him.

"Whatever you may believe, this time the Aterniens will

succeed in destroying the Union," Morrow began, speaking with an impassioned voice. "They will eradicate the human populations of all inhabited worlds, sparing only those who are marked for ascension." He paused then clenched his hand into a fist and shook it, like a senator addressing a room of dignitaries. At the same time the man's augmented eyes glistened with a devotion to his cause.

"Once humanity is eradicated, the god-king will create a vast, post-human empire populated by those who have transcended the limitations of flesh and blood. It will be a pure empire; one that will stand for all time. One that you can still be a part of."

Morrow finished his speech and waited for the reaction; fist still clenched. Based on how fervently he had delivered his pitch, Carter wondered if the man was perhaps expecting applause, or raucous cheers, but all he was met with was a stony silence.

"I've heard this elaborate fairytale already, straight from the fake lips of your lord and master himself," Carter said, sounding bored. "If that's all you've got then you can leave now."

"This is no fairytale, Commander Rose," Morrow hissed. "Right now, beneath Enterprise Stadium, there is a device; a doomsday weapon if you will. When detonated it will unleash a bio-engineered virus that will be carried to the four corners of Terra Six by drones. Once infected, there is no cure. Death occurs within hours and is mostly painless; a mercy granted by Markus Aternus himself."

The mention of a device at Enterprise Stadium confirmed what Cai had already suspected. Carter's unique biology was able to suppress the natural 'tells' that revealed when a person was lying or trying to hide something. Cai was similarly unreadable, but Major Larsen, despite keeping a level head, could not fully conceal her reaction. Her heart was suddenly thumping harder, and if Carter could hear it then Damien Morrow could too.

"You already know this, or at least suspect something?" Morrow enquired, frowning at Carina.

"You could still be lying," Cai cut in. "You may have learned of my investigations and are simply using this knowledge to manipulate me."

Morrow shrugged. "I have no reason to lie you, Mister Cooper. I'm only telling you out of respect for our shared history. We were brothers in arms once and can be again. The Union is weak and deserves to die. You know that just as well as I do."

"Won't this engineered virus kill you too?" Carina asked. "After all, you're still basically human."

The suggestion that Damien Morrow and Carina were in any way alike seemed to disgust the man. "Your ignorance is insulting," Morrow spat. "My superior biology protects me, just as the purity of the Aternien form protects them. Only unevolved meat bags like yourself will be infected and die."

Morrow continued to leer at Carina for another second, before disregarding her like she wasn't even in the room.

"You can't win this war, Carter," Morrow continued, continuing to use Carter's given name, despite the warning that they weren't friends. "The best you can hope for is to die a noble death; one worthy of your name and reputation. Or maybe you'll survive the extermination of humanity, only to live the remainder of your days as an outcast; alone and without purpose."

Carter clenched his jaw; Morrow certainly knew how to paint a dire picture of his future prospects in ways that the man knew would strike at his very core. He glanced at Cai, wondering how the traitor's speech had affected him, but for once he couldn't read his old officer and friend.

"This doomsday device won't have a chance to detonate," Carina cut in, remaining dogged in defiance of Morrow's bombshell. "The Union fleet will level that stadium so that not even a microbe will remain alive, whether it's natural or engineered."

"Your human stupidity reveals itself once again," Morrow countered, mocking Carina with a patronizing tone of voice. "Of course, we've considered that possibility, which is why the device is buried in a chamber beneath the stadium, so that not even the most hellish orbital bombardment could touch it." He dismissed Carina with a waft of his hand. "That's assuming your fleet could even get into position to launch such a strike, which we both know they can't."

"What about my family?"

Carter turned to Cai, and this time he was unable to hide his shock, as was Damien Morrow. *Is he considering the offer?...* Carter wondered, suddenly fearful of the possibility that he might have to fight three Longsword officers at once. Even with Carina on his side, he couldn't hope to prevail against such odds.

"Markus Aternus has granted me the title, Viceroy of Terra Six, which means this planet will be mine after the cleansing," Morrow said, taking the smallest of steps toward Cai, who didn't flinch. "More importantly, the god-king has given me the power to mark people for ascension. Join me, Mister Cooper, and I will ensure that your wife and children ascend with you. Your family will live together in peace and harmony for all time."

Carter could feel that he was losing Cai. In other circumstances, he would have dismissed Morrow's promise of ascending Cai's family as a lie. Yet the ritualist severing and reattaching of acolyte's arms suggested that there was some truth to the man's assurances. If Morrow had marked those men and women for ascension, then he could do the same for Cai's family too.

"This is a great gift and honor that you are being offered," Morrow continued, clasping his hands above his heart. "You deserve this, Mister Cooper. We all do."

Cai remained solemn and silent, while considering the proposal. Carina, on the other hand, looked like her head was about to explode. She was staring at Carter, imploring him to intervene, but he would not. Everyone had to make their own choice. He'd already made his; now it was the turn of his Master Operator.

"I thank you for the offer, sincerely, but I must decline," Cai eventually replied.

Carina let out a heavy sigh of relief and looked ready to collapse. Carter, however, felt invigorated.

"Master Commander Rose is right," Cai continued. "I took an oath. I cannot ever be at peace knowing that I have a broken faith with everything I fought for."

Damien Morrow said nothing, his expression a mix of disappointment, anger and frustration. However, the former Master Commander did not express any of these emotions in words. Instead, he nodded his head once, and accepted the decision.

"Then the die is cast," Morrow sighed. "The next time we meet, we will be enemies." He bowed to Commander Rose then turned on his heels and headed for door at the rear of the house. Marco Ryan, who had silently stood sentry like a

King's Guard outside Buckingham Palace, followed, though without taking his eye off Carter even for a second, until he was out of the door. A motor sparked into life and a vehicle pulled out of the garage. The Doppler shift of its engine note told him that the car was moving away at speed.

Carter finally allowed himself to take a deeper breath, then tapped his comp-slate to summon JACAB. The bot hummed inside in an instant, as if his gopher had been lurking nearby, eavesdropping. Which, of course, he had.

"Keep an eye on that car, buddy," Carter said, tapping JACAB with his knuckle. "I want to know if turns back, or if anything else approaches the house."

JACAB warbled and nodded, then shot out of the open door and ascended high above the farm. At the same time, Cai and Carina gathered around him.

"I have to say, for a moment there, I thought you were actually going to join them," Carina said, shooting Cai a nervous smile.

"For a moment, I almost did…"

The deadly serious tone of the response did nothing to alleviate Carina's already soaring blood pressure.

"Morrow arrived before us, but your family clearly wasn't here," Carter said, returning to the subject of why they were at the farmhouse in the first place. "So, what now, Cai? Is there someplace else they might have gone?"

Cai shook his head, but the man looked oddly at ease. "There is nowhere else for them to go, Commander. But there did not need to be. My family has been here all along…"

THIRTEEN
HOME COMFORTS

CAI LED them into the basement of the farmhouse then headed toward the far corner. To Carter, the space appeared to be no different to any other basement he'd seen before, and there were certainly no indications of people hiding down there. His former Master Operator approached the heating system, which was a large biomass incinerator coupled to a heat exchanger, and opened the huge safe-like door, which was as tall as he was. To Carter's surprise, Cai then stepped inside.

"Don't light a fire on our account," Carina said, nervously. "It really isn't cold today."

"This isn't actually an incinerator," Cai replied. He rapped his knuckles on the floor of the spherical combustion chamber, tapping out a tuneful sequence that was both complex and elegant. "At least, it isn't any more."

A hard clunk reverberated through the floor, then the hatch opened and the head and shoulders of Lola Carney, Cai's wife, appeared.

"They've gone," Cai said, taking Lola's hand into his own. "We're safe, but not for long."

Lola nodded. "I started to pack some things in case we had to leave in a hurry. Why don't you come down and help us finish?"

It was then that Lola spotted Carter and Carina in the darkness of the basement. Her eyes widened and a pistol was pulled out from beneath the hatch door, but Cai was quick to deflect the weapon's aim.

"It's okay, they're with me," he said, softly.

"They're Union officers?"

There was an uneasiness to the way Lola Carney asked the question, as if she was hoping her husband's answer would be "no."

"It's a long story," Cai replied, guardedly. "I'll summarize as best I can, but we don't have much time."

Lola nodded again then disappeared back through the hatch. Cai then stepped onto the ladder and indicated for Carter to follow him. However, he felt apprehensive about delaying their departure, even for a few minutes. Despite the fact that Damien Morrow had kept his word and left without any trouble, Carter didn't trust the man and feared that he would try again to either capture or kill them.

Carina, on the other hand, had no such qualms. She strode inside the incinerator and climbed down the ladder. The lower half of her body had already disappeared beneath the floor by the time she realized Carter wasn't following.

"What's wrong?" his XO asked. "Do you sense danger?"

Carter shook his head, then took a moment to tune in to his feelings, just to be certain of that fact. "I don't sense any immediate threat. I'm just anxious to get moving again."

"Then get your ass down here and help with the packing," Carina replied.

Her answer was a little too snippy for his liking, but she ducked beneath the hatch before he could reprimand her. He took a step forward then her head suddenly popped up again, like a whack-a-mole game in an amusement arcade.

"What I meant to say was, get down here and help with the packing, *sir*..."

Carter grunted a laugh. "That's more like it."

The panic room hidden beneath the farmhouse turned out to be more of a 'panic apartment'. Cai gave them a brief tour, clearly proud of the fact that he'd not only designed and built the shielded safe space, but that it had served its purpose too, by preventing Morrow and Ryan from discovering his family.

There was a kitchen-diner, a small lounge, and separate sleeping quarters, along with a bathroom that Cai had designed so that all waste matter was processed and recycled. Carter was suitably impressed, though after learning of the recycling system, Carina seemed less keen to drink the glass of water that Lola had given her.

"This is some set up," Carter admired, leaning against the kitchen counter with his own glass of water in hand. Cai's two adopted children were playing a board game at the dining table, ably assisted by JACAB and TOBY, who appeared to be enjoying it even more than the children were. "To have built a place like this, you must have suspected the Aterniens would someday return?"

Cai shrugged with his eyes. "There is an old saying that goes, 'hope for the best, but prepare for the worst'. I had hoped we'd seen the last of the Aterniens, but it would have been foolish to assume the threat nonexistent."

"I wish the Union had thought as you did," Carter sighed. "A hundred years, and they're weaker now than they were back then. A hundred years of shunning technology and stunting advancement, all because of deep-rooted prejudices and fears."

The pair were quiet for a moment, during which time TOBY appeared to make a successful move in the game. The bot was warbling and bleeping excitedly and had raised its maneuvering fins like someone throwing up their hands in celebration. JACAB, on the other hand had blown a raspberry and was staring gloomily down at the table, its red eye sharpened into a vee.

"Are the Aternien forces really that much stronger?" Cai asked. "It doesn't surprise me that Terra Six was so easily overcome, given that it has never had a significant military presence, but I would have thought the inner worlds to be more resilient?"

It was a good question and one that until recently Carter hadn't known how to answer with any level of confidence. However, seeing how effectively the Aterniens had blockaded the Union fleet, destroyed its troop transports, and occupied the city, it was clear they were hilariously outmatched. And now there was the lingering threat of a doomsday weapon; a device that, once activated, would kill every human being on the planet, leaving it ripe for Damien Morrow to claim as its new Viceroy.

"Terra Prime could maybe hold out for a few months in a straight-up fight, but the others will fall much more quickly, like Terra Six," Carter replied, trying to answer in the most positive way he could manage. "If Morrow is to be believed, all the Aterniens need to do is take and hold a city long enough to construct their weapon. Then they'll wipe out the population of the planet, and move on to the next, like a swarm of locusts, moving from field to field, and destroying everything in their path."

Carter glanced at Cai out of the corner of his eye. He could see that his bleak assessment of humanity's chances had affected him on a deeper level. Unlike the traitors, Morrow and Ryan, the oath meant something to the crew of the Longsword Galatine. To know that their enemy was back, stronger than ever, would have grated on him, just as it had done Kendra and himself. Yet, it was also true that the Union had effectively released them from that oath when the Longswords were decommissioned, and their crews discarded. His old Master Operator had new obligations now, and he would not guilt-trip the man into setting them aside.

"None of that will happen, though," Carter continued, offering Cai what he hoped was a reassuring smile. "Kendra will fix up the Galatine better than ever, then I'll find Amaya and Brodie, and remind the Aterniens exactly why they lost the war a hundred years ago."

Cai still appeared uncomfortable, like someone who was protecting a secret, but was unsure whether keeping it or revealing it was for the greater good. He was about to speak when Lola and Major Larsen approached, both smiling and chatting as if the worries of the world were light years away.

"What are you two so chipper about?" Carter asked, as the two women slid a tray of snacks onto the counter beside them.

"I was just telling Lola about how you almost killed that conference attendee in the hotel on Terra Three," Carina replied, her eyes bright. "Carter strung him up like a thanksgiving turkey, and was about to gut him like one, before I pointed out his mistake. The poor guy was so shook up, he fainted and fell flat on his face outside our room."

"He passed out because he was drunk, not because of me," Carter grunted.

"So, you were staying in the same room together?" Lola asked. "I didn't realize you two were partners out of uniform as well as in it."

"We're not," Carter cut in, before Carina could beat him to the punch and make some snarky comment about his age. "The hotel was just full that night, because of the conference."

"Oh, I see…," said Lola. The twinkle in her eyes was not unlike that of Carina's, and it suggested she didn't quite believe him.

"I bet Cai has some great stories to tell too," Carina added, looking hopefully at Carter's old crewmate. "After all that time serving together, I'll bet you got into the odd sticky situation or two?"

"We did not," Carter replied, bluntly. That wasn't true, of course; he simply didn't want Cai to feed his XO with more ammunition to fire back at him.

"Come on, Cai, I'm sure that's not true," Lola chipped in, nudging her husband. "You never really talk about the war, and I sometimes forget you lived a whole other life before meeting me."

Carter kept a careful watch on Cai and tried to convey his deep desire for the man to keep his mouth shut with a simple raising of one eyebrow. He could tell that Cai still remembered their unspoken language of gestures and facial expressions that each of them had developed over years cooped up together. He also knew that the Cai Cooper who'd served on the Galatine would never have indulged in such frivolous banter, anyway. However, this was not the same man he'd served with, and Carter was mortified to realize that his old Master Operator also had a roguish twinkle in his eye.

"Do you remember when Amaya let you land the Galatine at Outpost Fifteen on Terra Seven?" Cai asked.

"Yes…" Carter replied, scowling at the man. "And I didn't need her permission. I was the commander, remember…"

"It was a blowing like a tempest that day, with rain like you wouldn't believe," Cai continued, despite Carter's obvious unease. "Even with scanners, we could barely see a hundred meters ahead of the ship."

"I know where you're going with this, but in my defense, it wasn't my fault," Carter interjected, but it was to no avail.

"Now, the Commander is a solid pilot, but a Longsword requires a unique skill set; one that he has never quite mastered." Carter tried again to object, but it was like he was invisible. "So, he takes the helm and heads for the landing zone, fighting the wind with the tenacity of Hercules performing one of his twelve labors. And to his credit, the Commander hit the landing pad almost dead on, and was quite pleased with himself."

"Now, wait just a damned minute…"

Carina again brushed off Carter's protest, but it was Lola's smile that disarmed him.

"The next thing we know, the base commander has charged outside into the raging storm, waving his hands above his head like a madman. It turns out that Commander Rose had landed the Galatine on top of the Colonel's brand-new sports car and pancaked it flat."

Lola cried out and clapped, while Carina merely shook

her head at Carter, in a gesture of mock scorn and disappointment.

"In my defense, the colonel was parked in the wrong place," Carter grunted.

That's a good story, but I'm looking for something a little juicier," Carina said, flashing her eyes suggestively. "I'm sure a stud like Carter Rose got up to plenty of shenanigans during your periods of shore leave?"

"We didn't take shore leave," Carter grumbled, glowering at his XO. "And I'm not a damned horse, thank you very much."

"Well, there was this one occasion on Terra Two…"

Carter sighed and his eyes rolled into the back of his head.

"We were sent to eliminate an Aternien platoon that had attacked a mall in the capital city." Cai paused and looked at Carina. "Back then, they didn't have the sort of numbers and technology they have now, so the Aterniens employed a lot of guerrilla tactics to terrorize the core worlds."

"Major Larsen is something of an expert on the Aterniens," Carter cut in. He then scowled at Cai. "Just where are you going with this?"

Cai smiled, which only made Carter more anxious, then resumed his anecdote.

"Anyway, I was monitoring with TOBY and providing tactical support to the commander and Brodie, our Master-at-arms. They were on the upper level, tearing through the Aterniens in their usual brutal manner."

"I prefer the word efficient, but I suppose brutal is accurate," Carter mumbled. He had now folded his arms tightly across his chest, resigned to his fate.

"They had the last three Aterniens cornered, which is

when Brodie decided to finish the job with a plasma grenade," Cai went on. "Unfortunately, the explosive didn't only destroy the warriors, but the floor of the mall too, and the commander fell through to the level below."

Carter winced. He now had a fairly good idea where Cai was going with his story, and he was desperate to cut it short. "I'm sure Lola and Major Larsen do not want to hear our old war stories," he cut in, fearing the worst. "And we really should be going."

However, his attempts to break up the party failed. Carina merely shushed him, while Lola took hold of his arm, so that he couldn't get away.

"I moved in with TOBY to check he was okay, and found the Commander flat on his back, with four dripping wet, naked women draped all over him."

Lola laughed openly, while Carina gasped and clasped her hand over her mouth.

"Now, wait a second, you're missing out some pretty important parts…" Carter cut in, but, unusually for him, he was fighting a losing battle.

"It turns out that the level below was a Korean-style naked bath house, and that the Commander had accidentally landed in the women's section." Cai grinned. "From what I saw, they were quite pleased to see him, and he them."

Carina snorted and Lola hugged his arm even more tightly, while shaking from laughter.

"Well, I did just save their lives," Carter said, feeling his face burn hot – a reaction even his augments couldn't prevent. "They were relieved, that's all!"

"I love it!" Carina exclaimed, beaming a smile from ear to ear. "I want more!"

Carter shook his head, but while the laughs were largely

at his expense, he discovered he didn't begrudge Cai telling the stories. He had never seen his old officer so relaxed and happy. In the presence of his wife and family, Cai was completely a different man to the pragmatic and serious officer he once knew.

However, Carter was also surprised to learn that this revelation made him feel strangely wretched. He'd spent the last century avoiding people like the plague, living alone in his cabin on the forest moon of Terra Nine. Looking at Cai, and how contented the man was, he wondered if he'd simply wasted his life, and denied himself the happiness that all people deserved, post-human or otherwise.

"I think that's more than enough, thank you..." Carter said, accepting his roasting magnanimously. He turned to Cai. "I'm glad we met again, Cai. It seems that I never really knew you at all."

"I never knew me, sir," Cai said, putting his hand on Carter's shoulder and squeezing gently. "I had no idea my life could be like this. Lola was a blessing."

His wife smiled then slipped from Carter's side and wrapped her arms around her husband; an act that made the man seem to glow.

"We really should go," Carter said. He felt guilty for being the one to put an end to their fun, especially as recent events had given them so little to laugh about. "We have a shuttle docked at Enterprise Stadium, but that area is far too hot to risk trying to reach it. Instead, I suggest we look for a private spaceport close by. With any luck, we can find a craft that will get you and your family off this planet before it's too late."

Carina nodded and was about to move out, but Cai remained, his head bowed low.

"Sir, I know you risked your life to find me, but despite what we have learned, and despite my oath, I still cannot come with you. I must…"

"It's okay, Cai, I understand," Carter said, interrupting his former crewmate. Surprised, Cai raised his gaze and met his eyes. "We'll be just fine without you. You need to take care of your family."

Cai smiled and nodded, but still looked torn. His oath to the Union and his oath to his family were two conflicting forces that were tearing him apart from the inside out.

"You don't need to come with us," Cai added. "I have a truck in the east barn, and I have TOBY and the weapons from the fallen acolytes. I will be fine on my own."

His instinct was to resist and to tell Cai that he would see them the rest of the way, but the truth was that he had to get back on mission. There was no telling how long it would be until the doomsday device was ready to detonate. Time, as always, was against them.

"Okay, Cai," Carter said, smiling. "Major Larsen and I will take the other vehicle and head to the Union Army Barracks in the city. Hopefully, there are still some troops left on this planet that can help us to destroy the doomsday device."

"They might also have a transmitter we can use," Carina chipped in. "With JACAB's help, we could cut through any jamming fields and get a message to Admiral Krantz."

Carter nodded then laughed weakly. "Maybe our information will make up for the fact we stole her personal shuttle, and she'll show mercy and pick us up."

"You disobeyed orders to come and find me?" Cai said. The man looked more embarrassed than shocked, confirming Carter's suspicion that Cai had largely figured this out already.

"Don't worry about it, Cai. Major Larsen has a special rapport with the admiral and will smooth things over with her." He looked to his XO. "Isn't that right?"

Carina merely snort-laughed, which was not exactly the response he was hoping for.

Suddenly, TOBY shot up from the dining table, where he and the others were still playing their game and raced over. The bot squawked and warbled and with each electronic phrase spoken, Cai Cooper's expression became graver.

"There is an Aternien squad approaching the farm from the south," Cai said, relaying the news. "And TOBY says a gang of acolytes is also approaching, including Damien Morrow and Marco Ryan."

"The bastards lied to us," Carina spat.

Carter shook his head. "No, they just said they'd leave here in peace. They didn't say they wouldn't come back." He checked that his 57-EX was loaded then drew his sword. "Major, get Lola and the kids into the truck and make sure it's ready to move. Cai and I will handle our uninvited guests."

FOURTEEN

TRAITORS WILL BE TRAITORS

CARTER CLIMBED the ladder out of the panic room, scaling it three rungs at a time, then ran to the nearest window and peered outside. Aternien Immortals were marching through the wheat fields, their armor almost the same color as the crop they were trampling beneath their feet. Then he saw the acolytes, creeping up on the farm like thieves in the night. Unlike the Immortals, they were disorganized and spread out, more like a mob than an army, but no less dangerous.

Cai guided his family out of hiding but kept them away from the windows. He had also drawn his sword and had a gauss assault rifle slung over his shoulder; a weapon claimed from one of the acolytes they'd already killed. "My truck is in that metal barn, directly east of the house," Cai said, pointing out the structure to Major Larsen, who had exited the safe room last. "Lola can get you inside, but please do not leave until the commander and I have dealt with the Aterniens. The truck is not robust enough to withstand Aternien particle blasts."

Carina nodded then helped Lola to shepherd the children into position. Carter checked the perimeter then gave his XO the okay, and the group ran outside, keeping low and quiet, and using the house to block the enemy's line of sight. Carter watched anxiously until Carina and Cai's family had slipped inside the shelter of the barn, then turned his attention to his old Master Operator.

"That gauss gun will be next to useless against the Immortals, and you're also not wearing a battle uniform, which makes you vulnerable," Carter began. "I suggest you handle the acolytes, while I deal with the goldies."

Carter had already settled on a plan in his own mind, but Cai was no longer under his command, and not subject to his orders. Even so, the man reacted as if they had never stopped serving together.

"Yes, sir," Cai replied, making the gauss rifle ready. "I can keep the acolytes pinned down to the North, but the Immortals will know that TOBY has spotted them and will use the farm buildings as cover. Most likely, it will come down to close-quarters fighting."

"That suits me just fine," Carter grunted. He activated his buckler and limbered up his sword arm. His engineered biology meant that he had no need to warm up like a regular human, but it was more a ritual than a necessity. "Watch out for Marco Ryan. That bastard has a mean streak, and he's your equal with a sword."

Cai nodded, accepting the warning without ego. Though the decades had mellowed his personality, they had not eroded his capability to assess the cold, hard facts of a situation and respond in the most logical and appropriate manner. This was what had made him such an effective Master Operator on the Galatine; Cai tempered

Carter's natural impulsiveness and provided much-needed balance.

Suddenly, Carter's senses spiked, and he ducked as the farmhouse was ravaged by gunfire and particle blasts. Cai had taken cover too, benefiting from the same augmented instincts that had saved their lives on countless occasions. They exchanged glances, communicating through the wordless language they had developed on the Galatine, and moved out.

Cai ran north, bursting outside and shooting three acolytes who had overestimated their chances and been too eager to press their attack. More particle blasts punctured the wooden walls of the house, setting fire to them and the furniture inside. An update arrived on his comp-slate, and Carter smiled as the positions of the acolytes and Immortals appeared on the screen, overlaid on a tactical plan of the surrounding area.

"Thanks, buddy…" Carter said, glancing up to where he imagined his gopher to be, hovering in the sky above the farm.

Then his early-warning system kicked into a higher gear, and time seemed to slow down as he watched an Aternien energy grenade smash through the kitchen window. He burst into motion with the speed of a cheetah and threw himself through the smashed windowpane, feeling the pressure wave from the grenade blast accelerate his already-rapid exit.

Rolling through the fall on the gravel outside, Carter skidded to a stop and spotted the grenadier. A single shot from his 57-EX put the Immortal down, but return fire prevented him from killing any more Aterniens. He raced toward the nearest farm building, chased by shards of energy, and pressed his back to the exterior wall, hitting it so hard the entire barn shook. Glancing at his comp-slate he saw four Immortals working their way toward him, two around the side of the building and two directly through it.

Using the data from JACAB as his guide, Carter aimed around the side of the barn and fired blind. The thump of an Aternien's body hitting the ground told him that his shot had landed true, even before the target marker had blinked off his comp-slate.

Turning on his heels he sprinted across the front of the building toward where the other Immortal was stalking around the opposite side. The Aterniens inside the barn opened fire and he suffered a glancing hit to his thigh, but he shrugged it off and continued. The warrior turned the corner at almost the same moment he reached it, and their two bodies collided. It didn't matter that one was flesh and the other synthetic; his dense muscles and gorilla-like mass bowled the Immortal over like a ten pin. Yet the Aternien kept hold of his rifle and soon the barrel was aimed at Carter's heart.

The Immortal fired, but Carter deflected the shot with his buckler, before igniting the blade of his cutlass and plunging it into the chest of the Aternien warrior. A particle blast then thumped into his back, and he felt the sting of pain bite hard before his sensation blockers kicked in. However, his armor spared him from serious injury, which meant that all the Immortal had achieved by shooting him in the back was to make Carter furious.

Spinning around, Carter shot the Aternien who had attacked him, then picked off another two with headshots, like they were coconuts at a fairground stall. Reloading his 57-EX, he checked the tactical display on his comp-slate, and mentally marked the locations of the other Aterniens. Six more Immortals were closing in, using one of the larger, steel-framed agricultural buildings to cover their advance.

As he moved out, Carter caught a glimpse of Cai Cooper, practically gliding through the fields to the north of the farm, using boundary walls and trees for cover. The rattle of his rifle was near constant, as he picked off unsuspecting acolytes before they'd even seen him coming. Cai was fast, efficient and professional – it seemed like not a day had passed since he last saw the man in action.

The shriek of Aternien particle blasts snapped his focus back to his own targets, and Carter dove behind a tractor, letting the machine absorb the brunt of the onslaught. Scrambling onto the roof of the vehicle, he took the Immortals by surprise, and mowed down the front rank in a torrent of gunfire. The other warriors were still moving through the steel-paneled agricultural building, and he charged toward them, aware that his best chance was to trap the warriors inside and fight them in close quarters.

Ignoring the main entrance, which was a natural choke point, Carter made his own door by kicking down a section of the steel wall. The heavy panel flattened an Immortal who had been lurking behind it, but the warrior threw it aside and fought to his feet, particle rifle still in hand. Carter cut the weapon in half with his cutlass before the Immortal could fire, then hacked the Aternien out of his way. Particle blasts flashed toward him, but the building was filled with machinery that supplied ample cover.

Taking the fight to the Immortals, Carter met the Aternien advance head on, slicing open a deep gouge in the closest warrior's chest, before narrowly avoiding a blast that smashed into the steel upright next to his head. Particle fire chased him until a shot struck his leg and sent him tumbling across the cold concrete floor. Cursing, Carter dragged himself into cover behind a grain trailer and inspected the wound, but it was shallow and already healing.

Five Aternien Immortals remained and two had Carter pinned, while the others redeployed in an attempt to flank him. His mind was racing at a million miles per hour, assessing dozens of strategies and outcomes in mere seconds, and selecting the strongest option as instinctively as breathing.

Setting down his sword, Carter grabbed the grain trailer and lifted, using the explosive power of his muscles to perform feats of super-human strength that even the Aterniens were unable to match. The trailer flipped and rolled over the warriors, crushing their lower halves, and trapping them to the floor.

A blast raced past his head, and Carter was forced to evade before he could recover his cutlass. He searched the ground for another weapon then grabbed a pitchfork and hurled it at the Immortal like a trident. The prongs became impaled in the Aternien's head, piercing both glowing blue eyes and blinding the enemy warrior.

Another Immortal charged, bayonet outstretched, and he was forced to block with his buckler, but the energy of the impact destroyed the shield and left him exposed. The bayonet was then thrust at his neck, but he caught the barrel of the weapon and smashed it like a Karate black belt breaking a brick.

Still the warrior would not relent, and it wrapped its synthetic fingers around his throat, squeezing with the force of an alligator bite. A brutal headbutt rocked the warrior and loosened the Aternien's grip enough that Carter could break the hold and gain the upper hand. He unleashed a left-right combo that mauled the Aternien's handsome face and allowed him to snap the warrior's neck like a rotten tree branch.

Only a single Immortal now remained, but this warrior was a Warden. By biding its time, the skilled Aternien fighter had stalked closer without Carter knowing, and the warrior now had him cornered. Blasts hammered against the steel uprights close to where Carter had been forced into cover, and soon the metal was melting. The roof creaked and groaned as it collapsed in on itself, and Carter was forced to make a desperate dive to safety.

The Warden was on him in a flash, and Carter took a blast to the chest and another to the back before he regained his senses and darted out of range. His battle uniform was burned and scarred all over, and the wounds to his flesh were healing more slowly, due to the sheer number of injuries he'd sustained, but Carter had faced worse situations, and come out the victor. This was no different.

The Warden continued to advance, like a predator that already had the scent of blood on its tongue. Carter looked for a weapon or anything he could use to fight back. Then he saw a rusted axe buried under a pile of scrap metal, and he reached for it. At the same time the Warden burst around the corner and thrust the bayonet into his side. His sensation blockers were no longer effective, and Carter felt the full agonizing force of the injury, which caused him to roar with pain.

Grabbing the blunted axe, Carter smashed it across the side of the Warden's head, which stunned the Aternien for long enough that he could pull the bayonet free of his flesh. The Warden recovered and the two fought for control of the rifle, like champions locked in a brutal tug of war, but Carter was stronger. He was *always* stronger. The Aternien succumbed and Carter forced the energized bayonet into the Warden's chest. As the blade sunk deeper, the warrior's glowing eyes grew wide with shock and embarrassment. The Warden convulsed like it was having a fit, and sparks erupted from the wound, but Carter held firm until the Aternien's convulsions had stopped and the light had faded from its eyes. Then he tossed the body to the floor and tore the Warden's Soul Block out from the back of its head.

"Here, I wouldn't want your friends to miss this," Carter grunted, dropping the block, which contained the soul and memory of the Warden, onto his chest. "When you wake up, I want my face to be the first thing you remember."

"Carter, are you okay?" Carina said, speaking through the comm system in his battle uniform.

"I'm here, Major, what's your status?" Carter answered, while collecting his cutlass.

"Cai has dealt with the acolytes, and TOBY isn't reading any more Aterniens on the farm, but a full platoon is heading this way, and fast."

"I'm on my way to the truck now," Carter said, though he delayed his departure to prepare a low-dose nano-stim. Without it, he wouldn't be moving particularly swiftly. "Buddy, did you copy the Major?" he asked his bot.

JACAB darted out of the clouds and soared toward the east barn like a guided missile, and Carter smiled. *I'll take that as a yes…*

Pressing the nano-stim into his neck, Carter clamped his jaw shut and waited for the pain and spasms to subside. At a low dose, the side-effects were manageable, and the rapid healing benefit of the extra nano-machines allowed him to move out without difficulty.

Carter reached the barn, but as he pushed open the door, he felt his senses sharpen. He knew there was danger nearby, but it was elusive, like a rainbow you could see but never reach. Then an energy sword fizzed into life and cut through the air toward him. The strike came so hard and so fast that he was barely able to parry the attack, and he was unbalanced. Another cut raced past his face then he was kicked to the chest and sent down hard.

Marco Ryan appeared above him; his sword held high. The glow from the energized war saber drenched the man's face with a ghostly saturation that made his twisted grimace look even more hideous. A fierce cut was aimed at his head, but Carter didn't need to parry the strike, because another sword intercepted Ryan's blade before it could reach him. The turncoat retreated, and Carter saw Cai standing between them.

Without a word spoken, the two former Longsword officers raised their swords and clashed. Both were masters of their own forms, and both were as determined as the other to win. Blades continued to clash and fizz, then Ryan scored a glancing hit, and without his battle uniform, Cai was hurt. The Master-at-arms went in for the kill, but a succession of focused energy blasts hammered into the traitor's back and shoulder, and Ryan was forced to withdraw, covering his already burned face and neck to prevent more serious injury.

"Come on!" Carina cried out.

His XO was leaning out of the driver's side window of the truck, smoking energy pistol in hand. Carter jumped to his feet and helped Cai into the vehicle, practically throwing the man inside. "Floor it!"

Carina accelerated, smashing through the door at the end of the barn and turning hard toward the road. The truck skidded across the drive, but its wide, fat tires bit into the gravel, and soon they were on course. Further to the west, Carter could see sunlight glinting off the scale armor of more Aternien Immortals, but they were too far away to be of concern.

"Damn it, that was too close," said Carina, turning onto the road and causing the rear of the truck to fishtail out, like a drift racer. "A couple more minutes and an entire company of Aternien Immortals would have surrounded us."

"In about a mile, take the right fork toward Carytown Lake," Cai said. His hand was pressed over the wound to his arm, but it was already healing. "There's a private airstrip in the town that might have a shuttle we can commandeer."

Carina nodded and kept a heavy right-foot on the throttle. Carter spun around and checked the road to their rear, but they weren't being followed. Then he saw Lola and the kids bundled up together, tucked down on the long rear seat. He smiled at the woman, and she smiled back, and Carter allowed himself to take a breath of relief. Then a dark sense of foreboding gripped him, as if the Grim Reaper himself had just taken him by the throat.

There was a crackle of gunfire, and the truck was hit. Windows smashed and slugs hammered into the hood and doors. Carina held her nerve and kept on the throttle, while Carter desperately searched for the sniper. Then he saw the gunman, as clear as day. Damien Morrow was crouched on a hilltop by the side of the road, scoped gauss rifle in hand.

Without thinking, Carter took the energy pistol from the

holster on his XO's hip and opened fire. The blasts cut through the darkening sky like tracer rounds and Morrow was hit and sent tumbling down the hill on the opposite side. It was a shot in a million, but Carter felt no gratification, knowing that the traitor's Aternien scale armor would have spared him from harm.

Carina turned right, still handling the truck like a getaway driver, and soon the hill and Damien Morrow were far in the distance. Finally, Carter allowed himself to relax his aim and believe that their ordeal was over.

"We're in the clear," Carter said, turning to check on Lola and the children. "You can sit up. The danger is past."

The two girls, both shivering with fear, pulled themselves upright, then Cai's wife slowly followed suit, but her face was drawn, and her body was shivering. Carter felt a chill rush down his spine as he spotted the blood on her hands. His heart sank into a pit inside his chest. Lola Carney had been shot.

FIFTEEN

NOT FOR YOU...

MAJOR LARSEN PULLED the truck off the road a few miles from the farm but kept the motor running, since they were still at risk of being found by the Aterniens. Carter threw open the door and hurried to the rear seat, where Cai was holding his wife in his arms. Their children were huddled at their side, faces buried in his old crew mate's chest, while JACAB and TOBY desperately tried to treat Lola's wound. However, neither bot was equipped to deal with human trauma, and the tools at their disposal were insufficient to the task.

"Can you give her a nano-stim?" Carina said, breathless with worry. "It worked for me, so it could work for her?"

TOBY conversed with JACAB, exchanging bleeps and warbles so rapidly it was little more than an uninterrupted drone of electronic chatter. TOBY then turned to Cai, and they spoke, but from the look on his Master Operator's face, it wasn't good news.

"TOBY's assessment is that in Lola's condition, the stress

of the nano-machines invading her cells would kill her, before they were able to repair her injuries."

"Then we need to find a hospital," Carter said. To JACAB, he added, "Buddy, find us the closest medical facility that has an ER or surgical unit, and relay the coordinates to the truck's nav."

JACAB nodded then the positions of two hospitals appeared on the trucks' navigation screen. One was five miles away, and the other ten, in the opposite direction, though the more distant facility was the better equipped. Carter believed that the closest was still their best choice, but he was painfully aware that Damien Morrow would know this too.

"Go for the closest hospital, and drive like your life depended on it," Carter said, jumping back into the passenger seat.

Carina floored the accelerator, kicking up a thick plume of dust and gravel in her wake. Outside of the city, the roads were narrow and winding, but his XO navigated the lanes like she was piloting a space fighter. Before long, they had climbed beyond the valley in which Enterprise City was built, giving Carter an unfettered view of the battleground. Scarab-like Khepri fighters and Aternien drones filled the skies above the metropolis, half of which was now ablaze. Union troop transports, drop ships and frigates lay ruined and burning all across the city and beyond. He'd witnessed scenes like it before, but he never expected to see them again. The city was lost, and its people either dead or on the run. Yet, if Damien Morrow's warning about the doomsday device was true, there was ultimately no escape for the millions who couldn't get off world.

Carina swung right and the smoke from a crashed troop

transport filled the air. She drove past the wreckage without even giving it a cursory glance, such was her laser-focus on reaching the hospital in the shortest possible time. Carter wished that his mind had been occupied too, because it would have spared him the sight of hundreds of Union soldiers, lying dead in the mud. Most were missing limbs, while some had been burned black like charcoal. The unlucky ones had survived the crash, only to die minutes later, crawling through the dirt in the vain hope of rescue. It was horrific, there was simply no other word for it.

The next few minutes felt like hours, until Carina pulled into the hospital and screeched the truck to a halt in front of the ER department. The place was in chaos, with ambulances, nurses and doctors all around them, ferrying wounded through the doors, which were permanently locked open. Some of the injured were civilians, but most were military, and even with his basic medical training, Carter could see that many were already beyond saving.

Carina took charge of finding them a doctor, while Cai lifted his wife out of the truck and ran her inside the hospital. Carter could hear that her heart was weak, but she was still breathing, and he had to believe she was strong enough to pull through. Carina returned at the head of a stretcher, with two ER doctors in pursuit, and Carter held back, knowing that his XO had everything under control. Still, he felt numb. He could only watch as his old friend tried to console his children and tell them the necessary lie that everything was going to be okay. He choked back tears as he saw them break down and weep while the doctors wheeled their mother through the doors and out of sight. Major Larsen held the two girls close and escorted them inside. He desperately wanted to go too, but his senses warned him of the need to stay vigilant, and Carter suddenly hated his augmentations more than ever.

"Sir, is something wrong?" Cai said. He'd held back, perhaps also sensing what Carter had felt.

"Maybe, I'm not sure yet," Carter replied. The tumult of the crowd combined with the wail of ambulance sirens was making it difficult to hone in on what his instincts were trying to tell him. "I'll stay out here and keep watch," he added. "Go, be with your family."

"I should stay too," Cai said, gripping the handle of his sword.

"No." Carter was firm, and Cai straightened. He held his officer's shoulders and met the man's gaze; it hurt to look at him, like staring into the sun. "Go inside and be with your wife and children. I'll be fine on my own."

He could feel that his old friend was conflicted, but Carter didn't give him a choice. He turned the man and gently ushered him toward the entrance to the ER, forcing himself to smile so that Cai would believe his lie. He watched and waited until the husband and father was inside then allowed the smile, which was already weighing heavy, to wane.

Behind him, Carter heard the thrum of a powerful vehicle pulling up, followed by the weighty thump of doors being slammed shut. He turned to see two men standing in front of a black SUV. They were both armed with pistols and knives, and though the weapons remained sheathed, neither was making any effort to hide them.

He studied the men as they strutted closer, both watching him as keenly as he was watching them. They had the cocky swagger and cruel eyes of playground bullies. Typical 'hard man' types, Carter thought, feeling anger swell inside him.

They were just the sort of people he liked to teach a lesson to.

The driver's door of the SUV then opened, and Marco Ryan stepped out. The traitor moved with the same casual swagger as the bullies, even taking the time to fasten the middle button of his tailored suit jacket and straighten it, as if he were making himself ready for a photoshoot. The lazy way in which the acolytes had arrived had given Carter ample time to escape, but Ryan knew that he would never abandon his people, which was why the man was taking his time. Ryan's contempt and arrogance just made Carter hate the turncoat more.

"Commander Morrow thought you'd go for the more distant hospital in order to throw us off your scent, but I knew you'd come here," Ryan said, wearing a smile that Carter urgently wanted to slap off the man's face. "I guess he was wrong, and I was right."

"That just makes you the unlucky one," Carter grunted.

Marco Ryan stopped a couple of meters short of Carter, and the two thugs postured behind him, as if they believed they held all the cards. Carter knew differently, and the thugs would soon find that out to their cost.

"You should have just left the human to die and kept going," Ryan continued. "You were in the clear."

"I'm in the business of saving human lives, traitor, not taking them."

Ryan laughed and it took everything Carter had not to drive his sword through the man's throat, but he swallowed the bile in his mouth and bided his time.

"It doesn't look like you're doing all that well in the 'saving lives' department," Ryan added, looking at the carnage surrounding them with a smirk curling his lips. "A few hundred thousand are dead already, and that's only the start. In a few hours, every human being on this world will carry a deadly infection, and Commander Morrow will take over as Viceroy. Terra Six will belong to us."

"You're not an Aternien, Ryan, and you never will be," Carter countered. "You're just a filthy traitor, and you're going to die today."

Ryan scoffed at him again. Arrogance and disrespect oozed from the man like blood from the bullet hole in Lola Carney's gut.

"Take him," Ryan said, waving the two thugs forward.

The acolytes drew their pistols and advanced, but neither of the men would live long enough to squeeze the triggers. Carter had already contemplated a dozen different ways to kill the bullies in the short time it had taken them to step past Marco, but the truth was that they were mere distractions, not worthy of his time. Ryan was who Carter really wanted, and the turncoat's time would soon come.

Carter grabbed his sheath with his left hand and pushed it back, allowing him to draw the cutlass and cut in one fluid movement. The speed of his strike was too rapid for a human eye to see, but the thugs felt its impact all the same. The first crumpled in a bloody mass, cut open from hip to shoulder, while the second had dropped to his knees, hands wrapped around his throat in a futile effort to stem the bleeding from a severed jugular.

Carter could have finished the acolytes quickly and spared them the pain and torment of their final moments, but any shred of charity that had remained within him had evaporated the moment Lola was shot. Instead, he left them writhing and moaning, all the while keeping his eyes locked onto Ryan, who had not displayed even a shred of remorse or anger over the death of his men. They were just humans, after all.

"You should have joined us," Ryan sighed, drawing his American Revolutionary Saber, and energizing the blade.

"And you should have chosen the other hospital," Carter hit back, flicking the switch to send plasma coursing along the edge of his cutlass.

Ryan pressed his left hand to his hip and adopted a traditional fencing-style pose. The man was smiling again, but this was not the deranged grin of sociopath, but the contented expression of man who enjoyed his work. They circled around each other for a moment, and Carter observed that Ryan's footwork was exemplary. He'd already fought the man once and knew his skill was equal to any Longsword officer he'd ever known. Yet he also knew that fighting wasn't just about skill, but who had the strongest will to win. Ryan believed he was the better swordsman, and maybe he was right. In the end, it wouldn't save him.

Ryan attacked first, using the advantage of his longer blade to full effect. Carter parried, but with his buckler destroyed and his battle uniform still in the process of repairing itself, his defenses were weakened. Ryan came at him again, and the blades of the energized swords clashed and sparked, like electrified wires coming into contact. People nearby cried out and ran, taking cover inside the hospital, or behind cars, while some simply fled down the street screaming.

Amidst the chaos, Ryan continued his assault, and Carter parried and counterattacked, but his opponent moved like the wind, and his shorter cutlass hit only air. A quick thrust from Ryan cut open his leg above the knee, then a follow-up split his side and scored a deep groove across his ribs. The traitor could have pressed his advantage further, but instead Ryan danced back and continued to mock him with his smile.

Arrogant fool, Carter thought, while clasping a hand to his wounded side. The cut was deep, but there were already additional nano-machines in his bloodstream, and the damage was healing quickly. *Arrogance can kill more quickly than a blade.*

Carter darted forward, trying to close the gap between himself and Ryan so that he could strike with his shorter blade, but the Master-at-arms always managed to keep his sword at bay. The traitor had mastered his style over decades, and his technique was polished, like a flawless diamond. Carter, on the other hand, relied on speed, power and brutality, but his opponent knew this only too well, and had schooled his defense accordingly.

His relentless pressure finally paid off, and Carter scored a glancing hit to Ryan's shoulder, but the traitor's Aternien scale armor repelled his blade, and the man was unhurt. Counterattacking, Ryan swung for his head, and Carter's parry came almost too late. Sparks flashed and burned his face, temporarily blinding him. He retreated in a hurry but felt the saber rake across his chest. Pain briefly raced through his body before Carter's sensation blockers numbed the effect. Even so, it was yet another reminder that he was losing.

"When I'm done with you, I'll kill that idiot Cai Cooper too," Ryan said, flourishing his saber while pontificating. "Then I'll deal with that bitch Major, and make sure she suffers for the trouble she's caused."

Carter gritted his teeth and glared at the traitor, wanting nothing more than to charge at the man and hack him to pieces. However, despite his rage, he was smart. If Marco Ryan wanted to gloat, then he'd let him, because for every second the man paraded in front of him like a victorious general, the stronger Carter became.

"I'll kill Cai quickly, out of respect for who he was, but the human will suffer," Ryan went on. The man's hatred was palpable, and Carter reflected it back at him like a mirror. "I'll humiliate her first, of course. Maybe, I'll drag her outside naked, and make people watch as I take her apart, piece by piece." Ryan paused and smiled, making sure he had Carter's full attention before continuing. "Would you like that, Commander?" he added with a sneer.

Carter didn't answer, and his silence only appeared to anger Ryan. Bitterness was seeping out of the man's every pore, as if a century of repressed anger had rotted his insides into a putrescent, festering mass of darkness. Carter understood the man's rage better than anyone, but he felt no sympathy for the man. Ryan was weak, and by succumbing to his weakness he had become cruel.

"Or maybe I'll just break her bones so badly that she'll beg me for death, before I leave her in agony," Ryan continued, now desperate to get a rise out of him. "I'll have some fun with her first, of course," the traitor added, sinking to lower depths in order to provoke a reaction. "It would be a shame to let such a pretty young thing go to waste."

Carter had heard enough, but importantly, he'd also healed enough. He gripped his sword tightly and marched toward Ryan, who simply flourished his blade and adopted his fighting stance again, ready to strike the killing blow. Carter knew now that couldn't take the Master-at-arms in a duel, even if he wasn't already hurt and angry, but Ryan had failed to account for one critical factor. Carter Rose didn't like to lose.

Pulling his 57-EX from its holster, Carter shot Ryan in the chest from only a couple of meters distance. The power of the 0.50 caliber armor-piercing bullet propelled the Master-at-arms into his SUV, like the man had been struck with a sledgehammer. Ryan tried to escape, but Carter fired again, striking the same location, and piercing the man's Aternien armor. Blood spurted from the wound like a leaky pipe, and Ryan's eyes grew wide. Death was coming for the man, and he knew it.

Ryan swung his saber, but Carter swatted the blade away then punched the man with the guard of his cutlass, piling all of his pent-up fury into the blow. Ryan's jaw and cheekbone were shattered like glass, and teeth spilled onto the asphalt, followed soon after by the man's energized revolutionary saber.

"You still can't win," Ryan mumbled, his mouth full of blood and bone. "Aternus is forever..."

"Not for you," Carter hissed.

He stepped back and swung his cutlass, cutting so powerfully that his blade not only sliced through Marco Ryan's neck, but the roof of the SUV too, opening it like a can of sardines. The turncoat's head thumped to the ground and Carter kicked it into the distance, tired of seeing the man's traitorous face, even in death.

"Sir…"

Carter turned to see Cai waiting outside the door to the ER. The man's eyes were puffy and red, and his face was tracked with tears. He'd never seen anyone in more pain in all his long years. Agony was radiating from his friend like a furnace, and he didn't need to ask why because he could feel the ache of it in his bones.

Cai fell to his knees, head in his hands, and wept openly. Carter threw down his sword and ran to his friend, kneeling beside him, pulling him close, and absorbing the shivers of the man's trembling body into his own muscles.

"Sir… she's dead…" Cai whispered.

Carter said nothing. There was nothing to say. But in that moment, he vowed that he would make Damien Morrow pay.

SIXTEEN
A PAIN THAT CAN'T BE NUMBED

CARTER RECLINED AGAINST THE TRUCK, feeling angry, restless, and completely at odds with the peaceful countryside location they'd chosen to lay Lola Carney to rest. The innocent always suffered most from the consequences of war, but he had never truly understood that until Lola died. As a Longsword Master Commander, he was no stranger to civilian deaths, but they had all been anonymous, nameless faces to him. He wasn't heartless, and he lamented the senseless loss of life, but he hadn't known anyone outside of his own small bubble, and this had isolated him from any personal trauma.

Lola's death had been different. He'd only just met the woman, but in those few precious hours inside the farmhouse, he'd felt a connection to her that he'd never experienced outside of his crew. It hurt like hell to know she was dead, and he couldn't begin to imagine the agony that his old officer and friend was suffering in that moment.

"You picked a good spot," Carina said. She was reclined

against the truck too, so close that their shoulders were touching. "It's a beautiful place for a funeral."

Carter looked at the tree beneath which they had buried Lola. It was a species native to Terra Six that was as mighty as an oak but as broad as an acacia. It had heart-shaped leaves the color of Merlot wine that never dropped or lost their sheen, even in the dead of winter. It sat majestically in the middle of a meadow in a quiet hamlet that had so far remained untouched by war. It was, as Carina had pointed out, a picture postcard scene of natural beauty. Yet all Carter could feel at that moment was the bile swilling in his gut.

Cai Cooper and the two young girls were sitting under the tree, while TOBY hovered beside them like a chaplain conducting a funeral service. To outsiders, the bot's presence would have seemed incongruous, but TOBY was as much a part of their family as Lola and the children. Carter didn't know exactly how machine intelligences experienced suffering and loss; only that they did.

He glanced at JACAB, who was tucked beneath Carina's arm; each providing a measure of comfort to the other. His gopher had not been the same since he'd heard the news. The tone of his bleeps and warbles had lowered; his maneuvering fins and antenna had drooped, and his solitary red eye stared vacantly ahead. He felt sorry for the machine. Whereas Carter could only guess at the pain Cai was experiencing, JACAB's unique connection to TOBY meant that he felt everything his counterpart felt, in bit-perfect accuracy.

Carter rested a hand on JACAB and stroked his cold metal shell, before returning his gaze to the tree and the children who were huddled up to their father, their heads covered by the hoods of their coats. The garments were vibrant, like the leaves of the tree, but their happy patterns and dazzling colors no longer inspired joy. He felt a sickness burning inside him; one that his augments should have neutralized. Grief was a rare emotion for him to experience, and he hated it.

Maybe that's why the Union sterilized me and forbade personal relationships. Carter mused. *Perhaps they knew that the crippling pain of loss was the one part of the human condition they couldn't strip away.*

"They'll be okay," Carina said, nudging him gently with her shoulder. "It won't happen soon, and it won't be easy, but they'll be okay." She paused then squeezed his arm. "You'll be okay too."

Carter grunted. He didn't want to feel okay. He wanted to bottle his rage and compartmentalize it inside one of his augments, so that he could draw upon its violent power the next time he came face to face with Damien Morrow.

"You won't be okay, unless you treat that wound though…"

Carter looked at the cut to his side that Marco Ryan had inflicted. It was healing, but because of the numerous other injuries he'd suffered, the nano-machines in his blood were stretched thin. Carina plucked out a nano-stim from a stow on his battle uniform and twirled it in her hand like a baton.

"Here, stick this where it hurts," she said, slapping the device into his waiting hand.

"I'm not supposed to use it too often," Carter replied, setting the dial to thirty percent. "Our engineered biology was designed to accommodate a fixed number of nano-machines, and while a sudden boost can aid healing, it also puts an immense strain on our bodies."

"Then you need to do a better job of not getting hurt," Carina replied, for a change without smiling.

Her lack of sympathy was surprising, but Carter also found it amusing. A little tough love was a good thing every once in a while. As a Master Commander, it was his job to dole it out, so to be on the receiving end for once was refreshing, and welcome. He pressed the nano-stim to the wound and the sudden rush of pain stole his breath away. It was like someone had chiseled into his brain, and he felt Carina's hold on his arm tighten as his legs momentarily wavered. Then as suddenly as the dizziness had hit him, it was gone.

"Are you okay?" Carina asked, apparently regretting that she'd insisted on the nano-stim.

"I will be," Carter replied. He lifted his arm so that his XO could see how rapidly his bone, muscles and skin were regrowing. It was admittedly quite unpleasant to watch, and Carina's scrunched up look of revulsion only highlighted this. He lowered his arm, already feeling stronger, and for a time the two of them continued to stare out across the meadow, allowing the cool breeze to soothe their faces.

"It makes you think, doesn't it?" Carina said, wistfully.

Carter raised an eyebrow. "What does?"

"How one death can affect so many people," his XO clarified. She was watching Cai and the children, her eyes distant. "It's not just Cai and his kids, but everyone they knew and who knew them. Their extended family; their friends. Us. It's like ripples in a pool."

Carter grunted his understanding. "This is the side of war that you don't see from the bridge of a Longsword. For all the thousands of Union soldiers that fell today, there are tens or hundreds of thousands more that will feel their losses as keenly as the sting of a blade."

"This must be hard for you to go through again," Carina said. "All those years of fighting and sacrifice, only to be right back at the start."

Carter's mind suddenly went to a darker place, one that he'd worked hard to forget. Yet the truth was that the horrors of war were a part of him, as inseparable as his flesh and bone.

"You have no idea how many people I've seen die, Carina. You have no idea how many times I've seen pain and suffering spread like a cancer, while I was left untouched."

Carina frowned. "You see your augments as a curse, but they're a gift." She squeezed his arm again, though her fingers barely made an impression on his hyper-dense muscles. "You're a gift, Carter. Without you and those like you, the Aterniens would have defeated the Union a century ago. And if you weren't here now, this new war would be a forgone conclusion."

Carter sighed heavily and placed his hand on top of his XO's. "If my augments are a gift, then why wouldn't I wish them on anyone?"

The familiar twinkle suddenly returned to her eyes. "Because beneath that gruff exterior, you're actually an okay guy, Carter Rose." She flashed him a smile. "Very unlike Morrow and his headless sidekick. That was a nice touch, by the way."

Carter laughed. It was brief and welcome moment of respite from the pain he was enduring, but a heavy blanket of melancholy quickly descended on him again.

"I didn't know Marco Ryan well, but he wasn't always

like that," Carter said, recalling how he'd once considered the Master-at-arms to be an honorable officer. "I knew Damien Morrow, though, and the man we met today might as well have been a stranger."

"We'll get him too," Carina replied, with feeling. "And anyone else fool enough to follow his lead. We'll take all of those bastards down."

His XO's conviction and determination was a tonic that he needed. It told him that he wasn't alone. "You'd have made a good Longsword officer, Carina," Carter said, genuinely. "And you'll make a fine commander one day."

Carina flashed her eyes. "A Master Commander?"

"Like I said, I wouldn't wish it on anyone." He nudged his XO and because of his mass, it nearly bowled her over. "Even pain-in-the-ass executive officers."

JACAB warbled and Carter looked up to see Cai and the children returning, with TOBY out in front, like a funeral director pacing ahead of the convoy. Carter and Carina both pushed themselves away from the truck and walked out to meet then. The girls' faces remained buried in their father's chest, heads still covered so that all but the merest glimpse of their tear-stained faces was visible.

"JACAB has scouted a private spaceport a few miles to the southwest," Carter said. As much as he'd have liked to allow them more time to mourn, Terra Six was a ticking time bomb, and he had to get them to safety. "It's under Aternien control, and they seem to be using it as a supply base, but it's lightly guarded. JACAB says there are at least two warp-capable shuttles on the pad. They might not be luxurious, but they'll get you to your brother-in-law's house on Terra Four."

Carter nodded to his bot and JACAB projected a holo

image of the facility in front of them. It was a typical private port, designed for wealthy ship owners to store their craft and mingle with one another. High society stuff. The facility consisted of a landing pad, several hangars and supporting structures, such as a comms tower and operations center, along with assorted recreation facilities, including a private members' bar. As a civilian port, it naturally lacked guard towers and sentries, but the high walls still made it difficult for unwanted visitors to get inside.

"This is the main landing pad, which is enclosed by a wall and accessed by a gate that even I would struggle to force open." Carter then pointed to two buildings that were directly connected to the main pad, and the image responded by shading those structures in a different color. "This is the control center and main comms tower, and this is the security office. We need to take both, in order to secure the facility and ensure the Aterniens can't call for help."

"How many guards are there?" Cai asked.

JACAB added more projections to the image, and ten red dots appeared, each one signifying an Aternien Immortal.

"JACAB picked up two in the control center and two in the security office. Eight walk the perimeter, in four pairs of two," Carter continued. "Major Larsen and I will handle securing the spaceport, while you provide support from the truck, using JACAB and TOBY to monitor. It'll be like old times."

Cai quickly looked down at the two girls, and while neither appeared to be paying attention, Carter guessed they were listening closely to every word.

"Are you sure it would not be better for Major Larsen to provide operational support, and I join you in the assault?" Cai said, trying to keep his voice low so that the girls had less chance of overhearing. "The Major is capable, but she is only human."

The 'only human' comment caused Carina to bristle, but Carter was quick to interject on his XO's behalf. This wasn't to spare her ego, however; he genuinely believed she was up to the task.

"The Major and I can handle this," Carter said, firmly. "You have other responsibilities now, Cai. The war is over for you."

Cai glanced back at the tree and its heart-shaped leaves, which were rustling softly as a gentle breeze flowed across the meadow and toyed with the branches.

"I am not certain that is true anymore," Cai replied, still with his head turned away.

"I'm certain," Carter said, with the same steadfastness. "All you need to concern yourself with now is getting on a ship and getting yourself and the girls to Terra Four. The Major and I will handle the Aterniens."

Cai said nothing and continued to stare at the tree. His friend was fighting his own internal war, but while the man was no longer under his command, Carter knew that Cai would still obey his order.

"Very well, sir," Cai said, finally meeting his eyes again. "But I suggest we attack without delay. This planet remains at grave risk, and your mission is more important than we are."

Carter shook his head. "Right now, nothing and no-one is more important to me than you and your daughters." He wrapped his hand around the back of Cai's neck, and the two men pressed their foreheads together. "I'm getting you off this rock, Cai. The war can wait."

SEVENTEEN
DIFFICULT FAREWELLS

UNDER COVER OF NIGHT, Carter and Carina stalked to a hedgerow alongside the road near the private spaceport. The air was still, and the sky was clear, which meant their approach had to be swift to avoid being seen by the guards. Carter also noted that there were security cameras covering every square inch of the grounds, but that was a problem he could easily mitigate. JACAB and TOBY were already hovering silently above the spaceport. TOBY was tasked with surveillance and relaying information back to Cai in the truck. At the same time, JACAB was poised to hijack the Aternien communication channels and blind the facility's security system, so that he and Carina could approach unseen.

"From the moment JACAB hacks the tower and interferes with their channels, the Aterniens will be alerted, so this has to go like clockwork," Carter said to his XO. "Let's go over the plan one more time."

"You've already drilled it into me a hundred times,"

Carina grumbled. "Anymore and I might actually start to lose my mind."

He scowled at his XO, and she backed down. "Fine, one more time. But then we do this. I hate sitting around."

Carina's right leg was shaking with nervous energy, like someone anxiously waiting to be called in for a job interview. She didn't have the impulse blockers that allowed Carter to control his emotions, rather than let them control him. He sometimes wondered how regular human soldiers dealt with nerves, since he never felt nervous.

"Stop shaking your leg, you're making the hedge rustle like a damned trash bag," Carter said. His XO's fidgeting was sorely testing his patience.

"It'll stop when we stop sitting around," Carina countered. "Now let's go over this plan again, so I can put all this pent-up energy to good use."

Carter pointed into the clear sky. "On my signal, JACAB will drop like a stone and latch onto the main comms array. It'll happen so fast that the aging Union sensors in that spaceport won't pick him up. From there, he'll hack the array and turn it against them, to jam all Aternien communication frequencies."

Carina nodded. "At that point, they won't be able to call for backup, or even talk to each other."

"Jamming their channels will put them on alert, which means the Immortals in the security office will be scouring the perimeter for anything out of the ordinary," Carter continued. "We stay low and don't make a sound while JACAB enters the security office and pops off a string of miniature EMPs. That will knock out the security system and stun the two Aterniens inside."

Carina scowled. "Stun or knock out?"

"Only stun, I'm afraid," Carter said. "Remember, Aterniens aren't robots. They may be synthetic, but they're as alive as you or me. To them, an EMP is like a flashbang; a temporary sensory overload."

Carina nodded. "How long will they be out?"

Carter was glad they had taken the time to go over the plan again. He had wrongly assumed that Carina understood the mechanics of the Aternien neuromorphic brain, when in actuality there was no reason why she would know. Until their sudden reappearance at the diplomatic outpost on the demarcation line, no living 'normie' human had ever seen an Aternien in the flesh.

"I'd say a couple of minutes at best, so as soon as Cai relays the message that JACAB has deployed the EMPs, I run like the wind, and take out the two Immortals patrolling the southern perimeter."

Carina blew out her cheeks then nodded. "Once they're down, I break in through the window to the bathroom block, on the southeastern edge of the compound. Aterniens don't pee, so it should be empty."

"Correct," Carter said. The time for action was near, and he could feel his muscles and mind starting to fizz with energy, as his augments prepared his body for combat. "The bathroom leads into the members' bar, through a short corridor. That will also be empty, since as well as not peeing, the Aterniens don't eat or drink."

"Let's hope. It would be a hell of a time for an Immortal to discover he has the case of the midnight munchies."

Carter knew that in times of stress, it was normal to break the tension with humor, so he let Carina's comment slide, and continued his recap.

"Once you exit the bar, head along the corridor and take

a right, then next left toward the main foyer on the right. Keep going until you reach a T-junction. Ops will be dead ahead, and the security office will be on your right."

"Damn it Carter, with all your left, right, left, right crap, I've forgotten where I'm going," Carina said, with a nervous smile. "I already had it mapped out in my head until a moment ago."

"This isn't the time to fool around. Major," Carter snapped. One quip he could let slide; two was one too many. "I need you to focus. These are Aternien Immortals we're facing, not acolytes. Each one has many times your physical strength, and they're faster and more resilient than you could ever be. You have to be on your A-game, because one slip-up against these bastards, and you're dead."

His dressing down took Carina by surprise, but to her credit she soaked it up without complaint or irritation. If anything, she looked embarrassed.

"I'm sorry, Commander," she said, returning to a formal manner of addressing him to highlight her shift in attitude. "But you should know that I've got this. Once I reach the T-junction, I detour into the Security office, which JACAB would have unlocked, and double tap the Aterniens before they come around. From there, I hit the operations room and take out the two Immortals while they're still trying to figure out why their comms are down. JACAB follows, hacks the system, then we unlock the gate and release the mooring clamps on the two warp-capable shuttles."

Carter listened carefully, to make sure she hadn't missed anything, but she was focused and to the point. He considered apologizing for snapping at her, realizing that his own feelings had influenced his reaction, but decided against it. His relationship with Carina was Longsword-like, in that they were more than just commander and XO, but their familiarity and kinship could not interfere with their jobs.

"At the same time, I'll deal with the remaining six Aternien guards patrolling the perimeter, before opening the gate so that Cai can drive the truck inside," Carter said, bringing the re-cap to a close. "Are you ready?"

Carina nodded then coiled up, like a sprinter ready to burst out of the starting blocks. Carter looked up and tapped the comp-slate on his left forearm.

"We're all set here, buddy. Are you good to go?"

An old-fashioned thumbs-up emoji appeared on the screen of his comp-slate, which made him smile.

"Then take it away…"

Carter's augmented vision allowed him to see JACAB's suicide dive toward the comms tower, like an eagle swooping in on its prey, though to a regular human eye, the bot was nothing more than a blur at best. He drew his cutlass and coiled up like Carina, ready to rush out and take down the two guards on the southern edge of the spaceport. The wait to receive the go felt like an eternity, when in reality it was only a few seconds.

"Comms are down. Commander Rose is go…" said Cai's voice, through the bone-conducting transceiver in his battle uniform.

Carter exploded into the hedge, using his cutlass to carve a path through it like an icebreaker splitting a frozen sea, then accelerated like a space fighter. The ground was torn up behind him, but the Aternien guards were also not ordinary beings. Their synthetic eyes and sharp wits allowed the Immortals to spot Carter, despite the eye-watering pace of his advance, but even with their hyper-fast reactions, there was not enough time stop him.

He ignited the blade, cutting through the first guard before the Aternien woman had a chance to fire, then shoulder-barging the second and sending him through a low wall. He glanced back, intending to call out to his XO to start her run, but she was already on-mission, sprinting toward the bathroom block. The distance she'd covered suggested that Carina had moved out even before Carter had dealt with the guards. It was a calculated risk that had paid off, because now they were ahead of the clock. Using her energy pistol, Carina cut the lock on the bathroom window and dove instead. There was nothing he could do to help her now; she was on her own.

Then the exterior cameras went dead, and he heard Cai's voice in his head, confirming that JACAB had reached the security office. Referring to his comp-slate, Carter could see that the other guards on the perimeter had become alerted to the strange goings-on inside the spaceport building. They were all heading toward the main gate, which would soon put six Aternien Immortals in his path. Even with his speed and brutality, it was a tough ask, especially given the lack of cover, but nothing short of an act of God was going to stop him from completing his mission.

Carter grabbed an Aternien particle rifle and slung the weapon across his back then engaged the bucker on his battle uniform. The nano-machines in his unique armored clothing had regenerated and repaired the holes that Marco Ryan had put into it, along with rebuilding his buckler. He deployed the shield, knowing that, in all likelihood, it would be melted and useless again within a matter of seconds.

With his gear and weapons primed, he hustled along the

side of the building and peeked around the corner. The two Immortals that had been patrolling the east side where the gate was located were trying to unlock it, but they'd already been frozen out. Carter smiled as Cai confirmed that his XO's assault on the interior of the spaceport was going to plan. Marching out, he drew his 57-EX and shot both Aterniens in the head, before they knew he was coming. That left four, except that now he lacked the element of surprise.

Particle blasts lit up the night sky and Carter zig-zagged toward the two Aternien guards from the north. He dodged at least a dozen shots then took a hit, which forced him to take cover behind a low wall lining the driveway that led to the main gate. Blasts continued to rain down on him and the wall was obliterated. Sharp fragments of brick and mortar pelted his face, which was numb to the pain, and he returned fire with the three remaining rounds in his revolver. One of the immortals fell, but the other evaded and tagged him with an accurate shot to the chest, which knocked him to the flat of his back.

Carter rolled to the side, making use of another part of the wall to shield him from the blasts that continued to harass him, like a swarm of angry hornets. A section of his battle uniform six inches in diameter had been completely melted away, and the skin covering his sternum was burned red, but his flesh was intact.

More shots came at him, this time from other directions. The guards from the west had circled around behind him, and Carter was now caught in a crossfire. Blocking the blasts with his buckler, he dropped prone and returned fire with the particle rifle he'd taken from the first pair of guards. The Aterniens withdrew, using the corner of the building for cover, but he was outgunned three-to-one and in a bad position.

"Cai, I could use a little help," Carter called out, as the wall to his rear was rapidly chipped away by blasts from the Immortal closing in from the north. "Have Toby harass the two guards behind the wall, while I deal with the asshole who gave me heartburn."

"Copy that. Raining fire…"

Flashes of needle-like energy spat from above, like a shower of icicles. The Aterniens to the south were consumed in the downpour, but TOBY's blasts were not nearly powerful enough to take out the Immortals and could only deal limited damage.

Even so, the bot's timely distraction allowed Carter to focus on the adversary to his rear. He glanced at his comp-slate and saw that the Aternien was almost on top of him. Leaving the rifle on this ground, he grabbed his sword and jumped up, buckler held out in front. The Immortal opened fire, destroying his shield, but not before he'd been able to swing his cutlass and remove the warrior's left arm. With no hand to support the rifle, its aim dropped and the Aternien simply lit up the dirt at its feet. A second swing of his sword removed the Immortal's right arm, leaving the fighter incapacitated and in shock. He felt a little like a cruel child, pulling the wings off flies, but this didn't stop him from taking the Aternien's head with a final, fateful swing of his cutlass.

A blast hammered into his back and pain raced through his body. His dropped flat to the ground and rolled behind the wall with more shards of particle energy chasing him. The pain was soon numbed, and he touched a hand to his back, feeling the bone of his exposed thoracic vertebrae. The energy of the blast had melted his flesh and from the sick feeling of nausea that began to overwhelm him, he feared that it had cooked his kidney and maybe even damaged his liver.

Cursing, he grabbed a nano-stim and hovered the device over the gaping wound but hesitated. It had only been a few hours since he'd last administered a stim, and he remembered his warning to Carina about the potential side-effects. Yet, his body was telling him that he was dying, and his human instinct for survival overrode any logical fears. Setting the stim to fifty percent, he pressed the device into the gaping wound, delivering the nano-machines directly where they were needed. Immediately, he began to convulse, and he clamped his jaw shut, for fear he might bite off his own tongue. Pain rippled through him in waves and his vision was tainted with a kaleidoscope of colors and patterns that merged chaotically into one other. The pain briefly eased then another wave overcame him, even fiercer than the first.

Carter reached out and grabbed the wall that he was still cowering behind. Another wave pulsed though his muscles, and the bricks exploded in his hands, like brittle, dry clay. A scream escaped his lips that must have sounded like the howl of a werewolf, and another brick crumbled in his grasp. Then, when he felt sure he was going to die, his vision began to clear and the pain vanished, leaving him entirely numb. He tentatively reached behind his back and touched the area where the wound had been, but the flesh had completely healed over. His nausea was gone and his strength had returned. He was royally pissed off.

Grabbing one of the loose bricks, Carter got up and hurled it at the closest of the two Immortals, hitting the warrior in the face and knocking her flat. The final Aternien opened fire, but Carter had a new shield to protect him. Instead of his melted buckler, he was using the armless and headless body of the Immortal he'd just killed. Its scale armor proved an effective barrier to the particle energy, and before long he was within striking range.

The swing of his sword cut the Immortal's rifle in half, while a second blow opened up the warrior's chest, like unzipping a cushion cover. The Aternien staggered back and stared in dismay at the crater in his body, but Carter wasn't done yet. Stabbing his sword into the ground, he dug his hands inside the Aterniens' synthetic body and ripped it apart, like a strong man tearing a telephone directory in half. The two parts of the enemy fighter thudded into the ground twenty meters apart; a distance that surprised even himself.

"Hey, how about you use that strength to push open the gate?"

Chest heaving and blood still coursing through his veins like river rapids, Carter looked up to see Major Larsen standing on the wall surrounding the landing pad. JACAB was by her side, and Carter smiled as the bot waved a maneuvering fin at him. He waved back.

"I take it all went well?" Carter said, recovering his sword and walking up to the gate.

"It went like clockwork, just as you said."

Sheathing his sword, Carter pushed open the gate with ease thanks to his boosted muscles. A horn honked, and the truck containing Cai and his daughters rolled up, with the windows down.

"Are you okay, sir?" Cai asked, a look of concern furrowing the man's brow.

"Just a scratch," Carter replied, smiling.

Carina appeared by his side and rested on the sill of the open window. "I've unlocked both shuttles, and JACAB has had them fueled, but I'd take the X-774, if I was you. It's a pretty sweet ride."

"Thank you, Major, I will do as you suggest," Cai replied, with a gracious nod of his head. The man looked Carter in the eyes, and he could tell his old friend had so much to say, but no time in which to say it. In these circumstances, Carter felt that saying nothing at all was better. Or, at least, easier.

"We'll see each other again," Carter said, patting his friend on the shoulder. "When this is all over, we'll come visit you on Terra Four." He laughed. "After all, we have a whole century to catch up on."

Cai nodded. "I will hold you to that, sir."

"It's just Carter now," he said. "I wish we'd met again under better circumstances. I feel like this is all my fault."

Cai's expression twisted with anger. "Do not say that. Don't even think it. There is only one person to blame for what happened, and we both know his name."

"I'll get him, Cai," Carter growled. "Even if it takes me another century, I'll get him. I swear that to you now."

Cai nodded again, then the face of one of his daughters appeared at the rear window. He felt shame that he didn't even know their names. Then he noticed that she was looking at the hole in his battle uniform from the Aternien particle blast. The wound had healed thanks to the addition of more nano-machines, though his skin was still a little raw.

"It's okay, it doesn't hurt," Carter said, smiling at the girl. She looked just like her mother, and he suddenly felt nauseous again.

The girl frowned then removed a necklace that she'd been wearing. It was comprised of a thin leather strap and ruby-red stone, that looked to have been rough-cut and polished by hand. "Here, take this," the girl said. "Mom made it. It'll keep you safe."

Carter choked down tears as he shook his head. "Thank you, but you don't have to do that. It belongs to you."

The girl was adamant. "Dad will keep me safe, and you need this more than I do, so you can get the bad people who did all this. You will, won't you? Get them, I mean?"

Carter nodded. "I will. I promise. You don't need to worry about that; not even for a second."

The girl managed a weak smile. "Then take this, please. I want you to have it."

Carter couldn't argue any further. He took the necklace, released the clasp and fastened it around his neck. "Thank you."

The girl suddenly reached out of the window and pulled him into an embrace. Despite his super-human strength, he was powerless to resist her. When the hold was finally released, he stepped back, then smiled and waved as the truck pulled up next to the shuttlecraft. He should have felt happy and relieved, but in that moment, he'd never felt more broken in his entire life.

EIGHTEEN
A MOMENT TO REFLECT

CARTER ENGAGED the parking brake and switched off the truck's motor. He'd stopped on the edge of a nature reserve in the hills above Enterprise City. It was an oasis of tree-lined trails, lakes and wildlife that seemed a million miles away from the war in the distance, but his choice of location had nothing to do with its natural beauty. The spot also provided an elevated view of the city, in particular the barracks that were their next destination.

"The fighting seems to have eased up a bit," Carina said, jumping out and closing the passenger side door with a weighty thump. "There are pockets of resistance, but it looks like the Union has been largely driven out."

Suddenly, a barrage of rockets was fired from a Union position west of the city. Carter's keen eyes were able to spot the launchers, which means that the Aterniens would have had little difficult spotting them too. Sure enough, particle-based anti-aircraft guns soon lit up the sky and the rockets were intercepted before they'd made it much beyond the outskirts of the city. A squadron of scarab-like Khepri fighters then diverted from their patrol route and a quick skirmish ensued, in which the Union position was strafed and destroyed.

"It's all too easy for them," Carter commented, shaking his head. "They're not even trying, anymore. All they're doing is containing the Union forces, until they're ready to deploy the doomsday weapon."

Carina strolled up next to him, boots crunching on the dry stones and dead twigs beneath her feet. Her arms were wrapped around her body to stave off the chill wind that was whipping over the hill. It was three in the morning, local time, and the crystal-clear sky meant that the temperature had dropped to a cool thirty-nine degrees.

"Do you think we'll find anyone in those barracks to help us?" she asked, standing behind Carter so that his body functioned as a windbreaker. "It's odd that they haven't fallen already."

This was the question that had been plaguing Carter's mind too. The barracks were home to the First Infantry Brigade, Terra Six, or what was left of them, and they were surrounded on all sides by Aternien forces, but the Immortals showed no sign of attacking.

"Whether there's anyone that can help us or not, those barracks are still our best shot of getting a message to Admiral Krantz and the fleet," Carter said, parking his concerns for the moment. "Besides, it's on the way to stadium."

"Even if we can warn Krantz, I don't like her chances of breaking through the blockade of Khopesh destroyers so that she can launch an orbital assault." Carina sighed heavily. "Even then, the Aternien defenses are intercepting every bomb, rocket and rock we've thrown at them, so more likely than not, an assault would fail."

As if to prove her point, more Union missiles and rockets snaked toward Union positions in the city, but they were stopped by AA fire as easily as the first barrage was.

"We need the option, no matter how slim the chances of success are," Carter said. "But our best shot is to reach the stadium through the underground transport tunnels and disarm it manually."

Carina laughed. "Well, when you say it like that, it sounds easy."

"It won't be," Carter grunted. "But first, let's focus on getting inside the barracks."

JACAB hummed in front of them and projected a simple, wireframe schematic of First Infantry Brigade's station. As a city barracks on home turf, it was only lightly fortified, with five-meter-high walls, topped with razor-wire to deter would-be trespassers and the native pigeon species.

"There are guards patrolling the walls on all sides, including snipers and a couple of machine-gun emplacements that have been added recently," Carter said, highlighting the troops in question. "Inside the wall, they've set up some air defenses to ward-off attacks from Khepri fighters, and it looks like there's some light armor too, but all told, it's fairly deserted."

"The First Infantry Brigade was comprised of two battalions and about sixteen hundred troops in total," Carina added. "From JACAB's scans, it looks like the Aterniens have decimated their ranks, which makes it all the more unusual that they haven't finished the job. They could easily storm the barracks, or just obliterate them using Khepri fighters."

"One problem at a time, Major," Carter said, offering her a weak smile, before returning to the schematic. "My view is that it's safest to approach from the suburbs to the North, but the Aterniens are holding the road exits in and out, and are patrolling the streets. For now, we need to observe and learn their patterns. Maybe we can even catch a patrol napping."

Carina gave him a doubtful look. "Surely, Aterniens don't sleep?"

"I don't mean literally napping," he scoffed. "But, once the action is over, and all that's left is patrolling, boredom quickly sets in. There's a chance we can find a patrol that's slacking off, or just distracted, and sneak past them."

Carina still appeared unconvinced. "But they're machines, not people. Don't they just follow their programming?"

It was a common mistake to think of Aterniens as nothing more than simply machines, especially when it came to the rank-and-file Immortals. However, each and every Immortal had started life as a human being. Their consciousness had simply been transferred to a neuromorphic brain and synthetic body, but everything that made them an individual sentient being – their soul, in essence – was retained.

"Like I said at the spaceport, they're not robots," Carter explained, while continuing to study the schematic and the routes in and out of the city. "Beneath that armor, they're still people. Sure, living the way they do, without aging, tiring, or experiencing physical pain, or even hunger, changes a person. It makes them feel invincible. But while they look alien, they're not. They can be deceived, distracted, angered, and outmaneuvered. Sooner or later, one of those patrols will slip up, and when they do, we need to be ready."

Carina yawned loudly. It lasted for several seconds, during which time her mouth grew so wide that her hand barely covered it.

"I'm sorry, Major, am I boring you?" Carter said, with a suitable amount of snark.

"Sorry, Carter," his XO replied, rubbing her eyes and yawning a second time. "You forget that I don't have your unnatural ability to go without sleep or rest. I'm dead on my feet here."

Carter backed off, feeling a little guilty about his snippy comeback. It was easy to forget that Carina was an unaugmented human, which was testament to how well she had performed. However, he couldn't just jab her with a nano-stim to keep her on her feet, and since their next task was remote reconnaissance, he determined that a short break was in order. And looking at his own battle-scarred uniform, he figured it wouldn't hurt for him to rest, either.

"Take five, Major, I need you sharp," Carter said. "I can keep lookout, while JACAB continues his surveillance."

"Now that's an order I can get down with."

Carina thumped him on the shoulder, which he barely felt, then returned to the truck to recover her rucksack of equipment and provisions.

"Don't you need to eat?" she asked, jumping up onto the hood of the truck and sliding back so that she could rest against the windshield. "I've got some of those high-calorie protein bars in my bag somewhere."

Carter checked his comp-slate and assessed his bio-readings. Most levels were off the chart, thanks to his use of nano-stims, but his metabolizable energy levels were low.

He'd already exhausted his considerable glycogen reserves and lost some body fat. If he didn't replenish his energy levels soon, he'd be at risk of losing muscle mass.

"Come to think of it, I am bit peckish," Carter replied. He jumped up onto the hood of the truck and slid back next to Carina. The metal bowed under his weight and the truck leaned to one side, as the vehicle's suspension was compressed unevenly.

"I think you could stand to lose a few pounds," Carina said, smirking. The sudden tilt of the truck had caused her to slide closer to him.

"I'm just built differently, Major," Carter replied, while snatching one of the protein bars from her bag. He tore back the wrapper and took a large bite. The bar was dense, sweet and cloying. "Damn, I'd forgotten how horrible these things are."

"If you don't like my cooking, then you can head off into the woods and hunt yourself a deer," his XO hit back, hooking a thumb toward the nature reserve. "I know how you like that sort of thing."

"I don't like it, as you well know," he grunted. Carter finished the first energy bar then grabbed a second, much to the displeasure of the bar's former owner. "Though Morsapri tastes a hell of lot better than this crap." He closed his eyes and lifted his chin. "If I concentrate, I can almost smell the sizzling fat from my open spit back at the cabin."

"Barbarian…" Carina said, with a flash of her eyes.

They continued to chat and eat for several minutes. Carter found his XO's prickly style of banter to be a welcome distraction from the harrowing events of the last few hours. She seemed at ease in his presence in a way that only his former Longsword crewmembers had ever been. And while she wasn't impressed when he snatched a fourth protein bar, she accepted that the calories were necessary if she wanted him at his best. They not only replenished his energy levels, but they fueled his augments too, and allowed them to accelerate the healing process for the many injuries he was still suffering from.

The respite also allowed the nano-machines in his battle uniform to catch up on repairs. Where it had been ripped, scorched, and melted, the super-fabric was now looking pristine again, though for how long, Carter couldn't be sure.

Suddenly, Carina yawned again, and this time it lasted so long that he wondered if her mouth would ever close again.

"You can kick back and take a nap, if you want," Carter said, while cleaning his 57-EX revolver. "I'll wake you if anything important happens, such a missile heading in our direction."

"Too kind," Carina said, sarcastically. She was fighting her fatigue, but as with all unaugmented humans, her will would eventually succumb to her body's natural needs. "But I'm okay, really."

"Take a nap, Major, that's an order," Carter said, more sternly.

"You're ordering me to sleep on the job?"

"Yes. I'm sick of hearing you yawn," Carter grumbled. "It sounds like out-of-tune whale song."

His unkind description of her yawning seemed to a have struck a nerve, though his XO's grouchiness was more due to fatigue. Or, at least, that's what he told himself.

"Fine, sir. I'll take a nap, sir," Carina snapped, throwing up a rough salute. She grabbed her rucksack, scowled at the number of empty wrappers inside it, then shoved it behind her head to use a pillow.

"You could sleep *in* the truck, you know?" Carter said, surprised that Carina had chosen the hard glass windshield of the vehicle as her bed.

"You could mind your own business, sir…" Carina hit back.

Carter choked back a laugh. Carina was normally the one to poke fun, so he was enjoying that the tables had been turned.

"I had imagined that our first night together would be a little more romantic," he said, intentionally trying to get a rise out of her.

Carina turned over and scowled at him. "What do you mean? We're camping under the stars on a clear autumn night, with tens of thousands of honed killers surrounding us. What could be more romantic?"

Carter did laugh this time and so did his XO. She then jabbed him in the leg and closed her eyes. "I won't be able to sleep if you keep yammering," she said, fidgeting in order to get comfortable. "So, unless you want to be the cause of me disobeying your own order, I'd kindly request that you button it. Sir…"

"Yes, ma'am," Carter replied, returning a salute, not that his XO could see it.

She smiled, still with her eyes closed, then shuffled around on the hood on the truck for a few seconds more, before finally lying still. It wasn't long before the slowing beat of her heart and the rhythmic nature of her breathing told Carter that she'd dropped off.

The sudden absence of her voice combined with the stillness of the air was eerie. Even the fighting had stopped, and the city was dead silent as a result. He found the quiet to be unsettling. It provided him with far too much opportunity for his mind to wander, and his thoughts were quickly filled with Cai Cooper and his family. The pain of his friend's loss was still with him, like the lingering throb of a wasp sting. It was a pain that people of their kind were never supposed to experience.

That he and Cai were destined to outlive and outlast regular human beings was an intentional consequence of their design. The Longsword program was complex, time-consuming and fiendishly expensive, made worse by the fact that only one in a hundred of those who began the trials survived to the end. Because of this the Union wanted to get the most from their investment and have Longsword crew serve in a front-line capacity for two or three times longer than an unaugmented human could manage. As a result, personal attachments were strongly discouraged, if not outright forbidden. In short, families were a complication and a distraction the Union simply couldn't afford.

Yet, even if the Union had encouraged Carter and his fellow Longsword officers to have relationships, society would not have stood for it. Post-humans were considered dangerous and unnatural abominations. For a human to be in a relationship with a post-human was sacrilege, harking back to the periods of human history, when interracial and cross-cultural mixing was forbidden by law.

None of this had stopped Cai. Though it sounded corny, his love had overcome the barriers that had been put between him and Lola. Even so, he couldn't help but think that even if Lola had survived, and his family had lived long, happy lives, Cai would have still eventually lost her. In all likelihood, he would have outlived even his children, and maybe even their children. He couldn't image the pain of burying entire generations of his family, while he remained fit and strong. *Surely, it's better to not love at all...* he wondered.

He suddenly realized that he was twirling the stone pendant that Cai's daughter had given him between thumb and forefinger. He stopped to look at it more closely. As an item of jewelry, it was wholly unremarkable, but it meant more to him than anything he'd ever owned. It was a symbol of incredible kindness and selflessness – deeds that he was rarely subject to – as well as a stark reminder of the callousness of war.

Carter blew out a heavy sigh and glanced at Carina, who was still soundly asleep. He needed something to take his mind off the darker thoughts swirling around his augmented brain, and without his XO to distract him, he decided to go for a walk. This was something he did often on the forest moon of Terra Nine, where he'd learned to embrace the stillness and allow it to fill him up. It was how he'd survived so long without losing his mind or turning to Trifentanil to take the edge off.

Carter slid carefully off the hood of the truck so as not to wake Carina, then directed JACAB to keep watch over her. The bot happily obliged and guarded his XO like a loyal dog, while he headed into the woodland. However, unlike his isolated forest moon, the sounds of the city and the suburbs were never far away. He tuned out the rumble of traffic and the distant roar of Khepri fighters so that it became a white noise that helped to clear the fuzz in his head.

He didn't know for how long he'd been walking when his augmented hearing began to isolate a specific sound from the jumble of white noise. His senses climbed and he focused on the noise, filtering everything else out. It was the sound of a starship falling through the sky, out of control, and it shattered his calm like clashing cymbals.

Carter locked on to the source of the noise, then raced out of the woodland and back to the truck, so that the canopy of leaves wasn't obstructing his view of the sky. Then he saw it, a Union drop ship, heavily damaged and on fire. The stricken vessel was out of control and falling fast toward the city, pursued by three Aternien Khepri fighters, which continued to hammer it with particle blasts. The scream of its broken hull as it tore through the still night air grew deafening before the ship exploded in mid-air.

The bulk of the vessel's burning carcass fell like a stone and bombarded the streets close to the military barracks. Then Carter saw dozens of parachutes glinting in the moonlight, like twinkling stars. However, they weren't the drop ship's crew, but union paratroopers. He watched intently as the soldiers landed North of the barracks and quickly began to organize. At the same time, Aternien forces that were garrisoned close to the barracks moved out to intercept them, leaving a gap in their defenses. It was the opportunity they'd been waiting for.

Carter grabbed Carina's ankle and shook it vigorously, causing her to grumble sleepily and try to pull her leg away. Incredibly, his XO had managed to sleep through it all.

"Carina, wake up," Carter said, continuing to shake her until she finally roused. "It's game time."

NINETEEN
BREAKING AND ENTERING

CARTER GRABBED Carina's rucksack and began to rummage through the contents, waiting for his XO to awaken from her deep slumber, and by the time she was sitting upright, bleary-eyed, on the hood of the truck, he'd found what he was looking for. He popped the cap of the innocuous looking tube and shook out two tablets.

"Here, take these," he said, as Carina slid off the hood and onto the stony ground. Her hair was pressed flat on one side, where she'd been lying on it, but he managed not to laugh.

Carina scowled at the pills then at Carter. "Why, what are they?"

"They're your caffeine tablets," Carter explained. "The human equivalent of a nano-stim."

"I'd have preferred it if you'd brewed me a coffee," Carina complained, but she took the tablets anyway and tossed them into her mouth, before spotting the carnage that had resulted from the crashed drop ship. "I slept through that?"

"You were pretty out of it, but you managed a solid three hours, which will hopefully set you up for what comes next."

"And what comes next?" Carina asked, nervously.

"Union paratroopers landed to the North, and the Aterniens laying siege to the barracks have redeployed to engage them," Carter answered. "That gives us an opening."

Carter worked his comp-slate and a magnified image of the barracks appeared on the screen. It was purely for his XO's benefit since his augmented eyes could see clearly without the need for magnification.

"There's a route open to the south-east corner of the barracks," Carter continued. "Then it's just a standard five-meter wall between us and the courtyard."

Carina nodded while ruffling her hair to even it out. "Okay, but won't the Union guards and snipers try to take us out if we rampage toward the barracks?"

"I don't think so," Carter said. "I think they'll be too pre-occupied with the Aterniens to notice us, or care about one stray truck."

Carina didn't appear to be reassured by his plan, and he accepted that he was taking a risk, so he didn't want to sugar-coat it.

"Okay, we might take some friendly fire, but this is still our best shot," Carter added, meeting his XO half-way. "It's either this, or we forget about trying to warn Admiral Krantz, or getting help from the battalion, and go for the doomsday device by ourselves."

Carina sighed and nodded. "Okay, let's do it. What's our best route into the city?"

Carter worked his comp-slate again and a 3D map appeared, similar to the navigation displays that were built in to domestic cars and flyers. The highlighted route took them along a main road that ran directly past an Aternien anti-aircraft site.

"It would be nice to take that down on the way, if possible," Carina said, jabbing her finger into the holographic map where the AA cannon was located. "With it gone, the Union might be able land some more troops on this side of the city."

"My thoughts exactly, though we probably won't get a choice," Carter replied. "The site is manned by five Immortals, who will surely take issue with a truck racing toward them at breakneck speed."

"If it's breakneck speed you want, then let me take the wheel," Carina said, deadly serious. "I learnt how to drive in a city like Enterprise, and believe me, I can navigate these roads like a street racer."

Carter raised an eyebrow. "Is that because you *were* a street racer?"

Carina smiled. "I wasn't always a Union officer and an upstanding citizen."

"You're still only one of those things," Carter said, causing his XO to roll her eyes. "Start her up, Major. But let's keep the neck breaking to a minimum, okay?"

Carina climbed into the driver's seat; her eyes bright from the stimulant effect of two potent caffeine tablets. The engine roared into life as Carter climbed into the cabin next to her, then she floored the accelerator, pressing him back into the seat, as if they were being launched into space on a rocket. Huge plumes of dust trailed behind them as she powered the vehicle back onto the main road into the city, at one point drifting around a bend like a rally driver.

"You weren't kidding about your misspent youth, were

you?" Carter said, hastily fastening his seat harness. "Just don't feel like you have to impress me, okay?"

Carter wasn't concerned about their velocity, since his augmented senses processed the world at a higher sample rate, which tended to make everything feel slower. He was, however, concerned about crashing.

"If I try to impress you, you'll know about it," Carina replied, swerving to avoid a burned-out car in the middle of the road. "I'd suggest you concern yourself with how to take out that AA-site, rather than commenting on my driving. In that regard, feel free to impress me…"

A section of the road ahead was pockmarked from a battle that had occurred at some point in the past, and Carina was forced to take a detour. The tires screeched as she turned the truck hard to the right then left, still managing to avoid smaller obstacles as though she had pre-cognitive knowledge of their location. Suddenly, Aternien drones buzzed overhead, and Carter watched them, keenly aware that the machines were watching them too.

"We've picked up some friends," he warned, drawing his 57-EX revolver. "Three bogies, at six o'clock high."

Carina glanced up and scowled at the drones. "Tell me if they follow us…" She yanked the handbrake and slid the truck around a tight, ninety-degree bend, before reapplying the power and drifting down a narrow side-street. The maneuver was the truck-driving equivalent of threading a needle, and it would have been enough to lose all but the most skillful purser.

For a second, there was no sign that the drones were taking a continued interest in them, then the remote flyers sped up behind the truck in a diamond formation. The lead drone opened fire, hitting the roof with needle-like blasts of particle energy that thumped dents into the metal, like hammer strikes.

"Keep on track, I'll deal with our pest problem," Carter said.

With more needles of energy peppering the hardy vehicle, Carter released his harness then jumped into the rear cab, before kicking-out the glass that separated the passenger section from the truck bed. Activating his buckler, he climbed outside while shielding his head from the blasts that were already raining down on him.

Suddenly, Carina swerved to avoid more wreckage in the road, and Carter was almost thrown off the truck, but just managed to grab the roll bar above the cabin to steady himself. Tires wailing like a banshee, she wrestled the vehicle back on course and straight away the barrage of particle fire resumed.

"Try to give me a heads-up before you do that again," Carter called out.

"I'll try…" his XO called back, though without much confidence.

Carter focused on the drones and bulls-eyed the closest, causing it to explode like a firework. Three needles of energy struck him in return, though the energy wasn't sufficient to damage the nano-mechanical fabric of his uniform.

"Hold on!"

Carina's cry came barely in time for him to grab the roll bar again, before the truck braked hard and turned sideways. The passenger side clipped a drop ship, which spun them a full three-hundred-and-sixty degrees in the opposite direction. Incredibly Carina kept the motor running and used their forward momentum to get back onto the road.

"Sorry!"

"Next time, I'm definitely driving!" Carter complained.

With the truck relatively stable again, Carter shot at and missed the second of the pursuing drones, which responded by thumping blasts into his legs. His next shot winged it, and the machine spiraled out of the sky and crashed into an advertisement hoarding for a new fragrance that was apparently all the rage.

"Carter, the AA site!" Carina yelled. "We have a problem!"

Carter turned his back on the final drone, giving it a free shot. The sting of pain was instantly numbed, but as his XO had highlighted, they now had bigger fish to fry. They were closing fast on the anti-aircraft battery, but to his surprise, and his XO's evident horror, the particle cannon that usually pointed skyward was turning toward their truck.

"Floor it, Major!" Carter said, quickly shooting the last drone before it needled him again. "I need you to pick up as much speed as you can."

"We won't reach it before it gets a lock on us," Carina called back, though the truck was accelerating, as per his command. "One blast from those guns and we're dead."

"When I give the order, brake hard and turn onto 14th street," Carter said, holstering his revolver and drawing his cutlass.

"Why, what the hell are you going to do?" Carina asked, stress building in her voice.

"There's no time to explain. Just be ready!"

Carter kept his eyes fixed on the anti-aircraft gun, while his augmented brain constantly processed and updated the angle and timing of his jump, without him needing to give it any conscious thought. A blast of particle energy from the

AA cannon raced past and tore up the road to their rear. The weapon wasn't designed to target vehicles on the ground, and the Aterniens were modifying the mechanism on the fly. Their first shot had barely missed; their second wouldn't.

"Now, Carina! Now!"

His XO slammed on the brakes and the wide tires of the truck, already sticky from running hot, gripped the surface of the road like glue. At the same time, he launched himself into the air like a missile, pressing his arms back to make his augmented body as aerodynamic as possible.

Behind him, Carina was back on the power and making hard for the junction to 14th Street. The cannon fired again, tearing through the rear section of the cabin and blowing off half of the roof in the process. Then the truck sped out of view, and he knew his XO was safe. The rest was down to him.

Tapping his collar to activate his head covering, Carter ignited the blade of his cutlass and unfurled his body like a sail. He locked his eyes onto the base of the AA cannon and swung hard, cutting through the metal and severing the gun from its mooring. His momentum carried him onward, and he cut down two dumbfounded Immortals, before hitting the road, and bouncing along it like a boulder hurtling down a mountain.

Metal screeched and groaned and the ground shook, then the gun emplacement toppled and exploded in a ball of golden flame. Using his buckler as a brake, Carter finally came to a stop, and climbed to his hands and knees. His battle uniform was scuffed all over, but the material had resisted the friction of his fall, in the same way that motorbike leathers protect riders in a crash. Even so, his head covering was compromised, and a savage burn marked his left eyebrow and forehead, like the tire tracks that Carina had left on the road.

Carter tapped his collar to retract the damaged head covering then got to his feet. Secondary detonations rocked the destroyed gun emplacement, but three Aternien Immortals had survived its destruction. The warriors were also getting to their feet and slowly regaining their bearings, but he wasn't about to let them spot him. He drew and aimed his 57-EX, but the weapon did not fire. Cursing, he dropped to a crouch and tried to clear the jam, but the revolver stubbornly refused to comply.

Finally, the Aterniens marked his position, and Carter looked for cover, but he was in the middle of the highway and completely exposed. Particle rifles were aimed in his direction, and he huddled into a ball, pushing his buckler out front, but the blasts never came. Instead, there was a screech of tires, and the truck piloted by his XO sped around the corner and rammed the Immortals, bouncing them off the bumper like squash balls striking the back wall.

One crashed through the window of a store, another was embedded into the side of a car, while the final Immortal skidded down a side street on its back, leaving a trail of sparks in its wake, like an angle-grinder deburring metal. The truck itself then ploughed headfirst into a convenience store, but the rugged vehicle had survived surprisingly unscathed. His XO reversed out of the store, and pulled up next to him, arm hanging casually out of the window.

"Can I give you a ride, mister?"

"If that was you trying to impress me, then it worked," Carter said, jumping into the passenger seat.

"After your daredevil antics, I think I'm going to have to try a little harder," his XO replied.

She plucked a chocolate bar off the windshield – spoils from her earlier crash – then started out again toward the barracks. Tearing open the wrapper with her teeth, she took a bite then offered the snack to Carter.

"Nice to see you've got your priorities in order," Carter said. Though, he didn't refuse the offer.

"I'm starving," Carina replied, taking another bite. "We skipped breakfast, remember?"

There was a string of bleeps and warbles from the rear of the truck, then JACAB emerged from beneath a pile of top-shelf holo magazines.

"What's up, buddy?" Carter asked.

His bot appeared unusually agitated, then his comp-slate vibrated, and he saw that JACAB had updated his map with new data.

"The paratroopers have pulled back," Carter said, absorbing the information then lowering his wrist to his side. "The Immortals are resuming their siege, so we need to hustle."

Not needing to be told twice, his XO put her foot down, and within a couple of minutes, she'd turned onto the road leading toward the barracks. Carter used the time to fix and reload his revolver, but he knew how many Immortals were inbound, and five shots, no matter how powerful the rounds, weren't going to cut it.

"We've got another problem," Carina said, ominously.

Carter looked up and saw that a barricade had been erected across the road, twenty meters from the perimeter wall surrounding the barracks.

"I could try to ram it?"

Carter shook his head. "This truck is tough, but not that tough. We'll have to go the rest of the way on foot."

Carina stopped the vehicle at last possible second, then they both bailed out and worked their way through the barrier. The thump of Aternien boots on the ground was already audible, even to his XO's regular human ears, then the guards on the wall of the barracks opened fire.

"Quickly, we can still make it," Carter said urging his officer on, while sprinting even harder so his XO was left in the dust. He hit the wall deliberately hard and used his fists to hammer clumps out of the brick. The indentions were slight, but enough for him to gain a handhold. "Climb onto my back!" he called out, as Carina finally arrived, flushed and breathless.

"You can't be serious?" Carina said. "You can't climb the wall with me weighing you down."

Particle blasts began snaking along the road and one smashed into the wall barely a few meters away, showering his face with shards of rubble.

"You'd rather stay here?" Carter answered, scowling at his XO. "Besides, you don't weigh much."

Carina still looked doubtful, but another blast convinced her that Carter's plan was their only option. She jumped onto him, like a kid playing knights and horses, and wrapped her arms and legs around his body.

"Hold on!"

"You're kidding?"

Carter started to climb, while smashing fresh footholds into the brick with each alternating hand. He quickly gained height, but the Immortals were closing fast.

"Keep going, just another couple of meters," Carina said.

Carter appreciated the encouragement, though as a comment, it was just as dumb and pointless as his order to 'hold on!' had been.

A meter from the top, a volley of particle blasts hammered into the wall, and he heard Carina yelp. Her grip around his neck loosened, but his super-human reactions allowed him to catch her, before she fell.

"Carina!" Carter shouted. His XO's battle uniform was not burned through, which meant that she was only stunned. But while he was forced to hold onto her, he was unable to climb. "Carina, wake up, damn it!"

Carina's eyes flicked open then she jolted as if she'd been poked with a needle. "What the hell?!"

"Climb back onto me," Carter growled. Her skin was clammy, and his grip was slipping. "Quickly, I can't hold on much longer!"

Carina spun her body around and grabbed him around the waist with her legs. He let go and felt her arms wrap themselves around his chest.

"Go!"

Gritting his teeth, Carter climbed hard and cleared the final meter to the top of the wall, as if he'd been propelled by a jetpack. Carina clung on as he dragged himself over the razor wire, using his body as a bridge for his XO.

"Climb over me," Carter grunted, as the sharp blades grazed the skin on his face and neck.

He felt the weight of Carina on his back, then his XO hesitated.

"What now?"

Carter took a deep breath. "Now we jump…"

"But it's a five-meter drop. You might be able to survive that, but I can't!"

Carter looked over the other side of the wall. By sheer luck, there was a cargo truck parked beneath them. It only shaved maybe a couple of meters off the drop, but it was better than nothing.

"I can take the hit for both of us," Carter said. He was certain of the fact, but his XO was still stuck in the mindset of a 'normie' human.

"Are you sure?" she said, dithering. "You're not indestructible!"

Particle blasts were shredding the bricks beneath them, and they were in danger of falling back into the road. The time for questions was over, and Carter made the decision for both of them. Spinning himself around so that he and his XO were face-to-face, he wrapped his arms around her then rolled off the wall.

Carina didn't scream as they dropped, though that may have been because of how tightly he was compressing her lungs. The fall lasted less than a second, though to his accelerated senses, it felt longer, and allowed him to rotate and take the tumble on his back. They crashed into the roof of the truck, which was pancaked flat by the force of the impact, before their momentum carried them to the gravel floor of the barracks courtyard. Again, Carter took the brunt of the impact for both of them, and he instantly regretted his earlier confident assertion that he could take the hit.

Carter released his XO but she just lay there on his chest, gasping for breath. Her body was shaking, but her eyes were open. Then, to his astonishment, she laughed.

"You are one crazy bastard; do you know that?" she said, her voice trembling like her body.

"It's only crazy if it doesn't work," Carter grunted. Despite the agony shooting through his back, he managed a smile.

Suddenly, the barrels of four gauss rifles were pressed into his face.

"On your feet!" a soldier demanded.

Carina rolled off Carter, wincing and groaning in the process, then climbed unsteadily to her feet. The soldiers saw her uniform and rank, and quickly pulled up their guns.

"I'm sorry, ma'am, we weren't told to expect you," the corporal said.

"We're not expected," Carina replied, offering Carter her hand, and helping him up. "But we need to see your commanding officer, right away."

TWENTY
HIDDEN TRUTHS

THE CORPORAL STEPPED AWAY to relay Major Larsen's request for a meeting with the battalion's commanding officer. In the meantime, Carter and his XO were forced to wait in the courtyard, under guard. Carter could feel the eyes of the soldiers on him at all times. They didn't consider Major Larsen a threat, but he was different. Tall, powerfully built, and wearing a sword on his hip, Carter didn't doubt he looked imposing, but it wasn't his striking appearance that was making them nervous, but the fact he was a post-human. By now, most soldiers would have heard of the Galatine rising phoenix-like from the ashes, and it would have stirred up long-held prejudices and fears. However, it was one thing to hear about the fabled Longsword officers on the grapevine, and quite another to have one standing before you.

"Colonel Bell has agreed to see you, ma'am," the corporal said, continuing to be nothing but professional and respectful to his XO. "However, because of the unusual circumstances of your arrival, I have been ordered to escort you and your associate."

Carter huffed under his breath. The unusual circumstances the corporal referred to could have simply been the fact they'd tumbled over the wall and flattened a truck, but he suspected it was more to do with his unwanted presence.

"My 'associate' is Master Commander Carter Rose, and you will address him as, 'sir'," Carina responded, taking offense on Carter's behalf.

"Of course, ma'am," the corporal said, meekly. The soldier then leveled his gaze at Carter and the man's eyes sharpened. "My apologies... sir."

"Let's hurry this up, please," Carter grunted. The corporal's half-assed, forced apology had done nothing to allay his suspicions. "Our information is time-critical, and there is not a moment to lose."

The soldier nodded then asked Carina to follow him, which she did without delay. Carter stayed by her side, and the other armed guards filed in behind them, though as before, they were focused only on him and not his pure human XO. Suddenly, JACAB flitted down over the wall, and one of the guards panicked and raised his rifles.

"Don't shoot, damn it, he's with me!" Carter barked, quickly deflecting the barrel upward.

"What is that thing?" the Corporal demanded, rifle now trained on Carter instead. "It looks Aternien."

"It doesn't look anything of the sort," Carter snapped. "It's Union tech; just tech you're not familiar with."

"It's okay, Corporal, I can vouch for the robot," Carina cut in, intervening to diffuse the tension. "It's not a threat."

JACAB let out an aggrieved warble then peered over

Carter's shoulder and blew a digitized raspberry at the corporal. The soldier was not impressed.

"Fine, but make sure it stays with you at all times," the Corporal said. "If it goes snooping around the base, I can't promise the guards won't destroy it."

"Understood, Corporal, now can we please continue?"

Carina had remained calm, though Carter's anger was already bubbling under the surface. It hadn't taken long for old prejudices to assert themselves.

The corporal set off again, though the soldier was now watching JACAB even more closely than the man was watching Carter. Before long, they had arrived at the door of Colonel Harvey Bell, commanding officer of First Brigade, Terra Six. The corporal knocked and was permitted entry, before announcing Carter and Carina to the brigade commander.

"Come in, come in," Colonel Bell said, waving them over from his seat behind a plain-looking but busy desk. "That'll be all for now, Corporal. You and your men can wait outside."

"Yes, sir," the corporal replied, crisply.

As he entered, Carter at once sensed that Colonel Bell was wary of him, though it was JACAB that initially drew an inquisitive scowl from the senior officer. However, the bot quickly settled down in the corner of the office, interfaced with a power outlet and went into charging mode, and Bell chose to ignore him. Carina entered last then closed the door behind her.

"I'm surprised you didn't have the guards stay to keep watch on me," Carter said, as the Colonel rose from his chair.

The officer scrutinized Carter carefully before answering.

He was a round-faced man in his late forties, with a perfectly bald head, curving to a prominent brow with intense, deep-set eyes that gave him an imposing bearing. His unsmiling expression added to his hard-boiled look.

"You broke into my barracks, Master Commander, so you'll forgive me if I don't roll out the red carpet," Colonel Bell replied, sternly.

"Technically, we scaled the wall, so we didn't break anything," Carter answered. The Colonel's passive-aggressive hostility was already rubbing him up the wrong way.

"My flattened truck says otherwise," Bell countered.

Carter nodded, accepting the point. "Fair enough, Colonel. I'm sorry about that."

"An unhappy accident, just like your arrival here, it seems," the colonel grunted. "What is it that you want? As you probably know, I'm fighting a war, and don't have a lot of time."

"What is the tactical situation in the city, sir?" Carina cut in.

His XO's interjection was artfully designed to reset the tone of their conversation, and it was immediately obvious that the colonel was more comfortable dealing with Carina than her post-human commander. Carter decided to stop poking the angry bear and let his XO take the lead. The point of them being in the barracks at all was to gain the colonel's support, and he was simply an impediment to achieving that goal.

"Enterprise City hasn't fallen yet, but we're on the brink," Colonel Bell replied, somberly. "When the Aterniens invaded, we had three full battalions here: close to three thousand soldiers. Now, we're down to one hundred and eighty-five, all of whom are within these walls."

Carter was surprised at the brigade's swift losses, and his expression seemed to convey this to the colonel, who was now scowling at him.

"I don't need any silent judgement from one of your kind," Colonel Bell added, making his distaste for post-humans plain. "The bastards took us by surprise and hit us hard. They already knew our tactics, our numbers, our deployments... everything. It was a massacre." Bell growled a sigh and shook his head. "We were lucky that anyone made it back to the barracks alive, but we're still here and still fighting."

Carter was about to comment that hiding behind the walls of his barracks was hardly what he'd call fighting, but he bit his tongue.

"What about the forces that landed on the drop ships and troop transports?" Carina asked.

Colonel Bell snorted. "What about them? The Aterniens hunted them for sport, shooting them out of the sky like they were clay pigeons." He pressed his hands to the small of his back and stared out of his office window, which overlooked the courtyard. "The last we could tell, a few hundred troops are still in the city, but most have retreated into camps in the outskirts. The Aterniens know exactly where they are, and they have air superiority. They're trapped, just the same as we are." Colonel Bell turned back to Carina. "If you came here looking for my help, Major, you're going to be disappointed."

"We do have a request, sir, but we've also come with information," Carina said, trying to keep the momentum going, since it seemed clear that the colonel was in a defeatist frame of mind. "We've learned that the Aterniens have built a doomsday weapon in the city, beneath Enterprise Stadium. If detonated, it will release an engineered virus that will kill everyone on the planet. We need soldiers and equipment to help us destroy it, before it's too late."

The Colonel's eyes narrowed, casting them deeper into shadow. "Where did you hear about this so-called doomsday weapon?"

Carter was intrigued by the officer's response. He'd expected a bombshell of the nature that Carina had just dropped to be met with shock and a sense of urgency, rather than skepticism. Even coming from the lips of Major Larsen, it was clear that Colonel Bell didn't believe a word she'd said.

"We've had a couple of run-ins with the Acolytes of Aternus," Carina replied, calmly. "We acquired this intelligence from one of their members."

Carter was impressed that his XO had picked up on the Colonel's latent hostility toward him and post-humans and had smartly left out the part about who the particular acolytes were.

"Acquired how?" Colonel Bell answered, his voice laced with anger. "In fact, forget that question. First, I want to know why you two are even on Terra Six in the first place. I ran your names through the system, cross-referencing with all the ships and units that were sent here, and there is no mention of you anywhere."

"Our mission is classified, Colonel," Carina replied, more stiffly. "That's why you won't find any mention of us."

"Unacceptable," the officer snapped. "You break into my barracks, and request men and women from my brigade for an attack on a doomsday weapon that for all I know doesn't exist. You will have to do much better, Major."

"We don't have time for this." Carter had remained silent for long enough. "Even if the acolyte was lying, we have to assume the threat is real. If this weapon detonates then everyone on the planet dies. Can you really afford to take that chance, Colonel?"

"I can't afford to send my men and women on a wild goose chase, on the say so of a rogue Union officer and a post-human," the man fired back, standing tall. "I take my orders from my commanding officers, not you. If you want to waste your time trying to reach the stadium then be my guest, but you will do so without my help."

Colonel Bell reached for the control panel on his desk to call for the soldiers outside to enter.

"Colonel, wait," Carter said, taking a step toward the man.

The colonel jerked back, and his hand clasped around the grip of his gauss pistol. Carter froze and his senses climbed sharply. Out of the corner of his eye, he could see that Major Larsen had tensed up too. Her hand had also instinctively gone to her hip, despite the fact her energy pistol had been confiscated.

"Step back, Commander," Colonel Bell insisted.

Carter remained where he was but kept his hands where the colonel could see them. "What the hell are you doing?" Carter said, challenging the officer to explain his hostility. "We're not your enemy."

"I don't know who you are, that's the problem," the officer replied. "All I know is that you're not supposed to be here, and that you've been consorting with Aternien spies and conspirators." Colonel Bell tapped the panel on his desk. "Corporal, come inside."

The door opened and the soldiers that had escorted them to the Colonel's office hustled inside. Carter could see that more soldiers had gathered outside.

"So, you're just going to sit here, behind your walls, and do nothing?" Carter said, exasperated. "The Aterniens could overrun this base in seconds, and the only reason they're waiting is because they don't need to risk any more of their warriors. All they have to do is keep you inside, and when the bomb goes off, you'll all be dead."

"I've heard enough of your lies," Colonel Bell growled. He looked to his corporal. "Take them to the conference room and detain them for further questioning. Post guards outside; no fewer than eight men, understood?"

The corporal uttered his compliance then grabbed Carter's arm and tried to drag him out of the office, but it was like trying to push around a stone obelisk.

"At least help us to get a message to Admiral Krantz on the Battlecruiser Dauntless," Carina cut in, also staying rooted to the spot. "She'll confirm our mission and vouch for us."

Carina would have known this was a risk since their presence on Terra Six was in contradiction to Krantz's actual orders. However, Carter felt confident that once she heard about the doomsday weapon, and how they had learned of it, the admiral would give them her support.

"I've wasted enough time on you, already," Colonel Bell said, with a dismissive waft of his hand. "Now, get out of my office, before I order my men to use force."

The corporal yanked on Carter's arm, but he remained statuesque in his defiance, and turned to peer down at the smaller man. "I'm going to need you to unhand me, Corporal," Carter said. His tone was threatening, and his threat was sincere.

The corporal ignored him then made the mistake of grabbing Carter by the scruff of his neck, like he was a stray kitten. With a burst of power, he shrugged the man off him and sent the corporal crashing into corner of the room. In a flash, the colonel and two of the other soldiers outside had drawn weapons and aimed them at him.

"Woah, take it easy!" Carina said, getting between the colonel and Carter. "We're on the same side."

There was series of bleeps and warbles and JACAB suddenly hummed into the air. The corporal that Carter had sent flying had bumped into the bot and roused him from his recharging mode. His gopher was squawking and waving his maneuvering fins and antenna, while keeping his red eye rigidly fixed on the colonel.

Carter quickly checked his comp-slate and saw that JACAB had sent him an analysis. It was a bio-scan of Colonel Bell, and at first, he didn't understand what the bot was trying to tell him. Then he looked more closely, and his augments kicked in, combating his natural human fight-or-flight response and ensuring that he showed no physical tells that would reveal to the colonel what he'd just discovered.

"Control that machine before I have it broken down for scrap!" Bell yelled.

JACAB shrieked and hummed in front of Carina, who hugged the machine to her body, like a childhood teddy bear. The situation was escalating out of control, and there was only one way to recover a sense of calm. Carter had to comply and surrender.

"Fine, we'll come quietly," Carter said, holding up his hands.

Carina looked understandably shocked, but she had learned to trust his instincts and quickly submitted too.

"While you have us detained, I suggest you contact Admiral Krantz," Carina said, as the soldiers jostled her toward the door. "She'll confirm who we are and why we're here."

"I'll do that, Major, don't you worry," Colonel Bell replied, with obvious sarcasm.

One of the soldiers snatched JACAB into a bag, like a kidnapper covering someone's head before driving them away. The bot resisted and shocked the soldier, but Carter was quick to intervene. "It's okay, buddy, go with them," he called out, trying to soothe his gopher. "I'll come and get you soon, I promise."

JACAB complied and Carter remained quiet while the soldiers marched them through the corridors of the barracks and into the conference room. The corporal quickly checked the space, disabling any communications devices and making sure there was nothing inside that could be used as a weapon, or a tool to escape. It was a pointless exercise, considering Carter still had his comp-slate, but he allowed the corporal to believe he was making a difference. The man then breezed past Carter and slammed the door shut. A moment later the lock thudded into place.

"I don't suppose you're going to tell me what the hell is going on?" Carina said, perching herself on the edge of the conference table with her arms folded across her chest.

Carter accessed his comp-slate and sent her the analysis from JACAB. "Take a look at that and tell me if you spot anything unusual."

Carina continued to scowl, but she played along and studied the scan reading on her comp-slate. Like himself, it took his XO a moment to understand what she was looking at before the realization hit her.

"How is that even possible?" she said, the shock of the discovery taking her breath away.

Carter shook his head. "I don't know, but these scans don't lie," he said, looking at the analysis again.

On a cursory level, everything seemed fine. There was flesh, a heart, flowing blood, and neural activity consistent with a human being, but beneath it all hid a disturbing truth. The colonel's skeletal structure was actually an alloy coated in a compound that mimicked the appearance of bone. This was suspicious enough in itself, but JACAB had found more. Deep inside the folds of brain tissue was a synthetic device designed to look like the thalamus, though its true purpose was quite different. It was a neuromorphic brain. Colonel Bell was an Aternien.

TWENTY-ONE

SKIN DEEP

"I TAKE it that you have a plan for getting us out of here?" Carina was pacing up and down the length of the conference room, cracking her knuckles like she was spoiling for a fight. "I don't understand why you didn't just take out Bell when you had the chance?"

"Slow down and take a breath, Major," Carter said. Her pacing was already driving him to distraction. "Bell had a dozen soldiers around him. I could have snapped his Aternien neck in a heartbeat, but then what? You'd have been gunned down in a second."

Carina stopped pacing. "Just me? What would have happened to you?"

"I would have jumped through the window into the courtyard and scaled the wall, before any of the colonel's soldiers had picked their jaws off the floor." He folded his arms. "That wouldn't have been all too helpful for you, though, would it?"

Carina wrinkled her nose. "Point taken. But we're still in a pickle, so what's our play? I take it this conference room can't really hold you? Hell, *I* could probably break down that door."

"And then the same thing would happen; you'd be shot, and I'd be in the market for a new XO." Carter looked through the window, which provided another view onto the courtyard outside. "Right now, imposter Colonel Bell isn't aware that we know his secret, and that's the only reason we're still alive. But he'll want us gone, as soon as possible."

Carina joined him at the window and managed to stay still for a moment, though her heart was still racing. "You think he'll send for a ship to pick us up?" his XO said, correctly guessing why he was scouring the skies beyond the window.

"That's my belief. I don't know what bullshit excuse he'll come up with, but he knows who we are, and who is looking for us."

"Damien Morrow…" Carina cursed under her breath. "But how will Colonel Bell manage to pull that off?"

"I don't know, but I suspect it won't be long before we find out."

Carter continued to watch the skies for a few more seconds, but while there were dozens of craft flying over the city, none of them were yet heading in their direction. He sighed and stepped away, then dropped into one of the well-worn conference room chairs. His mind was racing faster than his XO's heart, but he had far more questions than answers.

"At least this explains why the battalions on Terra Six were so quickly overcome," Carina said. She had returned to pacing up and down the room. "Phony Colonel Bell has been working for the Aterniens this whole time, probably passing them information on troop movements and god knows what else."

Carter had already been thinking along the same lines, but he worried that the problem was much deeper than Enterprise City alone or even the whole of Terra Six.

"The man we met might have looked and sounded like Colonel Bell, but it wasn't him," Carter said, rubbing his silver beard. "Not only did the Aterniens manage to replace him with a facsimile, but they did it so convincingly that no-one noticed. If his orders had been stupid or illegal, or if the imposter had acted too out of character, he would have been quickly exposed. The trick is to walk that line carefully, so that you can still do damage, but not compromise your identity. Bell managed all that." Carter laughed and shook his head. "Hell, even I didn't notice he was a fraud. It took JACAB to warn me."

He suddenly remembered that JACAB had been snatched away, and a twinge of guilt, fear and anger gripped him, but he wrestled it back. There was nothing he could do for his bot while he and Carina continued to be labelled as suspected Aternien sympathizers.

"This fake Colonel Bell could have been there for years for all we know," Carina said. "And in all that time, he's been secretly passing information to the enemy."

Carina stopped pacing and leaned forward on the conference table. The fingers on both of her hands were drumming on the surface so fast and hard that Carter could feel the vibrations rattle his teeth.

"We know they have brain scanning tech that lets them transfer the consciousness from a human mind to a synthetic," Carina continued, thinking out loud while still drumming on the table. "It wouldn't be a stretch to think they could extract knowledge and memories, and even personality traits, and blend them with another mind." She cursed again and shook her head. "It's the perfect recipe for creating a double agent. Who knows how many more there are in the Union?"

Carter raised an eyebrow. "Something you want to tell me?"

Carina wasn't amused. "I'm supposed to be the one who cracks jokes. I'm surprised you're taking this so lightly."

"I'm not," Carter grunted, returning to massaging his beard. "But this is a hell of a can of worms, Carina. Once word of this gets out, trust in the chain of command will break down. People will start questioning who is Aternien and who is real. In the chaos that follows, the Aterniens won't need to break the back of the Union; it'll crumble under its own weight."

His little monologue hit Carina like a ton of bricks, and she flopped into the chair opposite. "I preferred it when I thought you were taking this lightly."

"Who else is an Aternien mole is a problem for another time, and it's also not our problem. We have our own mission," Carter said. "But we need to let Admiral Krantz know about this as soon as possible, and we have to do it in person, once we've established that she's the genuine article, of course."

Carina snorted a laugh. "Oh, she's the real Clara Krantz, alright, you can trust me on that."

Carter regarded his XO with inquisitive eyes. "Why do you say that? I know you two are well acquainted, but I didn't think you knew her that well?"

Carina stopped drumming her fingers, but only so that she could use her hand to brush off his probing comment.

"That's hardly important right now," she said, hurriedly. "What we need is a plan to get out of here and expose Bell, before we're shipped off to an Aternien interrogation center."

Carter noticed that his XO had looked down as she spoke, and from the flush of her skin and the pulse of the veins in her neck, he could tell she was hiding something. For a moment, he wondered if his earlier flippant comment about her being an Aternien might have actually been accurate, before dismissing it. It made no sense for the enemy moles to retain the physical tells that revealed when a person was lying, simply because their entire existence was a fabrication. Even so, there was more to Carina's relationship with Admiral Krantz than she was letting on, and he was determined to get to the bottom of it. Carter was about to quiz his XO more sternly, when his senses began to climb, and he swiveled his seat around so that he could see out of the window. The smoke trail of a shuttle caught his eyes; the ship was heading in their direction.

"It looks like we're going to have a visitor," Carter said, rising out of the chair.

"Do we make a run for it?" Carina asked. She had also stood up and was now drumming on her thighs instead of the table. "They likely locked up JACAB in the stores. We could storm past the guards, bust in there then steal one of the trucks in the courtyard and make our escape."

"There are one hundred and eighty-five Union soldiers in this barracks, Major," Carter said, still watching the shuttle. "Even if we made it to a truck, we'd be riddled with holes long before we got anywhere near the main gate."

"Then what do we do?"

Carter sighed and turned around. "For starters, you can

stop tapping your fingers on anything in your reach, before I'm minded to break them off."

Carina stopped fidgeting but shot him a look of pure thunder. "Maybe you're okay with confinement, but I'm not. And I'm not about to just sit on my hands, while Bell gifts us to Damien Morrow."

"That's not going to happen, Carina, but you need to trust me," Carter said. "When you've lived and served as long as I have, you learn when to be patient. Not everything can be solved by breaking down doors and crushing skulls."

Carina finally took his advice and inhaled a deep breath, and at the same time she also stopped tapping her fingers, giving his rattling brain some blessed relief.

"My guess is that Morrow is on that shuttle," Carter continued, cocking his head toward the window. He could hear the craft's engine now. "That means fake Colonel Bell will be back soon to escort us into the courtyard. He'll want to make a show of handing us over himself; to prove he's still in control."

"Okay, then what?" Carina asked.

"Then I expose him."

His XO was itching to learn how he planned to do this, but the bolts on the door suddenly unlocked, cutting his explanation short. Four soldiers filed inside, rifles aimed at their chests, while a dozen more were waiting outside, along with Colonel Bell.

"I've spoken to Admiral Krantz and she has no idea who you two are," Bell said, speaking from the corridor outside. Carina scoffed and shook her head but didn't argue; she knew there was no point. "As such, I'm transferring you to military intelligence. They can get to the bottom of who you really are, and what you're doing on Terra Six."

The colonel motioned to his soldiers and the four in the room, barked orders at them to move out. Carter did so calmly, as did his XO, and as soon as they set foot in the corridor more guns were leveled at them.

"My suspicion is that you're in league with these Acolytes of Aternus," Colonel Bell continued, as they were frog marched to the courtyard. "I also suspect this nonsense about a doomsday device at Enterprise Stadium is a fabrication designed to lure our forces out into the open."

"Heaven forbid you might actually order your soldiers to do some fighting," Carina quipped. Her comment earned her a jab in the back from the butt of the corporal's rifle.

"There's no point arguing, Major, the colonel has clearly made up his mind," Carter said, coolly. "I'm actually glad that we're being transferred to the custody of military intelligence, since there's clearly a lack of intelligence here."

"Watch your tongue," the corporal barked, jabbing him in the back. However, unlike with Carina, the punch of the man's weapon had no effect, much to the man's annoyance.

Bell said nothing further and soon their boots were crunching across the gravel of the courtyard. The shuttle was in the process of landing, and more soldiers had been gathered to bear witness to the colonel's great victory in capturing Aternien spies. Carter noticed that one of those assembled was another senior officer; a woman wearing the silver oak leaf of a Lieutenant Colonel. Her name badge read, *Ortega*.

"It's curious how a Union shuttle managed to fly in here without being shot down," Carter said, speaking loudly enough for the Lieutenant Colonel and the other soldiers to hear. "In fact, I didn't see the Aterniens take a single shot at it."

Bell narrowed his eyes, but said nothing in return, presumably since doing so would only draw further attention to Carter's comment. The side hatch of the shuttle hissed as the pressurized cabin equalized with the atmosphere outside, then the door swung open. Damien Morrow stepped out first, still in the same civilian clothes he was wearing when they'd last met, followed by four other armed men.

"I'm Major Owens, from military intelligence," Damien Morrow said, offering fake Bell his hand, which the Aternien spy shook without hesitation to cement the rouse in the minds of his officers. "I hear you have a couple of unwanted visitors?"

Morrow's eyes flicked across to his and the man smiled. Carter, however, didn't react.

"They're all yours, Major," Colonel Bell said, speaking loudly like Carter had done earlier, so that all those assembled could hear. "Watch out for that one, though," he added, pointing to Carter. "He's one of those post-human freaks."

"Thanks for the heads up, Colonel," Morrow replied, putting on a good show for the crowd. "I'll be sure to pay very special attention to him."

Colonel Bell stepped back, and Morrow waved his acolytes on, but the traitors didn't even have time to blink before Carter made his move. With his senses and augments already primed, he exploded toward the colonel and wrapped his left arm the around the Aternien spy's neck. Weapons were raised, but not before he'd dug his fingers into the fake flesh beneath Bell's chin and pulled back, ripping the man's face clean off in one swift and brutal motion.

Carter tossed the mask of synthetic skin to the ground, but continued to hold Bell in place, as stunned faces peered upon the colonel's golden, Aternien metal skull.

"Here's your traitor," Carter said, holding Bell tighter as the Aternien struggled in vain to free himself. He then pointed to Morrow. "And there's another."

The other soldiers in the courtyard were too stunned to speak or even move. Then the golden skull of fake Colonel Bell turned to Morrow and screamed a command.

"Don't just stand there, kill them!"

The sight of a talking skull continued to stupefy the soldiers, but Damien Morrow was quick to act, and the leader of the acolytes drew his weapon and opened fire. Carina hit the ground, but the energy blasts were aimed at Carter, not his XO. Using Bell as a shield, he fended off the shots then, out of the corner of his eye, he saw Lieutenant Colonel Ortega draw her sidearm. Her next action would determine whether they lived or died.

"Engage the imposters!" cried Colonel Ortega.

The soldiers sprang into action, but Ortega held her ground and raised her weapon. To his relief, she aimed it at Damien Morrow and squeezed the trigger.

Morrow was hit, but the Aternien scale armor beneath his clothing repelled the slug with ease. The traitorous former Master Commander gritted his teeth and tried to run for Carter but was quickly beaten back by gunfire. The acolytes also began shooting, but they lacked the benefit of Morrow's advanced armor and biology and were quickly gunned down.

Putting on a burst of speed, Damien Morrow dove back inside the shuttle and slammed the hatch shut. The engines fired and the shuttle lifted off the ground, but Ortega and her soldiers continued to pelt it with gunfire. The ship was hit, but not badly enough to put it down, and Carter cursed as the craft sped over the walls and accelerated into the city, smoke billowing from its engines.

Feeling relieved, Carter lowered the body of Colonel Bell, which was now limp in his hands. Morrow's energy blasts had destroyed the imposter, precluding any possibility of interrogating the enemy spy. Frustration took hold and he stomped on the Aternien's golden skull, hammering it flat with his boot.

"What was it you said earlier about crushing skulls?" Carina asked. She was now at his side, dusting down her hands and the front of her uniform.

"I said not everything could be solved by doing it," Carter grunted. He pointed to the facsimile of Colonel Bell and smiled at his XO. "This was an exception."

"Do you mind telling me what the hell just happened?" Lieutenant Colonel Ortega was looking at them both, weapon still in hand, and with the other soldiers clustered behind her.

"Your commanding officer was a Aternien infiltrator, Colonel, that's what happened," Carter said, not mincing his words. "Are you next in command?"

"Yes, I am," the woman replied, moving closer and tentatively kicking Bell's body with the toe of her boot. "I'm Lieutenant Colonel Adriana Ortega, commander of Two Battalion, or what's left of us."

"My name is Master Commander Carter Rose, and this is Major Carina Larsen," Carter replied, nodding toward his XO. "I need my command assistant bot, Colonel. Can you arrange that for me?"

Ortega's eyes had grown wide, though this was no

longer due to the shock of finding out that her CO was an Aternien spy. "You're a Master Commander?" Ortega asked. "A Longsword commander, from the time of the first Aternien war?"

"That's right," Carter grunted, bracing himself for Ortega's reaction to the news that he was a post-human. "My bot, Colonel. It's important."

"At once, sir," Ortega replied. She was respectful and professional, which surprised both himself and his XO. Outside of Admiral Krantz and maybe one or two others, most people reacted with disgust when they found out who and what he was.

Colonel Ortega spoke to a lieutenant, who was far too young to look as battle weary as he did, and the man hurried away.

"With respect Master Commander Rose, I'm going to need some answers," Ortega said, while they were waiting. "Not least of which is why my commanding officer's head is made of Aternien metal."

"I'll explain what I can, Colonel, but there are some things I need your help with first," Carter replied.

JACAB's familiar bleeps and warbles suddenly floated across the courtyard, and the bot whizzed up beside him, twirling his antenna and waving his maneuvering fins. Carina hugged the bot, and JACAB coyly sunk into her arms.

"Hey buddy, are you okay?" Carter asked. JACAB warbled his answer, brightly. "Good. Now can you scan the colonel here and let me know what you find out?"

JACAB nodded and hummed in front of Ortega, who recoiled from the bot in the same way someone might recoil from a snapping dog.

"What's this all about?" Ortega demanded.

Carter didn't answer and simply stared at his comp-slate, waiting for the analysis to come through. The data arrived and another wave of relief washed over him.

"I just had to make sure you were human," Carter said, lowering his arm. "Which you are."

Ortega now looked painfully confused, but Carter didn't want the colonel to highjack the conversation with more questions.

"Colonel, before I tell you what I know, it's imperative that I speak to Admiral Krantz on the Dauntless," Carter continued. "Can you give me access to your comms array? With JACAB's help, I'll be able to defeat any Aternien jamming systems and get a message through."

He could tell that Ortega was all over the place, but to her credit she had patience and presence of mind enough to acquiesce to his request.

"Sergeant, take the Master Commander and the Major to the comms room and give them full access," Ortega said, speaking to a craggy-looking soldier to her side. "Then bring them to the conference room, so we can get to the bottom of all this."

"Yes, ma'am," the soldier replied, grunting the words with a bulldog-like gruffness. "Sir, if you'll please follow me." The sergeant hurried them away, and soon they were at the base of the comms tower.

The door was locked, and the sergeant stopped to hunt for the keycard. "I wish you would have jumped over our walls a few days earlier," the veteran soldier said. "The Colonel's orders were crazy, like he was trying to get us all killed." The man grunted a laugh. "It turns out he was."

The sergeant found the key and unlocked the door.

Carter was about to grab the handle when his senses spiked, and an awareness of imminent danger gripped him like vice. Grabbing Major Larsen, he bundled her away from the comms room just as an Aternien particle blast ripped through the structure. Brick and metal crashed down around them, but his instincts had kicked in just in time to move him and Carina out of harm's way.

Carter waited for the deluge of raining debris to end then pushed himself up and checked on his XO. She was covered in loose rubble and hacking up dust from her lungs but was otherwise okay. Rushing back to the tower, he tore through the wreckage, searching for sergeant before finding the man, crushed to death. Anger swelled inside him, and the brick in his hand exploded from the pressure of his grip. Damien Morrow had claimed yet more lives, and the sickening truth was that the traitor would claim more still before the day was done.

TWENTY-TWO
FIGHTING RETREAT

CANNONBALL-SIZED ORBS of Aternien particle energy soared over the walls of the barracks and hammered into the courtyard, cratering it like the surface of the moon. Carter dashed into cover with Carina at his side, and watched the next volley of blasts as they arced through the sky. His augmented brain instantly calculated their trajectories so that he knew where the energy projectiles would land without even having to think about it and selected his route inside the barracks accordingly.

"What are they hitting us with?" Carina asked, as the ground shook beneath their feet.

"It's the Aternien equivalent of artillery," Carter replied, guiding his XO toward the room where they were to meet Colonel Ortega. "They're spheres of focused particle energy contained within a magnetic field. Trust me, you don't want to be nearby when they land."

"That much I already knew…"

The barracks building was hit, and loose plaster and dust fell from the ceiling as the structure was shaken to its foundations. Carter spotted the conference room, and burst inside, taking its occupants by surprise. Pistols and rifles were thrust in their direction, but Colonel Ortega was quick to intervene.

"Lower you weapons; they're with me," the colonel ordered. Carter already liked her a hell of lot more than any other Union officer he'd met recently, simply on account of the fact she didn't talk to him like shit on her shoe. "Master Commander Rose, I would welcome your input."

Carter stepped up to the table and saw that Ortega and her officers were hastily forming a new plan to defend the barracks. He shook his head and turned to her.

"Colonel, this position is lost," Carter said, laying it on the line. "Now that Bell has been exposed as an Aternien mole, there's no reason for the forces outside to hold back. Your imposter commanding officer was the only reason they hadn't already wiped you out. Now that he's dead and no longer able to feed intelligence to the enemy, the Aterniens will hit this barracks with everything they have."

His assessment was grave and the reaction of the officers and NCOs in the room was equally bleak. However, Ortega again showed her mettle. "Very well, we will evacuate immediately." To another officer, Ortega added, "Major Grant, co-ordinate an immediate fighting retreat, and rendezvous with Second Brigade, Terra Prime, North of the city."

"Yes, ma'am," the Major replied, before immediately springing into action.

The barracks was rocked by another heavy volley of Aternien artillery. Windows shattered and the very fabric of the walls began to crumble under the strain. Carter expected

Ortega to call a close to the meeting, but she and two senior NCOs remained.

"Was what you told Colonel Bell about the doomsday device true?" the new battalion commander asked.

"I wish it wasn't, but yes," Carter grunted. "I actually came here in the hope of gaining Colonel Bell's support. I need equipment, and a demolitions team to help me take out the weapon."

"I suspected as much." Ortega turned to the two NCOs to her rear. "This is Sergeant Isaac Marsh and Sergeant Walter Fischer. Both have experience in this sort of operation, at least in training, as do I." She turned back to Carter and fixed him with a determined stare. "We will accompany you on the mission."

For the first time since arriving on Terra Six, Carter felt that the tide was finally turning in their favor. His senses then suddenly spiked.

"Take cover!" Carter practically hurled Carina under the heavy briefing table, then activated his head covering before darting toward Colonel Ortega and shielding her with his body. Aternien energy orbs battered the building and the room collapsed, raining brick, metal and other debris onto his back. Each thump stole his breath, but the sensations blockers were fast to act. Soon, the room stopped shaking and Carter disengaged his helmet, waving dust from his face as if it were cigarette smoke.

"Is everyone okay?" Carter asked, flexing his shoulders and back muscles, and shaking off more debris in the process.

"I'm okay," Carina said, staggering out from underneath the table.

Carter helped his XO to stand, then the two sergeants,

who had also both dived underneath the briefing table, called out to indicate they were unhurt. However, despite him acting as her shield, Ortega had been struck on the back of her calf, which was bleeding, though not badly.

"Thank you, Master Commander," the colonel said, ignoring the wound and instead choosing to brush the dust off her shoulders. "I think that is our cue to leave."

"I tend to agree," Carter replied. "But we need to gear up first, including enough explosives to level a football field."

Ortega looked to Sergeant Fisher and the man took the cue, leading them through the door and toward the armory. The remains of the brigade were all now outside and were split between those fighting to repel the advancing Aterniens and those who were readying the vehicles they needed to withdraw.

"Do you have a plan to disable this device?" Ortega asked, while the sergeant unlocked the armory.

"I'm afraid I don't," Carter admitted. "In truth, Colonel, we have no clue what it even looks like, but JACAB can get hold of the city plans, and the construction blueprints for the stadium. The Aterniens have it under heavy guard, so we'll need to make our way inside through the network of subterranean transport tunnels."

"Will the Aterniens not also be guarding the tunnels?" Ortega replied.

"Most likely, but JACAB can look for older or disused tunnels that are perhaps not on any recent plans."

The colonel looked at JACAB, who was hovering dutifully beside Carter, watching Ortega just as closely as she was watching him.

"And do you trust this machine's ability to accurately gather such information?"

JACAB wasted no time in blowing the colonel a loud, electronic raspberry, which stunned the officer into silence. This was the first time Ortega had hinted at a latent mistrust of technology. That she had not treated him like a leper was to her credit, but Carter was under no illusion that the colonel, and her soldiers, were still influenced by the biases Union society had harbored for more than a century.

"JACAB isn't just a machine, he's a command assistant bot, and he has feelings," Carter replied.

"Feelings that you just hurt..." Carina chipped in, while patting JACAB on top of his spherical shell.

Ortega frowned at the bot, then at Carter. "How can a machine have feelings? It is not alive."

"The Aterniens are synthetic, electromechanical machines, Colonel. Are they alive?" Carter asked the officer.

Answering a question with a question had been designed to put Ortega on the back foot, and he wasn't sure how she'd react. A normal Union officer would simply scoff and dismiss his statement as nonsense. However, it was already clear that Colonel Ortega was cut from a different cloth.

"I apologize to you and to... JACAB." The bot warbled and seemed to accept the apology. "This is all new to me, Commander."

"It's old tech as far as I'm concerned," Carter replied, offering the colonel a forgiving smile. "And to answer your earlier question, I trust JACAB with my life. He'll get the job done."

More artillery blasts rocked the barracks, and Ortega quickly excused herself and helped the two sergeants to gather the equipment they needed. Carter left her and her soldiers to it and joined Carina, who was busy outfitting herself with a new rifle and a belt of EMP grenades.

Meanwhile, Carter recovered his plasma cutlass and 57-EX revolver, which Bell had confiscated, and fastened them to his uniform.

While they were working, comm chatter crackled between Ortega and Major Grant, all of which Carter could overhear thanks to his superhuman hearing. In summary, the brigade was ready to withdraw, but the enemy were literally at their gates.

"The Aterniens will be inside the barracks within seconds," Ortega said, hustling back toward Carter. She looked at his battle uniform and grabbed a set of body armor from the rack. "I suggest you wear these. I don't think that uniform will stand up to Aternien particle weapons."

Carter grabbed a combat knife from the shelf and slapped it into Ortega's hand. She frowned and was about to ask what he was doing, when he took her wrist and plunged the knife into his belly. His uniform hardened, repelling the blade, and Ortega jerked back, dropping the knife in the process.

"I think we're good, Colonel…"

Not for the first time, Ortega shook her head in disbelief. "That is something we could have sorely used a few days ago."

"I suggest you pass that along the chain," Carter replied, moving to the door of the armory. His senses were spiking again. "If the Union hadn't turned their back on technological development, you'd all be wearing this now."

Suddenly, alarms sounded in the hall and a frantic voice boomed over the internal PA system. "Aternien troops have entered the base… Repeat, Aternien troops…" The announcement was cut short, then gunfire rattled along the corridors close to their location. Aternien particle blasts were returned and soon the soldiers were retreating.

"Is there a vehicle or APC in the courtyard we can use?" Carina asked. There was an appropriate sense of urgency to her question.

Ortega nodded. "Yes, I reserved an infantry squad vehicle specifically for our mission. It is parked just outside."

JACAB warbled and Carter saw the location of the vehicle appear on his comp-slate. It wasn't far away, but there were already a dozen Aterniens that were equally close by. Accordingly, his augments had flooded his bloodstream with chemicals, boosting his speed, stamina, strength, and metabolic rate. Carter's body was prepared for a fight, and so was he.

"Stay behind me and give me as much covering fire as you can" Carter said. He activated his buckler then drew his cutlass and ignited the blade "Don't get too close though," he added, flourishing the sword in his ritual way of limbering up. "I don't want to accidentally cut you in half."

Ortega raised an eyebrow. "I appreciate the thought."

Carter marched along the corridor, sword held ready, and elbows tucked in tight due to the confined space. Firefights were erupting all across the barracks, and he could see that some of the armored vehicles carrying the retreating soldiers had already left. Blasts shattered the windows, causing Ortega and the sergeants to duck for cover and scout for the enemy, but he already knew exactly where they were.

Putting on a burst of speed, Carter turned the corner and ran headlong into a squad of Immortals. He cut down the first with a hacking blow to the head then used his momentum to barrel through the others, sword whirling like a whip being cracked. Aternien limbs thudded into the ground and shots were fired, but he managed to block with his buckler. Then the rattle of gauss fire filled the air, as his companions caught up with him, and riddled the rest of the enemy squad with holes.

Pushing on, he turned the next corner and saw the vehicle they needed beyond the glass doors at the far end. He accelerated toward it then a blast destroyed the corridor only meters ahead of him. He was knocked to the ground, but unlike his human allies, his augments prevented him from being stunned. Four Aternien Immortals crashed through the hole in the ceiling, landing on the rubble and the bloodied bodies of half-a-dozen Union soldiers. Carter got to his knees as another blast rocked him, taking out one of the Aterniens in the process. He covered his face with his buckler as shrapnel from a frag grenade was repelled by his battle uniform.

There was a moment of confusion, then the remaining Immortals saw him and opened fire. Buckler outstretched, Carter sprinted at the enemy, absorbing a shot to the thigh in the process, before cutting one warrior in half above the waist, and decapitating the second.

The last Immortal was a Warden, and the warrior anticipated his attack and pinned his wrist to the wall, rendering his sword useless. Carter struggled as the Aternien head-butted him repeatedly, and hammered knee strikes into his ribs before he shook the Warden free and flattened his perfect nose with a savage left hook.

Anger was swelling inside him now, and Carter grabbed the Warden by its neck and smashed it first into one wall then the next, continuing to batter the warrior until it was limp in his hands. Tossing the Immortal to the ground, he picked up his sword and turned to the others. They were all on their feet again, with JACAB hovering close by Carina's side. The looks on the faces of Ortega and the sergeants were ones he'd seen before, many times. Shock and awe.

"We could have done with you a few days ago too, Commander," Ortega said, working her way over the rubble toward Carter.

"I'm afraid there aren't many of us left," Carter grunted.

Lights suddenly flooded through the smashed windows as a heavy volley of Aternien particle orbs arced toward the main barracks block. Carter would have called out to the others to take cover, but he knew the bombardment was of no immediate risk to them. Instead, everyone watched as the projectiles smashed through the buildings on the east side of the base, reducing them to smoldering wreckage.

"Major Grant, what is your status?" Ortega said into her comm.

The reply crackled back, and Carter heard it, though even if he hadn't done, the drawn look on the colonel's face told him everything he needed to know.

"Did they get out?" Carina asked.

"Forty-nine made it clear of the barracks," Ortega replied, in a matter-of-fact tone. "Forty-nine out of a hundred-and-eighty-five."

"I think you'll find the correct number is fifty-two," Carter said. "Because you three are also getting out alive."

Just as he spoke, a team of five Immortals clambered over the rubble toward him. Carina called out a warning, and the others rushed into cover, but Carter remained where he was, in plain sight of the Aternien soldiers.

"Commander, take cover!" Ortega yelled, but he was going nowhere.

Drawing his 57-EX, he aimed and fired, emptying the

powerful weapon in barely the space of a second, and killing all five immortals with headshots. The bodies of the warriors slid down the mound of smashed glass and brick; a mini avalanche of Aternien metal.

"Keep moving," Carter grunted. He holstered his revolver and pushed on, tossing aside fractured concrete blocks and twisted metal beams with inhuman ease. It was like the obstacles were foam replicas of the sort that might be used on the set of a movie. With artillery fire and particle blasts still flying, he finally made it to the end of the corridor and kicked open what remained of the door. Remarkably, the infantry squad vehicle that Colonel Ortega had reserved was still there, and still intact.

"Hurry, we're running out of time," Carter called out, trying to urge the others to push on harder.

More particle orbs flew overhead, and this time the west of the barracks was hit, including the section containing the armory. More than half of the facility had been destroyed, and the rest was on fire. Only the burning carcasses of destroyed APC and piles of rubble from ruined buildings shielded them from the squads of Immortals that were pilling through the gates and gaps in the walls.

"The exits are all cut off," Ortega said, arriving at the truck. Carina had chosen to drive; a fact that filled Carter with dread as well as hope. "I don't see how we can get out."

Carter checked their surroundings and decided there was really only one choice. "Sergeant Fisher, can you make us an exit?" He pointed to one of the few remaining intact walls.

"I believe I can, sir," the sergeant replied.

Carter and Sergeant Marsh stood guard, while Fisher planted charges on the wall. At the same time, Carina had started up the motor of the powerful infantry vehicle and lined it up, ready to make their escape.

The sergeant worked fast, but thanks to Carter's accelerated senses, even a few seconds felt like minutes. Aternien Immortals were crawling all over the barracks, and he knew they might be spotted at any moment.

"Sergeant, we need to hustle," Carter said, gripping the handle of his sword more tightly as the scrape of Aternien metal on rock drew near.

"I'm ready," Fisher called back.

The soldier ran to the vehicle and climbed inside, and Carter slapped Marsh on the shoulder, telling him to go too.

"Carter, come on!" Carina called out, revving the engine.

He turned his back and was about to jump into the vehicle, when his senses alerted him to danger, but it was a fraction of a second too late. An Immortal leapt over the rubble and impaled him through the side with the bayonet of her particle rifle. The suddenness of the attack even took his sensation blockers by surprise, and he roared as the stab of the blade bit deeper.

Carter pulled the bayonet clear and diverted the barrel of the rifle just as the Aternien squeezed the trigger, hammering a blast of energy harmlessly into the ground. Tearing the weapon from her delicate hands, Carter beat the Immortal senseless, until the rifle was little more than broken fragments of golden metal.

"I've had it up to here with his barracks!" Carter raged, storming back toward the vehicle. "No offense, Colonel."

"None taken," Ortega replied, though she was staring fearfully at the hole in Carter's body. "Commander, you're wounded."

"I'll be fine," Carter growled, sliding into the back of

their ride. "Blow the charges and let's get the hell out of here."

Fisher detonated the explosives, and the vehicle was showered with brick, which rebounded off its armor like giant hailstones. Carina floored the accelerator and within seconds they were on the open road. A squadron of scarab-like Khepri fighters roared overhead and a dozen energy bombs fell from their wings, razing what remained of First Brigade's barracks to the ground, as if it had never been there are all.

"Commander, let me see your injury," Ortega insisted. She had a med-kit in hand and an urgent look about her.

"I'm fine, really," Carter replied, waving her off.

"But you were stabbed…" Ortega inspected his side, but the cut had already healed over, and his battle uniform was knitting itself back together. "Well, I'll be damned." She shook her head and looked at him with disbelieving eyes. "How do you feel?"

"How do I feel?" Carter growled. "I'm mad as hell, that's how I feel."

Carina laughed and glanced over her shoulder; the rush of air through the open windows of the vehicle was whipping back her hair, like medusa's snakes. "Don't worry, Colonel, that's how he feels all of the time …"

TWENTY-THREE
GOING UNDERGROUND

CARINA EASED BACK on the throttle once it became clear that the Aterniens attacking the barracks had lost interest in them. With their imposter colonel dead, the enemy was focused on simply destroying the last Union military stronghold in the city, and they did so with furious efficiency.

The fighting continued beyond the walls of the barracks, however. The troops that Major Grant had managed to evacuate were being continually harassed by Khepri fighters and Aternien Immortals. Colonel Ortega had stayed in contact with her officer, but they were taking heavy casualties, and it wasn't clear that any of them would make it out of the city alive. As cold as it sounded, that wasn't Carter's problem. If the doomsday device was allowed to detonate, then millions more would die. War too often boiled down to a simple numbers game.

JACAB warbled, rousing him from the darker thoughts that were intruding on his mind. He checked his comp-slate and saw that his bot had uploaded the coordinates of a subway emergency exit point. The position was also showing on the vehicle's nav system, and Carina had already spotted it.

"We're still a couple of kliks from the stadium, are you sure there's nothing closer?" Carina asked, while following the highlighted route to the co-ordinates on the nav.

JACAB bleeped and squawked then rotated from side to side, like a head shaking.

"This is close enough," Carter said. He was reviewing a map of the subway tunnels that his bot had also sent him. "Any closer and we risk running into Aternien patrols, so it's better if we make our way to the stadium underground."

Carina continued to follow the nav, which led them onto Fourth Street; a straight road that ran from one end of the city to the other. However, she'd only just completed the turn, before she suddenly veered onto the sidewalk and hammered the brakes, causing the vehicle to come came to an abrupt, screeching halt. Carter slammed his hand onto the dash to prevent himself from sliding forward, denting it in the process. Colonel Ortega and the others were caught off guard too and rattled around in the rear of the vehicle like loose change in a pocket.

"Sorry about that," Carina said, getting her apology in first, before the inevitable raft of angry complaints. "But our plan has just hit a stumbling block."

Carter had already seen it. The subway emergency exit was on the street corner of an intersection, across from a café. On a normal day, the sidewalks would be filled with tables and chairs for locals and visitors to sit and enjoy a coffee. Now, the junction was littered with burned out cars and rubble from damaged buildings, and the exits were all barricaded. A single Aternien squad stood guard, but thanks to his XO's sharp eyes and quick intervention, it didn't appear that the Immortals had seen them.

"If those Aterniens clock us then the game is up," Carina said, resting her forearms on the steering wheel. She had pulled in behind a downed Union drop ship, which hid their vehicle from view. "One word from them and this place will be swarming with goldies before we can say 'Markus Aternus'..."

In many ways, Carina was right, though Carter didn't share his XO's pessimistic appraisal of the situation. "You took some EMP grenades from the armory in the barracks, right?" he asked.

"Sure, they're in the back," Carina replied. "But that squad has to be over a hundred meters away. Even you can't hit a target that far away with any accuracy."

"One hundred twenty-one meters, to be precise," Sergeant Fisher called out from the rear of the vehicle. The soldier was referring to a personal comp-slate, eyebrows raised.

"That's a hell of throw, Commander, are you sure you can make it?" Colonel Ortega asked, adding her voice to the chorus of doubt.

"I could throw one of those damn grenades all the way to Pallas City if I wanted to," Carter hit back, feeling set upon. "Hitting those goldies is no sweat, trust me."

From the way Colonel Ortega and her sergeants looked at one other, it was clear that he'd yet to earn their unequivocal trust, despite the feats he'd already performed. It shouldn't have bothered him, and he tried to tell himself that it didn't, but the truth was, he was itching to prove them all wrong.

Carter stepped out of the vehicle and Ortega jumped out beside him with two EMP grenades; one in each hand.

"How long do you want the fuse setting for?" the colonel asked.

Carter peeked around the burned-out drop ship to check the distance. He didn't doubt that Sergeant Fisher's scan was correct, but he needed to see it for himself, so that his augmented brain could process the calculations and feed those results subconsciously to his muscles. "I'd say six seconds should do it." He looked at JACAB. "That about right, buddy?"

JACAB pondered the question for a second then nodded. Carter's comp-slate updated, and he saw that his gopher had transmitted the optimal launch angle and velocity needed to hit the target, but he refused to look at the numbers. He knew that pride came before a fall, but on this occasion, he didn't care.

"Six seconds," Ortega said, adjusting the fuses then holding out the grenades. "I hope you're right about this, Commander Rose, because if you miss then we're in a whole heap of shit."

"Trouble seems to follow me around regardless," Carter grunted, taking the first grenade. He clicked down the trigger, released it to activate the timer then launched the explosive into the air. His arm swung so fast that the breeze blew back the loose strands of the colonel's hair. "But we won't be getting any trouble from that squad, at least," Carter added, taking the second grenade and launching it, snapping the throw like a whip-cracking.

Ortega, the sergeants and even Carina craned their necks to watch the two grenades arc through the sky in a perfect parabola. JACAB bleeped excitedly and seem to judder, as if the bot were giggling, which told him that his throws were on the money.

The first grenade hit an Immortal square on the nose with a satisfying clunk, before detonating and taking three more down with it. The second landed in the middle of the pack a split second later, paralyzing the remaining Aterniens with a focused blast of electromagnetic energy. The Immortals staggered around like drunks then fell flat on their faces, quivering as if connected to a live wire.

"I don't believe it," Ortega said.

Sergeant Fisher cursed and squashed a bank note into Sergeant Marsh's hand. The other NCO was grinning like a Cheshire cat.

"It won't keep them down for long, so we need to hustle," Carter said, jumping back into the vehicle.

Ortega slid into the rear and Carina pulled away, accelerating hard along the road to where the squad of Aterniens had been knocked down. By the time they arrived at the emergency exit hatch, the Immortals were already recovering, dragging their synthetic bodies off the road, and gathering their particle weapons. Carter jumped out before the vehicle had even come to a full stop and drew his cutlass.

"What are you going to do?" asked Carina, anxiously.

"What needs to be done," Carter answered. He ignited the blade and stabbed each struggling immortal in the back of the head, destroying their neuromorphic brains. It was over in seconds. Flipping the switch to deactivate the sword he turned back to his XO. She was looking at him like he was a demon risen from the fires of hell.

"Aternien Immortals don't surrender, Major," Carter said, sheathing his blade. "And these bastards aren't dead, not really. Their souls will just get transferred to a new body, and we'll end fighting them again."

"I know," Carina said, though it was clear she was shaken. "It's just a hell of a rollercoaster, you know?"

"I know," Carter grunted.

One moment, they were all smiles, betting on how far he could throw a lump of metal. The next, he was cutting down enemy soldiers with the nonchalance of a butcher at an abattoir. Carter turned to the two sergeants, both of whom were stony faced and silent.

"Get that emergency hatch open," Carter said, nodding toward their next objective. "It won't be long before the Aterniens send a drone to find out why this squad has stopped responding. We need to be underground before then."

The two soldiers acknowledged the order and set to work. At the same time, Carter returned to the vehicle, disengaged the parking brake and began pushing it further down the road. Once he'd picked up enough speed, he released it, and let it crash it through the glass frontage of a restaurant.

"If we need it again, it'll still be there," Carter said, dusting down his hands. "This way, it looks less conspicuous."

Metal hinges creaked and the subway hatch door swung open. The humid, stale air that drifted up from inside tasted like burned metal and oil.

"Check it out, buddy," Carter said to JACAB. The bot nodded then hovered a few meters down the steep staircase, antenna swiveling and lights flashing like a police squad car. A trio of Aternien Khepri fighters soared across the sky to their east, and Carter watched them for any sign they were turning in their direction, but the craft continued on course.

"Come on, buddy, we're exposed out here," Carter said, urging his bot to work faster. JACAB reappeared a few seconds later, and his analysis flashed up on Carter's comp-slate, but he struggled to believe was he was reading. "There's nothing down there?" he asked his gopher, who nodded. "Are you sure?"

JACAB nodded again then shrugged his maneuvering fins. Clearly, the bot had been surprised too, which was why he had taken so long to report back. JACAB had re-run the scan, but the results were the same.

"What's wrong?" asked Carina. Colonel Ortega had also gathered closer; a similar expression of worry and confusion furrowed her brow.

"The tunnel is clear of Aterniens, pretty much all the way to the stadium," Carter replied, still scowling at the comp-slate, and wracked with doubt.

"Isn't that a good thing, Commander?" Ortega asked.

Carter rubbed his silver beard. "I don't know. Maybe. Maybe not."

He'd expected the subterranean transport tunnels to be less heavily patrolled, but certainly not empty. Carter's senses told him something was wrong, but they were in a bind. It was either take the tunnel and risk walking into a trap or continue at street level and potentially end up facing down an entire company of Aternien Immortals. Neither option was good, but one of them had to be chosen.

"We continued as planned," Carter decided, disliking his own order as soon as he'd given it. "But stay on your toes. It's too quiet down there."

"Maybe they just overlooked the subway?" Carina suggested.

"The Aterniens don't make those sorts of mistakes, Major," Carter replied, gravely. "Everything they've done so far has been carefully coordinated. They've been planning this war for years."

"It may be a trap, but I don't see that we have a choice," Colonel Ortega added. "If we turn back now, we're effectively giving up on finding this weapon. We can't take that risk."

A solemn silence fell over the group. They all understood what they might be walking in to, but Carter also knew that traps worked best when you weren't expecting them. That gave them a chance; even if it was a slim one.

TWENTY-FOUR

ROUND TWO

"BUDDY, take the lead and scan ahead," Carter said, rapping his knuckles against JACAB's spherical shell. "Keep every sensor and detector you have running at full power. If so much as a rat scampers in our direction, I want to know about it, understood?"

JACAB warbled nervously then hummed back through the emergency hatch. Ortega and the sergeants followed next, then Carina. Carter waited until they had all traversed the first flight of steps, then grabbed the door handle and pulled the hatch closed behind them. It felt like sliding the lid shut on his own sarcophagus.

Tramping through the subway felt like exploring an abandoned mine. Using the maps that JACAB had retrieved from the city's central computer, they quickly worked their way off the main line and through access tunnels and disused sections, all of which remained devoid of Aternien patrols. With their progress unimpeded, it wasn't long before they'd emerged into the sub-level parking section of

Enterprise Stadium. Immediately, it seemed clear that they'd come to the right place.

"What the hell is that?" Carina said, cautiously stepping out across the parking lot, energy pistol in hand.

"That's a new one for me too, I'm afraid," Carter replied.

A narrow tunnel had been bored through the wall at the end of the car park, held in place by a perfectly smooth coating of golden metal. It sloped steadily downward into an oval-shaped cavern, which was also lined with Aternien metal, making it look like the inside of a giant golden egg. In the center of the cavern was a spherical object, which resembled an underwater mine from the old naval battles Carter had once read about at the Union Academy. The device was also built from gleaming Aternien metal, and had dozens of tubes sprouting from its surface, all of which snaked up through the ceiling of the cavern like roots.

"I've never seen one before in my life, but I'd say that certainly has the look of a doomsday device about it," Carina said, wide-eyed.

Carter felt his senses begin to rise, but there was no obvious cause for alarm, besides the appearance of what certainly looked like a large bomb. He checked his comp-slate, which was relaying the scan readings from JACAB, but while there were literally hundreds of Aterniens above them on the surface level, the sub-level remained clear. This was excluding the oval cavern, which JACAB's scanners were unable to penetrate.

"Can you get any sort of reading from the cavern, buddy?" Carter asked. JACAB scanned again, but the results were the same. He cursed, then a message from the bot appeared on his comp-slate, and he gritted his teeth. "Okay, but take it slow, and back out at the first sign of trouble, got it?" JACAB warbled then accelerated ahead of the group.

"Where is he going?" Carina asked.

"He's going to scout the cavern and report back," Carter said. The look Carina shot him made it clear she didn't like the idea of JACAB being used like a coal mine canary. Carter didn't like it, either, but there was little about their situation he did like.

JACAB hummed toward the cavern and Carter stopped at the tunnel entrance, always with an eye on his comp-slate. The readings started to clear up, but the data made no sense to him. "Colonel, do you or any of your men understand these readings?" Carter said, stopping and holding up his forearm so that the others could read his comp-slate. "Science stuff was my Master Operator's domain, not mine."

Ortega and the others gathered round, each frowning at the screen. It was Sergeant Marsh who spoke up. "I don't know what it is, sir but it's certainly not an explosive," the sergeant said. "At least, it's no kind of explosive device that I've ever seen before."

Carter balled his hands into a fist and let out a muted growl. The readings from JACAB's scanners continued to populate then the signal suddenly went dead. "JACAB, come in?" His senses climbed another notch. "Buddy, do you hear me? I need you to come back…" Still, nothing. Cursing again, Carter re-read the latest scan updates, but besides the device in the center, the cavern seemed empty. "I'm going in," he announced, setting out for the tunnel. "I don't care if that thing's a doomsday device or just a goddamn Aternien alarm clock, I don't like it, and we're going to blow it sky high."

"Don't you mean, 'we're going in'?" Carina said, though it was more of a demand than a question.

"No, you remain in the garage and guard the tunnel entrance," Carter replied. He turned to Sergeant Marsh and held out his hand. "Give me the explosives, sergeant. I'll rig them myself, while I fetch JACAB. There's no need for the rest of you to enter."

The sergeant obliged without protest, which was more than he could say for his XO.

"At least let me come with you," Carina said. "It doesn't need four of us to guard the tunnel entrance."

"Something about this isn't right, Carina," Carter said, pulling on the pack of charges. "No-one else needs to risk going inside, is that clear?"

Carina clamped her jaw shut and nodded.

"I need to hear it, Carina…"

"Fine, yes sir," Carina said, finally relenting.

Carter nodded then drew his 57-EX revolver and moved out. His boots clacked against the smooth metal floor, and the mirrored surface of the tunnel made it feel like he was inside a Christmas bauble. Reaching the device in the center of the cavern, he slid the bag off his shoulders and removed the demolitions components, before noticing JACAB. His bot was on the ground with an oval-shaped dent in his shell, but the cavern was empty and there was no obvious cause of the damage.

"Buddy, are you okay?" Carter said, running over to his gopher. JACAB's lights were still on, but the dent had clearly damaged his anti-grav repellers. "Don't worry, I'll get you out of here," he added, scooping up the bot and bundling him into the now-empty bag.

With JACAB stowed away, Carter returned to the

Aternien device. His comp-slate updated, and he saw that it was a message from his bot. The text was garbled, but from what he could make out, JACAB was trying to telling him that the mysterious object had nothing to do with the virus Damien Morrow had talked about. He pulled open the bag and peered into the bot's faded red eye.

"Are you sure about that, buddy?" JACAB warbled weakly, and Carter stood up. Nothing about the cavern or the device was making any sense. "But if this isn't the weapon then how do the Aterniens plan to deploy the damned virus, if there even is one?"

"Oh, the virus is real, as is the weapon…" The voice of Damien Morrow filled the cavern, but there was no sign of the man anywhere. Suddenly, a section of the smooth metal wall drew back then slid upward like a sash window. Damien Morrow stepped out, and Carter pointed his 57-EX at him, though the man wasn't armed.

"I wouldn't do that, if I were you," Morrow said, a smirk curling his lips.

A dozen more doors slid open in the chamber and a single Aternien Immortal emerged through each one. All of them were carrying standard Aternien particle rifles, with their bayonets energized.

Carter was seething with rage. "What happened to you, Morrow? You said you'd spoken the truth about this weapon, out of respect for our shared history and service. You've not only betrayed your oath to the Union, you've betrayed your promise to me too."

Damien Morrow was unrepentant. "Those oaths mean nothing anymore, Carter, and you're a fool to hold faith with them. You had your chance to join us, and now, you'll suffer the consequences of your stubborn loyalty."

"So, it was all a lie?" Carter said, as the dozen immortals aimed their bayonets at him. "If this isn't the doomsday weapon then what is it? And why lure me here?"

"The weapon is somewhere else, safe from you," Morrow said, resting against the smooth wall of the cavern. "This object is merely an interstellar communications array, nothing more. Just a way to keep the god-king informed."

"Well, why don't you dial him up right now, so I can pay him my respects?" Carter said, petulantly.

Morrow laughed. "I always liked you, Carter. Such a shame." Another door slid open in the chamber, but it was behind the comms array and his view of the new arrival was obscured. "Besides, there's someone else who wants to pay you their respects."

The final figure marched into the cavern and stood in front of Carter. The faces of the other Immortals, all perfect in their own ways, were unknown to him, but this Aternien was someone he'd met before.

"Aren't you dead?" Carter said, as the female Overseer approached, war spear in hand.

"I cannot die," the Overseer replied, staring at him with her shimmering eyes, dangerous and beautiful in equal measure. "You hoped I would be reintegrated into a new body, so that you could kill me again. Well, here is your chance."

Carter recalled their encounter on the exoplanet in the Piazzi asteroid field, but he never actually believed that the stubborn Aternien would actually come back for round two.

"So, this is why you've lured me here?" Carter said to the woman. "Revenge?" He shook his head at the Overseer, genuinely disappointed. "I thought you Aterniens were beyond all that? I thought you were more evolved?"

"This has nothing to do with revenge," the Overseer replied. The Aternien's delicate voice was somehow powerful enough to fill the cavern with sound, but Carter could tell a lie when he heard one, and the Overseer was deceiving herself as well as him.

"You remember what happened the last time you faced me, don't you?" Carter said, thinking back to the Overseer's comment about how her soul was permanently backed up on the Aternien homeworld.

"I remember," the woman answered, and her glowing eyes sharpened further.

Carter sighed and drew his cutlass. "Then maybe another death will finally teach you to stay out of my way."

"This time, I will not fail," the Overseer answered, spinning her weapon, and aiming the spearhead at him. "This time, I will honor my king."

Suddenly, Carter understood everything, and it was even more pathetic than he'd first thought. "So *that's* it," Carter said, mocking the Overseer with his smile. "You failed to stop me from recovering the Galatine, and it cost you a place at the god-king's side."

"A position that was rightfully mine!" the Overseer snarled. "You have no idea how long I have waited to ascend to the Royal Court!"

Carter energized the blade of his sword. "Then you can stand to wait a little longer."

He was about to attack when angry voices filtered along the tunnel behind him. He glanced over his shoulder and saw that Major Larsen and the other were being bundled down the passageway at gunpoint by a squad of Aternien Immortals.

"They're nothing to do with this," Carter said, glowering

at the Overseer. "You only need to beat me to regain your honor. Hurt them, and I won't give you what you want."

"You have no say in the matter," the Overseer replied, in a high-handed manner. "And you are correct. This has nothing to do with them." The Overseer nodded, then the Immortals threw Carina, Ortega, and the sergeants against the wall, before raising their weapons and shooting them all in the chest.

"No!" Carter cried.

He drew his 57-EX and killed the firing squad with pinpoint headshots, but it was already too late. Carina, Ortega, Fisher and Marsh were on the ground, smoke rising from their bodies. All of his pent-up rage suddenly exploded inside him like an atom bomb. He tossed the empty revolver to the ground and turned back to face the Overseer.

"If you want a fight then you've got one..."

TWENTY-FIVE

THIS IS WHAT I AM...

THE OVERSEER CLASPED her hand against the shaft of her Aternien war spear, and the twelve Immortals began side-stepping to their right. Carter spun around and was about to cut down one of the bayonet-wielding warriors, but none of them were advancing toward him. They were simply moving in a circular motion around the circumference of the golden cavern, like planets orbiting a star.

"They are only here to stop you from running," the Overseer explained. "They will not intervene."

Carter snorted a laugh and turned back to the Aternien. "I don't run from a fight." His gaze flicked toward Damien Morrow, who was watching from his cubby hole in the cavern, behind the wall of Aternien guards. "Just ask him."

Morrow smiled. "You should have listened to me, Carter," the traitor said, reclining against the wall, hands in pockets, as the Immortals stepped in front of him.

"I warned you to stop calling me Carter," he answered.

He was far more interested in taking down the turncoat Longsword officer than the Overseer, but Morrow had wisely stayed out of the fight. "When I'm done here, you and I are going have a little chat."

Morrow simply laughed and shook his head. "I look forward to it."

Rather than try to take advantage of Carter's preoccupation with Morrow, the Overseer had waited patiently while he and the traitor spat words at one another. She had more honor than the turncoat Longsword officer, Carter realized, but it wouldn't save her. If the Overseer wanted to die again, he'd gladly grant her wish. Carter flourished his cutlass and the hum of the energized blade cutting through the air was amplified ten-fold by the smooth cavern walls. The Overseer also spun her weapon and advanced, glowing eyes fixed unwaveringly onto his own. There was no hatred in them, he realized, just a thirst to prove herself.

The Overseer attacked first, using her reach advantage, and stabbing the spear at his neck, but even with the Immortals circling around them, the cavern was large enough that Carter could easily dodge back and evade. The Overseer didn't press her attack. She was testing him and biding her time. To stand any chance of regaining her mark of ascension, the Overseer's victory would have to be convincing, and clean.

The Aternien woman came at him again, with a combination of slashes and lunges, which Carter parried or evaded, each time stepping back to keep the distance between them. With each attack, the speed of the spear head moved faster, so that soon it was little more than a blur. The clash of his energized cutlass against the Aternien metal rang out as clear as a church bell on a winter's morning, amplified by the cavern, which was like an echo chamber. To anyone nearby, it would have sounded like two armies fighting.

Carter's bio-engineered eyes were augmented with extra rods and cones, and connected to implants that allowed him to perceive temporal gaps as low as a millisecond. As such, despite the ferocious speed of the Overseer's strikes, he could see the motion of the blade clearly and react in time, whereas a 'normie' human would have been skewered a dozen times over.

Suddenly, the Overseer overextended, and Carter counterattacked, deflecting the spear then leveling a combination of fierce cuts at her face and body. The Aternien warrior dodged and ducked as if she had a second sight, and his swings hit only air. Then his blade struck the spherical comms array, and for the briefest moment, his sword was stuck. The Overseer capitalized on the opening and thrust her spear into his leg, cutting through his battle uniform and slicing his flesh. Carter dodged back, parrying a follow-up thrust to his neck, but the blade still nicked his skin and drew blood. The Immortals circling around the fighters clashed their hands to their weapons twice, as if keeping tally of the score.

"I needed a shave anyway," Carter said, dabbing the blood away, though the wound had already sealed itself.

"Joke all you wish, Commander," the Overseer replied, growing in confidence. "But choose your next words wisely, because they may be your last."

"I prefer not to speak to subordinates who are outside of the Royal Court," Carter replied, remembering how easily the Aternien woman could be provoked. "A lowly Overseer like you is below my station."

The woman's eyes flashed, and she bared her perfect teeth, before jumping and thrusting at his neck, using the full extension of her arm to gain the necessary reach. Carter parried and the Aternien landed, crouching low and spinning a strike at his legs, which he barely managed to skip over, before the spear was whirled at him again. This time it struck true, cutting across his chest below his pectoral muscles, deep enough to scar his ribs. Sensation blockers kicked in, and his battle uniform rapidly adapted to seal the wound and add pressure, but it was a strong strike, and the Overseer knew it.

"I will soon regain my rightful station," the Overseer vowed, and at the same time the Immortals clashed their hands to their rifles in recognition of the hit. "But you will not live to see me ascend."

Out of the corner of his eye, Carter saw Morrow smiling. The traitor's sanctimonious expression made him want to break off the duel and skewer the man through his black heart, but he couldn't afford to take his eyes off the Overseer even for a second. She had learned from their last encounter and adapted her style, which was why she was winning.

What does it matter anyway? Carter thought, parrying, and jumping back to avoid another combination of thrusts and slashes. *Even if I beat her, Morrow and the Immortals will just cut me down, like Carina and the others…*

The Overseer capitalized on her momentum, and her movements became even more fluid and precise. A vicious thrust cut his shoulder and drew blood, causing the Immortals to cheer another point for their captain. Carter countered, but the futility of the fight was sapping his energy even more rapidly than the wounds the Overseer continued to deliver. His strike missed by a wide margin, and Carter was stabbed in the side and sent staggering into the wall of guards, who merely deflected him back into the arena like a pool ball bouncing off a side cushion. He tried to use the extra impetus to surprise his opponent, but she danced aside and used the energized spear tip to score a smoldering furrow across his belly.

"Yield, and I will grant you an honorable death," the Overseer said, as Carter dropped to one knee, dispirited, and hurting. "Yield, and I will ensure you will not suffer."

Carter used his sword as a crutch to push himself to his feet, then regarded the Overseer with curiosity. Though her offer might have sounded pompous, he sensed her good intentions. Whoever she was – whatever she had been before metamorphosing into an Aternien – she was not evil. In fact, he sensed she was more honorable than the turncoat watching them duel and the vipers lurking in the Royal Court, which she aspired to join.

"That's very gracious of you," Carter replied, genuinely. He circled around the spherical transmitter and saw the bag with JACAB still sealed inside. Flourishing his cutlass, he made sure to slice open the material as he moved past. "But my honor won't be served by quitting."

The Overseer bowed her head. "As you wish…"

Carter was about to attack when he caught a flicker of movement in his peripheral vision. He risked taking his eyes off his opponent to look more closely, then saw it again, in unmistakable clarity. Carina had stirred, and knowing that she wasn't dead gave Carter more of a boost than any nano-stim or drug could ever hope to achieve.

The whirl of the Overseer's spear snapped his focus back

to the duel, and he barely had time to dodge, feeling the breeze of the spearhead as it swept past his face. She came at him again, this time thrusting low at his gut, but Carter had been studying the Aternien's new technique, and he blocked while also moving himself into striking range. A ferocious backhand sent the Aternien crashing into the wall, pulverizing one of the Immortals beneath her metal armor in the process. They both fell, but while the Overseer quickly regained her footing, the Immortal's neck was broken and skull crushed.

"Where's my cheer?" Carter said, bullishly. The sound of the Immortals clashing their hands against their rifles was conspicuous by its absence.

"We do not cheer for our enemies," the Overseer said, approaching again, but more cautiously.

The interlude allowed Carter to hurriedly tap commands into his comp-slate, then he glanced toward the bag and saw his bot's red eye glowing inside it.

"Help her, buddy…," Carter whispered, while again stealthily moving past the bot. "She's hurt bad…"

JACAB hummed into the air, but the damage his gopher had suffered was still impairing his ability to fly. While the bot raced toward his injured XO, the Overseer resumed her attack, forcing Carter onto the back foot. He blocked her thrust, then whirled his cutlass like a lasso, accidentally striking an Immortal to his rear, and slicing its head in half above the nose. The other Immortals did not react as the body of their comrade hit the deck, and Carter had an idea.

Pushing the Overseer back, Carter attacked with a sudden ferocity that took the Aternien woman completely by surprise. She desperately tried to block and evade but couldn't stop a savage cut from gouging open her Aternien armor and synthetic flesh. Her shimmering eyes widened with fear, and her confidence was shaken, allowing Carter to wound her again, this time striking her side.

Carter fed on the hope that his XO might still be saved, and continued his belligerent assault, cutting down three more of the gatekeeper Immortals in the process. The Overseer tried to counter, but Carter had the upper hand now. He shook off her blows then hammered the guard of his cutlass into the woman's chest, crushing her breast plate and sending her down.

The war spear fell from the Aternien's faltering grasp, and Carter claimed the deadly weapon for his own. The Overseer reached for it, and for the first time since their duel began, he could sense her fear and desperation. The Overseer knew that her opportunity for redemption was slipping away, and that she could do nothing to stop it.

Carter stepped back and struck the Overseer across the side of the face with her own weapon, knocking her flat. She raised her arm to protect her face, and Carter hacked it off at the shoulder. Then a second cut broke the Aternien's back and left her incapacitated and beaten. However, Carter was not finished yet. Spinning the war spear, he aimed the powerful cannon-end of the weapon at the Immortals surrounding him.

"Kill him!" Damien Morrow yelled. "What are you waiting for, you fools? Kill him before it's too late!"

It was already too late.

Carter activated the particle cannon and swept the beam around the cavern, melting through the Aternien warriors like they were made of butter. Then he saw Damien Morrow racing toward him, energized sword held high, but Carter reacted faster, and thrust the spear into the traitor's gut.

Morrow's scale armor was defeated, and he drove the traitor back against the wall, pushing the blade deep into the man's abdomen.

When close to death, Carter's implants were designed to drive his body far beyond its already unnatural limits, and Morrow's bio-engineered physiology was no different to his own. The turncoat grabbed the shaft of the spear and yanked it from his flesh, overpowering Carter in the process. Morrow then hammered a punch into the side of his head, causing him to reel back. For a moment, they held each other's gaze, then Morrow snatched a nano-stim capsule from Carter's armor and vanished through one of the doors in the cavern, pressing a fist to the deep wound in his gut.

Carter threw down the spear and gave chase, then he heard Major Larsen's voice drifting past his ear. It was a feeble, fearful cry for help, and it disarmed him as effectively as Morrow had just done. He ran back into the cavern and dropped down at his XO's side. She was conscious, barely, and JACAB was doing what he could to treat the wound to her chest. Her advanced battle uniform had soaked up the majority of the particle blast, but she was still listless and barely breathing.

"Can we risk a nano-stim?" Carter asked, as the bot worked feverishly to save her life, employing every tool and limb at his disposal. "She survived one before, and the residual nano-machines in her system might cushion the impact."

JACAB thought for a moment, its maneuvering fins and antennas swirling, before its red eye fell to the ground. Carter checked his comp-slate – the bot's assessment was 60:40 that Carina would not survive. Despite this, he was willing to risk a very low dose.

"I don't see that we have a choice," Carter said. He reached for his nano-stim then his gut tightened as he remembered that Damien Morrow had stolen it. His augments were designed to ensure he never experienced crippling panic, but at that moment, he was terrified of losing his XO.

"I'm not a medic, buddy, what's wrong with her?" Carter asked, desperation creeping into his voice.

JACAB ran a medical scan and the result appeared on his comp-slate. It was a pneumothorax – a collapsed lung.

"Help me out, JACAB," Carter said, scrambling across to Colonel Ortega and the sergeants, and searching them for a medkit. "Battlefield medicine isn't my area, but I'm hoping that Union medical tech still isn't in the dark ages."

JACAB hovered over Sergeant Marsh and shone a narrow torch beam onto an item of the man's gear. Carter leaped on it and tore the satchel free; it had the word MED written on it in bold letters.

"Okay, show me what I need," Carter said, hurrying back to Carina's side and tearing open the kit.

JACAB sprouted two mechanical arms and began searching through the contents, flinging any items that were of no use into the corridor. Then the bot found what he was looking for and snatched it into his claw-like pincer.

"Hemofoam?" Carter said, taking the item and reading the label. Understandably, he'd never heard of it before. "What do I do with this?"

His comp-slate updated with instructions and Carter followed them to the letter, injecting the substance directly into Carina's chest cavity, before shuffling back and hoping to God it worked. According to the blurb that JACAB had sent him, Hemofoam was a blend of synthetic proteins and peptides that attached to the punctured lung tissue and congealed to prevented air from entering the chest cavity. *A nano-stim would be a lot simpler, even if they do hurt like hell...* Carter thought, as he waited anxiously for the treatment to take effect.

Carina suddenly began to breathe more freely and her strained expression and sickly hue rapidly improved. He blew a sigh of relief and gripped her arm to let her know she was okay. At the same time, JACAB whistled and warbled with happiness, and it was then that Carter again saw the dent in his shell.

"How do you feel, buddy?" he asked, guilty for not considering his bot's injuries sooner.

JACAB bleeped and shrugged his maneuvering fins; he seemed more interested in Carina's recovery than the damage to his own circuits. Carter took this as a good sign.

"I think we've all seen better days, buddy, but Kendra will fix you up once we get back to Station Alpha," Carter said, patting his bot affectionately.

Carter's senses sharpened, and his immediate thought was to look toward the doorway that Damien Morrow had escaped through, but the turncoat Master Commander was long gone. Then the scrape of metal against metal drew his attention to the center of the cavern, to where the Overseer was slowly dragging herself toward one of the exits.

Carter checked Carina's vital signs, but she was getting stronger by the second, and she managed a nod and a smile to let him know that he could leave. He squeezed her arm again then stood up and approached the crippled Overseer, watching her eyes shimmer with fear as he drew closer.

"Don't kill me," the Overseer called out, holding up her

only hand and pleading with him. She was humiliated, and also deeply afraid. "Just leave me. Please. I can be healed."

"What does it matter, either way?" Carter said. Despite what the woman had done, he felt sympathy for her. "Your soul is backed up, anyway, so once you die here, you'll just upload into a new body, right?"

"Yes, but it is not that simple," the Overseer replied, dragging her broken back up against the comms array in the center of the chamber. "Rebirth is like a nightmare, but one where the pain is real. Time stops, and confusion reigns, and in those seemingly endless moments, all that exists is agony."

Carter crouched beside the Overseer so that their eyes were level. "I know what pain feels like, Overseer," he said, staring into her flickering, blue eyes. "Pain is what you, and those like you, are inflicting on millions of people as we speak." He came closer and the woman flinched. "Pain is a man losing his wife, shot dead in front of her children. Pain is living with that loss for the rest of your life. You don't feel pain, Overseer. You are pain."

The Overseer had nothing to say in response, and Carter got back to his feet. He saw his 57-EX revolver on the ground and recovered it, before slowly emptying out the spent cartridges and reloading.

"I'll give you a piece of advice, lady," Carter said, closing the cylinder with a snap. "Give up on your dream of ascending to the Royal Court. From what I've seen, you wouldn't fit in there anyway, because unlike those cruel bastards, you might just have a sliver of humanity left in you."

"You cannot understand," the Overseer whispered. If it were possible, Carter felt sure that tears would be welling in her synthetic eyes. "This is what I am. This is all I know. Without ascension, I am nothing."

Carter aimed his revolver at the Overseer's head and placed his finger on the trigger. "Maybe it's better to be nothing than what you are now."

He squeezed the trigger and shot the Overseer dead.

TWENTY-SIX

TIME TO LEAVE

CARTER HOLSTERED his revolver and returned to check on his XO, who was already sitting upright, and looking more like her old self. JACAB was by her side, sifting through the leftovers of the med kit that Carter had recovered from Sergeant Marsh, and separating out a selection of drugs for Carina to take.

"How are you feeling?" Carter asked, while checking an updated medical scan of his XO on his comp-slate.

"I feel like I've been repeatedly kicked in the chest by a mule, but otherwise okay," Carina replied, with an encouraging smile. "JACAB is busy sorting me out with some of the good stuff, so I'll be on my feet before you know it." She nodded toward the Overseer. "Unlike her, I might add. Do you think she'll take the hint this time?"

Carter also glanced at his adversary. "Sadly, I doubt it. I'm her ticket to the Aternien Royal Court, and I don't think anything will convince her to give that up. She's obsessed about it for so long there is nothing else."

His XO's eyes then slid across to where Colonel Ortega

and her sergeants were lying dead on the smooth, Aternien metal floor.

"I actually liked her," Carina said, her voice low and regretful. "I liked all of them. It's such a waste."

"That's war, Major. Wasting lives, until one side can't afford the body count anymore."

Carter moved over to Colonel Ortega and arranged her body and the bodies of the two sergeants into more dignified poses. He then drew his fingers over their eyelids to cover their vacant stares, stood to attention and saluted.

"We have to make sure it wasn't for nothing," Carina said, after a few seconds of somber silence. "There are millions more people on this planet. They need to know what's about to happen. We've got to give them a chance to escape."

JACAB finished dosing-up Major Larsen with pain meds and healing accelerants, and Carter could sense that she was a lot stronger, without needing another bio-scan to prove it.

"Can you stand?" he asked, extending a hand toward his XO.

"I can try…" Carina grabbed Carter's wrist and he was comforted by the strength of her grip. She then hissed like air escaping from a dinghy as Carter hauled his XO to her feet, highlighting that Carina was still hurting, despite the brave face she was putting on.

"Are you good to go?" he asked. "We're still in a tight spot." Carter was conscious that Damien Morrow had escaped and would likely return with reinforcements. He surmised that the only reason the traitor hadn't already done so was because of the war spear he'd stabbed through his body.

"Well, my ears won't stop ringing, I ache in places I

didn't know could ache, and I need to pee, but otherwise, all good." Carina replied, smiling.

Carter snorted a laugh. "I'm afraid I can't help with any of those." He shrugged. "Well, besides peeing. I guess I could turn my back while you go."

"I'll hold it, thanks," Carina replied, sarcastically.

"Suit yourself." Carter checked his comp-slate, but the chamber was still interfering with his scans. "We need to reach the fleet and warn Admiral Krantz what's about to happen. There's nothing more we can do on the surface now. The real doomsday device could be anywhere, and we have neither the time nor the resources to do anything about it."

While Carina was collecting her weapons, Carter had an idea and recovered the Overseer's war spear from the floor of the cavern. "Here, you can use this as a crutch," he said, offering the Aternien weapon to his XO. "Just be careful where you point it, because one blast from the end of that thing will take your head clean off."

Carina took the spear, though not without some reticence.

"Thanks, I'll bear that in mind," she replied, careful to plant the cannon end of the weapon into the ground, so that the worst that might happen was that she lost a foot.

Then, together, they walked back along the sloping metal tunnel until they were on the familiar concrete surface of the underground vehicle parking garage. Carter checked the signs and referred to his comp-slate to locate the shuttle garage relative to their position.

"Assuming Marco Ryan didn't destroy it, our ship should still be docked at the stadium," Carter said, programming the comp-slate to find them a quick route to the docking garage. "And if it's not then we'll find another.

There were a couple of other shuttles up there when we arrived, assuming they've not been taken since."

Following the map on his comp-slate, Carter found a stairwell that led most of the way up the shuttle parking area. It would have been quicker to take an elevator, but he didn't want to risk that the Aterniens would notice the moving car and trap them inside.

"It looks clear, at least for a couple of levels," Carter said, starting up the first flight, covering three steps at a time. Carina followed, but even with the spear as a crutch, her face crumpled with pain, and her progress was slow.

"Shit, at this rate, we'll still be here tomorrow," his XO complained, compelling her weary muscles to move by sheer force of will.

"I could carry you up?" Carter suggested.

He was being serious, but the thunderous look on Carina's face made it clear his XO was less than enamored by his suggestion.

"Don't give me that face, Major, you know it's the right thing to do," Carter added. "It's not like I'm carrying you over the threshold or anything."

Carina continued to glare at him, but she'd only made it half-way up the first flight and already seemed broken. "Fine, just don't make me look like some kind of feeble fairytale princess."

Carter snorted a laugh then maneuvered his XO into position. "I think Prince Charming would run a mile within seconds of meeting you," he said, hoisting her up, ironically, exactly as if he was about to carry her over the threshold of their marital abode.

"What the hell is that supposed to mean?" Carina

growled, as Carter started climbing again, two-steps at a time. "Prince Charming never had it so good!"

Carter scowled at his XO. "So now you're angry that I don't think you're the ideal woman for a clichéd fairytale prince?"

Carina smiled and flashed her eyes at him. "I'm the ideal woman, full stop."

Carter laughed. "I think the drugs have gotten to your brain," he said, already on the third flight of stairs.

After several minutes of hard climbing, Carter was finally closing in on the shuttle garage, and not a second too soon. Despite his augments and enhanced natural strength, carrying a full-grown woman to the top level of a sports stadium had proved as challenging as wrestling a Morsapri with his bare hands. Carina, meanwhile, looked factory fresh, as if she'd just finished an intense spa session and was ready for the day ahead.

"You'd better not be faking those injuries," Carter said, setting Carina down then hunching over and resting his hands on his knees. They still had two more levels to traverse, but he needed a break. "I'm not as young as I used to be."

Carina looked ready to respond with one her usual wisecracks, but the sound of footsteps on the other side of the door, caused them both to take cover and listen hard.

"Alert all Wardens and lead acolytes that we have an intruder," Damien Morrow said. Carter glanced through the porthole window in the door and saw the man hobbling along the corridor outside with Aternien Immortals to his rear. "Commander Rose is to be detained if possible."

Morrow and the Aterniens were gone as quickly as they

arrived, then Carter checked his comp-slate, but the coast seemed clear.

"Morrow seemed hurt," Carina said.

"I stabbed him with the Overseer's war spear, while you were still out of it," Carter replied, nodding toward the golden weapon in his XO's hand. "So be careful where you point the sharp end too."

Carina nodded but appeared angry. "I know the bastard will heal, but I hope it hurts like hell in the meantime. First, Lola, then Ortega, Marsh, and Fischer…"

"He'll get what's coming to him," Carter grunted. He'd already vowed to take revenge for Lola's murder, and he intended to follow through, just not yet. "Right now, we have bigger problems."

JACAB hummed closer and bleeped. The bot sounded distressed.

"What's up, buddy?" Carter asked.

JACAB warbled again and Carter checked his comp-slate, but the bot's scan readings had become garbled and difficult to read.

"I can't make heads nor tails of this, buddy," he said, scowling at the screen. "The Aterniens must have just put up a jammer net once they found out I escaped."

"At least that will also blind the stadium's internal security system, so we don't have to worry about cameras or other sensors," Carina pointed out.

Suddenly, the doors at the top of the landing flung open and a team of Aternien Immortals burst through, led by a Warden. The leader slid to a stop as soon as he spotted Carter and raised his rifle, before being engulfed in a beam of particle energy. The stream continued unabated, slicing through the walls, and cutting down the entire team, who were concentrated into the confined space of the stairwell. The beam disengaged and Carter saw a startled Carina, Aternien war spear in hand, staring at the carnage in disbelief.

"That was a bit more powerful than I was expecting…"

"No shit…" Carter eased the cannon end of the spear away from him. "But good shooting. Not that you could really miss with that Aternien blunderbuss."

Frantic voices began to echo up the stairwell, and Carter chanced a look over the handrails. A small army of acolytes were flooding into the lower levels.

"That blast will have let them know where we are, so we have to move, double time."

Carter scooped up Carina, much to her indignation, and ran up the stairs. Molten metal clung to the soles of his boots, but soon he was on the next landing up, then the next. Then the stairs ended.

"Damn it, we're still one floor below the garage," Carter said, setting Carina down. "JACAB, how do we get to the shuttle from where we are?"

The bot's light flashed and its glowing red eye flickered from side to side, before the information was relayed to his comp-slate. Carter checked the new map layout, which was a venue space, filled with bars, restaurants, and a conference area. The emergency staircase they needed was directly on the other side of the building.

"We're going to have to make our way across," Carter said, drawing his sword, but not igniting the blade, for fear it would attract attention. "We stay low and move through the bars and restaurants to keep out of sight."

Carter inched open the door and peeked through, but the coast seemed clear. Without accurate scanners, he couldn't be certain, and had to rely on his own sixth sense to warn him. Opening the door fully, he waved Carina through, and she stalked into the closest business unit, which was a cocktail bar.

"I don't suppose we can stop for a drink?" Carina whispered, while shuffling forward on her hands and knees.

"I'll buy you one on the Dauntless, once we make it back," Carter replied. "Besides, I thought you needed the restroom?"

"Oh, I'm sweating buckets, so that urge is gone."

"Good to know, Major," Carter said, giving back some sarcasm of his own.

Across from the bar was a restaurant; a typical stadium venue eatery that served burgers, fries and milkshakes, all made from engineered meats, starches, and proteins. It was a far cry from the hunting grounds around his cabin of the forest moon of Terra Nine.

JACAB chirruped softly, and Carter tapped Carina on the leg to alert her. His XO also glanced back, anxiously, as he referred to his comp-slate. It was showing a thermographic scan of the far end of the restaurant. A shape in the outline of an Aternien Immortal was clear against the cooler background.

Carter tapped the war spear that his XO still had in hand, and she slid the weapon back to him. Carina then mouthed the words, "What are you going to do?" but he simply pressed a finger to his lip. He didn't need to explain because it was easier to just show her.

Grabbing the end of the shaft so as to maximize his stabbing range, Carter slithered forward like a sand snake, then jumped up and thrust the blade of the weapon through the back of the Aternien's head and out through its mouth.

The warrior flailed its arms and convulsed like a speared fish, then Carter yanked it back, dropping the Immortal out of sight behind the welcome counter. It was a brutal takedown, but also completely silent.

"It's a shame he won't remember this," Carter said, yanking the spear free of the Aternien's skull. The Immortal's soul block had been split in half, which meant that the warrior would be reborn from an earlier backup, with no memory of being skewered.

"I can see the door," Carina whispered, pointing between two booths. "But it's guarded, and pretty heavily too."

Carter maneuvered himself into a better position, then cursed under his breath. The door to the garage level was guarded by a full squad of ten Immortals, which included a Warden.

"We could just blast them to smithereens, like I did the others?" Carina suggested.

"We'd be swamped with goldies within a minute if we did that," Carter replied. The thought had crossed his mind, however. "What we need to do is lure them away."

Carter then had a thought. He grabbed the spear and looked it over, before turning to JACAB. "Can you overload the energy core in this thing?" he asked his bot. "I'd imagine that a weapon this powerful would produce a pretty big bang?"

JACAB warbled and chattered then began scanning the spear in earnest.

"Are you sure you want to do this?" Carina asked. "It might blow the entire roof off the stadium. Or worse, vaporize it entirely."

"I'm sure that's an exaggeration, Major," Carter replied,

dryly. Then he reconsidered. "Well, I'm fairly certain, anyway..."

JACAB bleeped with excitement then waved its maneuvering fins at him.

"What's the deal, buddy? Can you set this thing to blow up?"

JACAB chirruped happily and Carter checked his compslate. There was a number counting down from ten.

"Wait, have you already set it to overload?" he asked his bot, his senses spiking. JACAB nodded and smiled with his glowing eye and Carter felt his gut tighten. "Damn it, JACAB!"

Spinning around, Carter grabbed the spear and hurled it along the corridor in the opposite direction to the squad of immortals. It flew perfectly flat and jet-fast before thudding into a door fifty meters away. Another second ticked by, then the spear exploded, taking out the entire corner of the level with it.

The floor shook and Carter pressed his body flat as the squad of Immortals raced past the restaurant, led by their Warden, to investigate the cause of the carnage.

"I can't believe that actually worked," Carter said, smiling. "Come on, we don't have a second to lose." He went to scoop up his XO, but she waved him off and started toward the exit under her own steam. Carter was still faster and reached the door first, yanking it open ready for Carina to move through. Pushing on into the garage, Carter quickly spotted Admiral Krantz's personal shuttle, parked exactly where they'd left it. The maintenance bots they'd set to work on the damaged craft appeared to have done a decent job of patching it up, and they'd even given it a wash and wax polish too.

"The shuttle looks good," Carina said, running her hand along the polished metal. "Maybe the admiral won't even notice the damage?"

Carter unlocked the hatch and it opened slowly, creaking like a rusted barn door.

"Okay, she'll probably notice," Carina corrected herself. She jumped inside then JACAB followed and settled down on her lap, which his XO appeared to appreciate as much as the gopher did. Carter was about to slide into the pilot's seat when his senses hit high alert. Drawing his 57-EX revolver, he turned to see Damien Morrow. The traitor and former Master Commander was standing on the outer ledge, half hidden by a support pillar, and with a sheer drop to the lower level beneath him.

"I'm not here to fight, Commander," Morrow said, smiling and holding up a hand, while the other gripped the support pillar.

"I should kill you now," Carter said, holding his ground. It was an idle threat, and they both knew it, since Morrow's augmented reactions would allow the man to literally dodge a bullet.

"I'm genuinely sorry for lying to you," Morrow continued, and Carter stayed quiet to let the man speak his piece. "I'm also sorry for the death of your Master Operator's wife. It was an accident. It was never my intention to hurt them." Morrow huffed a weary laugh. "I actually wanted to take them all to a better place."

"Your apologies don't mean shit, Morrow," Carter answered, his voice cold as steel. "You chose your side and threw your lot in with the enemy. You don't get to brush that off with a little, 'I'm sorry'. It doesn't work that way."

Morrow nodded. "Fair enough, Commander." His

expression hardened. "But don't mistake me, I make no apologies for joining the Aterniens. Their vision for the future is the right one, and I only wish you could see that. I wish you could be a part of shaping this new future; a better and more tolerant future."

Carter shook his head at the man. "Tolerance isn't wiping out anyone that disagrees with you, Morrow. It's learning to live together. You know, forgiveness and all that crap."

Morrow wasn't amused. "You don't believe any of that. You've lived in the Union as long as I have. There's no tolerance; not for people like us."

Carter shrugged. "Maybe you're right. But I know who I am. And an oath breaker is not it."

Damien Morrow smiled; a reaction that surprised him, because it was a warm smile, the sort often exchanged between friends, rather than the cruel smile of an enemy. "Till we meet again then, Master Commander Carter Rose."

Morrow bowed his head, then slid behind the support pillar. Carter felt his senses climb, and he rushed over to where the man had been standing, buckler engaged and revolver ready, but Morrow was nowhere to be seen.

TWENTY-SEVEN
ESCAPE VELOCITY

"EVERYTHING OKAY OUT THERE?" asked Major Larsen, as Carter swung through the hatch and into the pilot's seat of the shuttle. He could see that his XO was drifting in and out of consciousness and hadn't been aware of his conversation with Morrow.

"Everything is fine," Carter said. It wasn't a lie, just a convenient omission. "Hang tight, we'll be underway soon." He powered up the shuttle's reactor, which responded strongly, then fired the engines. The status indicators on the consoles began to climb and he was relieved to see that they settled in the green. "The shuttle seems fine, but run a quick diagnostic from your panel too," Carter said to his XO.

When Carina didn't answer, he glanced across to find his XO staring vacantly out of the window, like she was drunk. Accessing his comp-slate, he ran a bio-scan. Her vitals were stable, but the cocktail of meds that JACAB had given her were kicking her ass.

"Buddy, I'm going need your help to co-pilot this bucket," Carter said, turning to his gopher.

"I can manage," Carina said weakly, slurring the words. She tried to sit up and focus on the consoles, but her head was lolling from one side to the other, and her eyes couldn't focus clearly. Carter fastened her harness then reclined her seat, and she was too drowsy to resist.

"I've got it from here, Carina, just sit back," Carter said, running the diagnostic himself. "This is just a casual flight back to the mothership. Nothing to worry about."

Carina finally relented and relaxed. "I guess I could do with taking five. Getting blasted by an Aternien particle rifle kinda takes it out of you."

"You took it like a champ," Carter grunted, focusing his attention on the nav controls, and trying to plot a safe course to the Union fleet. "I'll let you know when we're nearing the Dauntless. I'll need your help to explain all this to Krantz."

The navigation system began to populate, showing all of the ships close to the stadium. Activity in the skies above Enterprise City had diminished significantly, but there were still regular patrols of Aternien Khepri fighters, along with dozens of recon drones, any one of which could spot their launch and relay their position to the enemy.

"JACAB, can you do anything to boost our reactor output and engine power?" Carter said, turning to the bot, who was plugged into the auxiliary station in the aft section of the cabin.

The bot warbled and bleeped his usual mix of cheery-sounding responses, then Carter felt the deck plates of the shuttle begin to vibrate at a higher frequency. His engineering console updated, and he saw the reactor output was one-fifty above standard and peak engine power was almost double the rated value.

"Holy hell, JACAB, what did you do?"

The bot's red eye smiled and he waved his maneuvering fins. Carter was aware that such a cocky response was not actually an answer to his question, but he also figured that it was perhaps best he didn't know.

"So long as we don't blow ourselves up, trying to avoid things that want to blow us up, I guess I don't care." The bot remained suspiciously silent. "We're not going to blow ourselves up, right?" Carter added, hopefully.

JACAB shrugged then turned back to the console. The bot didn't actually need to be looking at the bank of switches and displays, since he was directly interfaced with the ship, so turning away was simply his gopher's attempt to ignore him, and his question. Carter blew out a heavy sigh, checked on Carina again, who was out like a light, then grabbed the controls.

"Here goes nothing…" The shuttle lifted off the parking deck and Carter maneuvered the craft in front of the docking garage door. It should have opened automatically, but the slab of metal remained in place. "Buddy, can you get the door, please?"

His bot bleeped, but at the same time another door opened, and team of acolytes burst onto the garage floor. They saw the shuttle and immediately opened fire.

"Any time today would be good…" Carter added, with a necessary sense of urgency.

JACAB grumbled and blew a raspberry. Then the garage door unlocked and began to slowly whir open. Slugs continued to dent and ricochet off their hull armor, then a shot cracked the cabin glass to his side.

"Is that rain?" Carina said, dreamily. "I love the sound of rain on my bedroom window."

"Sure, it's rain," Carter replied, hurriedly applying a

sealing patch to the crack. "It's actually a little stormy outside, so if you feel a few shakes and bumps, don't think anything of it."

"Okay, mom…" Carina replied, wispily.

An acolyte appeared at the window and thumped his fist on the glass.

"Shut it down!" the man bellowed, holding up his pistol for Carter to see. "Shut it down, or we'll shoot you down."

Had it been an Immortal making the threat, Carter might have taken it seriously, but short of shoving their heads inside the shuttle's engine exhausts, there was realistically little the human traitors could do to stop them leaving. Even so, the man's angry face was pissing him off, and he'd been pissed off enough for one day, already.

Grabbing the controls, he thrust the shuttle toward the man, crushing the acolyte beneath their hull. Six others scrambled to get out of the way, but Carter turned his engines to face them and ramped up the throttle, while keeping their grav brake engaged to stunt any forward motion. The screams and cries of the men as they were consumed by a thousand-degree furnace were frightening, but mercifully short-lived.

"Was that thunder?" Carina asked, head lolling toward him.

"Yes, it's pretty wild out there," Carter said, aiming the shuttle back at the door. "We'll be out of the atmosphere soon enough, then it will be smooth sailing."

Carina smiled and her eyes fluttered then closed. At the same time, the garage door opened fully, and Carter punched the throttle, propelling them outside like a bullet from a gun. A pair of Aternien Khepri fighters was streaking across the horizon on the far side of the city, but otherwise it was eerily quiet. The gunfire was absent and many of the buildings that had been ablaze were now little more than smoldering carcasses.

If there is a storm brewing, then this is the calm before it… Carter mused.

JACAB bleeped urgently and the navigation array lit up with red markers. The Khepri fighters he'd seen on the horizon were turning toward them, and they weren't the only ones. Another patrol had diverted from outside the city. Four fighters was less than he was expecting, but still more than he needed.

"I guess we made an impression," Carter said to his bot. However, while he felt sure that Carina would have appreciated the sarcasm, his bot wasn't in a joking mood. "Can we just turn skyward and outburn them?"

JACAB shook from side to side and his response was relayed to the shuttle's comms screen. The short answer was no, but not because the Khepri fighters had the performance to pick them off, but because every surface-to-air weapon in the city would attack and obliterate them before they even reached cloud level.

"In that case, we'll have to get outside of the city first," Carter said, holding position and using the bulk of Enterprise stadium as a shield. "But I need to shake off these Khepri fighters first."

Widening the view on the nav map, Carter surveyed the city, paying particular attention to the tallest buildings and narrowest avenues. Then he spotted exactly what he was looking for.

"Hold onto your transistors, buddy, this is going to be a little bumpy…"

Carter rammed the throttle forward and shot over the

city, skimming across the tops of the buildings like a free runner. Before long, needles of particle energy were chasing them, crashing into the buildings, and racing past their hull so close that their brilliance flooded the cabin with light.

Carter had once admitted to Carina that he wasn't the best pilot in the galaxy, but he'd also never explained on what scale he was measuring himself. His old Master Navigator, Amaya Reid, had a superhuman level of spatial awareness. Combined with her cognitive interface that linked to a Longsword's navigation scanners, she could fly a ship like she was the ship. And while he lacked such natural prowess, when his augmented senses were ramped up to maximum, like they were then, he could still fly faster and harder than any human could ever hope to manage. What he didn't know was how his skills stacked up against the Aterniens who were chasing him.

Small arms fire from the surface joined the blasts of energy from the Khepri fighters, and soon the enemy ships had him zeroed in. Braking hard, Carter swung right, looping back the way he'd come and cutting so low past Enterprise Stadium that he could have reached out and touched it. The first pair of Khepri fighters followed, but pushed too hard, and one of the ships clipped the building. It spiraled out of control, taking its wingman with it.

"That's one patrol down," Carter said, speaking to his bot, even though the machine was too preoccupied to answer. Rolling the shuttle by ninety degrees, he pushed between two ad hoardings, before straightening up and aiming the nose of the boosted ship at his next target. Sure enough, the second flight of Aternien Khepri fighters was following in his engine wake. The Aternien fighters opened fire and a blast tagged the shuttle. Carter checked the damage readout and saw that life support had been knocked out. In other circumstances, this would have ended any hopes of a trip to space, but their battle uniforms would protect them both, at least for a time.

With particle blasts coming at them thick and fast, Carter kept his flying loose and squirrely to keep his Aternien pursuers guessing. A second volley barely missed their engines, peeling the paintwork off their starboard wing as the energy scorched past, but Carter only had to hold his course – and his nerve – for a few more seconds.

"Why are we still in the city?" Carina had woken up and tilted her seat forward enough to see sky instead of stars.

"Because we've still got company," Carter replied. As if to make his point, particle energy rippled over the top of their canopy, melting a railroad straight streak through the synthetic polymer. The canopy held, but had it been an inch closer, Carter knew that they would be breathing real air, rather than recycled oxygen from the shuttle's tanks.

"I don't know about you, but I've had enough Aternien company for one day," Carina said, much more alert.

Carter aimed the shuttle at mouth of a long underpass and increased speed. "Don't worry, I'm about to show them the door..."

Carina's still glassy eyes grew wide. "Carter, that's an underpass for ground vehicles, not shuttles!"

"I know," Carter grunted in reply. "Let's see if these metal-framed bastards have balls of steel too."

The shuttle rocketed through the tunnel like a high-velocity rifle bullet. Carina cried out and gripped the arms of her seat, but her screams of terror were consumed by the roar of the shuttle's engines, which were magnified tenfold due to the confined space. Suddenly, flames lit up the tunnel behind them, and Carter checked the navigation system and smiled. His pursuers were no longer in pursuit.

"I take it back, you are a good pilot," said Carina, collapsing in her chair.

"As with most things in life, you don't need to be the best." Carter looked over to his XO and smiled. "You just need to be better than the other guy."

Exiting the tunnel, Carter turned along the main highway out of the city and pushed the throttle to full. The shuttle punched through the sound barrier twice and soon they were beyond the city limits and flying over lush fields and grassy plains.

"Buddy, are we beyond the range of the Aternien surface to air weapons?" Carter said. His bot nodded, though he was also shaking. "Are you okay?"

JACAB merely narrowed his red eye at him, and turned away, huffily.

"I guess someone doesn't like your flying very much," Carina quipped.

It was good to hear his XO's humor again, though after her rude awakening and the shock of his daredevil maneuvers, she was looking frazzled. Carter's comp-slate updated with the all-clear from JACAB, though the bot had also highlighted two dozen other craft that had now been alerted to their location.

"I think we've outstayed our welcome," Carter said, pulling back on the controls and climbing vertically toward Terra Six's silver moon.

"We still have to get past the Aternien blockade," Carina pointed out.

"I've already thought of that," Carter replied. The planet's blue sky was giving way to black. "Our life support systems is shot, so you'll need to engage your head covering. It's going to get cold in here."

Carina nodded then activated the helmet device, which grew from her armor like ice crystals forming. With his XO all set, Carter activated his own head covering then set the shuttle on a course for the Dauntless. The Union flagship was holding position close to Terra Six's moon, but there were hundreds of enemy warships between them and their final destination. He couldn't fight them and couldn't outrun them, so there was only one thing he could do. Carter made sure they were pointed in the right direction, then shut down everything on the shuttle, and coasted.

TWENTY-EIGHT

SECRETS REVEALED

THE JOURNEY back to the fleet seemed to drag on endlessly, but despite the urgency of their mission, Carter couldn't risk drawing attention to the shuttle. This meant that drifting through the cosmos like space junk was the only way to get past the enemy blockage unseen.

"We're almost there, buddy," Carter said, speaking to his gopher, since Carina had long since slipped into unconsciousness inside the protective cocoon of her battle uniform. "In a few minutes, we'll be too far from the Aternien fleet for them to do anything about us."

JACAB bleeped and warbled, but the bot was distracted by the worsening condition of Major Larsen. Carter checked her vitals on his comp-slate to make sure she was still merely unconscious and not dead, but it turned out to be somewhere between the two. His XO had slipped into a coma.

"Buddy, is there anything more you can do for her?" Carter asked, but the bot merely shook from side to side, his eye looking down.

JACAB had spent the journey sitting in Carina's lap, using the heat from his power core to keep her warm, as well as prevent the insides of the shuttle from becoming a frostbitten nightmare. Carter's augmented and bio-engineered anatomy meant that he could survive in extremes of temperature that would kill a normal human within minutes. This included the ability to rapidly dissipate energy into the environment to ensure he didn't overheat. As such, he'd wrapped himself in emergency blankets and any other insulating material he could find, to increase his body temperature and force it to 'vent' the excess energy into the ship. In effect, he'd turned himself into a multi-kilowatt radiator. It was deeply uncomfortable, but necessary to ensure they didn't freeze to death before reaching the Dauntless.

"I imagine you'd make some bullshit remark about me being 'hot stuff', right now," Carter said, from beneath his mountain of coverings. "I can't believe I'm saying this, but I actually miss hearing your wiseass remarks and inappropriate jokes." He grunted a laugh. "At least you won't remember me admitting it."

JACAB warbled and bleeped then interfaced with the co-pilot's station. Carter checked his comp-slate and saw the message from his gopher stating that they were in the clear.

"Bring everything back online," Carter said, hurling the blankets off himself, like a boxer throwing off his robe before entering the ring.

The shuttle's main dashboard activated then the reactor stirred, and their engines began warming up. Before long, a comforting blast of hot air was spewing from the heater core, raising the icy internal temperature to something much more civilized. Carter continued working to reinitialize their systems one by one, then as soon as the scanner console flickered into life, an alarm began screaming at him like a strangled parrot. He checked the panel and recoiled from the screen; a squadron of Union frigates had flagged them as hostile and locked weapons.

"Raise the lead frigate on comms, buddy," Carter said to his gopher, trying to further accelerate the reboot cycle, since they didn't yet have full maneuverability. "And make sure we're transmitting a friendly ident."

A frantic babble of bleeps and warbles came from the bot and Carter read his comp-slate, feeling despair creep into his bones. Their comm system was still rebooting. "What about pulsing our running lights or using some other way to signal them?" he suggested.

JACAB's lights flashed chaotically as he considered the option, then the bot suddenly became motionless, and his red eye grew wide. Carter was about to grab the gopher and shake some sense back into him, when he realized why JACAB had frozen like a statue. The lead frigate had launched a missile, and it had them dead to rights.

"I'll try to evade it," Carter said, grabbing the controls, but the main engines were still down, and he knew that thrusters alone couldn't hope to dodge a missile.

With only a few seconds to act, Carter was about to resort to truly desperate measures, and attempt to shoot the warhead through the cockpit glass, when the missile exploded, peppering the shuttle with shrapnel. More alarms sounded and lights on the dashboard flashed red to indicate they'd taken damage, but miraculously, their already-battered hull remained intact.

"What happened?" Carter asked, flopping back into his

seat. Then the comm system cycled on and connected to the fleet channel.

"Master Commander Rose, is that you?" It was Admiral Krantz.

"Yes, yes, it is!" Carter blurted, unable to hide his joy and relief at hearing the admiral's voice. "Would you mind telling the rest of the fleet to stop shooting at us?"

"What are you doing on my shuttle, Commander?"

Carter winced. The admiral sounded furious.

"It's a long story, but right now I don't have time to explain. Major Larsen is injured and needs urgent medical attention. And there's another big problem we need to discuss."

"Carina is hurt?" the admiral said, oddly ignoring the second part of Carter's statement, while also referring to the major by her given name.

"Yes, she's in a coma but currently stable," Carter replied, setting aside the admiral's unusual reaction, and focusing on what mattered. "I suggest you have an emergency medical pod prepped and waiting for us once we've docked."

"You are cleared for hatch four, port-side," Admiral Krantz said. Though calm, Krantz couldn't hide the obvious stress indicators in her voice. "It is the closest dock to the surgical bay. I order you to hurry."

"Understood, Admiral, I'm going as fast as I can," Carter answered, though the comm channel had already gone dead. The engines cycled online, and he pushed the shuttle as hard as he could toward the Dauntless. At the same time, the Union's flagship advanced toward him, flanked by two heavy cruisers. He was thankful that the admiral was taking his XO's injury so seriously, but the use of her given name during their brief conversation was irregular, and this gnawed at him.

The docking maneuver went swiftly, and a hard seal was formed. Carter unfastened Carina's harness then scooped her out of her chair and hurried aft. A green pressure indicator was glowing above the door, and he hit the button to open the hatch, which swung back with a pneumatic hiss. Admiral Krantz and a medical team were already on the other side, and he rushed through, placing his XO gently inside the waiting medical pod.

"She took a blast from an Aternien particle rifle at close range," Carter said, ignoring the admiral to inform the medical team about Carina's injury. "Her right lung collapsed, and she was treated with Hemofoam, and a bunch of meds that my gopher can transmit to your comp-slates."

"How is she even still alive?" the surgeon said, as the other doctors worked on Carina, and hurried the pod toward the surgical bay. "A hit at that range should have killed her."

"Her battle uniform protected her to a large degree," Carter replied, while running alongside the stretcher. "But you won't be able to cut through it." He touched his finger to the collar of Carina's uniform and drew his finger down to her sternum to unlock the jacket and allow it to be removed. "She lost consciousness and dropped into a coma a couple of hours ago, but she's alive, and I expect her to stay that way."

The surgeon, who held the rank of Commander, glared at Carter like she was about to tear him a new one, then Admiral Krantz rolled in like a hurricane.

"Doctor, you are to do everything within your power to save this patient, and that extends to the use of post-human technology, if necessary, is that clear?" The doctor opened her mouth to protest, but Krantz's bark was easily as strong as her bite. "Is that clear, Commander?"

"Yes, Admiral," the surgeon replied, meekly.

"Consult with Master Commander Rose, if necessary," Krantz added. "He will be with me on the bridge if you need him."

The team reached the surgical bay and the pod containing Carina was sped inside. Within seconds, she was in theatre and the doors were closed. He hated being shut out; it made him feel even more helpless, but barging in and watching over the surgeon's shoulder would not help his XO.

JACAB then hummed up beside Carter and aimed his red eye toward the closed-off surgical bay, before releasing a sorrowful warble. Carter rested what he hoped was a comforting hand on his gopher, but said nothing, since he didn't want to make empty promises.

"She is my niece."

Carter was turned around by the sudden and unexpected admission. "I'm sorry, what?"

"You are wondering why I am so invested in saving the life of Major Larsen," Krantz answered. "I'm sure my slip during our earlier conversation made you suspicious, so I am choosing to make you aware now."

Carter stared at her blank-faced. "I knew there was something between you two, but I honestly never expected that."

"It is not something I publicize," came the stern reply. "Carina did not want to risk being given special treatment on account of her relationship to me. Her mother and I were never especially close, and even as children, we argued more than most siblings. I joined the Union military when I was eighteen and didn't see or hear from my sister for more than fifteen years, until I learned of her death. Carina was already seven years old by then."

While they'd been talking, JACAB had slipped away and was now hovering above the admiral's head, stealthily scanning her at a safe distance. Carter knew what his gopher was doing but was too wrapped up in the admiral's story to dwell on the possibility that Krantz might be an imposter.

"She never told me any of this," he said, more than a little taken aback. "In fact, I hadn't even thought to ask her anything about her family. I guess I've been remiss in that regard."

"She prefers not to talk about that time, much like me," Krantz replied, sounding suddenly like a normal human being, instead of the hard-nosed and pigheaded admiral Carter was used to dealing with. "The accident killed her entire immediate family, so I was all she had left."

"She lived with you, since age seven?" Carter asked, and Krantz nodded. He blew out an exaggerated sigh. "Damn, that must have been hard."

"Sometimes, though in many ways, it would have been much harder without her," Krantz replied. The admiral suddenly turned her attention to JACAB, and she scowled at the bot, who meekly retreated, looking like a scolded child.

"What is that infernal machine doing?" Krantz snapped. "It's been buzzing around my head like a bluebottle for the last minute."

JACAB hummed to his side and Carter checked his comp-slate for the results of the admiral's bio-scan.

"It's okay, Admiral, you'll be pleased to learn that you're human."

Krantz scowled at him; it was remarkably Carina-like in

its intensity, and now he understood why. "Of course, I am human, Commander. You'd better explain yourself."

"We can walk and talk," Carter said, ushering Krantz toward the bridge. "There's a lot I need to explain."

"Yes, there is," the admiral replied, ominously. "Including why you stole my shuttle and disobeyed my direct orders."

"You can court-marshal me later," Carter said, in a dangerously dismissive tone, given the admiral's pugnacious mood. "But right now, the population of the entire planet is in danger of being wiped out."

Krantz was suitably cowed by Carter's statement, and en route to the bridge, he showed the admiral the scan data of imposter Colonel Bell and explained how the Aternien spy had managed to slip by undetected. The realization that there could be potentially dozens, hundreds or even thousands more Aternien infiltrators embedded in the Union hit her as hard as he expected it would. Then he had to tell her about the doomsday weapon and what Damien Morrow had revealed. By the time they set foot on the bridge of the Dauntless, Admiral Krantz had gained several more gray hairs on her head.

"Morrow lied to you once, so how can you be certain this doomsday device is not another fabrication?" Krantz said, adopting a stately posture in the middle of the command deck. Carter noticed that everyone on the bridge was sitting a little more upright since she'd entered.

"Truth be told, Admiral, I've had doubts about myself," Carter admitted. "But after Morrow lured me to Enterprise Stadium for the duel with the Overseer, he specifically said that the virus and the weapon were real. At that point, he'd already snared me, so I don't see why he'd lie again."

Krantz thought for a moment then turned to the ship's ops and science station. "Show me the locations of any objects or structures the Aterniens have landed on the planet, since their invasion."

The officer responded then worked his station for a few moments before a map of Terra Six appeared as a hologram in front of Krantz. Pallas City and Enterprise City were the population centers, and both had been the focus of the Aternien invasion. However, the enemy had landed all over the planet's surface, making it almost impossible to narrow down potential locations for the doomsday weapon.

"Focus in on Enterprise City, around the stadium," Carter said.

Krantz nodded to the ops officer and the display updated.

"The Aterniens built an interstellar comms buoy beneath the stadium, but it's not showing on your map," Carter said, prodding the holo with his finger. "If your scans missed that, who knows what else they missed?"

JACAB bleeped, which made Krantz jump. She had evidently forgotten the bot was still with them.

"What's up, buddy, do you have an idea?" Carter asked.

JACAB nodded then transmitted his thoughts to Carter's comp-slate. He studied the bot's suggestion, though the finer details were lost on him.

"What did the machine say?" Krantz asked, still regarding JACAB with suspicion.

"It's a whole load of science gobbledygook that I could really use my Master Operator to decipher…"

"A Master Operator who is conspicuous by his absence," Krantz cut in, eyebrows raised.

"That's another story," Carter said, sheepishly.

Krantz snorted then nodded toward his comp-slate. "Go on…"

"Anyway, the short version is that JACAB believes he can use his analysis of the Aternien comms device to reveal more objects on the planet," Carter continued. "If the comms unit was important enough to keep hidden, then it's no stretch to think they'd do the same for a doomsday device."

Krantz nodded. "Very well, plug your bot into the ops computer and have it run the necessary scans."

The operations officer jerked back, and Carter noticed a half-dozen other officers do the same. "Admiral, is it safe to allow that machine to interface with the ship?" the operations officer spoke up.

Carter looked at the man. As a senior lieutenant, he was probably no more than twenty-five or twenty-six years old and had almost certainly never seen combat before that day. He had to admire the man's balls for questioning an admiral on the bridge of her ship, but he expected the hairdryer treatment that he would receive later would stymie any future outbursts.

"Interface the bot with the ops computer, Lieutenant," Krantz repeated. Each word was like the stab of a dagger, and this time the lieutenant did not answer back.

Carter nodded to his gopher and JACAB hovered over to the ops console, bleeping merrily to himself in response to the admiral sticking up for him. The ops officer stood close by and watched the bot like a hawk, clearly uneasy with an external computer system taking control of his station. Carter stifled a laugh as the officer tried to make a suggestion, only to receive a loud electronic raspberry from JACAB in reply.

Soon, the holo image updated, removing all of the structures except for two. One was sited directly over Enterprise Stadium, where the secret comms device had been built, and the other was located in a hangar in an industrial spaceport on the outskirts of Pallas City.

"Lieutenant Commander Trevilian, do we have any assets in the vicinity of that spaceport?" Krantz asked, directing the question to the tactical officer.

"Yes, Admiral, the remains of Seventh Battalion, Terra Five are camped ten miles away. They have recon drones listed amongst their assets."

"Send them in, now," Krantz barked. "Everything they have, all at once. We need eyes inside that hangar, if only for a few seconds."

The officer acknowledged the command and set to work. The next few minutes remained tense, and Carter found that his thoughts were dwelling more on Carina than on the hasty recon op the admiral had just ordered. He used one of the ship's consoles to interface with the medical system, but his XO was still in theatre and there were no updates.

"The battalion commander reports that the recon drones have come under heavy fire from concealed anti-aircraft positions." Trevilian announced.

The update from the tactical officer refocused Carter's mind, and he looked at the main viewer, hoping to see a camera feed from inside the hangar.

"We managed to get two drones into position before they were destroyed," the tactical officer added.

"On screen..." Krantz said, waving the holo map away.

The viewscreen activated and everyone on the bridge

went silent as images from inside the hangar were shown. They lasted for only a few seconds, before squads of Immortals destroyed the drones, but it was enough to confirm there was something inside.

"Is that all?" Krantz said, disappointed. "We can't make any determinations from that."

"I think we can, Admiral," Carter said. "Go to frame 179,765 and hold the image."

Krantz nodded and the order was carried out. The frame appeared on the viewer.

Carter stepped closer. "Enhance the figure in the lower right quadrant, at roughly 75, 25."

The image zoomed in and enhanced. Carter turned to Krantz, and it was clear she recognized the importance of the figure too. It was the Aternien Grand Vizier.

"Buddy, can you get a reading on that hangar?" Carter called over to his bot, who was still interfaced at ops. "Anything that might tell us what that object is?"

JACAB warbled and nodded then Carter realized his bot had already run the analysis and sent it to his comp-slate. He raised his wrist, read the data, and sighed.

"That's our bomb, admiral."

An alert chimed from the tactical station and Lieutenant Commander Trevilian leapt into action. The man's heart rate doubled in an instant.

"Admiral, the Aternien fleet is reconfiguring," Trevilian reported. "They are assuming battle formations and advancing."

"I think we got their attention," Carter grunted, returning to Krantz's side. "It's now or never, Admiral," he added, casting her a sideways glance. "We either throw everything we have at that weapon or accept that Terra Six is lost."

TWENTY-NINE
BAIT AND SWITCH

"LIEUTENANT COMMANDER TREVILIAN, signal the fleet to execute operation Blockade Runner, on my mark," Admiral Krantz said. "And get me Strike Force Sigma on the viewer."

The admiral had made her decision without any doubt or dithering; a trait that Carter admired. There was no question in her mind of allowing Terra Six to fall, despite being opposed by an Aternien force that was unquestionably stronger.

"The fleet has responded and is standing ready, Admiral," Trevilian replied.

"Execute, Mr. Trevilian."

The order was given, and the Union fleet began organizing into taskforces, with the Dauntless at the center.

"I have Captain Rankin for you, ma'am," Trevilian added.

Krantz nodded then the viewer switched to display the unsmiling face of a warship commander. Carter could tell by the tautness of the man's expression and the way he carried himself that this captain had seen action before. On that front, he was a rarity inside the Union military.

"Captain Rankin, I have sent you details of a priority target," Krantz began. "You are ordered to destroy it at all costs."

"I understand, Admiral," the captain replied, coolly. Rankin hadn't even batted an eyelid in response to the, 'at all costs' part of the command. "My strike force is in position. I will report back when the mission has been accomplished."

The link was terminated at the receiving end, but Krantz seemed satisfied that her officer understood the task. Whether Captain Rankin could complete it was another matter.

"Do you trust him to get the job done?" Carter asked.

Krantz shifted uncomfortably on the spot. "Sigma is the best we have, Commander." She then reconsidered her statement. "At least, they are the best we have available right now."

It wasn't really an answer to his question, but Carter understood the admiral's meaning, all the same.

A battle management console then rose out of the deck in front of the admiral and a holographic tactical map was displayed high above it. Between the map and the console, Carter was able to quickly piece together what 'Operation Blockade Runner' involved, and Captain Rankin's part in it.

The bulk of the Union ships had adopted a tight conical formation, like the pressure wave of a cannon shell, with the Dauntless and other heavy cruisers at the point. Behind this protective front wave was the strike force led by Captain Rankin.

"You plan to punch a needle through the enemy lines

then inject Rankin into orbit above Pallas City, so that his strike force can launch on the weapon?" Carter asked.

"Very good, Commander," Krantz replied, without taking her eyes off the battle console.

"It's a gutsy move," Carter admitted, with admiration, and no small measure of unease. "It might be enough to get them through, but we could lose a third of the fleet in the process, maybe more."

"My projection was thirty-four percent," Krantz said, still without taking her eyes off her console.

Carter nodded. She had clearly devised the contingency plan some time in advance, and trusted that the situation would not become dire enough to need it. Though Krantz had been wrong about that part, at least she had been prepared for the worst.

"Admiral, we have engaged the Aterniens," Trevilian said. "They are already adapting to our strategy and are focusing fire on the spearhead of our fleet."

"On screen," Krantz replied.

A wide, panoramic view of the battle appeared in front of them, with a dozen inset displays showing specific engagements in more detail. Flashes of particle energy were crisscrossing space like a laser light show, and already the Union was taking losses. For every ship that fell, another from further out in the cone moved in to plug the gap. The problem was that the Aterniens were creating holes faster than they could plug them.

"Continue on course," Krantz said, as the Dauntless also began taking fire. "Focus only on the Aternien ships that break our line and target Strike Force Sigma. Captain Rankin must reach his objective."

The tactical officer acknowledged the order briskly and

continued working, while Carter concentrated on the battle console and tactical map. The Aternien redeployment, which had happened before Krantz had even executed Operation Blockade Runner, had focused their most powerful Khopesh-class Destroyers at the center. These vessels were ignoring any attempt by the Union to draw them away, and to Carter, this suggested only one thing.

"They already know your plan," he grunted, casting another sideways glance to Admiral Krantz. "Someone has been passing information to the enemy."

"So it would seem," the flag officer replied, irritably. "That is a problem for another time, however. We must push through."

This time Carter didn't nod his agreement. It was true that the Aternien spies already nestled within the fleet couldn't be rooted out before the conclusion of the battle, but that didn't mean staying the course was their best option.

"Pushing on won't work, Admiral," Carter said, offering his opinion discreetly, so as not to openly challenge Krantz on her own ship. "We need to adapt a new strategy on the fly. One that the Aterniens, and even your own taskforce commanders, won't expect."

Carter accessed the battle management console and highlighted the location of an Aternien formation. That he had done this without asking Krantz's permission appeared to irk her. She was glowering at him and had puckered her lips, presumably to stop herself from chewing his impertinent ear off.

"That's Markus Aternus' ship, the Mesek-tet," Carter said, choosing to pretend he hadn't noticed Krantz's dagger eyes. "That Solar Barque and its Royal Court escorts are the most valuable pieces on the board, but they've held back to observe from a distance. These aristocrats prefer not to sully themselves with actual fighting if they can help it."

"They are also nowhere near where our fleet needs to be, Commander," Krantz replied. "What is it you are suggesting?"

"If we attack the Mesek-tet, the Aterniens will rally to protect their god-king." Carter continued, making his point quickly to ensure Krantz's temper didn't boil over. "But to pose a credible threat, the entire Union fleet must redeploy."

"How will that help us destroy the doomsday weapon?" Krantz asked.

"If the Aterniens believe that we've abandoned the mission to destroy the biogenic weapon, and are targeting the Mesek-tet instead, it will throw them into turmoil," Carter continued. "We advance in stages, using short-range soliton warp jumps to drop in dead ahead of the Mesek-tet. First, we send a hundred ships, then another hundred, and keep building until the Aterniens panic and run to their leader's aid."

Krantz was silent for a moment as she considered his idea, then raised an important point. "But even if we kill the god-king, won't he just be reborn on New Aternus, or someplace else?" Krantz said. "If we can't truly harm him then we're not a threat."

Carter had already thought about this, and while his answer was supposition, he was confident he was right. "If mere humans beat Markus Aternus, then it would destroy the entire 'god-king' mythos that his rule and his empire is built on," Carter replied. "I've witnessed first-hand how the stain of defeat can undermine these high-ranking Aterniens. The god-king couldn't survive the shame and humiliation of losing a battle. He won't risk it. I know he won't."

The admiral was silent again, and even the thump of Aternien particle blasts hammering into the ship didn't rouse her from her deliberations. Carter knew not to push her, despite feeling the urge to do so. Krantz had to come to the decision on her own, one way or another.

"Go on…" the admiral finally said, and Carter knew he'd hooked his fish.

"As soon as the Aterniens break ranks, the Dauntless and Strike Force Sigma will turn and burn for Pallas orbit, running our engines hotter than the fires of hell," Carter continued. "Even Aternien warp drives have a cool down period before they can be used again, which will buy us some time. Hopefully, enough that we can launch a bombardment against the weapon."

The deck of the Dauntless shook hard and the crew were feverishly working to shore up the damage. Carter reviewed the battle map and saw that they'd already lost more than fifteen percent of the fleet. Operation Blockade Runner was going to fail faster and harder than even the admiral's pessimistic estimate had predicted.

"Admiral, we can't sustain this level of fire for much longer," Trevilian reported, and the deck shook again as if to highlight his point. "Captain Rankin also reports his strike force is taking heavy damage."

The voice of the Lieutenant Commander at tactical had been unwavering up until that point, but Carter could sense that the pressure was finally getting to the man.

"I'm also picking up boarding pods in flight," Trevilian added. "They are targeting the Dauntless and Strike Force Sigma."

Carter instinctively placed his hand on the grip of his cutlass. Boarding pods were compact shuttles that were fast, maneuverable, and hard to shoot down. Each was capable of deploying a team of five Aternien Immortals inside a Union ship. It often didn't require more than fifteen or twenty to commandeer a vessel then use it against its own forces, typically by ramming it into nearby ships. The Immortals on board would all be killed too, though their souls would survive to fight another day.

"New orders," Krantz said, while using her long fingers to hammer commands into the battle console. She then turned to face her tactical officer. "All ships are to break now and attack the Mesek-tet. Taskforces twenty through twenty-four are to make an immediate, short-range soliton warp and engage the enemy. Further task forces are to follow, as per my orders."

Trevilian looked stunned, but unlike the greener lieutenant at operations, the officer didn't question the command. "Yes, ma'am, the order has been relayed," the tactical officer replied, his voice shaky. "All ships have reported in and are making course corrections now."

Carter stroked his silver beard and watched the Union fleet redeploy against the Mesek-tet. The Aterniens didn't react, though Carter could practically hear the transistors fizzing inside the neuromorphic brains of the High Overseers, as they tried to work out what the hell the Union was doing.

"Admiral, the lead task forces report that they will require a minimum of four minutes to compute the soliton warp parameters." Trevilian called out.

Carter turned to JACAB who was still loitering by the ops console. "I think we can help to speed that up a bit, can't we buddy?"

JACAB warbled then saluted with a maneuvering fin,

before taking over the operations console, much to the annoyance of the lieutenant who was supposed to be in charge of it. Within a matter of seconds, Trevilian's console chimed with an update.

"Soliton warp parameters received…" Trevilian said, frowning at his console in disbelief. "I have forwarded them to the fleet. Task Forces twenty through twenty-four are preparing to jump."

The viewscreen updated and Carter watched the first group of warships blink away then reappear instantly in front of the division of Royal Court destroyers. The elite vessels responded by closing ranks and protecting their god-king.

"Task forces twenty-five through twenty-nine are away…" Trevilian updated.

The second task group blinked into position and joined in the attack, and suddenly the Aternien fleet sprang into action. The Khopesh destroyers that had been bludgeoning through the middle of the Union formation broke off and jumped away, followed quickly by squadron after squadron of enemy warships.

"It's working," Carter said, his senses tingling. "They're taking the bait."

"We're also being massacred!" Krantz said. She was looking at the holo map, which was showing the Mesek-tet and Royal Court ships tearing through the Union taskforces with frightening ease. It was like a twenty-first century naval armada fighting ships from the age of sail. "We have to alter course and make our run, before there's no-one left."

"Not yet, Admiral," Carter cut in. He was pushing his luck by telling Krantz what to do, but ranks aside, he was more experienced by far. "They need to believe we've abandoned the planet to its fate, in favor of killing their king. Our losses are necessary to maintain that illusion."

Krantz clenched her jaw then leant on the battle console and began drumming her fingers on it. Carter almost remarked how a certain relative of the admiral's often did the same thing but thought better of it.

"Boarding pods have already breached ten ships, and are continuing to penetrate the fleet," Trevilian called out. "Our close-range guns are struggling to take them down out. I estimate impact on the Dauntless in sixty seconds."

"Prepare to repel boarders, and get a trooper squad in here, now," Krantz called out, before turning back to Carter. "We're out of time, Commander. We attack now, or not at all."

Carter studied the battle map. More than half of their fleet had already jumped away, and the Aterniens were following in even greater numbers, desperate to protect their god-king. His senses told him they had a chance.

"Turn and burn, Admiral," Carter said, fixing Krantz with a determined stare. "We'll get one shot. Let's make it count."

THIRTY

STAND YOUR GROUND

"HELM, resume course for Terra Six at flank speed," Admiral Krantz called out, barking the order at the pilot, and making the ensign literally jump out of her seat. Spinning on her heels the admiral then aimed her index finger at the tactical station, pointing it like a pistol. "Mr. Trevilian, have Strike Force Sigma follow us in. Hell, have them beat us there, if they can. Full power burn. Everything we've got!"

"Yes, Admiral!" The tactical officer replied, sweat pouring from his brow.

Suddenly, a squad of soldiers piled onto the bridge, sealing the hatches behind them, before assuming defensive positions. Carter surveyed their drawn, pallid expressions, and almost all of them looked ready to piss their pants, but he had no intention of relying on Union troopers to protect the ship. He'd single-handedly cut down more Immortals than any man or woman living or dead, and he fully intended to add to his tally. Carter drew his sword and engaged his buckler, and suddenly all eyes were on him.

"When the Aterniens break in, stay behind me," Carter said to the admiral.

"I do not cower from my enemy, Master Commander Rose," Krantz hissed, drawing her sidearm. "Nor do I take orders from you."

"Call it whatever you like, Admiral, so long as you stay at my back," Carter countered. He didn't care that she was an admiral; he'd be damned if Clara Krantz would die on the bridge of her own ship on his watch.

Enemy warriors began cutting through the hatches and Carter flicked the switch on the handle of his sword, sending plasma energy coursing along the blade. The rhythmic thump, thump, thump of Aternien footsteps began drumming through the deck, and Carter's augments kicked in to make him battle ready.

"Whatever happens, stand your ground!" Carter called out, his powerful voice filling the bridge of the ship as if it were amplified through every speaker and console. "Immortals are weakest at the base of their necks. Don't waste ammo shooting at the body because your gauss weapons won't penetrate their armor."

There were a few scattered replies of, "yes, sir…" but Carter doubted if half of the terrified officers had even heard him. Suddenly, the doors on either side of the bridge blew inward and smoke filled the room. Carter dropped to a crouch, dragging Krantz down with him, much to her irritation, then particle blasts flashed through the smog. Four soldiers were hit and went down straight away, too dumbstruck to get out of the line of fire, but soon the rattle of gauss rifles added to the frenetic commotion of combat. Atmosphere processors cleared the smoke, and Carter got his first good look at his enemy. Ten Immortals had entered, five from each door at the aft of the command center, and none had yet seen him. That was about to change.

"Stay down, Admiral," Carter said, speaking to his superior like she was an officer under his command. "I'll deal with this."

Krantz looked furious at being spoken to like a first-year cadet, and Carter knew he'd get a roasting after the battle, assuming she survived. His mission now was to ensure she did.

Pushing away from the battle console, Carter soared toward the Immortals like a cruise missile. His senses and augments were fully primed, and his body was operating at peak efficiency, providing him with an explosive level of power no Immortal could hope to match.

Carter ran down the front rank of Immortals like a nuclear-powered linebacker, then unleashed his energized blade with unrelenting fury. He cut through the Aterniens like he was deadheading daisies, leaving a trail of severed limbs scattered on the deck in his wake. The rear rank opened fire, and Carter was blasted at close range, but his buckler and armor absorbed the energy, allowing him to unleash another devastating assault.

With the first wave cut down, he found himself confronted by a Warden, but the Aternien's enhanced reactions couldn't stop Carter from smashing the guard of his cutlass into the warrior's face. The Warden staggered back but recovered fast and thrust his bayonet into Carter's side. The brief stab of pain only served to enhance his strength, and he swung so hard that he split the Immortal down the center, like he was peeling a banana.

Battling onward, Carter cut down two more Immortals and fought his way to the east hatch. A particle blast cooked the flesh on his thigh and a second slammed into his gut, but his armor held and so did his resolve.

"Hold this corridor!" Carter bellowed, grabbing a stunned Union corporal and shoving the man toward the hatch. "Aim for their heads and don't stop firing until these so-called Immortals are scrap at your feet!"

The combination of his rallying cry and his savage display of swordsmanship had the desired effect of boosting the troopers' morale, and for the first time they began to fight as a unit, with the belief they could win. However, Carter knew they had a long way to go yet.

Suddenly his sixth sense warned him of mortal danger, and Carter ducked and covered his head as particle blasts raced along the corridor. His buckler absorbed some of the energy, and he moved into cover to avoid further shots, but not everyone on the bridge had been so alert, or so lucky. Lieutenant Commander Trevilian was down, his chest hollowed out by an Aternien particle blast. Carter pulled the man into cover, but Trevilian's eyes were staring blankly into empty space, the man's expression still conveying the shock he must have experienced as his heart literally melted inside him.

Glancing across to the battle console, Carter saw that Admiral Krantz had ignored his advice to stay down and was engaging the enemy. The deck around her was on fire and flames were licking at her feet, but Krantz showed no sign of letting up her assault. He admired her courage, even though it was liable to get her killed.

Racing out from behind cover, Carter deflected three particle blasts with his buckler then severed an Immortal in half above the waist, before ducking behind the operations station. He'd secured one corridor, but the second was still unguarded, and Immortals were streaming inside like a stampede of cattle. Carter looked for JACAB, but his gopher had smartly hidden himself inside a maintenance crawlspace.

"Stay there, buddy, I'll have you out in a moment," Carter said to the bot, by way of reassurance. JACAB nodded and warbled something in reply, but he could barely hear it.

Steeling himself again, Carter charged at the fresh influx of Immortals, catching them by surprise, and hacking down four before taking a solid blast to the chest. It was a fluke shot, but it managed to defeat his battle uniform and scorch his flesh. Sensation blockers numbed the pain, but he knew it would hurt like hell in the aftermath.

More blasts flew at him, but Carter dodged and weaved a chaotic course toward the remaining invaders. Two Immortals came at him with bayonets, and for a few seconds his cutlass clashed against Aternien metal, as he parried and counterattacked, but the ferocity of his strikes quickly overpowered his opponents and left them mutilated at his feet.

Pulling up behind the west door, Carter drew his 57-EX and waited. Another boarding pod had connected a few seconds earlier, and the Immortals were storming his way, expecting to find the bridge already under Aternien command. Instead, the warriors walked into a barrage of .50 caliber armor piercing bullets that tore through their armor like it was made from egg crates.

With the immediate threat diminished, Carter took a moment to check his comp-slate. Only three Immortals remained on their deck, and all the other boarding pods had been destroyed. *Three more Immortals, and we're in the clear.* Carter told himself, urging his body and mind to stay strong.

The last of the Immortals overpowered the guards at the east hatch and burst inside the bridge, particle rifles blazing. Two were heading for Admiral Krantz, while the third – a Warden – came for him, and the skilled Aternien warrior didn't even have his finger on the trigger.

This bastard has the arrogance to take me on hand-to-hand… Carter thought, flourishing his sword, and beckoning his opponent on.

The Warden slashed his energized bayonet at Carter and split open his battle uniform from collar to belt. A swift follow-up glanced his hip and he twisted just in time to avoid a thrust to his heart, before catching the barrel of the weapon and immobilizing it. The Warden's glowing, beautiful eyes grew wide, but the Aternien barely had a second to contemplate his mistake before Carter cleaved the warrior's head from his body and left him in ruin on the deck.

Only two Immortals now remained, and they had Admiral Krantz pinned down. Finally, she had taken his advice and gotten into cover, but the battle console was being blasted to shreds and Carter knew it wouldn't protect her for much longer. He put on a burst of speed and attacked the closest of the two Immortals, but the Aternien had seen him coming and dodged his cut. The butt of a particle rifle was smashed across his jaw and for a moment Carter was dazed; long enough for the Immortal to spin around and thrust his bayonet into his gut.

With lightning reactions, Carter grabbed and crushed the barrel of the rifle at the exact same moment the warrior squeezed the trigger. The weapon exploded, taking the

Immortal's arms with it, and blowing Carter to the far side of the bridge. His body thudded through a wall panel, leaving him tangled in the wires and conduits behind it.

Admiral Krantz, two troopers and the operations lieutenant all ravaged the Immortal with gunfire, but the slugs merely ricocheted off the Aternien's golden armor and did little to stay his advance. The soldiers were killed first then the admiral screamed as her right arm was disintegrated below the elbow. She went down, and the Immortal stabbed the lieutenant through the heart, before turning its weapon on Krantz, but the warrior would not get a chance to pull the trigger.

Carter powered his scorched body to his feet and hurled his energized cutlass at the warrior with all his augmented might. The weapon spun through the air so fast it looked like a comet's tail, before impaling itself through the warrior's back all the way to the hilt. The Immortal was confused at first and tried to dislodge the weapon, before dropping to its knees as its body was melted from the inside out.

Krantz was now standing, weapon in hand. Carter expected her to look afraid, but instead she looked furious. Pressing the barrel of her pistol to the back of the Immortal's neck, she fired until the magazine was empty then tossed the weapon onto the deck beside the fallen Aternien soldier.

There was a cry of, "Bridge secured!" from a sergeant who was pressed up against the west hatch, clinging to the frame like his life depended on it. Carter checked his comp-slate and confirmed that the Aternien assault had been repelled, but as battered and beleaguered as they were, they still had a job to do.

"Master Commander Rose, assume the tactical station,"

Krantz ordered. "I will handle operations." The admiral then turned to the helm, but their pilot was dead, splayed out over her console with a dozen burns cratering her back. Krantz looked defeated, but Carter had an idea.

"JACAB, are you still with us?" Carter said, speaking into his comp-slate.

A distant warble echoed around the bridge, then the bot hummed out of a service crawlspace and flew in front of Carter, before saluting with a maneuvering fin.

"Do you know how to fly this bucket, buddy?"

JACAB shrugged them hummed across to the navigation station. He grabbed the dead pilot with a claw, dragged the body out of the seat then set himself down on the console.

"I'll take that as a yes," Carter said. If the situation hadn't been so dire, he might have laughed. The tactical station chimed an alert, and he ran to it, trying to ignore Trevilian's blood, which was splattered over the panels like a gruesome Jackson Pollock.

"Admiral, Strike Force Sigma is in range and has a target lock," Carter reported. "I'm ordering the attack." He was about to give Captain Rankin the green light when the tactical console lit up with alerts from the planet. Carter scanned the data and cursed under his breath. They were already too late.

"I'm picking up massive energy readings over Pallas City," Carter said, delivering the news to a sullen-looking Admiral Krantz. "The Aterniens have activated their weapon."

Krantz stood tall then forced down a hard swallow. "On screen…"

Carter entered the commands and the viewscreen switched to an aerial view of Pallas City. Thousands of vapor trails were snaking across the sky, heading in all directions. Some remained low, while others arced higher, adopting trajectories similar to an intercontinental ballistic missile. Then one of the projectiles burst open directly over the city and a swarm of drones flowed out from it like a murmuration of starlings.

"Damn it!" Krantz roared, hammering her fists against the operations console. Then her resolve hardened. "We launch the strike anyway. There is still a chance we could prevent some of the virus carriers from being deployed."

Carter heard the admiral, but his senses had latched onto another danger, yet it was elusive, like the memory of a dream.

"Commander Rose, did you hear me?" Krantz called out. "Order Captain Rankin to launch!"

Carter's senses sharpened, and the danger he'd perceived became clearer in his mind. He swept the planetary launch program off his console and scanned for soliton warp signatures to confirm his hunch, before releasing another bitter curse into the air.

"JACAB, swing us around, and spool up the soliton warp drive, now!" Carter called out to his bot. "And warn Strike Force Sigma to do the same."

"Commander, what the hell is going on?" Krantz snarled, marching toward him. "I remind you this is my ship, and my fleet!"

"I'm sorry, Admiral, but there won't be a ship soon, not if we don't get the hell out of here!"

A warp distortion rippled through space a few kilometers from the Dauntless, and shrill alarms sounded across all stations. Carter focused the viewscreen directly aft then watched as the Mesek-tet and its seven Royal Court escorts jumped in behind them. Strike Force Sigma engaged the new enemy vessels, but their cannon fire and torpedoes crumpled against the Aternien flagship's near impenetrable armor. Krantz could only stand and stare in disbelief.

"It's unkillable..." Krantz said, in awe of the god-king's seemingly unconquerable power.

"No, it's not," Carter fired back, growling the words. "But today, the god-king wins."

The Aternien flagship returned fire, splitting Captain Rankin's cruiser in half and reducing two of its escorts to molten slag, before the Royal Court Khopesh Destroyers swooped in behind to devastate what remained of the strike force. Carter gritted his teeth and checked the status of the warp drive, knowing they would be next.

"Buddy, I need you to get us out of here, right now..." Carter said, resisting the urge to yell the order at the top of his lungs.

The bot squawked and Carter heard the distant beat of the soliton engine spinning up deep within the ship. *Come on!...* he said to himself, silently urging the Dauntless to move faster. Never more than now had he wished he was on the bridge of his Longsword. The Galatine was their only hope against the might of the Mesek-tet, but first he had to make it back to her alive.

"This is Admiral Krantz to all ships," Krantz said, calling out on a fleet-wide channel. "Fall back and rendezvous at position Zulu. Repeat, all ships fall back and rendezvous immediately at position Zulu."

Krantz closed the channel just as the last of the ten strike cruisers was obliterated by the Mesek-tet, leaving only the Dauntless behind. Carter couldn't know for certain, but he felt sure that the god-king had intentionally left them till last.

Perhaps Markus Aternus knew that he was on-board, or perhaps the god-king just took pleasure in toying with his prey. Either way, the leader of the Aternien Empire would not claim his scalp today.

The Mesek-tet's guns flashed and beams of particle energy powerful enough to melt their hull to slag hurtled toward them but hit only empty space. The Dauntless had already jumped. The battle for Terra Six had been lost, but Master Commander Carter Rose was far from beaten.

THIRTY-ONE
I DON'T LIKE LOSING

CARTER RUSHED through the door of the medical center, knocking into a nurse en route and almost sending her flying into a storage cupboard. He caught the woman's shoulders, apologized profusely to her, then continued inside. Understandably, the station's medical center was teeming with the most seriously injured crew from all the Union vessels that had returned from Terra Six.

"Major Carina Larsen," Carter said, grabbing a doctor by the arm and holding him in place with the strength of Hercules. "Can you tell me where she is?"

"Do you mind?" the medic snapped, in the high-handed manner than people of a certain social class tend to use with those who they consider beneath them. "Enquiries should be made at the reception desk. Now, release me!"

Carter had left his social graces behind on the Dauntless, after the near-crippled warship had docked at Forward Operating Base Zulu, a station between Terra Six and the inner union worlds. "Look, doc, I'm in no mood to be messed around," he said, pulling the medic closer. "Where is

Major Carina Larsen? She was recently transferred over from the Dauntless."

The man considered protesting again, then Carter physically lifted the doctor so that only the tips of his shoes remained on the ground, and the medic rapidly backed down.

"Bay seventeen, east wing," the doctor blurted out.

Carter dropped the man and smoothed down his coat. "Thanks, doc," he said, feeling immediately guilty for manhandling him. "Sorry for rushing you. It's been a hell of a day, you know?"

The doctor stormed off, muttering something about post-humans under his breath, but Carter didn't care. He was already heading in the other direction, like a runaway steam train. Other medical staff wisely kept out of his way, presumably having witnessed his brusque handling of the doctor, and not wishing to receive the same treatment.

The medical bay was a literal maze, and Carter found that knowing Carina's bay number wasn't as much of a help as he'd hoped. Finally, after several minutes of bustling along halls and bursting into the wrong rooms, he eventually found her. She was unconscious and hooked up to more monitors that were required to pilot a battlecruiser. The devices all bleeped softly, showing different arrangements of swirling patterns and waving lines.

Carter looked at her prone, fragile body, then was bombarded by strange and unwanted sensations that caused his gut to churn and his pulse to race. His augments immediately reacted by flooding his body with chemicals and hormones designed to counteract such reactions. Fear was not something he was designed to experience, but sometimes the power of human emotion was simply too great. The same thing had happened when Cai Cooper had collapsed in his arms outside the hospital on Terra Six. He hated it and was relived beyond measure when the sick feeling went away, as if he'd taken a strong painkiller that had just kicked in.

Feeling more under control, Carter moved to Carina's bedside and took her hand in his. An IV was inserted into her arm, and she had an oxygen mask covering her face. Two medical drones were standing by the bedside, though neither was currently active, and neither reacted to his arrival.

"Damn it, I hate all this medical crap." Carter tried to make sense of the different readings on the monitors, but it was like another language. "It's simpler when your body just repairs itself." He even hated how the medical center smelled. It was mixture of bitter disinfectants and sickly artificial fragrances that somehow could never quite mask the pungent odor of death, disease, and decay. He tried to expunge these thoughts from his mind and focused on his XO's closed eyes. He huffed a laugh and squeezed her hand a little more tightly.

"Just look at me, would you?" Carter grunted. "The big, tough, post-human commander, afraid of hospitals."

"It's because you never have to frequent them."

Carter dropped Carina's hand like it was a hot coal and spun around to see Admiral Clara Krantz by the door of the bay. Her right arm, which was missing below the elbow, was bandaged up and in a sling.

"Shouldn't you be in bed?" Carter said, eyeing the sling.

"I also detest hospitals, Commander Rose, though I do, at least, respect those who work in them." It was an obvious dig at his rudeness only a few minutes earlier.

"Word travels fast," Carter said. "I was out of line. I'll apologize the doctor on my way out, assuming he doesn't run at the first sight of me."

"I would put good odds on that being the case," Krantz replied, walking over to Carina's bedside. "She will be okay, if that's what you're afraid of."

Carter was about to gruffly respond that he wasn't afraid of anything, but it dawned on him that this was no longer true. "Why is she still out?" he said, dodging the admiral's question.

"They are keeping her sedated to accelerate the healing process," the admiral explained. There was no concern evident in her answers. "Apparently, the medicines work more effectively when the patient is less physically and mentally active." Krantz checked the comp-slate by the bed, appearing to understand it better than he did. "She should come around shortly."

"That's good," Carter said, folding his arms. He felt more at ease knowing that Carina was out of danger, though he still hated seeing her all wrapped up in tubes and wires.

"You saved her life," Krantz added, settling down beside him. "If she had been with anyone else, Carina would have died on Terra Six."

"It's me who put her in danger," Carter grunted.

"Duty and orders put her in danger, Master Commander, not you." There was an unusual degree of warmth to the admiral's voice. Normally, she would enunciate each word with the bite of a Victorian schoolmistress, but it was a different Clara Krantz with him now. A grateful one, perhaps, he wondered.

"What about you, Admiral?" Carter said, pointing to the sling.

"They are building me a replacement limb. Apparently, it will feel and function largely as if it were my own, but I'll never be whole again, as it were."

Carter had an idea, though he doubted the admiral would go for it. "I could give you a low dose nano-stim once the prosthetic is installed. The nano-machines would probably transform it into something closer to your own flesh and bone."

Krantz shook her head. "From what I have heard about the effect of nano-machines on unaugmented humans, I think I would prefer the prosthetic."

The two of them smiled then Krantz spent a few moments looking at Carina. She delicately moved her hair away from her eyes and adjusted the position of her hand and how some of the wires fell around the bed. Then she stood up, and Clara Krantz the aunt gave way to Krantz the admiral.

"I need to update you on Terra Six," she said, now speaking to him in formal capacity.

Carter also got up, and the admiral unfolded her comp-slate and set it down on the table beside Carina's bed. He moved closer so that he could see the screen more clearly, and also so that neither had to raise their voices to be heard.

"Data from the battalions that were still active on Terra Six confirmed that the explosion of drones we witnessed was the biogenic weapon being deployed." Krantz scrolled through multiple images, taken from the ground and from the few aerial drones that the Aterniens hadn't destroyed. It showed clusters of baseball-sized drones spreading across the sky and dissipating like an aerosol.

"Early estimates suggest that ten million have already

succumbed, and that more than three-quarters of the planet's population has been exposed."

Carter cursed under his breath. "Did any of the ground forces make it off-world before they were infected?"

Krantz shrugged. "We're not sure. We believe some transports managed to launch, but none would have gotten past the Aternien defenses, let along the orbiting fleet."

"What are the effects of this biogenic weapon?" Carter was almost afraid to ask, but it was important he knew how the virus acted, and how quickly.

"As you might expect, we know little at this stage," Krantz admitted. "It appears to target the circulatory system and causes sudden cardiac arrest."

"At least it's relatively quick," Carter grunted, grateful for the smallest of mercies. "I half-expected those sadistic bastards to engineer something grotesque and painful."

"Slow is inefficient," Krantz said. "They want their worlds back, so in their eyes, the quicker they can eradicate us the better. There is, however, once piece of good news."

Carter straightened up a little at hearing this. He genuinely didn't believe there could be anything positive to come from the incident at Terra Six.

"Before they succumbed, Twelfth Brigade, Terra Three managed to gather a sample of the virus and blast it off world in a short-range shuttle. The craft was damaged by Aternien fire, but by pure chance its momentum carried it into the path of a cruiser from the Third fleet. They picked it up, thinking it might contain survivors." Krantz sighed, wearily. "Half the ship was infected, before they realized what it actually contained and instigated quarantine procedures."

"Where is this sample now?" Carter asked, setting aside the inevitable fate of the unfortunate cruiser.

"It was taken to an off-world research facility in orbit of Mars, far away from where it can do any serious harm," Krantz answered." In all honesty, Commander, we're not hopeful of developing an antidote or serum any time soon. The virus uses nano-technology way beyond our understanding."

Carter nodded and stroked his beard. He caught a glimpse of his disheveled appearance reflected in the window and realized he was starting to look like the wild, forest man he'd been before Carina had found him.

"Cai would probably understand some of the tech used in the engineered virus," Carter said, turning away from his unkempt doppelgänger. "Maybe once he's settled down a bit, we can have the lab send him their data."

The mention of Cai Cooper had caused the admiral's ears to prick up, and he realized it might have been a mistake to mention him. Carter had disobeyed orders by traveling to Terra Six in search of his Master Operator, and while he'd gotten away without being grilled on that subject so far, he figured his luck was about to run out.

"Master Operator Cooper should be by your side, right now, Commander Rose," Krantz said. The old schoolmistress was back. "I have sympathy for his loss, but this is a fight for the very survival of our species, and he does not get the luxury of sitting it out."

Carter found himself suddenly angry. "He doesn't owe the Union a damned thing, Admiral, not after what they did to him. I made a choice to come back, as did Kendra, and I gave that same choice to Cai. It's up to him and him alone what he does."

Krantz was also now angry. "Commander, we lost more than half of the ships we sent to Terra Six, not to mention tens of thousands of troops. We're running the factories and yards non-stop trying to ramp up production of new vessels and weapons, but with every loss we suffer, the Aternien advantage grows. We do not have the luxury of choosing whether to fight or not."

Carter listened respectfully to the admiral, and in truth, he accepted everything Krantz was saying. Yet, so far as Cai Cooper was concerned, it didn't matter. The Union had betrayed him, and he wouldn't force him, or any other Longsword officer, back into their service.

"Then it's all the more reason for me to get back to Terra Prime and get the Galatine into the fight," Carter countered. He figured that trying to change the subject was a wise move. It wasn't.

"That is precisely why you should never have gone to Terra Six in the first place!" Krantz roared, jabbing a finger into his sternum. Eyes turned to look at them, and the admiral controlled her white-hot rage and lowered her voice. "I should throw you in a cell for disobeying my orders."

"You don't have a cell that could hold me," Carter grunted. "But thanks for the stay of execution." His attempt at sarcasm was also unwise. When it came to pissing off Admiral Clara Krantz, it seemed he was on a roll.

"Look, Commander, the only reason you're not being court-martialed is because I need you. It does me no good to lock you up or stand you in front of a damned firing squad, even though that's what you deserve!"

Carter raised an eyebrow; he considered the last threat to be a little excessive.

"That you uncovered valuable intelligence about the

Aterniens posing as Union officers and officials went in your favor, but don't push your luck," she continued.

"It's vital that you start testing every senior officer and high-ranking civil servant," Carter said. The admiral's comment reminded him about fake Colonel Bell, and the damage the man had caused. "We have to start from the top and work our way down. Eventually, everyone wearing the uniform needs to be scanned, and it's a process that has to happen regularly. The Aterniens could replace any one of us, at any time."

Krantz held up a hand to stop him mid flow. "It is all being taken care of as we speak, Commander. Obviously, no-one objected to the proposal; to do so would have appeared a might suspicious." She sighed again. "Central government might prove problematic, however."

Carter snorted. "Send me to Terra Prime, and I'll scan the president myself. No-one gets immunity, Admiral. This is too important."

"Let me worry about that, Commander Rose," Krantz replied. She appeared calmer now and was merely radiating red-hot heat. "I have already discovered three more imposters, all in military positions at the rank of Colonel or above. Who knows what damage they've already done, and what intel they've provided to the Aterniens, but they are contained now."

Carter felt reassured that Admiral Krantz had the problem of the Aternien spies in hand, which left him one other major matter he needed to discuss with her.

"The moles aren't the only problem, admiral. Marco Ryan and Damien Morrow may not be the only Longsword officers to turn their coats. The fates and locations of many others are still unknown. Morrow will try to recruit more, just like he tried to recruit me and Cai."

This time it was Krantz who raised an eyebrow. "I believe your original assignment was to find and recruit Master-at-arms, Brodie Kaur and Master Navigator, Amaya Reid. Can I assume that this time you will actually follow orders?"

Carter scowled at the admiral. He didn't appreciate being talked to like a kid, especially seeing as he was three times her age. "I'll find them, Admiral," he grunted, keeping his answer short so that he didn't put his foot in it again.

"Then you are dismissed, Master Commander Rose," Krantz said. "Since you've already ruined it, you may as well take my shuttle to Terra Prime to rejoin with your Master Engineer."

Carter looked at Carina and the admiral appeared to read his mind.

"You can come back for Carina," Krantz added. "It will give the doctors time to fix her up." She then looked at her arm. "And me, for that matter. Besides, I would like to see the Galatine warp over here. The sight of a Longsword would give the troops a much-needed morale boost."

Carter nodded. "I'll do that, Admiral, thank you."

Krantz also nodded then gently squeezed Carina's hand before taking her leave. Carter felt like he should let his XO rest, but there was nowhere for him to go. Other than Carina and Krantz, he didn't know a soul on-board FOB Zulu, or any of the other ships docked to it or nearby. Instead, he sat in the chair beside her bed and listened to the bleep of the machines and the sound of her breathing in and out through the oxygen mask.

"I bet you're sorry you ever came looking for me," Carter said, running a hand though his tousled, silver hair. "All I've done is almost get you killed a half-dozen times or more, and for what? We still got our asses handed to us." He kicked the floor, cracking a tile in the process. "I hate losing. It pisses me off."

"Do you mind keeping it down?"

Carter looked up and saw that Carina was awake and had removed the oxygen mask. Her voice was slurry and slow, like she was still half-asleep.

"Sorry, I didn't mean to wake you," Carter said, feeling embarrassed for talking to himself.

"Forget that. Why were you watching me sleep, you creepy old bastard?"

Carter burst out laughing, and it felt good to do so. "So, I take it that you're feeling more like your old smartass self again?"

"Never better," Carina replied, smiling. "I mean, all of these tubes and wires are really just for show. Just give me a shot of Trifentanil, and I'll be on my feet in no time."

"Given your current condition, I could waft a Trifentanil pill under your nose and it would probably kill you."

Carina laughed then winced in pain and hugged her body. "Ow, don't make me laugh. I feel like my insides have been used as punching bags by a family of gorillas."

"Ah, you're not that bad," Carter said, facetiously. "I've taken more short-range blasts to the gut than I can remember. You'll be fine."

Carina looked over her eyebrows at him. "I think you might have one or two physiological advantages that I don't. The doctors say it's a miracle I'm still alive. So, there you go. I'm a modern miracle."

"You're full of shit, that's what you are."

Carina laughed again before again being forced to hug the pain away. "Stop, I mean it!"

Carter raised his hand by way of apology then a team of doctors and nurses entered Carina's medical bay, looking purposeful.

"I should leave you to it," Carter said, suddenly worried that he might have worsened his XO's internal injuries by making her laugh. "I'll be back to get you in a few days, by which time the healing boosters should have you right as rain again."

Carter smiled at her then turned to leave, but Carina called out for him to stop.

"Hey, what do you mean you're leaving?"

"I need to pick up the Galatine and Kendra from Terra Prime," Carter explained. "The admiral gave me her shuttle, since we busted it up, anyway. Thanks to the damage, its jump-range is limited, so I'll be hopping from planet to planet for a while."

"Wait up, I'll come with you." Carina threw off the sheets and slid her legs off the bed. The doctor immediately rushed to her, looking concerned.

"Carina, it's okay, let the doctors do their work," Carter insisted.

"Like hell," Carina hit back, wrestling with the medics, who were trying to steer her back into bed. "You've spent far too much time trying ditch me, for me to let you out of my sight now."

Carter returned to her side and the medical staff parted to allow him through. He held her shoulders gently to make sure she didn't stand up and tear a stitch or ten. "I'll come back for you, Carina, I promise," he said, with feeling.

Carina still looked unconvinced. "How can I be sure?"

"Because you're on my crew," Carter replied. "You might not be a techno-fueled, post-human freak like I am, but you're still one of us. You're Longsword, through and through. And I need you."

Carina smiled. He felt like a father telling his daughter than she'd 'done good' and was worried that she would consider him condescending. She didn't.

"Thank you, Carter," she replied, before smiling again. "I mean, sir…"

"Your orders are to get back in bed and do whatever the doctor tells you," Carter said, stepping back, and adopting an officer-like pose; chest puffed out and shoulders back.

"Yes, sir, Master Commander, sir," Carina replied, saluting, and sliding back under the sheets.

Carter returned the salute then saw the doctor looking at him.

"Don't worry, we'll take good care of her," the medic said.

"You'd better," Carter grunted. He grabbed the man underneath his arms, lifted him off the floor like he was a toddler, and set him down again closer to the bed. "Because if you don't, I'll pull your arms off."

The doctor's face fell, and blood drained from his features. The nurse looked like she might faint. Carina, naturally, was stifling a laugh.

"I'm only joking!" Carter added, slapping the doctor on the shoulder, and knocking him half-way across the room.

Carter then winked at Carina, which he did consider might be a little condescending, though didn't care, and left the room. He didn't feel like being cooped up in a small shuttle just yet, so he found himself walking the decks of FOB Zulu for a while. Carter politely nodded and smiled at the crew as they passed by in the halls, though all of them looked nervous around him, and gave him a wide berth.

Eventually, he found himself on a deserted viewing platform, staring out at empty space. He'd spent most of his life alone, and was accustomed to the feeling, but something had changed. He found himself missing the company of others: of Carina Larsen, Kendra Castle, and Cai Cooper, even Admiral Krantz. It made him realize the importance of company – of family.

He fought in the first Aternien war because it was his duty, and because fighting was all that he knew. Now, he was fighting for something more. The Aterniens had won the battle of Terra Six, but the war was all to play for. And Master Commander Carter Rose didn't like losing.

The end (to be continued).

ALSO BY G J OGDEN

Sa'Nerra Universe

Omega Taskforce

Descendants of War

Scavenger Universe

Star Scavengers

Star Guardians

Standalone series

The Contingency War series

Darkspace Renegade series

The Planetsider

Audible Audiobooks

Star Scavengers - click here

The Contingency War - click here

Omega Taskforce - click here

Descendants of War - click here

The Planetsider Trilogy - click here

G J Ogden's newsletter: Click here to sign-up

ABOUT THE AUTHOR

At school, I was asked to write down the jobs I wanted to do as a "grown up". Number one was astronaut and number two was a PC games journalist. I only managed to achieve one of those goals (I'll let you guess which), but these two very different career options still neatly sum up my lifelong interests in science, space, and the unknown.

School also steered me in the direction of a science-focused education over literature and writing, which influenced my decision to study physics at Manchester University. What this degree taught me is that I didn't like studying physics and instead enjoyed writing, which is why you're reading this book! The lesson? School can't tell you who you are.

When not writing, I enjoy spending time with my family, walking in the British countryside, and indulging in as much Sci-Fi as possible.

Printed in Great Britain
by Amazon

25254747R00202